ADVANCE PRAISE FOR
TO LOVE A STRANGER

"*To Love A Stranger* by Kris Faatz is a novel full of all kinds of love—big, messy, secret. It is a novel full of music and juicy orchestra drama rivaling *Mozart In The Jungle*. It is a novel full of both sweetness and sadness. Readers are safe in this author's thoughtful hands, amidst these gorgeous words, in this world rich with the heady sounds of darkness, honesty, forgiveness. *To Love A Stranger* is written with the harmony of humanity in mind. *To Love A Stranger* is a song."
　　- Leesa Cross-Smith, author of *Every Kiss A War*

"How well do we know the people we love? This question is at the heart of Kris Faatz's beautifully written first novel. With Sam and Jeannette, Faatz has created two sympathetic, deeply flawed characters, driven by loneliness and a desire to belong. Set in the 1980s, at the height of the AIDS epidemic, their story unfolds with tragic inevitability. Compassionate and emotionally engaging, *To Love A Stranger* is a page-turner, a story that will resonate with the reader for a long time to come."
　　- Geeta Kothari, author of *I Brake For Moose and Other Stories*

"*To Love A Stranger* captures your attention and heart immediately. I had to finish it in one sitting. Ms. Faatz writes with such vividness and her characters are so genuine that you are swept into their world, and you can't wait to read what happens next."
　　- Cecelia Prinkey, pianist

"Sam Kraychek is the Maestro, in total command of the small city orchestra he conducts. But the rest of Sam's life refuses to give in to his control, and throughout this gentle, moving book, Sam struggles to get along with his father; he struggles with his religion; he struggles to come to grips with the impending death of his gay lover; and he struggles to keep secret the deepest parts of himself, especially from his soon-to-be-pregnant new wife. More than anything, Sam struggles to accept himself. *To Love A Stranger* is a novel filled with decent, loving people all seeking acceptance, of and from others, and from themselves most of all."
　　- Mark Farrington, author of *Manion in Darkness*

1

COPYRIGHT INFORMATION

To Love A Stranger

Copyright 2016 by Kris Faatz

ISBN: 978-1-988279-19-0 All rights reserved

Cover design and graphic: DigiWriting

Published in Canada by Blue Moon Voices, a division of Blue Moon Publishers, located in Toronto, Canada.

The author greatly appreciates you taking the time to read this work. Please consider leaving a review wherever you bought the book, or telling your friends or blog readers about To Love A Stranger, to help spread the word. Thank you for your support.

First Printing November 2016

ACKNOWLEDGMENTS

Writing is solitary work, but getting a novel into the world takes a community. I owe so much to the writers, musicians, readers, and friends who offered encouragement and help as I went down this path.

Special thanks to Mark Farrington, of the Johns Hopkins University MA program in Fiction Writing, who decided to take a chance and accept me into the program in December 2007, and in doing so inadvertently kickstarted this project. Many thanks also to Geeta Kothari, Nancy Zafris, and the faculty and participants of *Kenyon Review*'s Fiction and Novel Workshops. Without Geeta, Nancy, and our summer 2012 Novel Workshop, this book would never have shaped up into a real story. Many thanks as well to Erin McGraw, Richard Bausch, and my workshop mates at the summer 2013 Sewanee Writers' Conference.

The idea and context for this book would not have existed without the inspiration and guidance of many musicians. I would especially like to thank Marcantonio Barone, James Freeman, Brian Ganz, and Edward Polochick.

Over the past decade or so, patient friends have suffered through novel draft after novel draft. Nicole Koller and Stacey Zyriek saw some of my very earliest work and were kind enough not to tell me how awful it was. Susan Ingram, Heidi Roosa, and Deirdre Johnston read about Sam more times than anyone could possibly want to and provided fantastic feedback. Profound thanks to Emily Bliss, who listened to huge amounts of writer angst from the other side of the Atlantic, and to fellow novelist Debby

Kevin, who for ten years and more has been an amazing ally on this crazy artistic journey.

When I started working on *Stranger*, I daydreamed about writing this page one day. I can't express how grateful I am to Blue Moon Publishers, especially to Heidi Sander, Talia Crockett, and Allister Thompson, for believing in this project and bringing it into the world.

Beloved critters Max (1999-2015), Robin (d. 2013), Alafair, and Templeton have shown me that cats are essential for a good writing life. Max in particular, with his diesel-engine purr, was the best writing buddy I could ask for.

And last, and most: thanks to my husband Paul. Eleven years ago, you didn't know you were marrying a writer (neither did I!). Thank you for sticking with me through all the life changes and for always encouraging me to do what meant the most to me. Thank you for weathering the storms, giving me hugs every time I needed them, and always accepting me as I am. I love you.

CHAPTER ONE

S am couldn't land a decent job. He knew he shouldn't expect any different; he had picked the world's least practical line of work, and he got what was coming to him. A young nobody-from-nowhere conductor with a Pennsylvania backwater twang in his voice and a tiny résumé to his name should consider himself lucky to get the lowest-tier orchestra that had had ever hacked through a song or two. Sam knew that. Even so, as he went through round after round of auditions during the wet grey spring of 1986, he dared to dream about a job that would let him stand up on a stage in front of a crowd and make the kind of music that would change the world. Music could do that, if you held the threads of it in your hands and gave it your soul to take into itself.

Sam dreamed about that kind of job. He didn't dream about one that would make his father proud. That couldn't happen, especially now. For what he did want, you needed a real group with real players and an audience that came to listen. In the end, he got the Richmond Symphonic Artists, a once-thriving group now one step away from oblivion.

Maybe he could save it. Maybe he couldn't. Sam got the impression that the Symphonic Artists' board of directors didn't care one way or the other. One afternoon in early June, when the city's pavements had already started to bake in heat that felt more like August, Sam sat in the conference room at the Linden Row Inn on Richmond's Franklin Street with a heavily condensing pitcher of ice water in the middle of the table and the "gentlemen of the board" in a semicircle on the other side. The gentlemen, a line of bland sweaty faces above stiff shirt collars and interchangeable striped ties, obviously wanted to get this ceremony over with so they could go home and change into shorts and T-shirts. Sam heard their thoughts between lines of jargon like *ready to usher in new energy and ideas* and *every confidence in your ability to contribute*. What they really meant was, *So the kid wants to jump on a sinking ship? It's his funeral.*

Sam hadn't bothered to wear a tie himself. He had put on a long-sleeved shirt and carefully pressed slacks, and he ought to have been sweating as much as the gentlemen, but he wasn't. Something cold and heavy sat in his stomach.

On the one hand, he had a job—his own orchestra, the one thing every conductor wanted—and Sam knew he ought to feel an explosion of excitement. On the other hand, this meant he would leave Philly behind. He would leave so many things, and he would do that for this little group that might or might not live out the year.

The meeting ended when the chairman of the board handed over a contract for Sam to read through "at his leisure," sign, and return. Sam thought the pages of legalese might go on longer than the orchestra's life span. The gentlemen all stood up in relief. Sam followed them to the door, but before he could make it into the anteroom, the chairman took his arm. "One moment," he said. "I'd like a word."

Bayard Keating looked like a daguerreotype out of one of the Civil War books in Sam's apartment. He had a white beard, an aquiline nose, and bushy white brows over dark eyes that regarded Sam with a drill-bit stare. His fingers didn't relax their grip on Sam's arm until the anteroom door closed behind the rest of the board. Then he motioned to one of the conference room chairs. Sam sat down again. Keating took the chair next to him and planted his hands on his knees.

"Let me tell you something," he said. He had the right kind of voice, too, Virginia blue-blood with enough of an edge to bark orders to a regiment. "Half of those boys you just talked to don't want to keep the RSA alive for another season. The other half think even if we do postpone the death, we'll be caught with our pants down bringing in a conductor nobody's ever heard of." He stared at Sam without blinking. "But I trust you. You do this fall what you did in that audition, and you'll show them all. They'll find out what the RSA is good for."

Sam couldn't tell whether the chairman actually gave a damn about the orchestra folding or whether this was a personal vendetta against his fellow board members. Keating did look like the kind of aristocrat who would settle his grievances with a pair of duelling pistols. Sam knew he ought to feel nervous, taking on the weight of this man's expectations, but with the cold weight already in his stomach, he didn't feel much else. "Yes, sir," he said. It seemed appropriate to use the same flat, level voice he used to put on when he talked to his father. "I'll do the best I can."

Within two weeks of that afternoon, he had signed the contract, packed up his few boxes of clothes and books and kitchen supplies, and made arrangements to have his spinet piano shipped to the bare-bones apartment he would live in when he got to Richmond. He didn't much care about trying to make the new place comfortable or homey. It didn't matter now that he had to leave behind the things he loved: all the things he had already lost.

Two days before he left, he wrote a letter. He sat at his beat-up spinet to write it, propping the paper up against the music stand and hoping the ink in the pen would hold out. *Dear Ma.* Once upon a time he would have written in Lithuanian, the language he used to share with her. He had stopped using that language because he didn't know when or if he might see her again. *Dear Ma, I'm writing to tell you I'm moving to Virginia.*

The words sounded so formal on paper. They always did. He and Ma used to talk so easily. When the two of them teamed up in the kitchen, the joking and teasing during their long cooking sessions had flavoured the pierogies and kielbasi as much as the actual ingredients. Nobody used to laugh like Ma.

Sam put the tip of the pen back to the paper. *The Richmond Symphonic Artists have hired me to be their conductor this season.*

Her face would light up when she read that, but her eyes would fill with tears, too, the same way they had the last time he saw her. Five years' worth of days, and that memory hurt no less. How many more would it take?

He wrote, trying to avoid the bumps and scratches on the wood underneath the thin paper, *The RSA is a small group. They've been having some financial trouble, so we'll see how this season goes.* He had to tell Ma that so she wouldn't picture anything too spectacular. He dug the pen point in harder. *I'll do my best for them.*

He wrote down the address of his new apartment on Regina Street. She would send him a line back. They didn't exchange letters often. It probably felt as wrong to her as it did to him, writing instead of talking, and she probably knew, too, how the sight of her handwriting made him feel. He deserved that ache. She had hurt so much, and it was his fault.

He stared at the paper. Five years' worth of days. He wanted to say *I'm so sorry. I'd take it all back if I could.* Or, *I miss you so much, Ma, you know that, right?* Or, *I would come home, if…*

But that was just it. If *home* had room in it for Sam and his father both.

He finished the note with, *I'll write again once I get settled. I love you.* It wasn't much to say, not when he couldn't at least pick up the phone and say the words out loud to her, but he meant it. He signed the name only she called him by: *Liudas.*

He always addressed the notes just to her. *Mrs. Anna Kraychek, 519 River Street, Westbury, PA.* If she showed them to Dad, Sam didn't know it. None of the notes he got back had anything in Dad's writing. Only once or twice, early on, she had written, *Liudas, your dad misses you too.* Sam didn't believe it. Not after the things he and his father had said to each other.

On his last day in the city, he mailed the letter. Then he did the last thing he had to do before he left: the worst thing.

Pennsylvania Hospital was the oldest hospital in the country. Sam had learned that fact at some point, along with the additional fact that it had been founded in 1751 to serve in part as an insane asylum. The Colonial-style brick building looked more like William Penn's mansion than a place where people scrubbed out bedpans and back in the bad old days had probably strapped the loonies to the furniture.

Sam walked in grey drizzle from his apartment to the old building, about a mile's worth of city blocks. Gil wasn't always at the hospital. It only seemed like it. The complications kept happening, the general deterioration that Gil said was "only to be expected." After each too-short stint in the outside world, he ended up back at Pennsylvania, in a different room each time, but they all looked the same.

Sam didn't know about the rooms from experience. He had never visited before. During Gil's first hospitalization back in March, Sam, staggered by his phone call and the weight of his news, had asked when he could come over. Gil had gently but firmly said not to. "I'm not at my best. I'd rather you not see me like this." In truth, the thought of seeing Gil at all, much less whatever the last four years had done to him, made Sam's hands shake so much that he had a hard time hanging on to the phone. He had agreed to stay away.

They had talked regularly since that first call. Gil always sounded like himself. The same way he had sounded like himself back in March, when that one word, AIDS, beat against doors in Sam's mind that he slammed and held shut with all his strength. Sam couldn't understand how Gil could say, "I don't want you to worry about me. I just want to know you don't have it."

AIDS. Five years ago, no one had heard the word. Now it carried the same weight of terror as the old words *smallpox* and *plague*. It killed as unstoppably as those ancient nemeses, with no cure or hope of any on the horizon, and it destroyed not just the elderly and weak but the young and healthy. People didn't know where it had come from or why it was so deadly. They did know that certain people were likelier to get it and carry it than others: people who were and always had been outcasts, not "normal," not "right." Sam knew about that. Those outcasts were people like him.

No, he didn't have the disease, but he should have. It should have been him instead of Gil.

In the hospital lobby, Sam brushed collected raindrops off the sleeves of his windbreaker and went to the front desk. The nurse on duty pointed him down a narrow white hallway to the right.

Room number 16 did look like all the others. They were like tissue boxes, Sam thought disjointedly, two long rows of plain white tissue boxes opening into the fluorescent-lit hall. The door to Gil's room stood open. Sam stopped on the other side of the hall, a hair too far away to see in.

Eight years. How could so much time have gone past already? Eight years since Sam had first met a young choir director named Gil Hart. Sam himself had only been a college freshman. He hadn't learned, yet, how fast and how drastically the world could change.

Now he did not want to go over to the open door. His feet felt like they had been mired in concrete.

He could turn around. He could leave right now. Gil didn't know he was here, because Sam hadn't told him he was planning to come by. Sam could go back to his empty apartment, and then when he got to Richmond tomorrow, he could pick up the phone and tell Gil guess what, he had an orchestra of his own, not much of one, but it was a start, right? They could both pretend he had called Gil at home, and they were chatting the way any two friends would.

"Sir?"

Sam looked around. A young man in blue scrubs had stopped on his way down the hall. "Yes?" Sam said.

"Are you here to see Mr. Hart?"

"Well, I…"

For a second Sam thought he could say he was visiting somebody else and had gotten the wrong hallway. He hesitated long enough for the truth to seep out in the silence.

"I'm glad," the young man said. "Mr. Hart doesn't often get visitors. I know he'll be happy to see someone." He took a step toward Sam. "You're a friend of his?"

Sam fought the urge to step back. The hospital garb and the other man's nearness made him nervous. "Yes," he said. "We haven't seen each other in a while." The words sounded so casual, as if Sam and Gil were two friends meeting at a bar or a high school reunion.

The other man put out his hand. "I'm Jonas Caruso. I'm one of the attendants on this floor."

Sam shook hands and let go as quick as he could. "Attendant? You mean like a nurse?"

Jonas Caruso smiled. "You could say that. Most men won't use the term yet."

A radar in Sam's head started to whine. He moved toward the door of room 16. "I'll go and see Gil now."

"Of course," Caruso said. "Glad to meet you, Mr...?"

"Kraychek." Sam threw it over his shoulder, turning away, hoping he spoke too fast to be heard. "Nice to meet you too."

He ducked inside room 16. For a second he felt like he'd gone to ground in a safe burrow. Then he looked around.

Gil had a room to himself. At least they hadn't doubled the misery by putting two hopeless cases in here. Although maybe it would have been better to have someone to talk to while you lay on the white bed and stared at the white ceiling, or out the small square window at the parking lot and dripping grey sky.

Bare walls. Bare windowsill. No flowers or cards or balloons. Those things usually looked like they were trying too hard, but didn't they mean somebody cared? Sam stared at the emptiness to avoid the sight of the bed.

Gil must be asleep. Otherwise Sam would have heard his voice already.

Finally he had to look. The bed had metal handrails up at the head, like the bars of a cage. The blanket, one of those cheesecloth institutional things, wouldn't keep anybody warm. At the foot of the mattress, Sam's eyes found the shape under the blanket, and then he couldn't stop them from moving, sliding up the bed, taking in the slow rise and fall where the chest must be, and then up a little farther, the last piece.

Gil's cheekbones and jaw stood out in too-sharp definition. His eyes were closed. The lids looked bluish and too thin to keep out the light.

A touch on his shoulder might make those eyes open, or if Sam said his name. But Sam didn't want to feel that papery blue hospital gown or the contours of the bones underneath. His throat had gone too dry to let any words out.

One of Gil's hands lay on the blanket. His arm, naked except for the short sleeve of the gown, looked shrunken. His fingers, though, looked almost the way they used to, except for the blue-purple veins that stood out darker than Sam remembered. Long, strong, lean fingers.

Sam reached out. His chest felt like somebody had wrapped elastic bands around it and now yanked them as tight as they would go. He laid his palm over Gil's fingers. The skin felt cool, but alive.

"Gil," Sam whispered. "I'm so sorry."

There was silence, broken only by the faint beeping of some hospital machine and a distant voice in the hallway outside. Then: "Sam?"

Gil's voice sounded sleep-logged and incredulous, but exactly like himself. "Sam Kraychek, is that you?"

For one stupid moment, Sam still did not look up. As if he couldn't see the cheesecloth blanket under Gil's fingers and didn't know what the face against the pillow would look like. Finally he raised his head.

Gil's eyes had not changed. Sam looked at the same shade of blue that, eight years ago, had taken his breath away.

"Gil." It came out as a whisper. "Hey."

He would have expected "What are you doing here?" or even "I told you not to come." Gil didn't say either of those things. Instead he turned his hand over and closed his fingers around Sam's. "My God," he said, "you haven't changed a bit."

How did you answer that? Giving the same compliment back would be the worst kind of lie. Before Sam could find any words—if he could have, with the touch of Gil's hand on his—Gil went on, "Unfortunately, I can't say the same of myself."

He could laugh about it? Sam swallowed and managed, "How are you feeling?"

"Oh, I've been better. Now, mind you, I've also been worse."

They could have been any two people having a casual chat, except that their hands did not let go of each other. Sam's throat ached. "Are they treating you okay in here?"

"You bet. They always do, you know. I'm one of their best customers."

Oh, Jesus, Gil. Gil had always been able to laugh. His smile had looked like the sun coming out. Sam's eyes burned.

Gil said, "Now, if my memory serves, I said you shouldn't come here."

That was more like it. The tone, though, was nothing like what Sam deserved. Before Sam could explain why he had disobeyed, Gil added, "Now that I see you, I'm so glad you didn't listen." He nodded toward the plastic beige chair at the foot of the bed. "Pull up a seat. Tell me what's going on in the wide world."

Sam disengaged his fingers and dragged the chair around to the side of the bed. The chill of the plastic bit through his jeans. He put his hand back over Gil's. Such a long time ago, their fingers had laced together as if they belonged that way. Sam remembered the first time Gil had held his hand, how he had touched each finger and said, "I've always noticed your hands. They're so small to be so strong."

Sam knew he shouldn't think about that now. The box of tissues by the bed didn't look anywhere near big enough. Gil said, "So tell me. What's new?"

Sam cleared his throat. "Well, I just got a job."

"Did you? Doing what?"

"I..." Sam hesitated. It sounded too proud. "I sort of got an orchestra."

Gil's smile looked like the sun breaking through clouds. "I knew that would happen! Where?"

"In Virginia. Richmond." It sounded so far away.

Gil nodded. "Tell me more. Who's it with? What are they like?"

"It's the Richmond Symphonic Artists. They're a chorus and orchestra." Sam had to rush on, the same way he had in his letter to Ma, to dim the enthusiasm in those eyes. "It's tiny. And it's headed down the drain."

Gil raised an eyebrow. "What do you mean?"

"They're on their last leg." It was kind of funny, really, when you thought about how glamorous the whole conductor gig was supposed to be. Sam guessed he was "the Maestro" now, but did that mean anything? "They think maybe I can turn things around," he said, "but they don't really care." Thinking of Bayard Keating's stare, he added, "Except the chairman. He'll probably beat me with a stick if I screw up."

Gil's mouth twitched. "He'd better not."

"You should have seen him," Sam said. "Seven feet tall, with this handshake that could crush concrete. The way he looked at me, it was like he could squash me like a bug, and I'd better not forget it."

Gil burst out laughing. Sam joined in. The grey sky outside didn't look as hopeless anymore.

A new voice came from the doorway. "It's good to hear somebody cheerful in here."

Jonas Caruso stepped into the room. Sam felt his eyes fix on the joined hands on the bed. He resisted the urge to let go and push his chair back.

Caruso said, "Gilbert, how are you feeling?"

Gilbert? Really. "Better, thank you." Gil nodded at Sam. "Jonas, this is my friend Sam Kraychek. We're old music colleagues."

"Yes, I met Mr. Kraychek a few minutes ago." Caruso smiled at Sam. Sam didn't return it. "I was glad to see you had a visitor."

"It's about time, right?" Gil's tone made it a joke. To Sam he added, "You wouldn't know I have a brother."

How could he laugh about something like that? Sam said, "You wouldn't know I have parents."

He shouldn't say that, especially in front of Caruso, who had no business hearing anything. Gil said, "You don't talk to your parents these days?"

"No."

The blue eyes rested on his face. "I'm sorry."

"Don't be. It is what it is."

Gil squeezed his hand. "Your father," he began.

"No," Sam said. "Let's not talk about him." He glanced sideways at Caruso, who was still watching them. *Think whatever you fucking well want.*

Caruso said, "I'll leave you to your visit. I'm so pleased to hear you sounding better, Gilbert."

Gil smiled. "Thanks, Jonas. See you later."

After the attendant left, Gil said, "So, you're moving to Richmond."

Sam swallowed. "Yes. Tomorrow."

Gil pressed his fingers again. "And you're here today."

Words rushed out of Sam from some deep place inside him. "I should have come sooner. I should have come more often, Gil, I'm so sorry."

Gil's smile looked just like him, if you didn't have to see the rest of the face. "I told you not to," he said. "You only followed directions, for once in your life."

Sam couldn't laugh. "Gil, I wish it was me in this bed. It should have been me."

Gil's smile disappeared. "Don't ever say that."

If I hadn't left. The same four words had pounded into Sam's head over and over, like a jackhammer into concrete, ever since the phone call in March. They started up again now, louder and angrier than ever, but Gil interrupted them. "Now," he said. "Tell me about Richmond."

As if Sam were the one who needed cheering up. Gil shouldn't have to do that. Sam forced out small talk about his new apartment ("about five feet square") and the hall where the Symphonic Artists performed ("the Robert E. Lee and Maria Day Lewis Center for the Performing Arts; that's a mouthful, huh?"). Gil's eyes asked for more, and Sam told him how his northern accent made him feel like a penguin in a flock of flamingos. "They all have these great voices. When they talk it sounds like singing, but I sound as exciting as a lawnmower."

Gil grinned. "Penguin?" he said. "Sure. Especially in your tux."

They had too few minutes to make up for so many hours and days and weeks apart. When Sam finally had to leave, he tried to ignore the steady drip of grey rain down the window. He wrote his new address and phone number on the notepad next to Gil's phone. "Make sure you take this with you. When do you get to go home?"

Gil tore off the paper and held it between his fingers. "Soon. Another day or two, I think."

"Keep me posted."

"I will."

Sam's wouldn't lose it now. Gil didn't need that. "I'll call you as soon as I have something to report," he said. "And don't worry. If you're sure you don't mind seeing me, I'll be back up here before you know it."

"I would never mind seeing you."

Sam shook Gil's hand one more time—such a tiny, empty thing to do—and made it out of the room. In the hallway, he stood and stared at a blank patch of wall.

"Mr. Kraychek?"

Sam whipped around. Jonas Caruso gave an ingratiating smile that rasped on Sam's nerves like a nail file on a raw cuticle. "Mr. Kraychek," he said, "I'm afraid we've gotten off on the wrong foot."

"I don't know what you mean." For God's sake, Sam should at least try to keep his voice down. This was a hospital.

Caruso came a step closer. "I don't mean to pry with respect to you and Mr. Hart."

"We're friends."

"Yes, I know." Caruso was so close now that Sam could smell his aftershave. Sam's fingers twitched, wanting to curl into fists. "It seems to me, though"—Caruso lowered his voice—"that you have an interest in his welfare which others don't share."

Listen, you... Sam forced air into his lungs. "I don't know why the fuck I am telling you this, but I was not the one that got him sick. Do you understand?"

Caruso didn't seem offended. "I didn't think you were. If you had been, at this point you would likely be in much the same condition he is. Mr. Kraychek, I would like to help you."

"How the hell can you do that?"

"Let's walk down this way a moment."

He touched Sam's elbow. Sam snatched his arm out of the way, but Caruso had already started walking away, and Sam had to go in the same direction to get back to the lobby. He followed, reining his anger in as hard as he could.

At the end of the hall closest to the nurse's desk, a supply room door stood open. Caruso ducked inside and motioned for Sam to follow.

As soon as the door shut behind them, Sam rounded on him. "What is this about?"

Caruso stood with his hands at his sides, as relaxed as if he and Sam were neighbours having a friendly chat over the back fence. "It would be best if we're not overheard," he said. "I wanted to tell you that hospital policy ordinarily would not allow you to receive information about Mr. Hart's state of health, since you are not a relative."

"I know that."

"And in this respect I would like to help you. When Mr. Hart is here, I can keep you apprised directly of his status, as necessary."

"As necessary? What's that supposed to mean?"

"For instance, if his health deteriorates suddenly. I feel sure you would want to know in that event."

The closet held extra linens, piled on shelves. The heavy floral smell of laundry detergent made Sam feel sick. "Yes," he snapped. "I would."

Caruso nodded. "And as I said, hospital policy ordinarily would not allow you to be informed, if, say, Mr. Hart could not contact you himself."

Why the hell call him *Mr. Hart* when apparently it was *Gilbert* to his face? "So, what, you'd call me instead?"

"Yes. With your permission, of course."

"What would happen if somebody found out you did that?"

Caruso shrugged. "It's a risk. My job might be compromised."

"Compromised." *Why can't you say, "I could get fired?"* Sam demanded, "Why would you do that for me?"

Caruso met Sam's eyes. Under the glare of the fluorescent light overhead, his face looked open and tired. "For the purposes of this conversation, Mr. Kraychek, and without getting into unnecessary specifics, let's leave it that I understand what you are going through right now."

Sam didn't need to be told what he meant. The anger drained out of him so fast, he almost slumped down on the floor. "I'm sorry," he said.

Caruso nodded. "You didn't know."

Sam realized, for the first time, that Caruso didn't look all that different from himself. Almost the same height, dark eyes, dark hair, except in this light Sam could see traces of silver at the other man's temples and faint lines at the corners of his eyes.

Caruso said, "So I will notify you, when Mr. Hart is here, if there is ever a circumstance you should be aware of and he is unable to contact you himself. May I have your information?"

Thirty seconds ago, Sam would have refused. Now he wrote his number and address on a piece of toilet paper wrapper Caruso produced. "It's a long-distance call," he apologized. "I'm moving to Richmond tomorrow."

Caruso seemed interested in the new job. "Mr. Hart is also a conductor, isn't he?"

Could you still say *is*? "Yes. One of the best."

Caruso turned off the light in the closet before he and Sam stepped out into the hall. He tucked the paper into the breast pocket of his blue scrubs.

"Take care, Mr. Kraychek." He held out his hand, and Sam shook it. "Safe trip tomorrow."

"Thank you."

Outside, the sky still dripped spiritless rain. Mist settled in Sam's hair and chilled the back of his neck. At the end of the block, he turned around for one more look at the hospital. The red brick bulk reared up into the sky, as solid and unyielding as a prison.

Tomorrow he would start over. If only he didn't have to leave so much behind.

CHAPTER TWO

Jeannette couldn't get inside the Lewis Center. She found the back door locked, and when she went around front and peered through the lobby's glass doors, she saw a field of red plush and gold braid and Corinthian pillars, and worse yet, a security desk with a burly uniformed guard behind it. At first she lifted her chin and reminded herself that she was going to work in this building and had as much right to be here as anyone else. Besides which, she did have on her best black skirt and a brand new silver blouse. She looked every inch a professional.

She put her hand on the brass door handle, but when she imagined pushing the door open and marching into the line of the guard's stare, she swallowed. No. It made perfect sense, really, to go back around the building and plant herself in a square of sidewalk, to keep an eye on the strip of parking spaces so she would see when her new boss arrived.

Standing in the hot sun, she thought she ought to have brought her boss's letter with her. A full month and more after she had gotten it, she still didn't believe the job offer was real, which was the biggest reason why she had decided to stand outside here like—yes, okay, call a spade a spade—a twit. If she had brought the letter, she could have waved it in anybody's face if they challenged her right to walk into this building. *July 24th, 1986. Dear Miss Reilly, I am pleased to offer you the position of choral accompanist...* Signed Maestro Samuel L. Kraychek, Director, Richmond Symphonic Artists.

Jeannette had daydreamed about what this Maestro Kraychek must look like. She liked to think that the clean, decisive signature on her letter meant that he would have distinguished grey hair and lean fingers, and a face like the portrait of Franz Liszt her piano teacher had shown her years ago. Maestro Kraychek ought to be impeccably dressed in a three-piece suit, and he would have, yes, a gold watch, the old-fashioned kind you stuck in your breast pocket so you could string the chain across the front of your vest.

Jeannette didn't have any watch at all, so she counted off her best guess at seconds and switched her choral music from hand to hand like a clock pendulum. Her fingers left sweat marks on the ivory cover. Tonight she would sit down at a piano and accompany a professional chorus for an honest-to-God conductor. People from Reckord's Mill didn't do that. Jeannette's decision to leave home for college and get a music degree— granted, only at Charleston Southern University, not three hours from home—had made people look at her as if she had announced an intention to move to Australia and herd dingoes for a living. Let those people see her now.

Across the street, next to the navy dumpster, a tiny maple tried to scratch a living for itself. It couldn't have much room to grow, shoving its roots into whatever cracks in the pavement it could find, but its handful of leaves made a brave little display of red and orange. The tree knew it was September, in spite of the heat.

Jeannette admired its persistence. She didn't care much for red: her own too-fiery hair, a liability all her life, made sure of that. Tonight, especially, she had twisted it up into the smallest and tightest possible bun. She did like the little tree for being tough, though, showing the world it would make a way for itself.

A battered grey Pinto pulled up behind the dumpster. Mozart's Mass in C Minor stopped moving, suspended from Jeannette's right hand.

The car didn't look right. A conductor should drive something grander, shouldn't he? Still, to be safe, Jeannette clamped her beat-up purse under her arm and rehearsed her lines again. *Maestro Kraychek? My name is Jeannette Reilly. Pleased to meet you.* Or, *Maestro Kraychek? So nice to meet you. I'm Jeannette Reilly.* Whatever she did, she had to breathe and concentrate on her voice so she would sound like a bona-fide Richmonder. No need to let this man know she was fresh off the bus from Nowheresville, South Carolina.

The Pinto's door opened. Jeannette braced herself. If it really was him, and he didn't see her right away, she could walk up as if she had just arrived and hadn't spent the last however many minutes hovering here like a fool. She had already taken a step forward when the driver got out of the car.

She froze. That boy looked barely older than her. Twenty-five, twenty-six at most? He wore a white short-sleeve shirt and, good grief, blue jeans. They had frayed cuffs. She could see the dangling fringe on them from where she stood. She stared as he reached into the back seat and pulled out a brown leather briefcase that looked more battered than her purse. When he turned around, she saw the shock of dark bangs that fell across his forehead.

He hurried across the narrow street to the back entrance. His keys clicked against the glass door. In another second he had disappeared inside.

The aristocratic figure in Jeannette's imagination had been so real that she couldn't make herself believe this was her new boss. But why else would he have a key, and why would he get here so early? At least he had left the door unlocked, and she could get out of the sun before she turned into a lobster.

Inside, the cool air hit her first, carrying the smells of old wood and floor polish. Halfway down the steps to the basement, something else found her too.

Piano music. Jeannette stopped on the second step from the bottom. She knew this piece: Chopin's third Ballade. She had played it herself, a long time ago now, but her fingers still remembered the quick jumps up and down the keyboard and the long, shimmering runs. She went down the last step and opened the door into the basement. The music rolled out to meet her.

It came from a room about halfway down the hall. The room's closed door made no barrier at all. Jeannette thought maybe the dark-haired boy had a tape deck in there, was blasting a recording by Rubinstein or

Horowitz. Except Horowitz would have had a tuned piano that wouldn't have jangled every time he hit that one low note.

Jeannette stopped two feet from the room's door. She had spent hours training her hands to coax enough strength and power out of her great-aunt's tired old spinet to make the music sound like something. In those days Jeannette had spent most of her time at the piano, because when she wrapped music around herself, for those precious minutes she felt quiet and safe. Now the same piece she had played back then sang under the unknown boy's hands. She had never made it sound like this. Suspended in the music, she closed her eyes.

When the last chord came, she held onto the sound an instant too long. Door hinges squealed. Her eyes snapped open.

He stood only a few inches taller than her. She could see that now, close up. She had always been the smallest person in any room, so she should have felt better, but the few bites of dinner her sister had made her eat earlier seemed to tap-dance in her stomach.

"Hello," he said.

He had brown eyes, Jeannette noticed, the rich colour of molasses. "Hello," she said. She had forgotten to concentrate on sounding like a Richmonder, and her South Carolina twang slid into the syllables. Her tongue froze in embarrassment.

After an interminable second of silence, he asked, "Are you with the chorus?"

"Yes." *Yay-us.* She had to do better than this. Pulling the shreds of her dignity around her, she said as politely as she could, "Do you know, is Maestro Kraychek here yet?"

He laughed. "That's me. Please call me Sam." He held out his hand.

Oh. Oh, dear. Jeannette shifted her grip on her music to return the handshake. Her jaw opened like a puppet's on a string. "So nice to meet you." *Nahs. Yew.* For pity's sake. "My name is Jeannette Reilly."

"My accompanist!" Jeannette realized he wasn't a Richmonder either. His accent put him from somewhere up north. "It's great to meet you," he said. "I was so glad somebody responded to my ad."

Per Jeannette's request, her sister Veronica had been scanning the paper for piano jobs for weeks before Jeannette followed her sister and their family to Richmond. Veronica was the one who had found the ad. But what did he mean, glad somebody responded to it?

He said, "I remember you're not a local, but where are you from?"

Jeannette couldn't say *Reckord's Mill* and drag that name and all the baggage that went with it out in front of him. "Charleston," she managed. At least it was the last place she had lived in.

"No kidding! I hear that's a great town. Did you like it?"

"Yes. It was nice." *Nahs* again. Jeannette bit her lip.

"And you moved here recently?"

"Just this summer."

"Really? Me too."

She ought to ask where he was from, try to talk like a human being. Before she could collect her wits, he said, "Anyway, I was thrilled somebody wanted to be my accompanist. You know we're on the skids here, of course."

Jeannette blinked. "No, I didn't know that."

He laughed. "Oh, sure. It's the only reason I got my job. Otherwise they would have wanted somebody with some qualifications."

Jeannette thought she heard a thread of bitterness in the words. She pictured the white-tie-sporting, silver-maned conductor again. Maybe that was what he meant by "qualifications." But this man, the way he played...

"Listen," he said, "I was going to go find a soda machine. Do you know if there's one down here?" She shook her head. "They must have one someplace. Anyway, right after that, let's go through my plan for rehearsal, okay?"

"Yes. Sure."

"Great. Do you want a soda, if I can find some?"

"No. Thank you."

"Okay. Be back in a minute."

After he disappeared down the hall, Jeannette blundered in the opposite direction toward a Ladies Room sign on the wall. The feeble light in the bathroom showed the cracks in the floor tile, the green rings around the drains in the old porcelain sinks.

Jeannette dropped her purse and music on the floor and leaned on the last sink in the row. She couldn't have explained to anyone, and wouldn't have wanted to try, why her heart beat so fast and her breath came so sharp and shallow.

In the grimy mirror, she stared at her reflection. Nylons and pumps and her best skirt and high-collared blouse. On top of the finery, her sister had made her put on makeup. Jeannette's eyes looked twice their normal size with all the silver shadow Veronica had painted on. You could see her wet-apple-red lips from the next block.

Jeannette held the faucet open with one hand and splashed ice-cold water on her eyes with the other. As she tugged at her eyelashes, trying to yank off the mascara, the piano started up again. He must have found that soda in no time. Jeannette found herself picturing his hands moving over the keys, the power and strength of each stroke.

A little voice in her head whispered, *On the skids or not, he did hire you.* It sounded like Veronica. *And you saw those brown eyes.*

No. Absolutely not. Jeannette scooped a handful of icy water and scrubbed at her lips, tasting the lipstick as it trickled between her teeth. This was just a job. Who cared how he played or what colour eyes he had or what he looked like when he smiled. Or what she looked like, ever, for that matter. She would do the best she could, get paid, and give her sister and brother-in-law something toward rent. She had no other reason to be here.

The music went on, wrapping around the splash of water into the cracked sink.

♫

He told the chorus to call him Sam. "I'm delighted to be here," he said, standing up on the podium with his score open on the music stand in front of him. "This will be a wonderful season."

Jeannette sat at the baby grand piano, which had clearly seen better days, and folded her hands in her lap so nobody would see them shaking. When he introduced her to the chorus—"our excellent accompanist, Miss

Jeannette Reilly"—she stared straight ahead at her own music and didn't chance a smile.

He, Sam, had told her more about his job while they ran down his plan for rehearsal. Ticket sales for the RSA, as he called it, had been bad for years. If the group couldn't turn things around this year, they would fold in the spring. He told her this matter-of-factly between sips of Coke from the machine he had discovered on the first floor.

His job could disappear. Hers—her first real one, the one she had hoped for and dreamed about for so long—could go right out the window along with it. Now, waiting for rehearsal to start, Jeannette knew she had every reason to feel nervous. In a few seconds she would have to put her hands on the keys and play in front of total strangers, and on top of that, she might have to start the job hunt again sooner rather than later. Somehow she couldn't focus on those things. She had sat here next to him on this piano bench, and his sleeve had brushed hers, and she had caught the spicy scent of his aftershave.

On the podium, he wrapped up his introduction. "Okay," he said, "let's sing. First movement, please." He turned to Jeannette. "Let's have the intro."

Jeannette had practiced this music over and over on Aunt Gretchen's old spinet, newly instated in her sister and brother-in-law's apartment, until Veronica begged her to stop. Right now she didn't know if she could find the first note.

Sam raised the baton. Jeannette's hands went to the keys because they had to. The room went quiet.

The baton came down. Jeannette's fingers moved on their own. The keys descended in perfect time with the white stick's pulse.

Sam guided her first phrases, shaping the music with free hand. He did not look at her after the first glance when he gave her the downbeat, but her eyes stayed on him. The sound of the piano filled the room. Inside it, she heard the orchestra: gentle bowstrokes of violins and celli, soft, solemn footfalls in a hushed funeral march.

Her fear went away. The singers breathed together the moment before their entrance. Jeannette breathed with them.

Kyrie eleison!

Sopranos, altos, tenors, and basses entered in turn, layering lines of melody over each other, building a tower. Jeannette had never heard anything like this. The sheer volume of the sound wrapped around her and took her breath away. She would have closed her eyes to drink in its power, but she must not break the connection with Sam's hands.

He leaned forward over the stand, feet planted, his free hand reaching out to the singers to ask for more. Intensity burned in his face, and the dark bangs fell across his forehead.

Dear God. He was beautiful.

In the final measures, he turned to Jeannette again. She pressed the piano's soft pedal to the floor and placed each chord exactly the way he wanted. One. Another. And soft as a breath, the last.

He curled his fingers gently into his palm, and she released the pedal. Just before he turned to the chorus, he looked at her and smiled.

"Okay." He turned back to the chorus, his voice brisk and cool. "Not bad for a first read-through. Let's go back to the top."

They spent an hour and a half working through the movement, note by note, phrase by phrase. Jeannette didn't feel the minutes passing. After they ran through it again, he called a break. "Good work. Let's take ten minutes."

Chair legs scraped the floor, and a babble of voices started up. Jeannette wanted to slump forward and let the piano hold her up. She couldn't do that in front of everyone.

It was going to be okay. She could play fine. She was tired right now because she'd never had to work so hard at a rehearsal before. College choir practice hadn't counted, not compared with this.

Sitting here on the bench, trying to summon the energy to get up and go out to the bathroom, Jeannette told herself those things so she would not think about how the guiding gestures of Sam's hands had felt as intimate as a touch on her skin. She could not afford to admit how much that scared her.

Somebody came up to the front of the room. "Sam?"

Jeannette couldn't help staring. The black man who walked up from the back row of chairs had to be the tallest person in the room. He was imposing, not heavy but muscular, with skin so dark that against his arms and neck, his sky-blue polo shirt seemed to glow. He had a mass of tight charcoal-coloured curls piled up half a foot deep on his scalp.

When he got to the podium, he said, "Sam, I have to tell you, I'm so glad to see you." His voice sounded dark and rich and made Jeannette think of chocolate. He held out his hand. "Seriously. You probably don't remember me, but I sang in the chorus for your audition."

The two men made a funny contrast: the tall, dark one and the small boyish figure. "I'm Nathan," the black man went on. "Nathan Woods. Your audition blew me away. I thought, man, if they don't hire him, that's some truly sorry shit."

Jeannette didn't care for swear words. "Ugly is as ugly says," her Aunt Gretchen had always told her, especially when Jeannette came home from school crying because of what the other kids had called her. But the fact that the man had said "shit" wasn't what bothered her. There was something else about him, something that tugged on the edge of Jeannette's brain and made her hands want to twist together again in her lap.

Sam laughed. "It's kind of you to say so," he said.

"I mean it." The black man still held on to Sam's hand, Jeannette saw. "You're exactly what this group needs."

Jeannette's bladder suddenly demanded her attention. She didn't want to get up in case either of the men noticed that she'd been listening, but she had no choice. She left the bench and hurried out of the room.

The air felt much cooler out in the hall. Jeannette hoped she would find the bathroom empty the way it had been before; she needed a minute to herself. When she got there, though, she found a squat woman in a bubblegum-pink sweater at the sink along with her neighbour from the alto section, a skinny, spidery blonde with faded hair and a skirt too short to hide her varicose veins.

Pink Sweater Lady beamed at Jeannette in the mirror. "Well, hello there!" she said. "Our new accompanist. I have to tell you, honey, you did a wonderful job."

Spider was touching up her mascara, opening her pink-lipsticked mouth in a huge O, the way women always mysteriously did when they put on makeup. She paused between eyes and said, "You sure did. I thought to myself, I wouldn't want to be that girl! How'd you ever keep up with him? He's a pistol, isn't he?"

Jeannette tried to set her face in a pleasant expression. "Yes. Excuse me."

She ducked into the nearest stall. One of the sinks started up. Pink Sweater Lady said, "What's your name again, honey? I know he told us, but I forgot already. Isn't that awful?"

"Jeannette," Jeannette managed. She would have to pee with both of them listening. She had always hated somebody hearing her bodily functions.

"I'm Matilda," Pink Sweater Lady answered. "Mattie for short, and this is my friend Gladys. We've been in the chorus forever."

Jeannette couldn't hold it in any longer. The stream started, even louder than the still-running faucet. One of them must take a coon's age to wash her hands.

Spider/Gladys said, "Our last director, Ian Scharbach, he was such a dear old thing. What a gentleman."

"I don't think this new boy is," Pink Sweater Lady answered. Jeannette couldn't remember if her name was Maggie or Millie. Both women tittered.

Jeannette sat on the toilet after she finished, but they made no move toward the door, even after the sink shut off. "What do you think of him, Jeannie?" Gladys asked.

Jeannette hated that nickname. Aunt Gretchen had always called her by it, and hearing it was almost as bad as saying the name Reckord's Mill out loud. She flushed the toilet and took longer than she needed to arrange her skirt, but the two of them were still waiting when she came out of the stall. "Well," she said, "I think he did a very nice job so far." *Fah-wur.*

Pink Sweater Lady said, "Maybe so, but it won't be easy to keep up with him. He's not very nice to us old folks!"

The cold water at the sink shrank Jeannette's hot fingers back to their usual size. Spider/Gladys smirked at her in the mirror. "But Jeannie here's young. I bet she doesn't mind having a young man to work with, do you, hon?" Her tone dug Jeannette in the ribs. "He's not bad-looking at all, you think?"

Pink Sweater Lady chimed in. "No, he sure isn't. In fact, if I was a year or two younger…"

Spider twittered with laughter. "A year or two? Honey, don't you just wish."

Jeannette's face burned as if she had stood out in the sun for hours. She had to squeeze between the two women to get to the paper towels, and she rubbed her hands on the sour-smelling paper and threw it out as fast as she could. "I think we're supposed to be back now," she said.

"We won't hold you up," Spider said. "You've got an important job to do." The *nudge nudge, wink wink* followed Jeannette out into the hall.

Back in the rehearsal room, Sam sat on a tall stool at the podium and leafed through his music. He glanced over at her. "How are you doing?"

Jeannette drew her aching shoulders back. She could handle this. "Fine, thank you."

He turned to face her. Those eyes hit her like a battery of sunlight. "You did a great job."

She would not go weak at the knees because of a compliment. "Thank you." In her own ears, her voice sounded chilly.

He didn't seem to notice. "I used to be an accompanist too," he said. "I started out with a church choir, a long, long time ago. I joined it to sing, believe it or not—well, you haven't heard me try to sing yet—but the director knew I could play, so that was that. They always do that to us, don't they?"

Us. She liked that in spite of herself. "Yes," she said, "I guess they do."

"The choir was pretty awful anyway. Little Catholic church, old ladies who sound like they're sitting on the washing machine during spin cycle. This was back in the town where I grew up."

"You're from a small town?"

The question came out before she thought. She shouldn't have asked it. He would have no idea why it mattered.

"Oh, yes." He laughed. "They don't get much smaller. I'm from Westbury, Pennsylvania, which nobody's ever heard of unless they live there. Sometimes not even then. It's way up in the northeast corner of the state, in the middle of nowhere."

Why, all of a sudden, did Jeannette want to tell him about Reckord's Mill? He should not hear how she been the only kid in town who played the piano, or how that had given all the others—as if they needed it— more ammunition to use against her. She should not hand him that piece of herself.

He glanced at his watch. "We should get started. Looks like pretty much everybody's here." She hadn't noticed the singers filing back in. "If they're not here"—he winked—"they'll know not to be late next time."

He went back to his score, and she had to fumble for the second movement of the Mass. She felt so tired.

This had been the longest night of her life, and it wasn't over yet. Sam rapped the baton against his music stand, calling the group to attention. Jeannette hitched her shoulders back again and put her hands on the keyboard.

In the back of her head, a small voice said, *I wish he would keep looking at me.*

♫

Jeannette stumbled on the stairs on her way up to her sister and brother-in-law's third-floor apartment. Her music wanted to drop out of her slack fingers. Drew had to get up at five for work, and Veronica spent all day trying to corral the kids, and now it was after ten. Everybody would be asleep. Jeannette tried to fit her key quietly into the apartment's front door lock, but the stubborn old metal scraped and rasped.

When she stepped into the living room, the silence hit her. No screaming baby, no shrieking four-year-old, no pots and pans clanging or vacuum running or record player blaring "Thunder Road." Most of all, no Veronica yelling down the hall, "Hey, little sister, how'd it go? Tell me everything!"

Jeannette relaxed. She managed to smile.

Light came from the kitchen. Her sister must have left the ceiling lamp on before she went to bed. Jeannette made her way carefully toward it, peering into the shag rug for stray marbles from Hungry Hungry Hippos. If you didn't find them by turning your ankle, Veronica would suck them up in the vacuum and then bring the house down with her wailing, opera-singer-esque laments about kids not picking up their toys. Jeannette suspected her nephew Ricky enjoyed watching his mother rip open the vacuum bag and swear at the dust inside, but she hadn't yet caught him in the act of setting up booby traps.

Jeannette stood her chorus music on the piano and stepped over the depression in the carpet next to the bench, where the wood squealed loud enough to bother the downstairs neighbours. The only face at the kitchen table belonged to Ricky's grubby jack-in-the-box. When Jeannette scooped it up and set it on the counter, the redheaded clown swung back and forth, squeaking sadly. She took off her shoes and lined them up on the floor by the table, heels and toes touching. Her feet drank in the cool from the linoleum tile.

At the sink, she filled the white ceramic kettle with exactly enough water for one cup. She propped herself up against the counter, because if she sat at the table she would fall asleep until the shrieking kettle woke everybody up. Her body felt like a deflated balloon.

What had she gotten herself into?

She had called Sam a boy. She couldn't have been more wrong. Again, thank goodness her sister wasn't here to ask a thousand questions. Veronica would never understand how that *man* was so far above Jeannette that Jeannette had to look up to see his shoelaces.

The kettle grumbled. Jeannette took it off the heat and got her favourite mug out of the cabinet by the stove. The white violet-patterned stoneware had been pretty once, but somebody had dropped it at some point and broken a piece out of the rim. They had glued it back together, but the crack looked like a stray hair you could never rub off, and the glue around it had turned yellow. The handle also had two chips missing, like a mouse's toothmarks.

Jeannette made the tea carefully, without spilling a drop of water on the counter. She wouldn't add sugar, because Veronica never sealed the bag properly, just folded the top down and shoved it into the cabinet. She never seemed to think about ants and whatnot getting into the food.

At the table, slowly sipping the tea, Jeannette replayed the rehearsal in her head. The steam from the cup warmed her cheeks. Maybe that was why the table seemed to blur, so that the grape juice stain on the yellow Formica swelled up to the size of an eggplant. Maybe the steam made her eyes smart too.

You didn't fall in love with someone when, as of twenty-four hours ago, you hadn't met him. You didn't hand that person a key to you, no matter if something about him spoke straight to your soul. Jeannette could not be that stupid. God knew she had reason to know better.

No, of course Jeannette didn't need her sister here right now. If Veronica saw her snivelling away like this, the questions and prying would never stop. Jeannette couldn't have tolerated that for five minutes. Except…

Saint Veronica, protector of helpless creatures. Who once, when she happened to glance out the window of her third-grade classroom and see kids cornering Jeannette yet again on the playground, the way they had done so often, had shot up out of her seat and straight past her staggered teacher to barrel down on those towheaded brats like the wrath of God.

Jeannette rubbed her eyes with the back of her wrist. It was so late, she might as well call it early. She poured the rest of the tea down the sink and neatly rinsed the mug out.

In her bedroom, she shut the door and sat on the bed to peel off her nylons in the dark. Her tiny room always smelled like boiled cabbage. The downstairs neighbours seemed to fix sauerkraut every day of the week. Jeannette reached behind her for the shade that covered her little window and pulled it down. Veronica laughed at her for doing that ("nobody's going to see anything, honey, unless there's some chipmunks out in that empty lot"), but you couldn't be too careful. Jeannette wormed out of the skirt and blouse and thought about hanging them up, but the mattress sagged underneath her, and it was too much work to stand up again. She folded the clothes neatly and set them on the floor by the foot of the bed.

She hadn't brushed her teeth, and she would probably have to pee in the middle of the night. It already was the middle of the night. In two or three hours, then.

Too bad. Jeannette found her nightgown under the covers and pulled the plain white cotton over her head. Veronica's nightgowns had a lot less fabric and a lot more lace, and what fabric they did have was that slippery satiny stuff. Jeannette didn't understand how she could sleep in those things. Of course, how anybody could sleep with somebody else right next to them, especially snoring the way Drew did, was beyond her.

She burrowed under the sheets. Her pillow felt smooth and cool. In too few hours, she'd have to open her eyes again.

Sleep closed over her. The last thing she saw behind her closed eyelids was Sam's hand holding the white baton.

CHAPTER THREE

Richmond was all right. Sam split his time between his box of an apartment in the brownstone on Regina Avenue, and when he got tired of looking at the same four walls, long walks in the city. The James River cut a steel-blue streak through the heart of downtown. In his well-thumbed copy of *The Civil War: Trial of a Nation*, Sam read again about the Confederate prison on Belle Island. The Civil War had fascinated him since high school. Now he lived in the city that had sat at the heart of that conflict. He read about Belle Island and went to see it, and when he looked at the spiky pine trees spearing the sky, he pictured the prison compound. He saw the Union soldiers trapped by water and slow starvation in the hands of their ragged, even hungrier enemies.

The RSA's orchestra started rehearsals at the beginning of September. When Sam stood onstage with his players for the first time, he learned something. Somewhere along the line, he had forgotten that the people who faced him now were the ones who had stuck with the RSA through thick and—lately, at least—a whole lot of thin. Audiences shrank, the board of directors didn't seem to care, nobody found a way to turn things around or even, as far as Sam could figure out, tried very hard, but these musicians kept showing up because the group meant something to them. The first time Sam stood in front of them, he realized how much it did mean. They sized up the kid on the podium, and their eyes challenged him. What was he going to do for them?

Rachel Morgan, the first oboist, had taught eighth-grade math for longer than Sam had been alive. When Sam met her stern expression above the glittering silver keys of her instrument, he had to remember she couldn't put him in detention. Bob Reed hunched over his tympani with a look that dared anybody to pry them away from him. Victor Goodstein, the diminutive concertmaster, had brought a roll of butterscotch Life Savers to rehearsal and transferred them to his mouth as furtively as a mouse. When he took his roan-coloured violin out of the case, he didn't put it down again until the last cutoff had been given and he could wrap the instrument back up in its cloth and lay it away like tucking a child into bed.

What could their new conductor do for any of them? Sam didn't know. For the first time since the board had dropped the job in his lap and washed their hands of it, he felt scared to find out.

After that first rehearsal, he wrote to his mother from the tiny kitchen table in his apartment. He didn't feel like turning the lights on, but the street lamp outside was good enough. *Dear Ma, Today I worked with my orchestra. It's not very big, but they all care a lot about what happens this year.* He remembered Rachel Morgan's expression. *Some of them probably don't think I'll be worth much.* Ma's mouth would set in a line at that. She would want to give them what for. *I don't blame them,* he wrote. They wanted a hero. God knew he had never been one of those.

Ma had written to him once since the move. One small, thin white envelope that somehow swelled up to fill his narrow metal mailbox. *Liudas, mielas, I am so proud of you.* Only a handful of words, but more than he deserved to hear, or could believe. Given everything he had done to hurt her, she shouldn't still feel that way.

Working made things easier. Time moved forward. Sam called Gil on the Saturday after the first orchestra rehearsal, when Gil was back at home. "Of course you'll win them over," he said. Sam imagined him at his kitchen table, putting his sockfeet up on a free chair, looking healthy and normal. "The kids at the college always liked you better than me."

Sam laughed. "Not true."

"Yes, it was. When you took the podium, the room would light up. Don't tell me you don't remember that."

"It lit up for you too," Sam told him. *So did the rest of the world, wherever you were.*

The Thursday night after that phone call, Sam got to the Lewis Center early. The chorus would arrive soon for their second rehearsal with him. At the first one, Sam had learned that only two people in the room besides him had much idea of what music was about: Jeannette Reilly, the accompanist, and Nathan Woods, the black baritone in the back row. The rest of the singers had barely followed Sam's lead and had wasted so many minutes hunting for the right places in their music that anyone would have thought they were getting paid overtime. Sam would have to get them into shape if he wanted them to sing a passable performance in October. Tonight, though, he didn't have much to give.

Last night he had dreamed about Westbury. He had been driving across the Lackawanna River, heading into the south end of town. The grey Pinto was right, the deep quick-moving river was right, the old concrete bridge was right. Sam had recognized it all immediately and didn't understand how he could possibly be there, but the sun was shining and, by God, he was headed *home*. He hit the gas, the car surged forward, and in exactly the same instant the bridge disappeared. No cracks formed, no concrete crumbled away: one second the span was there and the next it was gone. Sam looked down at the river below, farther away than it could have been in the real world, and then the car dropped like a stone.

He had jerked awake, sweating, staring at the dark ceiling. It was maybe four in the morning. He couldn't play the piano at that hour, so he sat on the bench and turned on the brass lamp and stared at his Mozart score while the sky turned grey outside.

Now he sat down at the rehearsal room's piano. With the memory of that dream in his head, he let his fingers choose the music: a gentle lament by Brahms. He lived inside it while it lasted, and at the end he let his hands stay on the keys for a long time. Music let you speak when words didn't do any good.

A knock on the door jerked him back to his surroundings. What the hell did anybody want? It wasn't nearly time yet.

When he opened the door, Nathan Woods smiled at him. "Hey," Nathan said. "I'm sorry to interrupt. I was hoping I could listen for a minute."

He was so tall. Sam looked up at the singer and remembered, with the speed of a punch, those strong dark fingers gripping his during Monday's rehearsal break. *Your audition blew me away. You're exactly what this group needs.*

The radar in Sam's head bypassed the whining stage, took a deep breath, and screamed. That was crazy. This man didn't know him from Adam. Sam said, "Actually, I just finished."

Nathan stepped into the room. He had two scores with him and, strangely, a woman's brown leather purse. He closed the door behind him soundlessly, oddly gently. "Please?" he said. "Something short. I'm sorry," he added, possibly seeing Sam's expression. "I'm coming off like some weird stalker, right?"

No shit. "Well," Sam admitted, "kind of."

Nathan laughed. "I'm sorry," he said again. "The truth is, I'm a sucker for good piano playing. I can't string two notes together myself, so I bum hits when I can."

That laugh was infectious. This still wasn't okay, but Sam felt himself starting to smile. "You could learn," he suggested.

"I doubt it. My sister tried to teach me way back, but my fingers don't get along with each other. I used to stand next to her and watch her play," he added. "Never could figure out how she did it."

I used to stand next to her and watch her play. Before Sam could prevent himself, he was back in Westbury, in his parents' house. Tall men brought in a long box that stood up on one end and had a brown sheen like silk. Ma had been Mama then, her hair pure gold in a long braid down her back, and she had sat down on the small brown bench and set her hands on the keys. Sam had barely been able to see those keys, even standing on tiptoe. But the sounds, oh, the sounds that had come out: he had stood at his mother's elbow and watched with all his might, as if he could suck this new magic in through his stare.

"Where did you just go?"

Nathan's voice brought Sam back. The singer was watching him. Why should he care what Sam was thinking about?

Sam blinked hard. "Nowhere."

Nathan held up the purse. "By the way, Jeannette's here too. She left this out in the hall. I figured I should bring it in so it wouldn't grow legs."

Jeannette was here too? And soon everybody else would show up. Sam shook himself. His problem was he spent too much time holed up alone in his apartment, and he had forgotten how to have a friendly conversation with somebody. He said, "Listen, I'll play something for you another time, I promise. Right now I should get my head together." He went up to the podium. "This could be a long night."

Nathan seemed to resign himself to the lack of piano playing. "How come?"

"No special reason. I'm just tired." Sam opened his music on the stand.

Nathan had brought Jeannette's things over to the piano bench. Now he sat down again in the front row. "And our singers, shall we say, have some issues?"

Sam looked up at him. A professional shouldn't agree with that kind of comment, but he wanted to laugh. Nathan was smart. They had one smart person in this group. Sam shook his head. "I'll plead the Fifth."

"I hear you."

Sam looked at the first page of the Kyrie. Would any of the singers remember all that work they did on Monday?

"Hey," Nathan said, "can I ask you something?"

Sam glanced up. "Sure."

Nathan looked about as relaxed as a person could get, leaning back in the chair and stretching his long legs out in front of him, but he said, "Can you come down here first? I feel nervous talking to the Maestro."

The radar woke up again. Where was Jeannette, anyway? Shouldn't she be here by now?

"Seriously." Nathan smiled. "One quick question."

Sam made himself get down from the podium. "Does this make me not the Maestro anymore?"

"It helps."

The smile drew Sam forward. He told himself he was being paranoid again. The chair next to Nathan felt cold when he sat in it.

Nathan said, "I realize this might sound pushy, but here's the thing. I can't tell you how good it is to meet someone who can talk music."

The radar whined in the back of Sam's head. He tried to ignore it.

"I'm an engineer," Nathan went on. "I work in a consulting firm, and the other guys are fine, but they wouldn't know Mozart if he bit them. They're all into football and that kind of shit. So I was thinking, it would be great to hang out with you sometime, maybe have a drink." He added, joking, "I told you, a singer couldn't say that to the Maestro."

The radar picked up speed and volume. *You shouldn't say it at all.* The muscles under Sam's scalp went tight. For God's sake, the man was asking him to go for a drink sometime and talk music. Who else had Sam met in this city that he could talk to? Why did he have to turn everything into such a big damn deal?

He might have gone with it. *Sure,* he could have said, *when's good for you?* He was that close.

Then Nathan leaned forward. "And now this is really pushy." His smile had disappeared. "You just met me. We don't know each other at all. But"—Sam sat frozen as the singer reached out across the tiny space between them—"I would really like to know you better."

Through the fabric of his jeans, Sam's knee burned. For one instant he stared at the strong fingers resting on it. Then his mouth opened, and he heard his own terrified voice.

"I can't. I can't. I'm sorry."

What the hell was that? He should have jerked away, told Nathan to go to hell, thrown him out of the chorus. If he had been strong enough, he could have done it. Instead, before he could get his breath back, or try, somehow, to collect his wits, the rehearsal room door flew open.

Nathan's hand went away. Sam felt the cool air on his knee again, and at the same time, something deep in his gut—no, no, not disappointment, not regret, it couldn't be!—that barely had time to exist before he slammed the door on it.

The girl in the doorway was a stranger. She wore a pale blue short-sleeved dress with a deep V-neck that showed off her creamy skin. Her red hair fell to her shoulders in a cascade of curls. Sam stared at her, wondering who she was and what she was doing there, until he saw the grey eyes. He had never met anybody else with eyes that pure sea-colour.

"Hi, Jeannette." He pulled himself to his feet. "Come on in."

His accompanist was wearing makeup. Lipstick, mascara, the works. On Monday, in a stiff blouse and skirt, she had looked like a kid dressed up in her mother's clothes, but not anymore. "I'm sorry," she said quickly. Her voice had the soft Southern lilt in it he remembered, but for some reason she seemed to try to clip the syllables off short. She said, looking distractedly around, "I can't find … I lost my…"

Nathan said, "You left your purse in the hall, and your music. I put them there on the bench for you."

Sam escaped to the podium. Nothing mattered except putting distance between himself and Nathan. His hands shook as he leafed through his music. *Get a grip, you bastard.*

Out of the corner of his eye, he saw Jeannette fumbling with a long white shawl, dragging it up to cover her bare arms. She thanked Nathan for bringing her things in. Sam thought her voice sounded chilly.

Maybe it was his imagination, but she had walked right in on the two of them. God only knew what she had seen or what she might be thinking. Sam knew how to handle this. Raising his head, he looked straight at her and said, "You know, Jeannette, you look lovely tonight."

He saw her thoughts scatter like marbles when the shooter slams into them. "Oh," she said. The lilt in her voice came out clear and strong. "Thank you."

Sam looked her up and down. "Your hair is a great colour," he said. It helped when you could say something true. "That style suits you." Then, to make sure, he added, "Do we get to see the dress without the shawl?"

He thought she might laugh or tell him off for flirting at work. He didn't expect the flush that climbed into her cheeks, or the way she clutched the shawl closer, or the way her eyes widened with something that could only be fear.

What was that about? He didn't have time to wonder. Out in the hall, the basement door opened. Footsteps and voices came toward the rehearsal room, a crowd of them from the sound of it.

Sam glanced at his watch. "Ah. Here they come."

Nathan moved to the back row. Jeannette went to the piano. Sam focused on his music again. *Get it together.*

♫

The Kyrie was a disaster. Less than a minute into the movement, Sam knew nobody had remembered anything from Monday's rehearsal. All the markings he had given, all the time they had spent painstakingly working on one note at a time: all of it was gone.

Nathan's head jutted up above the others in the back row. As Sam flicked the baton through the air, expressionlessly marking time, he felt sure the singer was trying to catch his eye. He glanced over that crown of hair and did not look directly at Nathan again.

The chorus floundered along, gaping at their music as if they had never seen all those little dots before. Okay, they didn't give a shit. Maybe Sam shouldn't either. What difference did it make?

And then it happened.

Out of all the people in the room, exactly one had stayed with the baton. One person had made music. Sam had held on to it without noticing it any more than you noticed your own breathing, until suddenly it wasn't there.

At the bottom of the second page, the piano part broke away. Sam felt the wrongness, as sharp and sickening as if the floor had disappeared under him. Jeannette had chosen not to stay with him. She was following the singers instead.

He crashed the baton down on the stand. Anger sluiced over him.

"No!"

He heard himself shout it. The piano part stopped instantly. The singers kept going for another note or two and then blundered into silence.

Sam rounded on his accompanist. He should not do this. He and Gil used to joke about diva conductors and their flameouts, but Gil was in Philly and Sam was here, and everything was so fucked up.

"Don't ever follow them!" he snapped at her. "Never!"

She stared at him, scared again. Colour flooded her face, and then her eyes filled with tears.

You jerk. You utter bastard. This mess wasn't her fault. He wanted to say he was sorry. If you did that in front of everybody, you would probably weaken your authority or something stupid like that. As calmly as he could, he said, "They have to get used to keeping up. The orchestra won't be able to follow them, you know?"

She nodded and tilted her chin up bravely, but he was sure he saw those tears still standing in her eyes. *Damn it.*

He kept his voice flat. "We'll take it right where we stopped. Measure sixty-three."

You could say one thing for Jeannette: she learned from her mistakes. The piece went on, and now she stuck with him like pollen when you got it on your clothes. Thank God for that, at least, because the chorus sounded uniformly and irredeemably horrible.

After the final cutoff, Sam set the baton down. No more flameouts. If nothing else, Gil would be ashamed of him. He said, "I've got to tell you all, I expected more."

They looked so clueless. Like sheep in a pen. Except in the back row, one pair of eyes met Sam's and looked sympathetic instead of baffled or simply bored. Sam could not let himself look in that direction.

He gripped the edges of his music stand. A woman in the front row, the one in the vile pink sweater, stared at him blankly. So did her insectoid neighbour in the ridiculous lime-green tank top. Why did these women dress to look decades younger than they were? Didn't they know how their clothes brought out every wrinkle in their silly faces? Sam clung to the stand and a level tone of voice as he told the group they had to do better.

"The audience has to think we're worth hearing." He shouldn't have to explain that. "Remember, we need to bring them back to hear our music."

A voice came out of the front row. "You're asking a lot, Sam."

It wasn't one of the women. It was a bass, a paunchy, balding sixty-something who for some reason couldn't find long enough pants to cover his short, stubby legs. A tendril of grey hair spiralled up out of one white sock. Sam stared at him. The man added, unabashed, "These old brains don't work like they used to."

In his head, Sam heard Gil's voice: *If you know what you're doing, you don't need to lose your temper. Your musicians will listen to you because they respect you.* But that had been one of those evenings Sam had spent in Gil's apartment, after they'd had dinner together, and they sat on the couch and Sam rested his head on Gil's shoulder and felt the world go quiet around him.

Now this bass sat there smirking as if he had said something clever. Sam tasted acid in the back of his throat. He said, "If they don't work, we'd better fix them."

For a second, the bass's wrinkly face looked blank. Then he opened his mouth and laughed.

The sound crashed into the room like a rock into still water. Sam barely heard what the man said next. Something about "we'll do the best we can," something about "bear with us." And then, "only a piece of music," and finally, rasping loud and clear, "Nobody's going to die if we make a mistake or two."

A mistake or two. Sam saw Gil's face on the pillow. *Nobody's going to die.*

The only solid thing in the world was the music stand under Sam's hands. His fingers tightened around it until the edges of the metal dug into his palms. For the space of a breath he relished that ache, and then he picked up the stand, music and all, and threw it down as hard as he could. It crashed onto the wood floor. The music slithered down beside it, pages folded over, the ratty old cover hanging off.

Sam's heart banged in his throat. His face felt ready to ignite. "No," he said. His voice was quiet now. "Nobody's going to die if you make mistakes." Every pair of eyes was fixed on him. Maybe he should be ashamed. For these few seconds, he was not.

In another time and place, Gil had told the college chorus how he wanted them to think about what they sang. That speech beat in Sam's head now. He heard himself say, "You might tell me, we know the notes, we've got the words. What does it matter if it's not perfect?" He answered the question the way Gil had. "It matters because this music will only live through us. What becomes of it is our responsibility."

Nathan was watching him. Sam felt the pressure of that stare, but in this moment he only thought of Gil, standing on the podium with the energy of the music all around him. *I'm sorry*, Sam thought to him, always. *I'm sorry*. "If you are going to be here in this room," he finished, "I want your absolute commitment. The music deserves nothing less."

Silence. Sam listened to his own pulse and realized how stupid he had been. They would never understand. All he had done was display how crazy he was in front of this roomful of faces.

Somebody said, "Amen."

Sam raised his head before he could stop himself. His eyes met Nathan's.

"Amen," the singer repeated. He didn't smile. "Sam, you're absolutely right."

He understood. That instant of connection and support, coming out of nowhere, meant more to Sam than he knew it should. A lump sprang up in Sam's throat, and he tried to swallow it down. "Thank you," he said. He swiped the back of his hand across his eyes, praying nobody would realize what he was doing, right there in front of them all.

With the last shreds of his self-control, he reached down for his music stand. "I'm glad you agree." Keep moving, that was the key. He set the stand up and found the right place in his music. "Now, here's what we're going to do. Measure eighty-six, on the downbeat."

Jeannette was there with him. The piano gave the pitches as soon as the words "measure eighty-six" left his mouth.

♫

By the break, Sam's arms felt as though somebody had unstrung his muscles and left them to dangle off the bones like stray pieces of twine. He needed something to drink, needed some fresh air. He couldn't even make himself stand up and get off the podium.

Nathan came up to the piano. He moved into the curve of it, next to Sam, and leaned against the wood as if he belonged there. "I wanted to apologize for interrupting before," he said. "I hope you didn't mind."

Sam should say he had. He should say a lot of things, but somehow, as clearly as he knew that, he couldn't do it. When he opened his mouth, what came out instead was, "No. I didn't mind at all."

Nathan smiled. "Also, I didn't mean to pressure you, back there before rehearsal. I just hoped maybe you'd think about it. My offer stands, if you feel like it sometime."

Sam could not take him up on it. He ought to say so right now. Before he could try to answer, he saw Nathan's glance shift to someone else. The singer said, "I asked our fearless leader if I could take him out for a drink one of these days. To talk music."

Jeannette. She must not have left the piano, and now she would have heard every word of this conversation. Sam didn't dare look at her. Fear tingled in the tips of his fingers and gnawed at his stomach.

That last morning in his parents' house, five years ago. The last fight Sam had with his father. He shouldn't have let it happen, but the secret had burned away at his insides until it finally rushed up his throat and out of his mouth. "You've always hated me! Let me give you something to hate!" He had heard his own voice, and it had been too late to stop, there in the kitchen with Dad's cold eyes on him and Ma standing silent with her hands twisted together. He had thrown the word *queer* down in front of them, and the raw ugliness of his own voice stabbed him all the deeper as he clung to the image of Gil's face in his mind. "Go ahead, Dad, tell me how fucked-up I am! Tell me how much you hate me now!"

Now, in front of his accompanist, sickness twisted in Sam's gut. He forced himself to turn and face her. She was looking at Nathan with—yes,

Sam was sure he didn't imagine it—plain dislike. Then her eyes moved to Sam's face.

"Sam! Are you okay?"

Did he look that bad? And, for that matter, why should she care how her boss felt? Half an hour ago, he had made her cry. She seemed to have forgotten that now. She seemed to have forgotten about Nathan too.

Sam tried to smile. "Sure. I'm fine."

She didn't look like she believed him. Sam noticed she had taken her shawl off to play. He couldn't help seeing how bright her hair looked against her creamy shoulders. A lot of women probably would have paid a lot of money for that gorgeous red.

From behind him, Nathan said, "You do seem pretty tired."

He touched Sam's shoulder. That light contact went through Sam's body like a bolt of electricity. He had to get away. Somehow he pulled himself up off his stool. One step toward Jeannette put him out of reach of Nathan's hand.

He went to the piano bench. Nathan was still watching him; Sam felt the singer's presence like a furnace, but he made himself focus on his accompanist as if she was the only person in the world. He slid onto the bench beside her. Any normal man would have admired the way her hair curled against her smooth neck.

A question came into his head. Asking it seemed like the right thing to do. "How would you feel about trying some four-hands?"

Her eyes widened. "Duets?"

"Sure. I thought it might be fun." To Sam's relief, out of the corner of his eye, he saw Nathan move away. The dangerous heat faded as the singer left the room.

For a second Jeannette looked as if somebody had turned on a hundred-watt light bulb behind her eyes. Then the bulb switched off. "I don't know if that's a good idea," she said.

Where had that coldness come from? Was she mad at him from before? "Why not?" Sam asked.

She studied him. She was barely younger than him, and she looked every inch a woman in that dress and makeup, but when she spoke again, her voice sounded small and oddly shy. "I'm not as good as you are."

"Not true," Sam said. She was quick and sensitive and understood music better than almost anyone else here. "I'd love to collaborate with you, if you don't mind."

She looked at him as if she still didn't believe it. Then her smile came out like the sun breaking through clouds. He hadn't seen her smile that way before. "Yes," she said. "That would be wonderful."

Her Southern lilt was clear and strong. She shouldn't try to hide it, Sam thought. It sounded lovely. "Excellent," he said. "How about we meet before Monday's rehearsal, say an hour early?" If Nathan barged in again, Sam wouldn't be alone.

She agreed. When Sam asked what she'd like to play, she blushed. "Oh, gosh, anything. Whatever you like."

"How about Brahms? I've always liked the *Hungarian Dances*."

"Sure," she said. She laughed. "I've never played them, but I'll do my best."

Sam made a mental note to bring his copy of them on Monday. Then he got up from the bench. "I'd better get ready for the second half. On the bright side, it can't get much worse."

She had a sweet laugh. "I hope not."

Sam went back to his stand. After a second or two, he heard her get up too. Her steps went the other way, toward the door.

Another minute alone. You took what you could get.

CHAPTER FOUR

Alone in the as-yet-mysterious upper floors of the building, Jeannette found a door marked "Backstage Access." She tried the handle and found it unlocked. She didn't have much time, ten or fifteen minutes at most, before she had to get back for the rest of rehearsal. At least she could get some room to breathe.

Duets. He wanted to play duets with her.

Veronica would be beside herself. Jeannette couldn't think clearly, if at all, but that much she did know. Her sister would shriek and punch the air and carry on like a crazy person.

Jeannette had ended up telling Veronica about Sam the day after that first rehearsal. The confused thoughts piled up in her head had felt like they might explode if she didn't let them out. Her sister had refused to listen to Jeannette's qualms about what a musician Sam was, and how anyway she, Jeannette, didn't know anything about him, and how you didn't go and fall head over heels for someone for no reason. To Veronica, always the brave one, the solution was as simple as two plus two equals four. "You finally found a boy you like. Let's make sure you get him."

Now, behind the Backstage Access door, Jeannette was alone in the dark. Somewhere around here, there was a stage. She hadn't seen it; she hadn't convinced herself yet to go in the lobby doors and explore the actual concert hall. She wouldn't want to get up on its stage anyway. As much as she had always loved the piano, putting herself on display had never appealed to her. Safer to be the accompanist, the background, to stay in the shadows and let people's eyes rest on someone else.

Now she took deep breaths in the cool silence. Duets.

Veronica had insisted on giving her a makeover before tonight's rehearsal. She hadn't approved of the silver blouse and black skirt combination, no matter what Jeannette said about its professionalism and appropriateness. She had lectured her sister: "You have to get him *interested*, honey. Nobody's going to look at you twice if you dress like somebody's old granny." And she had gone on, "You need to use your hair. If that boy is an *artist* and all, he'll just love that red hair. And your eyes. Nobody else has eyes like that."

Jeannette had heard before how her eyes and Veronica's were probably the only blessings they had gotten from their respective fathers. No other Reilly women had sea-grey or turquoise eyes. Veronica had never been afraid to work those eyes, or the curves of her body, or her pure black hair. She had bought makeup, smuggled it home over Aunt Gretchen's prohibitions, and hid it in her underwear drawer where even their nosy great-aunt wouldn't look (a decent woman did not paw through anyone else's "unmentionables"). Veronica had also smuggled the makeup to school in her purse and painted her face in the bathroom every day before homeroom. By the end of eighth grade, she'd had boys following her around in droves.

Jeannette had never understood that. To her, nothing felt more dangerous than being noticed.

She had gotten noticed too many times. Veronica had known how to fight back and stuff people's hateful words back down their throats, but Jeannette had never learned that skill. When the world came after her, the little world of Reckord's Mill that chose its victim and hounded her like a pack of dogs after a rabbit, she had only been able to huddle down small and duck her head and try to survive until it was over. Again and again, she had wished she could be invisible. Make it so no one would ever see her again.

And now Sam had noticed her. *Meet you on Monday an hour early. Brahms's Hungarian Dances.*

Jeannette felt her way along the nearest wall. Somewhere around here there had to be a dressing room, someplace with a sink and a toilet.

The little girl she had been wanted to huddle down here, alone in the dark, for the rest of the night or for good. Jeannette had to be stronger than that. She had to be a woman. At least she could find some cool water, put a damp paper towel against the back of her neck, and try to pull herself together.

She found a door. Again it swung open, and this time she found a light switch on the near wall. Fluorescent light filled the narrow space.

Sure enough, a dressing room. This might be where Sam got ready for concerts, but right now it didn't seem to belong to anyone. It had bare white cinderblock walls, an empty coat rack near the door, and an empty wooden table by the far wall.

And a mirror. A full-length mirror, so that anybody getting ready would be able to see themselves top to bottom.

Jeannette hadn't looked at herself before she left the apartment this afternoon. She hadn't wanted to know what Veronica had done to her. Of course she had known how the blue dress looked; Veronica had taken her shopping the day after the first rehearsal and insisted on buying something "more your age, honey." Jeannette had known about the tiny sleeves and low neckline, which was why she had insisted on bringing Aunt Gretchen's old white shawl with her tonight. She wasn't going to walk all the way from the apartment to the Lewis Center with so much of her skin out in the breeze. She hadn't checked the makeup Veronica had applied, though, and she hadn't looked at her hair.

Her hair. She had worn it in a bun for years, ever since she was thirteen and Aunt Gretchen told her she could let it grow as long as she liked. Jeannette did, not because she wanted that river of red down her back, but because then she could twist it away out of sight.

This afternoon, though, Veronica had sat her down in the living room and put a towel around her shoulders. "Just a trim, Nannie, I promise." And then, while Bruce Springsteen's voice blasted out of the stereo speakers, singing about finding the Promised Land at the other end of Thunder Road, Veronica snick, snicked with the scissors and cropped Jeannette's hair away.

Jeannette had known what her sister was doing. After all, she could feel the unfamiliar curls tickling her shoulders and neck. Still, as long as she didn't actually look at her reflection, she could pretend it probably wasn't as bad as all that.

Now she saw it. Standing in the empty dressing room, she looked at the woman in the mirror.

The woman had silver half-moons on her eyelids. The colour spread all the way up to her eyebrows, which, darkened with pencil, looked like slashes on her white forehead. Mascara had turned her lashes long and black. Her skin looked like cream, except where blush fanned out over the high cheekbones. Her lips were dusky rose. The deep V-neck of her dress showed off her white neck and throat, and the blue cap sleeves—plain, simple fabric, but somehow not so plain now—accentuated her soft, rounded shoulders.

And her hair. Rich, red curls fell to her shoulders, a tangle of fire.

She was lovely. Like an actress. Looking at her reflection, Jeannette heard Aunt Gretchen's voice in her head. *Looking for trouble. This family has had enough trouble, don't you think?*

In the mirror, the strange woman's eyes went wide.

Isabel.

The name came out of a past that Jeannette would have cut out of her memory, if she could. If Reckord's Mill had not been as much a part of her as her lungs and heart.

Isabel Reilly had left home when both of her daughters were too young to know. She had been driven out, though Aunt Gretchen had never said as much in words, by her shame. She had had first one child, then the other, less than a year apart and by different men who had abandoned her. Her daughters had never learned where Isabel went after Reckord's Mill shut her out. They had never seen her face in so much as a picture.

The town had never let them forget her, though. *You know what your mother was, don't you? She was a...*

Jeannette had always guessed that she herself looked more like her mother than Veronica did. It was the hair. Aunt Gretchen, for instance, had had silver hair since time out of mind, but you could still make out traces of copper in it. Reilly red.

Jeannette had never said the word "Mama" to any woman in her life. It floated into her head now as she looked at her reflection and brought another word with it, the filthy, ugly, stinking word Jeannette had so often tried to forget.

...your mother was a whore...

For a desperate second Jeannette wished she had brought the white shawl up here with her, but even if she extinguished her bare neck and forearms and scrubbed all the makeup off, no power in the world would give her back her long hair and twist it safely into a bun. Veronica had gone too far this time. Too, too far.

"We'll make him notice you," Veronica had said. But when you decided that someone had beautiful eyes, and when his smile made your heart jump stupidly in your chest, then you opened yourself up to all the pain in the world. Especially if you let him see who you were. If you let him know about you, if you gave him your secrets to use against you, he could hurl them at you like stones.

Jeannette turned out the light. The dark crashed in around her. For a second she thought again about how much she would like to stand here and let the rest of the world go on about its business. Stay here safely in the dark the way she had hidden at the back of her closet in Aunt Gretchen's house when she was very small, after she ran home crying from school because of the words the other kids had thrown at her.

...whore's baby...

...bastard...

Jeannette forced herself to leave the dressing room. The door swung shut behind her, a heavy noise in the dark.

She had to go back downstairs to rehearsal. She couldn't afford to be a child now; she had to be a woman and go and do this job she had wanted so much and had worked for so hard.

But it would be so much better to stay here alone, where it was safe. It would be so much better not to go back to the chorus and have to sit at the piano in front of all those people, all those eyes.

In front of the man who had noticed her.

CHAPTER FIVE

On Monday, Sam got to rehearsal at five. Jeannette would arrive at six. Nobody else, however persistent, would show up two hours early.

Sam didn't turn on the rehearsal room lights. At the piano, his fingers found the opening notes of the same piece he had played a week ago, before the first chorus rehearsal: Chopin's third Ballade.

A long time ago, he had also practiced in the dark every night in a silent building at college. Bond Hall had been empty at ten o'clock, except for the rows of aluminum chairs and the dusty grand piano. Sam had started going there when he realized that he shouldn't play for the college chorus anymore. He shouldn't work with Gil.

By then, he had known what he was. If Sam was honest with himself, he had known it for years, but he had fought it as hard as he could because his home had no room in it for people like that. Not just the actual house where he'd been born, though that was true, too. Sam had never thought his chilly, distant father liked him much as it was, and what would Dad say if he knew his only son had this "disease of the brain," as Dad called it? No, his parents' house wouldn't have room for Sam anymore, but it was more than that. The town where he had spent his whole life, the town that was as much a part of him as his arms and legs and heart, the place where he knew everyone and where the air itself said *home*: that place wouldn't want him either. Westbury, nestled up in the Pennsylvania mountains away from the rest of the world, had always been a couple of decades behind the times. In that place, people like Sam weren't just *wrong*. They didn't exist.

So he had known he shouldn't work with Gil. Sitting at the rehearsal room piano now, all these years later, Sam remembered how hard he had tried to kill the feelings that had overwhelmed him. He remembered how he had failed and what he'd had to do afterward.

In the tiny office, Sam in front of the desk and stared at the mess of papers on it to avoid looking up at Gil's face. He recited the words he had rehearsed until he could say them as flatly as he would have said them to his father. "I've been thinking, I shouldn't work with the chorus anymore. I'll wait till you can get a replacement, but I'd like that to be as soon as possible, please."

The music told Sam's fingers what to do. The left hand answered the right hand's tune, and the end of the phrase drifted away like smoke.

Gil wouldn't let him quit. Sam should have expected that. "What do you mean? You're the best accompanist I could ask for. You have to give me some reason." So in the end Sam sat at his desk in his narrow dorm room and stared at the cinderblock wall until he could control his hand enough to touch a pen to a piece of paper.

The tune didn't stay gentle for long. Sam's hands flew apart, reaching into the bell-like highest register and gonglike bass. This piano had seen hard use and needed tuning and voicing, but the keys answered his touch as well as they could. The strings sang.

Sam couldn't come up with a lie. At least he didn't have to say the words aloud to tell Gil why he couldn't, shouldn't, work for him anymore. He wrote the truth down on the paper and folded it in half, then went across the dark, empty campus to the music building and pushed the paper under Gil's office door. He touched the door one more time, the closest he would get to Gil again, and walked away as fast as he could.

The internal pulse of the music sped up. Sam remembered these glissandi; he had played them so often in Bond Hall when he barely had enough light to see the keys. He remembered when each separate keystroke had relieved the tiniest amount of the pressure inside him.

The next night, Sam didn't bother trying to sleep. He threw his jacket on over his T-shirt and went straight to Bond, empty-handed except for the keys in his pocket. He would sit here and let everything spill out in the dark where no one would hear it. When it got light outside, he would go back to his dorm and shower and shave and go to class. Nobody would see how something inside him bled as if somebody had taken a knife and hacked out a piece of him.

Now the melody dove deep into the low register and turned dark. The chromatic passage wound upward, climbing and twisting as the right hand began a harsh, insistent oscillating pattern.

Gil would not tell anyone. He would keep the secret. He would not want to see Sam again.

Dissonant notes clashed against each other like waves beating on rock. Sam's fingers raced over the keys. He threw the weight of his body behind each stroke, demanding more sound out of the dusty strings and scratched soundboard. Music beat against the walls and crashed around Sam like weightless water or streams of light.

No, Gil wouldn't want to see him again. Sam had no doubt of that. After all, he was sick; normal people didn't have the kinds of feelings he did. What was wrong with him? Why couldn't somebody take that knife, find the right piece and slash it out for good? The music poured out through his fingertips and wrapped around him. At least here, with the piano, he didn't feel so alone.

The piece was coming to an end. Sam didn't want to let go of it. He hung on to each passing note, but they were like beads on a string that slipped away and disappeared.

He lost track of time. Nobody would interrupt or find him here. The notes slipped away, and he didn't want them to go, but at least he could sit here with the piano until the sky went gray outside.

Soon, the crowd of faces would arrive. Sam would have to get up in front of them and try to be what they needed.

He hadn't thought to lock Bond's front door behind him. Who would come in? The last chord of the piece faded, and Sam kept his hands on the keys, holding on to the sound as long as it would last.

The music raced on to the final chord. Sam's fingers landed on the keys with all the force he could muster. The notes sang, rich and bright as polished copper.

And then somebody said his name. Gil's voice. Gil, here, this late at night.

Sam shut his eyes tight and grasped at the last echoes as they disappeared.

Sam thought he should get up and leave as fast as he could. Fear held him where he was. "I wanted to talk to you," Gil said. Sam saw the expression in the blue eyes and couldn't understand. It couldn't be true. "Sam," *Gil said,* "what you told me. The way you thought I'd feel…"

Door hinges squealed. A floor-polish-smelling gust of air came in from the hall.

Dragged out of the memory, Sam jerked his hands off the keys. "Who's there?" he snapped.

No answer. His heartbeat thudded in his ears. "I said, who is it?"

A voice came from behind him. "I'm sorry." Now Sam heard footsteps too. "It's me. Jeannette."

It wasn't time yet. No. It couldn't be.

"I'm sorry," she said again. "I'll go now." Her accent hung in the air, a melody in its own right.

Sam swivelled around on the bench and forced his smile into place, the one that meant nothing. "Jeannette. No, don't leave." He got up and hit the wall switch and tried not to flinch when light flooded the room. At first he only saw her as a blur of colour, the red hair, the black skirt he had seen before, a green top that showed off her pale arms. "You startled me, that's all," he said. "I didn't think you'd be here yet."

Her face came into focus, and he saw her look of consternation at the clock over the piano. "Oh, no, I'm still early. I really am sorry. I don't have a watch. I thought I was running late."

"It's okay," Sam said. He saw how she was carrying her music, hugging it against her chest like a shield. "Come on in," he said. "Let's get started."

He could have asked her to leave. That would have given him a few minutes at least to get himself in order. It would have looked strange, though, and it was better for him not to be alone. Better not to go back and remember the things he could never have again.

He did take the excuse to turn away from Jeannette and take the *Hungarian Dances* out of his briefcase. He opened the music and set it up on the piano's stand, delaying the time when he would have to turn around again, hoping his face showed nothing.

She came over to the bench. "My sister was cleaning the apartment today," she said. "She's… well, you can't imagine how she gets. I needed some peace and quiet, so I went for a walk down by the river." Her voice lilted and sang. "But like I said, I lost track of time."

As she sat down next to him, Sam decided he could trust himself enough to look at her. "You like to walk by the river?" he said. "Me too."

She smiled. "It's lovely. And quiet."

This close, he saw how striking her eyes were: pale grey near the pupil and deeper grey at the edge of the iris. And that hair, thank goodness she had taken it out of the tight bun she'd worn the first night. He said, "You know, I really like what you've done with your hair. That style suits you."

She blushed. Her hands twisted together in her lap. "Thank you. I'll have to tell my sister you said so. She did it." Then she shook her head. "I don't know, though. If I do tell her, I'll never hear the end of it."

Sam couldn't help smiling. "Is your sister a hairdresser?"

Jeannette laughed. "Oh, no. Not officially anyway. She got tired of the bun I used to wear, so she changed it."

"Cut it off in your sleep?"

"Not quite. She just didn't tell me what she was doing till it was too late."

Sam found himself laughing too. This sister sounded like a handful. "You live with her?" he asked.

"Uh-huh. And my brother-in-law and their two kids. Ricky's four and C.J.'s a toddler, so you can bet things get pretty loud sometimes."

Her voice sounded relaxed and cheerful now, but Sam noticed that she moved away from him on the bench, only by an inch or so, but enough that his sleeve couldn't touch hers. And her hands still held each other in her lap, so tightly that her knuckles had turned white. Maybe he had scared her more than he realized. God knew she had seen more than enough of his temper already.

He said, "You told me you were from, where was it? South Carolina?"

"Yes. Charleston." She hesitated. "Well, really I'm from this place called Reckord's Mill. It's tiny."

No kidding? It was just like him being from "Philly." "You're a small-towner? Me too."

"Yes, I remember. You told me, at the first rehearsal."

Had he actually said the word *Westbury*? He didn't remember. This was getting into dangerous territory. "Did I?" he said. "That seems like ages ago. What I wanted to say was, you have a great voice. I love your accent."

"You do?"

She looked so startled that he couldn't help smiling again. "Sure. Why is that a surprise?"

"If you're from a place like Reckord's Mill, and you move to Virginia … well, Virginians are blue-bloods, you know? And if you're from South Carolina, you're not. And everybody knows it."

He knew exactly what she meant. It was so familiar that he couldn't help saying, "When I moved to Philly, I was fresh from the sticks. People from Westbury have this accent." Oh, yes. The rounded vowels, the nasal point that harked back to the eastern European countries everybody's families had come from. Whether or not you had actually learned Lithuanian or Polish or Hungarian growing up, you got those vocal inflections passed down in your blood. Sam added, "Everybody in the city knew I was no Main Liner."

"What's a Main Liner?"

He shouldn't talk about this now. It brought everything he had lost too close. "A blue-blood, like you said." He hung on to his smile by his fingertips.

"Did you try to talk like them?"

"Not really. I didn't mind sounding like home." Enough. Sam turned to the open *Hungarian Dances*. "Want to start from the top and see how far we get?"

"Okay."

Sam had already put his hands on the keys when she said, "By the way, the piece you were playing. The Chopin. That's one of my favourites."

Sam made himself take his hands away. "Really?"

She nodded. Her hands had untwisted in her lap. "I heard you playing it the other night, too. I listened for a while. It was beautiful."

He didn't want to think about her listening, especially not given what the piece had meant to him tonight. She said, "I played it in high school. I was never as good as you are."

Her smile looked shy. Sam could imagine what she must have looked like as a girl. That clear skin, those wide eyes: she would have been as lovely and fragile as one of the first flowers you saw in the spring. He said, "I don't know. I bet you were pretty good."

Part of him wanted to ask her how she had gotten into music. If she came from a place like the one he had grown up in, she had probably stood out there, the same way he had in Westbury. That was dangerous ground too. The first hint of it brought the past rushing in: the Holy Roman Catholic Church of St. Francis, where Sam had accompanied the choir week after week; the commuter train he had taken every Saturday to his lessons in Scranton; and above all else, the honey-coloured upright piano in his parents' living room, which he'd sat at for hours on end. When you played, you talked to the instrument, and it answered. That piano had known him better than any person.

Jeannette said, "Are you okay?"

What had she seen in his face? She was too quick. That was dangerous. At the same time, something about her expression—why should she care so much about how he felt?—dragged a tiny piece of the truth out of him. "That piece, the Chopin," he said. "It makes me think about… stuff I miss."

"Are you homesick?"

The question hit him like a fist to the stomach. Yes, he was homesick, but not just for Westbury. For Philly too, for everything he had left behind.

Before he could try to answer, she said, "I'm sorry. It's none of my business."

You're right. It's not. Sam managed, "I think I'm a little stressed tonight, that's all." By this point they had gone several hundred miles past the *enough*-point. "Let's play."

He didn't give her time to find her starting notes before he launched in. This piece moved like the ocean. You surrendered to it, and the current dragged you out from shore in a heartbeat.

A page went by, then another. With every note, Sam left another shred of shadow behind. By the time he turned the last page, he felt as clean and cool as if he had swum a dozen laps in an Olympic-sized pool. He drove into the last chord without slowing down. In his head, the waves splashed, the clouds parted, and sun beamed through.

He could actually laugh. "We made it!"

Jeannette didn't answer. Sam realized she had taken her hands off the keys. The fall of her hair shielded her face, but he thought he saw, between the red strands, something glistening on her cheek.

Was she crying? Why would she do that? Tentatively, Sam touched her shoulder. "Jeannette," he said, "hey, what's wrong?"

Her head snapped up. One hand swept her hair out of her face, and he saw, yes, tears streaking her cheeks. "That was awful." Her voice sounded tight and fierce. "My playing. It was horrible."

But they'd been sight-reading. Mistakes didn't matter. Before Sam could point that out, she went on, "I wanted to do a decent job. I didn't want to foul up. Not in front of you."

She folded her arms across her chest. Sam didn't understand. Was she mad at him, herself, the whole thing? What was he supposed to say? "I didn't mean for you to stress about it," he tried. "This was supposed to be fun."

She unlocked her arms enough to scrub impatiently at her eyes with one hand. Her fingers came away smeared with mascara. "I would have practiced," she said. "I wanted to, but I couldn't get the music, and at home it's so noisy you can't think straight."

She still sounded angry. Sam asked the only question he could think of. "Why are you so upset?"

Her hands clenched and unclenched in her lap. "Well, I have this problem." The words sounded tight and cold. "I like you too much."

Sam didn't understand. She didn't know him. They had just met. Things like this didn't happen. They couldn't.

She went on, "I don't like to like somebody, especially somebody I don't know. It scares me. And you... you're..." Her eyes got bigger, brighter, and another tear snuck down her cheek. She brushed it away crossly. Sam felt paralyzed. Why in God's name should he mean this much to her? "You stand up there," she said, "and you make music happen, and I... oh, shit." She said it like spitting out a piece of gristle. "Excuse me," she said. He could hear the tears starting again. "I have to go."

She hid her face in her hands and made to get up. Without thinking, Sam caught her arm. "Wait."

This shouldn't happen. He should let her go, but something wouldn't let him. Maybe it was her fragility, or the way she cared so much that it pissed her off. Or maybe it was the way she had known he was homesick, and the way she had forced him to tell the truth about something.

She wanted to get away from him, but his touch on her arm held her back enough. He stood up and put his arms around her.

He didn't want her to hurt for him. He had hurt enough people in his life, the ones he loved most, and he knew he was committing another wrong in holding her like this. But her hair smelled like flowers and felt soft when he touched it. Any normal man would admire her. He said, "You're a beautiful woman, Jeannette."

She looked up at him, her eyes wide. Sam said, "You are. Don't think I don't see that."

She took a step back. This time he let go. She faced him squarely, her cheeks flushed. "I don't know," she said. He heard how tightly she controlled her voice, suppressing the tremor that wanted to come out. "We're colleagues. We shouldn't..."

Of course they shouldn't. But even while her words said one thing, her eyes said something else. Sam could see it. *I like you too much.*

She thought he was worth wanting. She cared so much about someone she barely knew. As he thought those things, Sam looked at her and thought too how one small, delicate woman could be a shield.

He reached up and touched her face. Her anger and fear fell away. There was nothing in those clear eyes now but surprise. And then her own hand came up and her fingers closed around his.

The world hung in the balance, as fragile as spun glass. Jeannette raised Sam's hand to her lips. Sam felt the lightest warm pressure on the backs of his fingers.

He was not a normal man, and he was no hero, and he was not what this woman deserved. Sam knew all of those things. He also knew that she wanted something from him. Those beautiful eyes, and the touch of her lips on his hand, told him how much. Maybe, in this moment outside time, he could give it to her. With his free hand he cupped Jeannette's cheek.He saw her fear wake up again, but she shaped her mouth into a kiss.

No, said the corner of his brain that never stopped being honest. *You can't do this.* For now, for this one moment, he didn't listen. Instead he leaned forward and let his lips meet hers.

CHAPTER SIX

Rehearsal went past in a blur. Jeannette didn't know how her fingers managed to find the right notes, but she couldn't have sounded too terrible, judging by the way Sam smiled at her at the end. That smile tightened her chest one more painful fraction and squeezed out the last of her breath.

She didn't dare let him see how scared she was. Fear pounded through her body, but she kept her hands on the piano keys as the singers dispersed, running through melodies lightly, as if she were practicing. She could have run as soon as rehearsal ended. But he stayed in his place on the podium, pretending to leaf through his music, and she knew he wanted to be alone with her. She couldn't deny him that. Not when she wanted it too: oh, so much, the way a plant kept in a dark closet might unfurl its leaves and shoot up joyfully tall at its first taste of the sun.

That black singer, Nathan Woods, hovered around a while at first. He looked like he wanted to talk to Sam, but Sam ignored him, and Jeannette was glad.

Yes, Nathan made her nervous. Now that she had seen him a few times, Jeannette knew why. People like that were twisted and dangerous. That disease, AIDS, was all over the news now, and everybody knew that people like Nathan were likelier to have it than anybody else. She also remembered something from the last rehearsal, something that had gotten swept away in all the drama since. That night, when she had left her music and purse in the hall while she went to the restroom—a stupid thing to do, but she had been distracted with the hair and makeup and nerves and everything else—and had come back to find them gone, she had thrown the rehearsal room door open in a panic in time to hear something strange. Sam had been saying something. Jeannette had practically forgotten it, but tonight, as she and Sam stayed by the piano and Nathan stuck around like a rock in a stream, she remembered.

I can't. I can't. I'm sorry.

He had sounded... what? Scared. Jeannette had come into the room, and next thing she knew she was facing them both, and her arms and neck felt awfully bare in the new dress, and Sam was telling her how lovely she looked. She hadn't had time to think about anything else. Now, though, she remembered. Had that man, Nathan, threatened Sam in some way? Had he said something he shouldn't?

Jeannette abruptly took her hands off the keys. She couldn't just sit here any longer. She had to do something. She would tell Nathan off, tell him to get out, say that she and Sam didn't want him hanging around anymore. And then whatever was going to happen when she and Sam were alone, could happen. And...

Another surge of fear stopped her before she could get off the bench. She had sat here, at this same piano, only a couple of hours ago and told Sam how she felt about him? She had handed him that much?

How could she?

She barely noticed the sound of the rehearsal room door closing behind her. Then Sam stood up from the podium, and she realized Nathan had gone.

Sam smiled at her. As he came over to the bench—dear God, let him not see her heart hammering in her throat—Jeannette stood up. Somehow that felt safer.

She had touched his hand, pressed a kiss on it. Really? Had that been her? Now he put his hands on her waist, and she tried not to flinch. She barely knew him. You handed your heart to someone, and you didn't know what might happen.

At the same time, though, his eyes were so lovely. And that smile was meant only for her. He said, "Can I drive you home?"

Jeannette felt something unfurling inside her, pushing the fear away. He was more beautiful than anything she had ever imagined, and he wanted her. *Her.* The girl who had been like mud under people's shoes.

She tried to think clearly. He had asked her a simple question, and she needed to answer it. If he did drive her home, she would have to invite him upstairs. Veronica had promised to stay up "so I can hear all about those *duets*, honey, you have to tell me how they went!"

No. Jeannette wasn't ready for Sam to see the apartment, oh, Lord, with Ricky's GI Joes strewn around the living room, and the dirty dishes stacked up in the sink, and Veronica in her black kimono with the red roses on it and her hair loose down her back. Not tonight. Jeannette said carefully, keeping her voice steady, "To tell you the truth, I'd like to walk. It's good exercise."

He actually looked disappointed. "Then can I see you again soon? I don't want to wait till Monday."

Jeannette tried not to go weak in the knees. "Sure," she said. "Okay."

She gave him her number, and he wrote it down on a corner of his music. Then somehow they were closing up the rehearsal room, and then they were outside the building in the fresh cool night air, and Sam was holding her again and leaning in to kiss her goodnight. Jeannette couldn't catch her breath until he had gone away to his car and she had started walking the opposite direction, heading for the Belvedere apartment building.

The first two times she had done this walk, Jeannette had worried about being out late alone. A well-dressed woman carrying a purse might as well have a bull's-eye painted on her forehead for every mugger and panhandler in the city to notice. Nobody had bothered her, though, and tonight she wouldn't have worried if an actual mugger had walked up and demanded her purse. She would have handed it over and kept right on going.

The cool air hadn't cleared her head by the time she got to the Belvedere. In the apartment, the smell of fresh cigarette smoke greeted her. Veronica was in the kitchen, sitting at the table in her red-and-black kimono.

She held a cigarette between thumb and forefinger and sent jets of smoke up to the ceiling like someone out of a glamorous old movie.

Veronica had always been the pretty sister. Those turquoise eyes, the long black hair and dark brows, the perfect curves and slim fingers: she could have had her pick of the Reckord's Mill boys, whatever their mothers had thought about it, and those mothers had thought plenty about their sons dating Isabel Reilly's daughter. In the end, they hadn't had to worry. Veronica had waited until community college. She didn't bother to finish a degree, but she got a husband instead.

Now she beamed at Jeannette. "You're *late*, Nannie. That means something good happened."

Veronica didn't try to hide her South Carolina twang, and she never, ever, showed a second's uncertainty about anything. Jeannette kicked off her shoes and set them side by side next to her chair. For a perverse second she thought about telling her sister that nothing had happened at all, or that in fact the duets had been such a disaster that Sam wanted to find a better accompanist. It got hard to live with someone who knew everything.

Veronica didn't deserve that, though. And as much as Jeannette didn't like to admit it, she very much wanted to slump down at the table and beg her older, wiser, always-stronger sister for advice about men and love.

She compromised by sitting down carefully and folding her hands in front of her on the table. That grape juice stain had never come out of the Formica, no matter how hard Jeannette had scrubbed it. She said, "Yes." *Yay-us.* "Something did happen."

Her voice sounded ridiculously small and shy. Veronica stubbed out the cigarette in the green ceramic ashtray in front of her and leaned forward. "So? Tell me!"

Jeannette tried not to think about Sam's hands on her waist, his lips touching hers. The memory alone would make her face fire up. "He," she tried. "Well, he…"

Veronica pounced. "He *what*? Come on, Nannie, the suspense is killing me!"

"Shh," Jeannette hissed. "The boys'll hear you."

"Then hurry up. Spill it."

"He..." Jeannette couldn't meet her sister's eyes. She stared at that grape-juice stain until it filled up her vision. "He liked my haircut."

"I *told* you so!" Veronica's impatient fingers drummed the table. "Now, I know that's not all he said. Not with the way you're acting. Come on."

Jeannette hesitated as long as she dared. Finally she managed, "And I... well, I told him I like him."

If she hadn't fouled up the Brahms so badly, if she hadn't gotten so mad, she never would have done it. Veronica reached across the table and took hold of Jeannette's chin. Jeannette had no choice but to look up.

"You told him?" Veronica said. "You actually did?"

Jeannette read pure admiration on her sister's face. It felt so refreshing that she couldn't help smiling. "Yes," she admitted.

Veronica goggled at her. There was no other word. "And?" she demanded.

"And he... he said he likes me too."

He hadn't, exactly, but Jeannette wasn't going to tell Veronica about the kiss. Not now. Possibly not ever.

Veronica sat perfectly still for two heartbeats, gripping Jeannette's chin, and then she shoved her chair back and shot to her feet. Next thing Jeannette knew, her sister had pulled her up out of her own chair and wrapped her in a bear hug tight enough to crack a rib.

"That's my girl! You wanted yourself a boy and you got him! That's how you get things done!"

"Be *quiet*, Vee. The neighbours'll hear you."

"So? I don't care if they do. My sister got a boy she likes!" Veronica let go of Jeannette to step back and look at her. "I'm proud of you, Nannie." Her voice was quiet now, and serious. "You go after the things you want. That takes guts."

Jeannette knew what she meant. Not just Sam, though that was the biggest and bravest thing Jeannette had done for a while. Veronica meant all of it: going to college, getting a piano degree, landing the job here in

Richmond. She knew how much it had taken for Jeannette to make a life for herself after Reckord's Mill.

Well, Jeannette guessed she could be proud of herself too. When she was finally alone in her room, after Veronica had stopped pumping her for details about Sam and gone to bed, Jeannette sat on her bedspread in her blouse and skirt and twisted a fold of the thin cotton quilt between her fingers. The little girl she had been, who had run home from school and hidden at the back of her aunt's closet, would never have had the nerve to do what Jeannette had done tonight.

She hadn't told Veronica all of it, though, or Sam either. Neither of them would know—Jeannette would not tell them—how, in the moment when she told Sam how she felt, Aunt Gretchen's face had loomed up in her memory. *Looking for trouble.* And another face, one Jeannette had recognized in a mirror days before, though she had never seen it that she could remember.

Isabel.

When she let Sam get that close to her, she had felt like she was walking into a lake, too cold, too dangerously deep. And when he had leaned in to kiss her, she felt the water surge up and close over her head.

Jeannette's fingers twisted the quilt tight as she looked out at the empty lot behind the building. A streetlight made a circle of orange on the cracked pavement. A chain-link fence separated the asphalt from the tangle of thistles and overgrown grass behind the building next door. Through the permanent light-haze of the city, she made out scattered stars far above the blocky shapes of buildings.

She didn't know enough about Sam. For instance, she didn't know where he lived, where he had headed tonight after they had gone their separate ways. She did know that he was out there somewhere in the dark city, and he had called her beautiful.

She let go of the quilt and stood up. The window shade was wide open. Jeannette looked straight out at the dark sky and drew the green blouse up and over her head, baring her skin to the starlight.

CHAPTER SEVEN

For Sam, the next few weeks went past in a blur. The RSA's first concert would happen on the second Saturday in October. Bayard Keating was worried. Sam fielded too-regular phone calls from the chairman "just to check up," "making sure you have what you need." Keating sicced his wife Geraldine on Sam too; the fragile, courtly-polite old lady called Sam early in September with a dinner invitation that he understood he couldn't refuse. He went to the Keatings' ridiculously grand house in the wealthiest part of town and ate food he couldn't remember afterward. The question the Keatings didn't ask, but that Sam heard loud and clear between the lines of empty conversation, was *Are you going to make this work or not?*

Sam didn't know. Ticket sales were sluggish, the same way they had been for years. The RSA couldn't afford to do any decent marketing. Nobody knew or cared about the new conductor. The first concert wouldn't, couldn't change much, but Sam knew he had to start somewhere. If this group was going to stagger back from the edge of the cliff, the Maestro would have to make the rest of the season count.

He couldn't afford distractions. For instance, the situation with Jeannette. Sam knew he shouldn't have gotten involved with anyone, much less his accompanist. Suppose it went bad and they couldn't work together anymore? Any normal man would have had to think about such things, or should have thought about them anyway. How much more responsible should Sam have been?

But.

Jeannette stayed late after every chorus rehearsal. Most times, she arrived early too, for duets. Her presence meant that nobody else could bother him. It meant safety. And maybe, more importantly, there was the way he felt when they were together.

He couldn't be the man she needed and deserved; he never forgot that for an instant. Somehow, though, things made sense when they sat at the piano and shared duets. Jeannette's tension and anger at that memorable first session had given way to laughter and joking. Sam liked the way her face lit up when she laughed. He liked the way their two duet parts could talk to each other, as easily as a pair of friends having a conversation. In the moments when he let himself forget all the layers and complications of the relationship between them, and all the reasons why it shouldn't have happened, it felt like spending time with the sister he'd never had.

The second or third time they played duets together, Jeannette brought a copy of Ravel's *Ma Mère L'Oye* with her. The Mother Goose Suite was a group of five short pieces that Ravel had written for two children, a pair of sisters. Sam knew the music but had never played the duets before. Jeannette was shy about suggesting them. "I know they're too easy for us. But I learned them when I was a kid, and I always wished I had somebody to play them with."

Sam didn't mind trying them. The music's simple beauty caught him and held him tight, and he could picture Jeannette as a little girl, working through the pieces alone, wishing she could share them with somebody. Apparently her own sister had never learned to play; Jeannette said Veronica wouldn't have had the patience. Sam was glad to give Jeannette what she had missed.

The two of them slipped into a pattern, stealing extra time on rehearsal nights and spending Saturdays together. Sam soon saw how shy Jeannette was about being touched. If he had been a different kind of man, he knew how frustrated he would have gotten when she didn't let him do more than hold her hand, give her a kiss, or put his arms around her for a goodnight hug. As it was, he was relieved. He also hadn't met her family yet. He had asked, but Jeannette wanted to keep their relationship private a while longer. He wasn't about to argue. As long as it stayed between the two of them, maybe the gentle, surreal magic of it could last.

On Saturdays, the two of them took walks by the river if the weather was nice, or went to a movie, or back to his place to talk and play music. The day always ended with them cooking dinner together. Jeannette had told Sam right away that she was no cook. He didn't mind. He had enough skills for them both, since he had started helping Ma in the kitchen around the same time he learned to walk and talk. Jeannette exclaimed over the roast chicken or meatloaf or fish he made and said that she and Veronica wouldn't be able to produce such a thing "if we had a month's worth of time and a stack of cookbooks." Sam tried not to let her see how much her admiration meant to him. It was such a little thing, after all. But when they worked side by side in his narrow galley kitchen, with her cutting up vegetables or watching a skillet for him it almost, almost felt like working with Ma again.

On the Saturday of the RSA's first concert, he didn't go to her place to pick her up as usual. He needed time alone to get ready for the evening, and besides, Jeannette was going to bring her sister and brother-in-law to the concert. Jeannette had to "make sure Vee gets her act together. I swear that woman will be late for Judgment Day."

In the afternoon, Sam tried to sit down with his music. He should care about this concert, get his head in the right place. His apartment felt so chilly end empty, the building around him so eerily silent, that he couldn't concentrate. He picked up the phone and dialled Gil's number.

Gil picked up on the second ring. "Hello?"

He always sounded like himself. His voice washed over Sam and felt as warm and sure as arms around him. "Hey, Gil," Sam said. "It's me."

"Sam!" He sounded so glad. If you didn't know how sick he was, you would have pictured his face the way it used to be, healthy and full of life. Sam pictured that now, leaning against his kitchen counter. The same way he had the last time they'd talked, he imagined Gil at home in his apartment, lounging on the couch with his feet up on the coffee table, looking the way he should. Gil said, "How's it going, Maestro?"

Maestro. Sam's title still felt like a joke, but coming from Gil, it made him smile. "I'm okay," he said. "How are you?"

Gil said he was feeling better. Sam hoped he could believe it. Then Gil added, "Now, what's up with your orchestra? You have a concert tonight, right?"

Trust him to remember, in spite of everything he was dealing with. "Uh-huh," Sam said. "And I have to tell you, I'm thinking I should lock the door and unplug the phone and go back to bed and stuff my blanket in my ears."

Gil snorted. "Come on. What are you so worried about?"

What *wasn't* he worried about? Sam said, "For starters, we'll have about five people in the audience." The kitchen floor felt chilly through his socks. He picked one foot up and kicked at the frayed edge on the other leg of his jeans. "Actually, exactly five, as far as I know." The only full seats he could guarantee were Jeannette's, her sister and brother-in-law's, and the Keatings'. Sam could imagine what the chairman would say about a pathetic turnout. "But that's okay," he added, "because the chorus is going to sound like a clogged toilet."

The explosion of laughter on the other end felt like a hot shower. Sam grinned. "I'm serious."

Gil pulled himself together. "I know you better than that. You've whipped them into shape."

"I wish. They can't remember anything." That wasn't quite true. One of them could, but Sam wouldn't mention Nathan. "Every week I feel like I'm fixing all the same shit again." That was a hundred percent accurate. "The orchestra's good, though. They've worked hard."

They had. By the end of the last rehearsal, Rachel Lewis had given Sam a look of frank respect over the keys of her oboe, and Bob Reed, at least twice Sam's age and as irritable as a shaved badger, answered "Yes, sir" immediately when Sam asked him to switch to softer mallets for one tympani entrance. Victor Goodstein had crept to the podium after packing up his violin to confide, in a butterscotch-flavoured whisper, that the strings had never before in his experience sounded so unified. All of them deserved a better chorus behind them tonight than they were likely to get.

"Okay," Gil said, "if the orchestra's good, tell them to play extra loud. Or, how about this, tell the chorus to turn around and face the other way."

All those tuxedos and black dresses with their backs to the audience. Perfect. "But then they won't be able to see the baton," Sam said. He thought about that and added, in the same second Gil said it too, "So what?"

Gil's laugh did sound exactly like himself. "I'll tell you, love, I wish I could have been there to increase your audience by... what would it be? Six instead of five. Twenty percent?"

Love. Sam tried to unfreeze his brain. "Uh, yeah. That sounds right."

"See, now, twenty percent would have been substantial. And I bet for the next show you won't need extra bodies. You'll have a full house."

Sam tried to match his tone. "As if. But you know, any time you want to come down, you've got a ticket."

"I'll remember that."

Gil could not travel. They both knew it. "I wish you could be here," Sam said and heard how whiny he sounded.

"I wish I could too." Gil sounded like a parent comforting a child. Jesus, Sam was pathetic. Gil said, "I know other people want the music, though. They'll be listening."

Jeannette would be listening. Sam knew how excited she was to hear the music they'd worked on come together in performance. He needed to focus on her. He shouldn't, for instance, think about Nathan standing in the chorus.

"Now," Gil said, "what time do you have to be there tonight?"

Sam looked at his watch. "Six thirty." He'd never bothered putting a clock in here; maybe someday he should. "In two hours."

"You're going to have dinner, I hope."

"I guess." Sam didn't much feel like eating. He ought to be on top of the world, going into his first show with his own orchestra, but somehow he didn't want to deal with any of it.

Gil made a *tsk* noise. "You have to have something. You'll need the energy."

Trust Gil still to care, still to worry about him. "Okay," Sam said. He had to push the word out past the lump in his throat.

"Promise?"

"I promise."

"And remember, I want a full report afterward. Tomorrow. You're going to call and tell me how well it went."

Sam tried to laugh. "Am I? What if it doesn't?"

"Then you can tell me how much better it'll be next time. And wait a minute, you called me today, so I'll call you tomorrow."

Whatever. Sam would talk to Gil again tomorrow. "All right."

They agreed on eleven in the morning. Sam didn't want to hang up the phone, but Gil ordered him to get ready. "I'll be listening tonight," he said, "from up here." So Sam pried the phone away from his ear, which he couldn't do until he heard the click on the other end and the buzz of the dial tone, and set the receiver back in the cradle.

If Ma had been here, she would have shooed Sam out of the kitchen with a dishtowel, the way she used to when she wanted him out of her hair. She would have exclaimed in horror over the contents of his fridge and cabinets, which were practically bare today because Jeannette wasn't visiting, but she would have scraped something together and made sure Sam ate it.

Sam didn't have a toaster, so he buttered some bread and put it in the oven. In a saucepan, he melted another pat of butter and cracked two eggs into it. The sizzling noise filled the apartment.

If Gil had been here… well, Gil's handful of efforts at solo cooking had always turned into something fused to the bottom of a skillet and a call out for pizza or Chinese food. So he would have told Sam to put some decent clothes on, and they would have gone out to eat.

The aroma of eggs in butter made Sam's stomach growl. He sprinkled a dash of pepper into the saucepan. Gil and Ma both would have taken care of him, but that wasn't why he wished, right now, that he could shut his eyes and open them again and see them both right here in his kitchen. Gil's tousled hair, Ma's silvering bun, and the two shades of blue eyes that had first claim on Sam's heart.

They could never have been here together, Ma and Gil. Instead, Sam didn't have either one, and maybe never would again.

He did have a job to do. The oven gushed warmth into the room when he opened the door and pulled out the bread. He slid the eggs onto one slice, put the other on top, and squashed the yolks till they ran. The sandwich smelled good, but when he picked it up and bit into it, the dry bread crumbled into dust and the egg sat in his mouth like a wad of slime. Sam made himself eat it anyway, chew and swallow, one bite at a time.

♪

The orchestra had set up onstage. Sam and Victor stood in the wings with Lydia Holland, the RSA's orchestra manager. Victor held onto his violin and crunched a Life Saver like a mouse crunching a sugar cube. You would expect a professional performer to have concert dress that fit like a glove, but Victor's tux hung on him the way a father's suit would hang on a kid.

Lydia stood by the stage door. She always had the look of a grade-school teacher waiting for a flicked spitball, especially, Sam thought, when she talked to the new Maestro. Tonight, her floor-length, high-collared black dress revealed not one square inch of skin. She had pulled her grey hair back so tight in its ponytail that her forehead looked stretched. "Not a bad house," she murmured, apparently to herself. "For the first show." Her voice was the one part of her image that didn't fit. The old Virginia lilt of it made Sam think of pressed flowers.

Sam had privately vowed not to look at the house before he got out there, and when he did get onstage, to stare at the lights so he wouldn't see all the empty seats. In spite of himself, he asked, "How'd we do?"

"About half," Lydia said. More than Sam had dared to expect. "I think they've been talking about you," she added.

Victor nodded. After one more crunch and swallow, he confided, "We sound better than ever this season. I've been telling everybody."

Everybody? Sam figured Victor knew about three people outside of the RSA. If so, he had scared up more ticket sales than Sam had, given that three of Sam's had been comps. For the first time since Sam had left his apartment, nerves woke up and twitched down his arms and into his fingers. It was one thing to think he wouldn't be able to do much for the RSA. It was another to realize that, just maybe, he could.

The RSA would have to rely on word of mouth for now. Sam knew they wouldn't have a critic in the audience for this show, but if people saw something they liked tonight, and if they liked it enough to go home and tell their friends, relatives, coworkers, whoever, and if those people then told some more, that was how you filled a house.

Had Sam done enough? Had he tried?

Lydia had taken his score and baton onstage earlier and set them on the music stand on the conductor's podium. Sam's fingers moved reflexively, wishing they had the smooth wooden baton grip to hold on to.

You can do this. You have to.

The house lights went down. Sam closed his eyes.

The stage door creaked open. Lydia said, "Good luck, Victor."

Sam heard the concertmaster's footsteps and the polite scatter of applause from the house and realized, all at once, how many times the people on this stage had done exactly this same thing together before. Lydia and Victor certainly had. All of them had stuck with the RSA because they loved it, watching the houses dwindle and the board sit on its hands, showing up anyway to play the music they cared about, whether or not they had any real hope of a future.

And now here came Sam, the Maestro. The outsider.

The orchestra was tuning. Sam heard the oboe's clear note and pictured Rachel Lewis in her long black skirt and black jacket, adjusting her glasses, giving one last tweak to her instrument's ligature as she waited for the show to start.

Sam's egg sandwich had solidified into a lump of ice in the pit of his stomach. He locked his hands together behind his back.

The tuning sounds faded. In another second the stage door would open again. Sam would have to go out there and bow to the audience, and turn to his players and…

The stage door creaked again. Lydia said, "Maestro?"

She had never called him anything but Sam, as if a whippersnapper didn't need a title. He forced his eyes open. She was watching him. The stage door stood open. Beyond it, the white light waited.

"They're all yours," she said.

He could not move. His thoughts scrabbled like a squirrel in a trap. Disjointed pictures flashed through his head. Bayard Keating, glaring at the stage. Jeannette, sitting with her hands clasped in her lap, waiting. And someone who wasn't here: a face just like Sam's but older, as still as ice, with dark eyes remote behind glasses. How did Sam plan to make good in his life? His father had asked him that so many times. Sam had no answer.

And then another face. A wasted one on a pillow.

I'll be listening tonight, from up here.

Sam's hands let go of each other. His shoulders went back and his chin lifted.

Okay, Gil.

His footsteps sounded like pistol shots. At the last instant before he stepped into the light, he felt a touch on his shoulder.

"Give them hell."

He thought that was what he heard, in Lydia's pressed-flower voice, but he couldn't be sure because the sound disappeared into the applause that beat against his eardrums like a clash of gravel. The white light poured down on him, and he went out to meet it.

♪

When you rehearsed, you treated phrases and even individual notes like pearls. You buffed them one at a time, strung them together with careful attention. There was no such thing as spending too much time on any one moment. All of them were essential.

In performance, you forgot all of that.

The notes were not pearls anymore. They were rubies and emeralds, amethysts and sapphires, or they were pieces of coloured tile in a mosaic, or they were drops of paint in the largest mural you ever saw. They flowed past and poured around you. You stood in a living stream of colour.

When Sam stood in front of the orchestra with the white light on him and the audience behind, he could not imagine anyone not wanting to give up their whole self, down to the last drop, to this.

Beethoven, the deaf genius, had felt like an outcast because his failing hearing isolated him from the world. He stormed and shouted, raged at God, lived in constant physical pain. Out of that, he wrote this music.

The strings were velvet, and the winds were silver. Their individual lines of melody met and blended at the podium. In the voices of the instruments coming together, Sam heard the voice of the other Maestro, the real one who had written this piece. By the end of his life, Beethoven couldn't stand up on a podium alone to conduct his own music, or sit down at a piano to play in public, because his ears would not tell him what his hands were doing. Sam could imagine that Maestro's voice in its gravelly roughness. *You, boy,* it said. *What are you going to do?*

The best I can, Sam told it. *Sir.*

The music went past too quickly. Too soon, much too soon, the end of the symphony came. Galloping chords charged straight ahead and dissolved one last time into a spiralling tune that wound around and around itself. The orchestra set the final chords down with Sam's beat, bows slicing across strings in perfect unison. The last notes rang for one final second, and then there was silence.

Sam heard the blood thumping in his ears. Energy tingled along every one of his nerves and pulsed in his hands and fingers.

The applause started. It sounded too thin and scarce for what they had just done, but Sam looked at the orchestra, his orchestra, and saw Rachel Lewis grinning and Bob Reed nodding, and Victor, timid little Victor, holding onto his violin with one hand and giving a thumbs-up with the other, and beaming until you thought the top of his head might split clean off.

Sam turned around to face the audience. Too many empty seats, like gaps in a mouth where teeth had fallen out. The people he did see, though, looked like they were clapping as hard as they could. In December, maybe they could fill more seats. Maybe.

By the time he got offstage and the house lights came up for intermission, Sam's arms seemed to have turned into cooked noodles. Lydia came to his dressing room with a can of Coke. "Thought you might need this," she said.

"You're a goddess."

Lydia actually blushed. Sam wanted to laugh. "Thank you," he said, popping the top open to take a long swallow. The liquid felt impossibly cold and good sliding down his throat.

So far, so good, but the chorus was up next. *They'll sound like a clogged toilet.* When intermission ended, when the house lights went down and Victor tuned the orchestra again, Sam focused on the rows of faces he could see in the chorus from his place in the wings. *Try not to screw up too much. Okay?*

When he got to the podium, he glanced at the back row of singers before he could stop himself. Nathan stood ramrod straight and held out his score like an offering. When Sam looked at him, the singer flashed a grin of pure comradeship.

Sam quickly looked away. *Focus.*

He picked up the baton. The hall went still. All the eyes onstage were fixed on him, waiting. The music took shape in front of him and around him. He brought the baton down.

The orchestra sounded exactly the way they should. Underneath their lines, in his memory, Sam heard the piano again. Jeannette had done so well. For a moment he thought of her out there in the hall, listening to this music that had been hers. Then the first choral entrance came up and Sam braced himself. *Come on, people.*

"Kyrie eleison!"

Perfect unison. Soprano, alto, tenor, and bass lines came together in a wave that sent chills down Sam's spine. What was this? Where had it come from?

They sang it the way it deserved to be sung. Mozart should have heard it. During the break of a few moments between movements, Sam pictured the young composer, young forever because in life he had never made it to middle age. Nobody else laughed the way Mozart had, like clear sparkling water, or better yet, bubbles in champagne.

You would have liked this, Sam thought to that young man during the seconds of silence. *You would have been proud.* Then it was time to turn the page in the score and pick up the baton again, and the music went on.

The last movement was the Benedictus, "Blessed is he who comes in the name of the Lord," with the double fugue, "Osanna in excelsis." Sam had pulled this section apart over and over in rehearsal. The singers couldn't keep up with his tempo, the sopranos stumbled and floundered for notes, the basses sagged disastrously flat. Sam had planned to slow down a lot for the Osanna in performance. It would sound shitty, but the slower speed would give the chorus more time to think.

The Benedictus ended. The baton danced without slowing down straight into the final section.

Sparkling water. Bubbles in champagne. They did it, by God: the pitch-perfect notes danced under the light in time with the white stick. Underneath the voices, the strings had never sounded so light and clean or the winds and brasses so pure.

You would have been proud.

As that thought went through his head, Sam saw another face: not the young composer's laughing one, but the older one, so much like Sam's own, cold and distant, with no hint of a smile.

The chorus and orchestra flew into the final measures. The stage shivered to the beats of the tympani. Sam drove his father's face out of his mind and pulled more sound out of the orchestra and the throats of the singers until there was no room for anything else in the world.

He sliced the stick through the air in the final cutoff. The hall rang with silence, and Sam stood still as the music drained out of him. Then the applause started, louder than the first time. What was this? Had somebody gone outside and hauled people in off the street? Sam could imagine Bayard Keating doling cash out of his billfold to fill seats. He dragged himself around to look at the house.

They were standing up. Every one of them. The applause filled the room, and Sam heard one voice, then a few more, shout "Bravo!"

We did it.

He made out a few faces. Bayard Keating, speak of the devil, was at least a head taller than anybody else and wore a pale grey suit that stood out in the dim light. Beside him, little white-haired Geraldine only came up to his shoulder. In a different row, Sam saw another board member whose name he had forgotten. And in the middle of the house, Jeannette. Her face was lit up with joy, and she held her hands up high, as if her applause were an offering. Sam smiled straight at her, hoping she would see it.

Sam stepped aside and gave the applause to the orchestra and chorus. The hall, half-empty though it was, roared. Sam did not look at the empty seats. He tried not to see the faces that weren't there.

You would have been proud.

Lydia propped the stage door open. "Congratulations," she said.

In her expression, Sam saw the grade-school teacher again, this time one who had sweated blood trying to pound information into her class's brains and finally given up in despair, and then one student raised his hand and came up with the most perfectly brilliant answer she had ever heard. She looked at Sam as if he were a hero.

He dragged out his smile and propped it on his face. "I'm just going to grab the rest of that soda," he said before he turned tail and fled for the dressing room.

The door clicked shut behind him. That wouldn't last. Give the Keatings and whoever else five minutes, tops, before they came back here. And Sam needed to be out there thanking the orchestra, too, and the chorus. God knew they deserved it.

For ten seconds he could be alone. He didn't let himself sit down, since he wouldn't get up again if he did. Instead he leaned against the dressing table to gulp down the Coke.

He must not think about the faces that should have been here. Ma's gold hair and blue eyes; Gil's long jaw and dishevelled mane; or—yes, he should have been here too, he should have!—the face that looked so much like Sam's, except for the lines carved into it as if into wood. *You would have been proud...* except he never had been, had he. Dad had never been proud of his son.

If Sam thought about any of that now, he would lock this door, turn out the lights, and sit here in the dark until the ceiling caved in. The knock at the door came as a relief.

"Just a minute," he called. The can felt heavier than concrete, but he dragged it up to his mouth for one more sip.

The door creaked open. Somebody's head appeared. "Hey. It's just me." Nathan.

Sam almost let go of the soda. Reflex made him set it carefully down on the dressing table. Any second, other people would show up. Sam had nothing to worry about.

Nathan stepped into the room and carefully shut the door behind him. "I was hoping I'd catch you," the singer said. "Just for a second."

He moved closer. Christ, he was so *tall*. Any second, somebody else would knock. Somebody would open the door. Sam's feet seemed to have glued themselves to the floor.

Nathan said, "Listen, I know this is crazy. Right now I feel kind of crazy, to tell you the truth."

Now the tiniest square of floor separated the two of them. What the hell was wrong with Sam? Why, oh, why couldn't he look away from those eyes? Nathan said, "Maybe you don't want to hear this. If you don't, I swear I'll never say it again, but I have to tell you, you blow my mind."

He reached out. Sam could not step back an inch. Nathan's arms slipped around him. The singer had not smiled once; he did not now. "Maybe you'll hate my guts for this. I can't help it. I've never known anybody like you."

Nathan leaned forward. The tiny part of Sam's brain that wasn't paralyzed screamed, *Don't just stand here! Get away from him!* He couldn't move. And then... oh, God...

Sam closed his eyes. It ought to feel terrible. It ought to feel wrong in every possible way, but it didn't. The kiss filled his head with light.

When he opened his eyes, Nathan was watching him. "Sam." Now a smile did touch the singer's mouth. "Do you—"

The knock sounded like a gunshot. Sam's heart leaped into his throat, and for a second he saw his own panic mirrored in Nathan's face. The singer let go and stepped back. At the same time, from outside, they heard, "Sam?"

Lydia. Sam couldn't move. Nathan went to the door and opened it.

"Hi, Mrs. Holland." He sounded as casual as if he had run into her at the grocery store. "I'm heading out. Wanted to catch Sam first."

Sam saw her eyes move between the two of them. Nathan went on, "So I'll see you at the next rehearsal." He nodded at Sam. "Congratulations again, Maestro."

He was gone. Sam still had not moved a muscle. He felt so cold all over that he ached.

"Are you okay?" Lydia said.

Sam reached for the soda again. "I'm fine." He brought the can up to his lips and tipped the last few drops of soda into his mouth.

Lydia said, "Why'd you have the door shut?"

Sam dropped the empty can in the trash and looked straight at her. "Keeping people out for a minute."

"That singer," she said. "Was he bothering you?"

"Not at all."

Lydia folded her arms. "You know, I haven't been sure about him. He's different."

He was a newcomer that year, like Sam, and a Northerner, from Cincinnati he'd said once. He was black. Whether or not Lydia knew the rest, in old-city Richmond those three factors were more than enough to make Nathan "different." She went on, "I have to say, I'm not all that comfortable with him."

Sam shrugged. "He's the strongest baritone we have." He turned away as if the conversation was over and stacked his scores in his briefcase.

After a pause that could only have lasted a second or two, but felt much longer, she said, "Well, I came to tell you there's folks waiting to talk to you. I don't think we can keep them out much longer."

"Okay." Sam turned around, and now the smile came back to shield his face from her eyes. "Let's have them."

CHAPTER EIGHT

On the night of the first RSA concert, Jeannette and Veronica and Drew left Ricky and C.J. at home with their "Auntie Rose," as Ricky called the neighbour who babysat, and climbed into the Datsun for the ridiculously short drive to the Lewis Center. They had to drive because of Veronica's gold-glitter-covered high heels, one of which she took off and brandished at Jeannette in the Datsun's rear-view mirror. "Maybe you don't mind walking in those shoes, honey," she said, nodding at Jeannette's flats. "I'm not taking one step on that pavement in these."

Jeannette led the way up the Lewis Center's front steps. After all the times she had spent in the bowels of this building, tonight would be her first real look at the red-and-gold sanctum. Veronica swept into the lobby as if she had seen this kind of thing every day of her life. "Not bad," she announced. She flourished the stub of her ticket like one of her cigarettes and grandly accepted a program book from an usher. "Nannie, didn't you tell me this place is pinching pennies?" She tossed her jacket casually over the counter at the coat check. Her blouse, a mass of gold sequins, practically screamed under the lights, and her short black skirt showed plenty of leg. Next to her, Drew looked reasonably tame and civilized in his one and only suit. Jeannette, who had been pleased with her own simple white dress, couldn't help feeling positively dowdy.

Their seats were five rows back from the stage and right in the middle of the hall. Veronica leaned back in her red plush seat and opened her program book. "This place is all right," she announced. "Just fine."

Jeannette sighed. Sam had been right, the house was only about half full, but most of the orchestra was already onstage, and Veronica's voice surely carried that far. Jeannette was convinced that a couple of the violinists looked right at her. "Vee," she whispered, "please keep it down."

Veronica patted her hand. "Don't fret. Once the music starts, I'll be as quiet as a mouse. That boy of yours won't know I'm here."

That boy. Jeannette put her head down and flipped grimly through the pages of her own program book. Drew, on Veronica's other side, turned through his book in his usual meditative silence.

When Jeannette had first met Drew Calhoun, she hadn't understood why Veronica, who could have had her pick of any of the boys in her community college classes, had chosen this square-faced man with the wispy blond hair and eyes such a light blue they looked almost colourless. He wasn't much to look at, which turned out to be a bigger drawback when you learned that he couldn't make conversation either. It wasn't until later, when Jeannette saw the way Drew massaged his wife's shoulders at the end of the day and the way he cuddled a sleeping baby to his chest, that Jeannette understood what her sister had chosen. Veronica would never have to worry about waking up one morning alone.

Now Veronica opened her own program. "So *that's* what he looks like!"

Jeannette knew this was her own fault. Veronica had asked her again and again to bring Sam over to the apartment on a Saturday afternoon. If Jeannette had done that, she could have avoided tonight. Veronica didn't normally go in for concerts and had only come to this one because Jeannette wouldn't let her meet Sam any other way.

Jeannette had wanted her sister to see Sam onstage, at his radiant best. Now she sat numbly as her sister scrutinized the black-and-white photo of him inside the program cover. "Not bad," Veronica decided. "Not bad at all, Nannie. I can see the appeal. *Maestro*, huh?" Her twang shoved at least three syllables into the word. "And what kind of name is Kraychek? You never told me."

There might still be a few people out on the street who hadn't heard her. Jeannette said, "It's Polish." Sam had told her once that his dad's parents had come over from Poland. That single piece of information was pretty much the only thing Jeannette knew about his family, and at the rate this evening was going, she might never learn anything else.

Fortunately, the house lights chose that moment to go down. Jeannette sank so low in her seat that the metal edge at the top of the back cushion pressed against her skull.

True to her word, Veronica did at least shut up. Jeannette stared out at the stage. The honey-coloured floorboards gleamed under the hot white stage lights, but from this close she could make out scuff marks. The black chairs and music stands for the performers made a wide, deep half-oval, with the copper tympani at the back and the two harps off to the side. The podium stood in front. The musicians, who had been warming up their fingers and instruments with slithery runs and trills, stopped playing. The hall went still.

The side door to the stage creaked open. The concertmaster walked out, carrying his violin. Jeannette straightened partway back up in her seat and joined the rest of the audience in the polite trickle of applause. She expected a nudge in the ribs and a "Why do we have to clap for him? He hasn't done anything yet," from Veronica, but either her sister remembered her couple of concert experiences past or honoured her promise to keep her mouth shut.

After the instruments tuned, silence settled back on the hall. Jeannette clasped her program book in both hands and sat up straighter. Invisible electricity prickled on her spine and dampened her fingers with sweat. The walls themselves seemed to hold their breath, waiting for the last person to come onstage. Finally, just before Jeannette couldn't wait any longer, the stage door creaked open again.

His footsteps rang on the floorboards. The lapels of his black coat made razor edges against his white shirt, and his gold cufflinks gleamed in the light. From the podium, he turned to face the audience, smiling. Jeannette caught her breath.

The same smile, the same eyes she knew, but he looked different up there, under the white light, above them all. He wore the formal dress as easily as the jeans and short sleeves she had seen on him so many times. She clapped until her hands burned, willing him to look straight at her and read what she felt in her face.

He might have. She couldn't quite tell whether his eyes found hers before he bowed to the audience, turned away, and took the baton up off his music stand.

Veronica's finger prodded her wrist. Jeannette spun around, ready to snarl, but Veronica patted her hand again and mouthed a word. *Handsome.*

Well. Jeannette nodded. Treacherous colour climbed into her cheeks, and she stared back up at the podium.

The baton was such a small thing. Jeannette had never thought about that before. You could break the wooden shaft with a simple twist, but when Sam fit the grip into its long-accustomed place between his fingers, the energy in the hall shifted. It converged into a single line and channelled itself straight into the white stick.

All sound drained out of the hall. Then, at the downward flick of the baton, the music began.

Jeannette stared at the man on the podium. He moved like a dancer, each motion clean and precise, so graceful her heart twisted. The music answered his every gesture. He held the threads of sound between his fingers and cupped them in his hands.

Or was it that simple? The white stick danced, and Jeannette realized she couldn't tell who was leading whom. Sam and the music were that closely wrapped together. Maybe the music had always been here in this hall, hanging in the air, waiting. He had only called it down for the audience to hear.

Jeannette didn't know. Only two clear thoughts formed in her head. One, that she had never heard anything as rich and vibrant as the sound that wove around her now. Two, that the man up there under the light, with his graceful hands and strong, slender body: he could not belong to her. Not to the bastard girl from Reckord's Mill.

How had Jeannette thought otherwise? She understood the mistake she had made, felt it in the deepest part of herself. Then the music called her, and she had to close her eyes and let it carry her away.

♪

At intermission, Veronica stood up. "I saw a drinks counter out there in the lobby," she announced to Jeannette. "Come on, honey."

Jeannette didn't want to leave her seat or for that matter feel like moving at all, but with Veronica levering her elbow, she had to get up. Veronica called back over her shoulder, "Keep an eye on our seats, Drew, okay? We'll be back in two shakes." Jeannette heard her brother-in-law answer "Take your time," before her sister dragged her away.

In the lobby, Veronica headed straight for the marble counter in the far corner, completely oblivious to the elegantly-dressed people she brushed out of the way. "They have *wine*," she said happily. An usher behind the counter, who wore the Lewis Center's mandatory red vest and black pants, looked up from cutting the top off of a bag of crystal-cut plastic glasses. "What can I get you, ma'am?"

Veronica thumped her beat-up purse down on the marble. "How much is a glass of wine?"

Jeannette found her tongue, which had gotten stuck to the roof of her mouth because of the stares they had gotten (*who is that creature in the gold shirt?*). "Vee," she whispered, "you don't need wine. Get a soda or something."

"One glass won't hurt," Veronica said. "How much?"

"Three dollars, ma'am."

Three dollars? For one plastic cup? Veronica pulled out her wallet and counted out the ones.

The bartender asked, "Will that be red, white, or rosé?"

"Rosé, thank you."

At least he filled it almost to the top, though it still couldn't be three dollars' worth. Veronica tugged Jeannette away into a corner of the lobby, where a pair of red plush armchairs sat in front of a long window overlooking Jefferson Street. One of the armchairs was occupied by a white-haired woman in a deep purple jacket and purple skirt. *Plum pudding*, Jeannette thought. The woman held a richly polished cane in one hand, probably made out of some mind-bogglingly expensive wood like mahogany.

Veronica pushed the cup into Jeannette's hand. "Okay. Drink up."

"What? Vee, I don't want this."

"Yes, you do. Your face looks like a toad's belly. You need some colour."

Jeannette should have gotten angry, but she heard herself quaver, "I don't look that bad, do I?"

"Nannie, you're pale is all. Have a couple of sips. It'll fix you right up."

Jeannette lifted the cup to her lips. The smell of the wine stung her nostrils, but not as much as the actual liquid going down her throat. She coughed.

"That's better," Veronica said. "One more swallow. There you go."

Jeannette had to have colour now. She was surprised sweat didn't break out on her forehead. Veronica drank the rest in a couple of easy swallows and tossed the cup into the faux brass trashcan nearby. "Now." She put her arm around Jeannette's shoulders. The smell of the wine mixed with her perpetual cigarette smokiness. "Tell me what's the matter."

Out of the corner of her eye, Jeannette saw the lady in purple looking at them. Why did everybody have to stare? You'd think they had never seen sequins before. "Nothing," she answered.

Veronica didn't bother to keep her voice low. "Not buying it. Try again."

Jeannette wanted to go home and crawl under the covers and go to sleep, except then she would miss the second half of the concert and seeing Sam afterward, and the two of them had planned to spend an hour or two together. But why would he want to give her his time? She wasn't worth it.

Veronica said, "I'll tell you what I think. I think you're deciding that boy's too good for you."

Plum Pudding was still looking their way. Jeannette could see the old lady's reflection in the dark window. Maybe it was Veronica's skirt, or rather the lack of it. Jeannette had asked her sister if she really wanted to wear such a short one, but Veronica had said, "I'm an example to all those other middle-aged moms out there." As if twenty-six counted as middle age.

Veronica went on, "Now, I don't mind telling you, I was impressed. He's good, all right. At least as far as I can tell before I talk to him face to face. But too good for you?" With her free hand, Veronica tilted Jeannette's chin up. "Honey, *nobody* is too good for my little sister."

Before Jeannette could answer, Veronica glanced past her at somebody else. "Don't mind us," she said. Jeannette realized with horror that she was talking to Plum Pudding. "Just giving some advice," Veronica said. "My sister here, that was her boyfriend up on the stage. The conductor," she added, to clarify.

Jeannette's knees turned to water. What were the odds she had a sinkhole right underneath her, and it would open up this second?

Plum Pudding smiled and got to her feet, leaning on the possibly-mahogany cane. She wore a purple brooch too, Jeannette saw. At least mostly purple. A gold peacock set with glittery stones. Amethysts?

"How lovely," Plum Pudding said. Virginia blue-blood, all the way. "Sam has a young lady now? I'm glad to hear it."

Sam. So Plum Pudding knew him, and well too, unless rich old ladies could gossip about anybody's life they felt like. And why, Jeannette wondered, didn't the old shrew just say she was sorry for eavesdropping and go away? Wouldn't that be the polite thing to do?

As if she had heard the thought, Plum Pudding said to Jeannette, "I do apologize for listening in. I noticed you looked a bit ill, dear. Are you all right?"

"Yes," Jeannette managed. *Yay-us.* "I'm fine. Thank you."

Plum Pudding held out her hand. Another purple stone glittered on a finger that looked too frail for it. "My name is Geraldine Keating. My husband Bayard is chairman of the Symphonic Artists board of directors. I can't tell you how delighted we are to have Sam with us this year."

"Oh. Um." Jeannette reached out to shake hands. "I'm Jeannette Reilly. This"—she nodded in her sister's direction—"is my sister, Veronica Calhoun."

"Very pleased to meet you both." Plum's skin felt papery, but her grip was surprisingly strong. "You're enjoying the concert?"

"Yes." Jeannette didn't trust herself to say anything else. She couldn't hang on to her Richmond accent, and every word out of her mouth would give this woman a clearer picture of what Jeannette was. Rich people had always had names for that kind of person. *Cracker. White trash.*

"Sam is exceptionally talented," Plum said, "and so charming. It's rare to see such grace and poise in such a young person." The woman actually twinkled, just like her amethyst brooch. She went on, "I am certain he'll be able to turn things around for Symphonic Artists this season. We are so fortunate to have a young conductor of his gifts."

Jeannette nodded mutely. Now would be the perfect time for Veronica to contribute something, anything really. Jeannette was past caring, but her sister stayed silent. For a horrible second the quiet thickened like butter. Then the lights in the lobby flickered.

"Ah, it's time for the second half." Plum twinkled again. "I wonder where Bayard's gotten to? I must go and find him, but I'm so pleased to have met you, Jeannette, dear." She had caught the name at once. "Both of you," she added, including Veronica in her nod. "I hope to see you again soon."

She turned away, hobbling—but in a stately fashion, of course—back toward the doors to the hall. The second Veronica judged she was out of earshot, she said, "Good thing that one's not your age, Nannie. You'd have competition!"

Jeannette couldn't smile. Veronica nudged her. "I was *kidding,* honey. Good gracious. Come on, let's go see what that boy of yours is going to do next."

Jeannette let her sister take her arm again and draw her back to the hall. Her legs felt so stiff, they could have been cut out of wood. She wished she could have let them take her out through the grand lobby and away from this place.

♫

In seven weeks of rehearsals, the Mozart Mass in C Minor had never sounded the way it did tonight. By the time it ended and the audience got to its feet, clapping and cheering, Jeannette felt entirely detached from the world. She could look up at *him* on the podium and understand that his universe and hers simply didn't intersect. The music filled her up more fully than any wine could, and she beamed up at the players and applauded along with everyone else.

Afterward, the house lights came up, people collected programs and purses and jackets, and onstage the chairs and stands scraped as the musicians packed up. "All right," Veronica said. "Let's go meet this boy."

Jeannette's energy drained out of her in a rush. Flat-sounding words dropped out of her mouth. "It's late. We should go home."

Veronica turned right around in the middle of the row to look at her. "Child, what on earth's the matter with you?"

"Nothing. I'm just tired." Jeannette studied her sister's shoes. They glittered like fool's gold. "I want to go to bed."

That strong hand found her chin again and tilted it up as if she had been no bigger than Ricky. "Jeannette Marie Reilly. You've finally got something you want. I am not going to stand here and watch you give it up." Veronica caught Jeannette's shoulder, turned her around, and marched her down the row. "We're going to find him this minute."

An usher tried to stop them, but Veronica, propelling Jeannette along and keeping Drew in tow, went straight up the stage-right steps and into the chaotic backstage world. Jeannette remembered this place from that night when she had come down here alone. She wondered if the room she had found had in fact been Sam's dressing room. God knew she didn't want to go there now, but Veronica kept walking, and Jeannette didn't have the energy to fight back.

She saw a flash of purple in the narrow hallway that ran behind the stage. Veronica muttered, "There we go," and elbowed past a few musicians to manoeuvre into that hall. At the other end of it, Jeannette could see Plum Pudding and a tall man in a grey suit standing in front of an open door.

Veronica prodded her from behind and made Jeannette keep walking. Plum Pudding had her back to the hall, but Jeannette saw the tall man's profile. He looked exactly like one of those old Southern generals you saw in pictures from the Civil War. Jeannette thought he ought to have a red sash tied around his waist and a sword.

Plum was saying, "Sam, that was magnificent. You did us proud, my dear."

His laugh. "I'm so glad you liked it, Geraldine."

Confederate General agreed. "It exceeded all my expectations. The board made the right choice. I will personally guarantee they know it."

"Thank you, Bayard." Sam sounded so confident, relaxed. *Grace and poise.* "Thank you for giving me a chance with this job."

Poke, right in the small of Jeannette's back. Veronica hissed, "Go on, child." Go where? Into the middle of their conversation? Confederate General's height blocked Jeannette's view into the room. Yes, it was the room she had found before. Now it belonged securely to Sam. Jeannette didn't want to budge another inch.

Plum Pudding glanced back into the hall. Her eyes met Jeannette's. "Ah! Here's that lovely young lady. Come along in, dear."

"Jeannette!"

Sam's voice wrapped around her, and then his arms and his familiar clean, spicy scent. Even then Jeannette couldn't look up into his face. She knew how stupid it must look, but she put her head blindly down against his shoulder and held on to him with all the strength she could find, the way a scared child would cling to somebody she loved, if she thought that person was about to disappear.

He laughed. "What's up, honey? Are you okay?" His voice sounded too bright, as if the white light from the stage still hung around him.

"She'll be fine now." That was Veronica. "I'm her sister, and this is my husband, and it's about darn time we met you."

Confederate General and Plum Pudding laughed. Sam joined in. He let go of Jeannette and touched her cheek.

She had to look up at him then, and no, this wasn't the Sam she knew. This man stood in a haze of light. His eyes bored into her, and his smile… she wanted to squint, shade her face, turn away. She had never felt the touch of his hand or his lips on hers. The room was too small and crowded to let her escape.

She didn't dare show how afraid she was. She straightened up and cleared her throat. "Sam, I'd like you to meet my sister Veronica and my brother-in-law Drew." She had no idea how she managed to sound so calm. "Vee, Drew, this is Sam Kraychek, but you know that already."

That got another laugh. Sam stuck his hand out right between Plum and the General to shake hands with Veronica. "Pleased to meet you," he said. "I've heard a lot about you."

Drew shook hands with the stranger, the Maestro, too. Veronica said, "So you've heard about me? I'm scared to ask."

The Maestro grinned. "Well, for one thing, I know you have a gift for styling hair."

"Is that so?" Plum Pudding asked.

"Now and then," Veronica said. "When Nannie will let me."

The Maestro raised his eyebrows. "Nannie?"

"That's what we call her at home. She didn't tell you?"

Oh, no. Jeannette didn't want to talk about this now and bring the deepest hurt of her life out right in front of these Virginia aristocrats. The Maestro reached for her hand. "No," he said, "I hadn't heard that nickname."

He drew her over beside him and put his arm around her. Through his coat sleeve and her dress, her skin burned at the touch.

Veronica said, "She told us we had to call her that when she was, oh, eight or so. Our aunt kicked up a fuss, but I said, why not? That's what sisters are for, right?"

Plum Pudding said, "Of course. And why did you choose that nickname, dear?"

No. Jeannette could not tell her. She found herself staring down at the white tile floor instead. "Honey," the Maestro said. His fingers touched her cheek again. "Why so shy?"

As if she were a child. Jeannette's face smarted with humiliation. A long time ago, he had called himself a nobody from nowhere and told her he was from a tiny town nobody had ever heard of. That couldn't have been this man. This man chatted as with people whose voices dripped money as if he had been born owning china and crystal.

Confederate General said, "I'll bet you impressed her, Sam." He sounded like the kind of plantation owner who would have set his hounds on any white trash he found snooping around his property. "Mrs. Calhoun, was it?" he said. "Where are you folks from?"

"South Carolina," Veronica twanged shamelessly. *Sahth Cal-Lyna.*

Plum asked, "Are you visiting Richmond for a while?"

"No, we live here. Drew works for Dominion Gas." She had to tell them that. "We just moved up a couple of months ago."

"How do you like it?"

"Oh, it's a great town. Real nice. Of course, we haven't seen too much of it yet, 'cause we have two little boys, and they keep us busy. Speaking of them, Drew honey, we should probably head home, don't you think? We promised the sitter we'd be back by ten."

Now Jeannette looked up. *Take me with you.*

Veronica said, "It was very nice to meet you folks." She turned to the Maestro. "And you too, of course." The arm around Jeannette's waist let go as Veronica pulled him into a hug. Where did she get the nerve? "You take care of my sister, you hear?" Veronica said. "Make sure she don't stay up too late tonight."

Jeannette tried to catch her eye. *No, please don't leave. Let me come with you.*

The Maestro returned the hug easily. "Don't worry. I'll get her home safe and sound."

If Veronica saw Jeannette's look, she ignored it. "'Night, folks. Drive safe." Then she and Drew were gone.

Lydia Holland, the orchestra manager, looked in to say good night too. Plum Pudding and the General didn't stay long after that. "I'm sure you young people want to be by yourselves," Plum said. She hugged the Maestro, and Jeannette saw her drop a kiss on his cheek. Then Jeannette was alone in the tiny room with the stranger.

He put his hands on her waist and looked into her eyes. "Honey. What's the matter?"

Behind the bewildering performance-light, she saw a tiny flicker of annoyance. She found her voice. "I don't know. I think I'm just tired."

"Well, tell you what. I'd like to get out of these clothes, and then I thought we could go back to my place for a little while. Is that okay?"

She nodded. She didn't have a choice, after all: he was her only ride home now, and—a tiny sane part of her mind woke up—for God's sake, she was supposed to be happy, supposed to want to be with him.

He disappeared into what turned out to be a tiny bathroom off the back corner of the dressing room. She heard him moving around in there, the zip and rustle of a garment bag.

Jeannette sank down on the room's one rickety wooden chair. When she had come down here before, the room had been dark until she turned on that accusing fluorescent light. She wanted find the switch again, right now, and turn it off. Maybe then she could disappear.

What a stupid idea. What was the matter with her, anyway? Sam's briefcase lay on the floor beside Jeannette's chair, open, with his baton and scores inside. In the bathroom, the toilet flushed. Jeannette leaned down and picked up the baton. She wrapped her fingers around the grip, holding on to the smooth wood that Sam had touched.

CHAPTER NINE

A fter five years, Sam understood that his last day in his parents' house could not have been easy for his father, any more than it had been for Sam himself. When you got right down to it, who would want a sick and fucked-up son, especially when that son was your only child?

"You've always hated me! Let me give you something to hate!"

Sam had said that to his father that last morning. The words beat in his head now as he got back to his apartment after his debut with the RSA and unlocked his building's front door.

Ma was crying. Sam could not look at her. He stared at his father across the white kitchen table, his eyes burning from the glare of light on that gleaming Formica surface, his head ready to explode. His father's expression did not change. The eyes behind the glasses were as frigid as water in winter.

The mailboxes lined the wall by the front door. Sam didn't bother checking his. He gripped his briefcase tighter and adjusted the drape of the garment bag over his arm. Jeannette followed him in silence up the two flights.

It could not be true. Dad could not hate him, not really. Sam's words rang in the silent room, and he held his breath and prayed with every nerve for something, something he couldn't say in words, but if God would listen just once to someone so messed up, maybe He would understand. Sam knew He probably wouldn't. All those Masses and Sunday school sessions had made it too clear that God hated people like him, but in this moment he couldn't help pleading for help anyway. Maybe God would hear him. Maybe.

Then his father's mouth opened. Quiet words dropped out. "Get out of this house."

Sam would have to write to Ma soon. She had known he had a concert coming up, and she would want to hear about it. How could he tell her now about tonight, with what had happened afterward?

You bastard. You son of a bitch. Sam couldn't find bad enough words to describe what he was. He had fucked up. He had stood there and let Nathan do what he had done. That kiss still burned on Sam's lips.

Inside the apartment, he didn't turn on the lights. He dropped his stuff on the unmade bed and went to the narrow window next to the spinet. Jeannette still didn't say a word. Sam knew he should open his mouth and say something to her, the woman he was supposed to care about. He should act like he was glad they had some time together.

He couldn't do it. In another life, he had stood in another apartment like this one, except it hadn't been his. It had been almost as bare, without a TV to relax in front of or family Polaroids on the walls, or a scrubby African violet or begonia on the windowsill. There had been a stereo, though, and a sprawling record collection, and the piano had been a sleek black grand, the one good piece of furniture in the place. And, most important of all, Gil had been there.

Sam forced himself to turn around. The smile felt like it would never come back, but maybe in the dark Jeannette wouldn't notice.

He didn't get a chance to open his mouth. She hurried over to him. "Sam, what's wrong?" Her warm hand touched his face.

She cared so much, and he didn't deserve it. "I'm all right," he said, trying to sound like it. "Kind of tired."

"You need to sleep. I should go home."

Three seconds ago, he had wanted that more than anything else. Now he fought down the urge to snatch her hand and cling to it. She would think he was crazy. *Please don't leave me alone.*

He put his arm around her instead. That steadied him. "No. I don't want you to leave." Over her shoulder he saw the shape of the spinet, half-buried under piles of music. "Do you think we could play some?"

That sounded pretty crazy too. It was almost eleven at night, and anybody would think he'd had more than enough music after this evening.

Jeannette glanced over at the piano and back at him, her eyes wide in the dark. "Now?" she said. "Won't the neighbours mind?"

To hell with the neighbours. "We won't be loud." On the top of the spinet he saw a pale rectangle and remembered what score that was. Yes: Ravel's *Ma Mère L'Oye*, the piece for children.

Children knew where home was. They knew how to get back to the place where they were safe.

At the piano, Sam opened the music to the fourth movement, "Conversations of Beauty and the Beast." Jeannette took off her shoes and came over to the bench. She reached for the switch on the brass stand lamp.

He caught her wrist. "Let's not."

"But it's dark."

"There's some light," he said. There was, from the street lamp outside. *Please. Just for now.*

She gave in. They sat on the bench together in the dark, and Sam looked up at the excerpt of the fairy tale written at the top of the page. *Beauty said to the Beast, "When I think of your good heart, you do not seem so frightening to me."*

The piece had a simple tune. Jeannette's part didn't even use the left hand. You could easily imagine two children playing it.

"Oh, yes!" the Beast said, "I do have a good heart, but I am a monster."

Sam felt the years drop quietly away behind him. All the times when he had hopelessly remembered home, it had felt as far away as the moon. Now it seemed that the thinnest, most fragile barrier stood between him and the place where he most wanted to be, the place where he used to be safe. He could melt that barrier with a fingertip.

"Many men," Beauty said, "are far more monstrous than you."

Sam's part changed. The gentle waltz of the opening faded away. His hands went down into the lowest register of the piano and struck harsh, clashing chords: the Beast's voice.

More monstrous than him? Maybe. Right now, Sam did not believe it. He would have closed his eyes if he could, but then he would have lost his place in the music, and the memory of Nathan would have jumped out to strangle him. He stared at the page and willed his fingers to keep moving.

"Beauty," the Beast said, *"will you be my wife?"*

Jeannette's part came back in. It was as gentle as it had been at the beginning, but now his part growled under it like the bogeyman in the closet.

"No, Beast! I cannot marry you."

She shouldn't, that was for sure. The sweet girl should not chain herself to the monster.

The two parts moved together. Ravel had skipped over the part of the story where Beauty left the Beast's castle and the villagers came with their torches and pitchforks. The narrative picked up again when the Beast lay dying, in the same garden where Beauty had walked among the flowers.

"I can die content," the Beast said, *"because I have seen you again."*

"No, my dear Beast, you must not die, for I love you!"

After the climax, there was a moment of stillness before Jeannette's hand moved down for a glissando. Sam's didn't move his fingers away in time. She brushed them lightly.

"The Beast disappeared. At Beauty's feet was a handsome prince, freed from his enchantment by love."

Sam and Jeannette did not need to look at each other in the last measures to set the chords down in perfect unison. They held the last one until the sound disappeared.

Now Sam could close his eyes. He let go of the keys and did it, and there was home, a million miles away, and Ma's face, and her tears. And Gil on the hospital bed. And Dad. What had Sam done to them all?

A touch made him jump. His hands had locked together in his lap. Jeannette's warm fingers covered them.

"Sam?"

He couldn't open his eyes. "I'm okay," he said.

"You're not. Please tell me what's going on."

He swung around. "Jeannette, why do you want to be with me?"

It came out like a snarl. Serve him right if she got up off this bench and walked away without another word.

Her clear eyes rested on him. "Why? Because…" She looked scared again, scared of him, but she didn't pull her hand away. After a long silent moment, she said, "Because I love you."

She had never told him that before. "I'm not worth it," Sam said. The words sounded as blunt as thrown rocks. He had to tell her while he could. "I'm not worth it at all."

Her fingers closed around his. "Sam, what are you talking about? That's not true."

Something was clawing its way up his throat now. She shouldn't be here to see him lose it. "You don't know. You don't know what I… what I've…"

The words choked off. Goddamn it. A hot tear slid down his cheek.

He saw the shock of it in her face. Then her other hand moved. Before he could do anything to stop her, she brushed the tear away and said, "Then tell me. Tell me what's so terrible."

Now he couldn't speak at all. He shut his eyes again, tight. In the dark—he couldn't stop himself—he reached for her hand. His fingers closed around it.

"Tell me," she said again. "Did something happen tonight? You did an amazing job. You know you did."

He couldn't let her believe such a lie. Not with the rest of what he'd done. "Please don't talk about that." His voice sounded like he was talking through gravel.

"Why not?" When he couldn't answer, she said, "Sweetheart, please, I need to know what's wrong."

Sweetheart. The word felt like a slap. Sam opened his eyes and told the only truth he could. "You shouldn't be with me. You deserve somebody better."

As he said it, he knew what he had to do. It swelled up in his head, huge and frozen.

Tell her what you are. She won't want you anymore.

If he thought about it, he would start to shake. He opened his mouth again and said, "Somebody who isn't…"

Another voice echoed in his head, cold and quiet. *"Get out of this house."*

Sam's voice cut off. He could not do it. Goddamn him, he could not.

Jeannette said, "Isn't what?"

He could not speak. If only she could cut a window in his skull and see inside his brain. She should know to run away from him as fast as she could.

She said, "Sam, listen. I don't want anybody else." Her free hand moved again and covered his. "You're so much more than I deserve."

She didn't want anybody else? Christ, she had no idea what a mistake she was making. But as Sam thought it, in the back of his head, a faint strand of music woke up. *No, my dear Beast, you must not die...*

She said, "I love you."

This beautiful woman. Holding on to his hands as if they were the most precious thing she had ever found, and she never wanted to let them go.

"I love you, Sam."

The Beast disappeared. At Beauty's feet was a handsome prince, freed from his enchantment by love.

The white house on River Street. The gray Lackawanna River. The crisp winter air of the mountains and a thick coat of sparkling snow on the ground. Ma. It was all here in front of him. Only the smallest, thinnest barrier stood between him and it, and he could melt that barrier with a fingertip.

When he opened his mouth, the words he had meant to say before did not come out. Instead he said something he never would have planned in a thousand years.

"Jeannette. Will you marry me?"

That floored her. No wonder, when they had only known each other for a handful of weeks. Sam would have laughed at his own craziness, but his life hung on her answer.

The girl should not chain herself to the monster.

No monster. Not anymore. If she said yes, he promised there would never be a monster again.

"Yes."

The syllable was no more than a breath of air and Jeannette's lips moving in the dark. "Yes," she said again, stronger now. "I will."

Sweet woman. Sweet, beautiful woman. He gathered her into his arms. She rested her head on his shoulder, and he closed his eyes and breathed the flowery scent of her hair.

♫

The next morning, the phone rang at eleven and woke Sam out of a dreamless sleep. He had driven Jeannette home sometime after midnight and collapsed into bed in the small hours of the morning. When the phone jolted him awake, he remembered two things: that Gil had promised to call him this morning, and that last night, he had gotten engaged.

He almost didn't pick up. The phone rang three times while Sam lay on the pillow and looked for answers on the bare ceiling. Finally, on the fourth ring, he threw back the blanket and stumbled into the kitchen.

"Hello?" Waiting to hear Gil's voice on the other end, Sam tried to collect himself. They could talk about the concert, not about anything that had happened afterward. That was a lie by omission. Two lies, if you counted what had happened with Nathan. That part couldn't matter anymore.

"Mr. Kraychek?"

The voice snapped Sam out of his thoughts. Not Gil. Vaguely familiar, but Sam couldn't place it. "Yes?" he said.

"Mr. Kraychek, this is Jonas Caruso at Pennsylvania Hospital."

Memory rushed in. *I will notify you when Mr. Hart is here, if there is ever a circumstance you should be aware of and he is unable to contact you himself.*

Gil was in the hospital again. He hadn't been able to call. "Yes?" Sam said stupidly. God, it was cold in this kitchen. He had never realized that before. He had goosebumps all over his bare arms and legs, and the linoleum tile froze his feet.

The voice on the other end of the phone said, "I am one of the attendants who works with your friend Mr. Hart. We met when you were here a few weeks ago. Do you remember?"

Sam's teeth chattered, and he had to pry his mouth open. "Yes. I do."

"Mr. Hart was admitted here last night. He advised me he was scheduled to speak with you this morning, but he is under observation and unable to call."

Under observation. What did that mean? Sam forced his mouth to open again. "Is he okay? I mean, why is he there?"

"He is in no immediate danger. He was admitted during the night with acute gastric distress, but has received palliative treatment and hydration. His condition has improved. He will most likely be discharged tomorrow."

Sam remembered the same voice saying, *For the purposes of this conversation, let's simply say that I understand what you are going through.* It was hard to reconcile that fact with the dispassionate words Sam heard now. One thing seemed clear: Gil was all right. No, he wasn't, he would never be that again, but this call didn't mean what it could have.

Sam hung on to the counter for support. "He's okay," he said. *Say yes. Let me hear a yes.*

"He is stable. He told me you expected to hear from him and was concerned that you would worry. I explained my arrangement with you, and he asked me to call."

A piece of what Caruso had said caught up with Sam: Gil had been admitted during the night. "But I talked to him yesterday." Sam realized he'd said it aloud. "In the afternoon. He seemed okay then."

"Yes. In his condition, sudden imbalances are common."

"You said he could go home tomorrow?"

"Most likely, yes."

Sam remembered something else. *My job might be compromised.* Where was Caruso calling from? Sam had a crazy image of that storage closet where he and Caruso had talked, a pay phone hidden in there behind the stacks of clean linen. Or maybe Caruso had gone to a pay phone on some street corner, though Sam didn't hear cars in the background. No matter what, every second the man spent on the phone was probably putting him more at risk.

"Thank you," Sam said. "Thank you for letting me know."

"Of course."

"Could you tell Gil I'll try him at home tomorrow? Or he can call me whenever he gets a chance."

"I will give him the message."

"And could you tell him, too…" Sam stopped. Tell him what? What could Sam say that would be any use at all? "Tell him last night went fine. I think he'll want to know."

Caruso promised he would without asking what that was about. Sam thanked him again, and they hung up.

Sudden imbalances. Gastric distress. Sam leaned on the counter and stared out the tiny window at the street outside. The fierce chill had left him, but he didn't trust his legs to hold him up. The edge of the yellow laminate dug into his stomach. Stable. Gil was stable. He would go home tomorrow. Sam would talk to him soon.

If he threw on some clothes and left right now, Sam knew he could get to Philly sometime between four and five in the afternoon. Gil was under observation. Sam should have asked what exactly that meant. Were they running some kind of tests on him? If Sam got there, could Gil have a visitor?

Sam flattened his hands against the countertop. *Think.* Gil didn't expect him to come, hadn't asked for him. Caruso would have said so otherwise. Sam didn't have gas in the car; taking Jeannette home last night had used up the last couple of drops in the tank. You could do a ten-hour round trip drive in a day, but if you started this late, you wouldn't have any useful time to spend up there. Sam could find a motel for overnight, but he had rehearsal again tomorrow, and he'd have to be back in time. And if Gil was going home tomorrow, who knew what time he would be discharged, or if he could see Sam beforehand?

Gil could have a "sudden imbalance" any time. Sam shook his head.

He had thrown a toothbrush and a change of underwear in an Acme bag and was yanking on last night's jeans when the phone rang again. He hauled the jeans up enough not to trip over them, ran back to the kitchen, and snatched the receiver out of the cradle.

"Hello?" It would be the one voice he wanted most in the world, calling to say "don't worry, I'm okay." It had to be.

"Hey."

Not Gil. Disappointment crashed down so hard that Sam wanted to slump on the floor. He couldn't say a word.

"Sam?" He could actually hear her blushing. "Sam? Are you there?"

Jesus. He had asked her to *marry* him.

The Beast disappeared. At Beauty's feet was a handsome prince.

"Jeannette. Hi, sweetheart." He couldn't tell what he sounded like.

"I'm sorry. Did I wake you up?"

"No. No, not at all." Sam propped himself against the edge of the counter again.

"Are you sure? You sound really tired."

She sounded odd herself. Like she was trying to whisper into the phone? Sam tried to pull himself together. He had to act glad to hear her voice. "No, I'm fine. How are you? Did you sleep all right?"

"Sort of." She hesitated. "Sam... last night, did you... I mean, did we really..."

Her half-whisper trailed off into a question. With somebody else, the question could have been, *did we really get drunk and fuck?* Not with her. Oh, God, never.

What had he been thinking? *Had* he been thinking? He stared at the piano bench in its corner. It had happened right there.

Her hands on the keys. Her pale face in the dark. The white house on River Street. The Lackawanna. *Home.*

Nothing but that last thought could have made him open his mouth. "Yes," he said. Thank God, he sounded happy, or at least happy enough. "Get engaged? Yes, we did."

He heard a laugh, but at the same time, a sniff. "I'm sorry. It's just, I woke up, I thought maybe I'd dreamed the whole thing."

"You know, I felt the same way."

"But we did. We really did." Another sniffle. "I'm sorry."

She shouldn't apologize so much. "Honey, it's okay." He tried to make his voice the caress it should be. "It's a big deal, I know."

A bigger deal than he had realized. *Marry.* That meant forever.

Jeannette laughed again. "No. I mean, I shouldn't get all emotional, because Vee's in the kitchen, and if she sees me she's going to ask what's going on, and I don't know. I'm not ready to talk about it yet."

Vee. Her sister, Veronica. Sam remembered the small, dark-haired woman with the mostly-bare legs and the, oh yes, glaringly gold blouse. "You didn't tell her?"

"Not yet. Does that bother you?"

Did he sound like it did? He had thought he must sound like he'd gotten a death-row reprieve. "No, not at all. You should tell her when you want." If nobody else knew yet, maybe none of it was real.

"Sam, can we... I know Sunday's not our usual day, but..." In a sick moment, he knew what she was going to ask and wanted to snap at her to spit it out. For God's sake, he was supposed to want to be with her. She finished in a rush, "I mean, I really want to see you."

Of course she did. Sam looked at the unmade bed where he had tossed the bag with the toothbrush and briefs.

She said quickly, "But I know you're tired after last night. And you probably have things to do."

He could have said yes, actually, he did have things to do. If he told her he was going to Philly, she would want to know why. He couldn't imagine saying Gil's name to her and didn't want to make something up. He had already lied to her, one lie by omission. He hadn't told her what he was.

He realized he was clutching the phone so hard that it dug into his hand. "No, I'm not busy at all." Was that a lie? Did it count? "What would you like to do?"

"I don't know. Anything."

Sam looked out the window again. It was misty and grey out. Not a good day for the river walk. "Tell you what. I'll come by and we can figure it out. Sound good?"

It struck him there was one thing they would have to do eventually. If this was real, she would have to have a ring.

"Sure."

She sounded so glad, it made him wince. "Say half an hour?" he said. "I need to take a quick shower. Is that too soon?"

"No. No. That's great."

"Good. See you in a few."

"Okay." He heard the catch in her breath. "I love you."

"I love you too."

They hung up. Sam started the shower running and peeled off the jeans again. When the water was as hot as he could stand, steaming in the narrow blue-tiled stall, he stepped in. Maybe the stream pouring down on him would flush his thoughts away.

♫

On Monday afternoon, before chorus, Sam called Gil's apartment. No answer.

The chorus was learning excerpts from *Messiah* now. At the beginning of rehearsal, Sam got up on the podium and thanked his singers again for their performance on Saturday. He outlined the sections of the Handel they would perform and told them, "I wanted to do the whole thing, but the board wasn't ready to cough up fees to hire soloists." A couple of people looked disappointed. Most of them had probably never done a complete *Messiah*. "Never mind," he said. "We'll give 'em a taste this year, and next year I bet we can do whatever we want." Next year. None of them, Sam included, might be here then, but for now Sam could pretend they would. He finished, "Sing this the way you sang the Mozart. They'll see how good we are."

With rehearsal under way, he did feel grateful that Jeannette had no ring on. That would have caused more consequences than he could handle. He and she worked together like the team they had become, and the chorus pulled together around them as best they could. Given that they were sight-reading, it wasn't half bad. Maybe the first concert had made a team out of them too.

They read through the "Hallelujah" chorus and a few others. Sam didn't look at the back row of singers, except for a fraction of a second here and there when he had to cue the basses. What had happened with Nathan after the concert did not matter. *No monster. Never again.*

Except that when he got home that night and found the phone ringing, Sam didn't stop to think. His briefcase hit the floor with a thump, and the receiver felt chilly when he snatched it up. "Hello?"

"Hey, you."

Sam didn't realize how tight his muscles had been until he heard that voice. He pulled out his chair at the table and collapsed into it. "Hey," he said. "How are you?"

"I'm here." Sam heard the laughter behind Gil's words. *"Here,"* Gil said, "meaning in my own kitchen, is an improvement after the excitement this weekend." Before Sam could ask what had happened, or how Gil was really feeling now, the voice went on, "How are you, Maestro?"

Sam could laugh too. "I'm all right."

"Jonas said the concert went well. Actually, he said you told him to tell me something went fine. I assumed that was it."

"Yes. It was." That didn't seem relevant right now. Sam wanted to say, *Are you sure you're better? When can I see you?*

That last thought pulled him up short. Jeannette's goodnight kiss, pressed on his cheek not ten minutes earlier, stung his skin.

"Yes?" Gil said. "Tell me more. I want to hear all about it."

Sam found his tongue. "Gil, are you... I mean, what happened to you? Caruso said..."

"I'm all right. They just had to reset my system. Now, tell me about Saturday."

Sam should have been nervous. He had more to tell than Gil would want to hear, and he had no idea how to bring up Jeannette, or whether or not he should. "Okay," he said, "I'll tell you. But first, when can I come up there?"

Gil hesitated. "Love, you're busy. Do you really want to?"

Love, again. He should not say it. Sam should not hear it. For the smallest possible slice of time, Sam thought he should say so: but he couldn't have done it if someone had held a gun to his head.

Instead he said, "You told me you wouldn't mind seeing me. So when? Next weekend?"

Something might happen. Gil might end up in the hospital again. Sam didn't care. He would go up anyway and pitch a tent outside those big glass doors if he had to.

"Next weekend?" Gil said. "Sure, if you're certain."

"I am. Deal?"

Gil laughed. "Deal."

Sam told him about the concert. Gil said "I told you so" about the chorus, and Sam could hear him grinning. They talked about the size of the audience and the length of the receiving line afterward. "I felt like I never wanted to be hugged again," Sam said. "Hugged, hell. I felt like nobody had better look at me for a week."

"You'd better get used to it, love. I have a feeling this is just the start."

How did time speed up so much when they talked? Sam forgot about the things he hadn't wanted to mention. They didn't seem important anymore. It seemed like he and Gil had only been on the phone for five minutes, but when Sam looked at his watch, it said midnight. "So, the weekend," he said. "When's good for you?"

"I'm always here," Gil said. Except when he wasn't.

Sam would have to tell Jeannette he was going out of town. For now he shoved that thought aside. "Sunday?" he asked. Jeannette could still have her regular Saturday. "If I came up on Sunday and went back Monday?" If he left Philly early enough, he could get back in time for rehearsal.

"Yes. Let's do that."

Hanging up got no easier no matter how often they did it. Six days, Sam told himself. Then, no matter where Gil was, Sam would see him again.

Lying in bed, looking up at the dark ceiling, he tried to hold Gil's face in his mind. Another kept slipping in front of it.

How could he explain things to Jeannette? Her kiss still tingled on his cheek. When he rubbed the place, it burned.

No monster.

CHAPTER TEN

On the Saturday a week after the concert, Jeannette had a headache. Needles poked up through her sinuses and jabbed the backs of her eyeballs.

Sam held her hand up under the lamp on the jewellery store counter. Two days ago, the band had been too big for her and the weight of the diamond had dragged it around. Now the stone sparkled bravely in place at the base of her finger. The jeweller said, "You have such small hands, miss." He had grey hair and deep lines etched at the corners of his eyes, and he didn't smile. "When we resized it, it looked like a toy."

Sam laughed. "A tiny little thing, for such a big deal."

White light glittered on her hand and in his voice. "It's beautiful," she said. She raised her eyes to his face and tried not to see the haze of white light around it too, just like in the concert hall a week ago. "Are you sure it's not too much money?"

"I want you to have what you like," Sam said.

The jeweller added, "Besides, miss, once we size it, it's yours."

Hers. This ring belonged to her and told the world that she, in turn, belonged to the man who stood beside her. The man who gave her the Maestro's smile as he took out his wallet to pay for this "toy" on her finger.

Why that smile here? Why now?

He had been the one who wanted her to have the ring right away. Jeannette herself would have been willing to wait, but he had insisted. He had said he wanted to "make this official."

Jeannette looked out the store's wide plate-glass front window. On Thursday, when she and Sam had come here the first time, the jewellery store had seemed like a mystical and lovely place, a cavern glittering with brightly coloured stones. Now, if it was a cave, Jeannette felt trapped in it. She wanted fresh air.

"Jeannette. Will you marry me?" No blast of trumpets or crash of cymbals could have stopped her breath as completely as those quiet words. She and Sam had sat there in the dark, and thoughts had scrambled through her head. She barely knew him. An hour earlier, less than that, she had thought there was no way he could want someone like her. The girl from Reckord's Mill, the one with the ugly red hair like a brand of shame, didn't get to have the hero.

Now Jeannette went over to the store window. It was a warm, sunny afternoon, and the sidewalk outside was crowded with a flow of foot traffic. A young couple sauntered along, pushing a blue baby stroller with a voluminous sunshade. The boy's leather loafers and the girl's bright new sneakers hit the pavement in unison. A woman in a yellow top and short pink skirt led a miniature poodle along on a leash. An elderly, silver-haired husband and wife, both dressed to the nines, walked slowly along, staying as much as they could under the awnings over shop windows. The man's honey-coloured cane tapped the sidewalk, and he held his wife's arm through his own.

That couple. Jeannette's eyes followed them down to the end of the block. Could that be her and Sam, someday?

Pain stabbed her temples. She had sat there in Sam's living room and told him she loved him. She had never imagined saying, *wanting* to say, those words to any man. She had never imagined letting someone get that close.

He had looked so sad. So lost, like someone out in a deep, dark lake, struggling to keep his head above the surface. She couldn't have done anything else. She had held out her words like a rope for him to catch on to, so she could take the other end and draw him back to the shore.

After, when he had asked the question, she couldn't have answered him any other way. When someone offered you the sun on a plate, you didn't complain that it was too bright, too hot. You didn't say you were scared to touch it.

From behind, Sam took her hand. "Ready?"

She looked around at him. *Marry. Husband.* The words swam and swirled in her head like quick fish and disappeared. "Sure."

Now they had to go and face her family. Tell Veronica and Drew what was going on. Sam held the door for Jeannette, and she stepped out into the sunlight.

The glare made Jeannette's headache worse. On her hand, the diamond glittered like a tiny firework. She kept her eyes away from it and followed Sam to the car.

♪

Jeannette had hustled around the apartment that morning, checking the carpet for marbles, plucking dead begonia leaves off the floor, brushing crumbs off the kitchen counter. Now, as she unlocked the lobby door, she decided it was good that she and Sam had gotten here early. Sam had asked if she wanted to go for a walk after the jeweller's, since Veronica and Drew and the kids wouldn't be back yet, but Jeannette needed an Aspirin. This way she could take her pill, and Sam could see the apartment without Nerf footballs and plastic building blocks and Ricky's latest proud acquisition, G.I. Joe action figures, strewn all over the place. That wouldn't be possible once the kids had been home for five minutes. Meanwhile, maybe the white-light glow would leave him, and Jeannette would know for sure who this man was.

The boiled-cabbage smell on the stairs didn't help her headache any more than the sun had. That might have explained why she didn't notice the noise in the apartment until she opened the door, and it smacked her in the face.

The TV was on, blaring some local newscast. The vacuum roared down the hall. Jeannette saw a confusion of flickering images on the TV screen and scattered plastic blocks on the floor, and then her nephew shrieked and ran across the living room to collide with her legs.

Ricky had his father's stocky build, Veronica's dark hair, and a round face covered with freckles, as if somebody had sprinkled cinnamon on him. "Mommy!" he yelled straight up at Jeannette. "Aunt Nannie's home!"

Jeannette tried to nudge him backward into the room. "Let me get inside, honey."

The TV newscaster, a solemn-faced young woman with a mass of sprayed curly hair, was saying, "...argument against discussing AIDS in schools. A group of parents here at Albert Hill Middle have signed a petition against in-school AIDS education, feeling that..." Ricky let go of Jeannette and ran to the end of the hall. "Mommy! There's a man here too!"

Sam had come in behind her. Jeannette shut the door, blushing furiously, her head screaming. Ricky came back. Jeannette heard him demand, "Who are you?"

"I'm your aunt's friend."

Jeannette turned around. Sam had been looking at the TV, but he crouched down to get on eye level with the little boy. "My name's Sam. What's yours?"

"Ricky. I'm four and a half. How old are you?"

"Twenty-seven. That's pretty old, isn't it."

"...CBS Local News met with some representatives of the parents' group, many of whom also object to the use of public tax dollars to fund AIDS research ..."

The vacuum shut off. "Ricky," Veronica's voice called, "I hope you're behaving yourself, now."

"I am!" Ricky ran down the hall toward her. "Mommy, Aunt Nannie's home, and..."

"I know. I heard." How she could have, over all the noise, was beyond Jeannette. "Just a minute."

"...individuals choose to engage in risky behaviour, the responsibility for it falls on them and the public should not be obligated to..."

Sam got to his feet. "He's a cute kid."

"He's a handful," Jeannette said. "He'll talk your ear off if he gets a chance."

"I don't mind."

He was looking at the TV again. Jeannette glanced at it in time to catch, "...possible late-stage effects of the disease include skin lesions, tumours in the lungs and gastrointestinal system, meningitis, and encephalitis. At present, of course, there is no effective..."

Jeannette went over and turned the TV off. "I wish they'd stop talking about that," she said. "It's so grim."

"It is."

"I mean, they make it sound like everybody has to worry about it." Jeannette tried to talk easily, to push back against the rising nervousness about what she and Sam had to tell her family. "I hope most people don't."

"A lot of people do."

Sam's voice sounded strangely flat. Jeannette looked around and saw him staring at the blank screen as if the picture were still there.

She went back over to him. "Well, sure, but most of those people, they do things." It was silly, but talking about it made her blush. "Things they shouldn't. You know."

She wanted him to look at her, but when he did, his face was so colourless and his eyes so dark, it scared her. She reached out to touch his cheek. "Sam. What's wrong?"

He didn't answer before Veronica appeared in the hall. "Hi, there!" she said. "You two are early."

Jeannette remembered about her left hand and jammed it into the pocket of her slacks. Sam's face unfroze into the white-light smile. He said, "You're early too, I think."

"Got that right." Veronica hugged him easily. She had tied her hair back with a faded pink and white kerchief, and she wore a bleach-stained yellow T-shirt with a black-and-white print of Bruce Springsteen's face plastered on the front, but she could have been a model in *Vogue*. "Meltdown city with C.J. today," she said. "Drew'll be out in a sec; he's putting him down for a nap. Plus my oldest got mud on his sneakers and tracked it into every square inch of carpet in the place. Kids." She tugged off the kerchief and let her hair fall loose down her back. "So what's new, you two?"

The ring burned in Jeannette's pocket. Ricky charged over with a yellow plastic bucket overflowing with G.I. Joe figures. "Lookit what I got," he ordered, holding it up for Sam's inspection.

Veronica scolded, "Ricky Calhoun! You know better than that. We don't interrupt folks when they're talking."

Ricky said, "He's not talking."

Sam caught Jeannette's eye. His seen-a-ghost look had vanished. Now he struggled not to grin and looked more like himself than he had all day.

Veronica said, "No, but Mommy was talking *to* him. Now go on over by the sofa and play with your Joes like a good boy." She turned back to Sam. "Anyway, come on in, make yourselves at home. What can I get you to drink? We've got water, apple juice, Pepsi, and I made some iced tea this morning."

"You go ahead," Jeannette said. "I'm going to run and find an Aspirin." She escaped down the hall to the bathroom.

With the door shut and the lights off, she drew her hand out of her pocket. The ring glittered, even in the dark.

Jeannette knew she should be happy. Thrilled. This should be one of the best days of her life. Shouldn't it?

Blinking hard, she looked up at the mirror over the sink. She could barely make out her reflection, just a vague oval in the dark and a faint outline of curled hair.

Maybe if Aunt Gretchen had been here. Goodness knew, her aunt had never been much for hugs or sympathy, but right now Jeannette would have been grateful for a glimpse of that hard, lined face. *I'm getting married, Auntie. That's good news, isn't it?* One word of approval. One brief, rare smile.

Or maybe if someone else had been here. Jeannette closed her hands tight around the edge of the sink. That was stupid. You could think "Mama" all you wanted: it wouldn't make her appear. That had been one of the first lessons of Jeannette's childhood.

Somebody knocked on the bathroom door. "Nannie?"

Veronica. "Coming. I'll be right there." Jeannette yanked open the medicine cabinet and made as much noise as she could, rattling the Aspirin bottle and tapping a pill out onto her palm. The bitter taste got stuck in her throat and stayed there after she took a swallow from the sink. She patted her face with a wet tissue.

Back in the kitchen, Sam and Drew sat at the table with tall glasses of iced tea. Jeannette manoeuvred around Ricky, who had stationed himself on the floor to bounce the Nerf football off the table leg, and sat down next to Sam in Veronica's usual seat. Drew was telling Sam about his job with Dominion Gas and Electric. "I started working there back on June fifth. The next week, no kidding, we had that hurricane. Remember? A hurricane in June, I ask you. People were calling in downed wires all over the place." Drew was never this chatty, especially with strangers. Jeannette stealthily took her hand out of her pocket under the table. "I couldn't fix them," Drew went on, "don't have the qualifications, but my boss sent me out anyway because the real experts were all chasing around like bluetailed flies, and somebody had to babysit those wires till a team could get there. Make sure no kids or pets fooled with them." He smiled. "I got paid for a lot of hours of reading magazines."

Sam laughed. "Sounds good to me."

"Sure was. I was hoping for a couple more hurricanes this fall"—it was even less like him to make a joke in company—"but no luck."

Looking at her brother-in-law now, his big square hands and mild eyes, Jeannette thought she understood better than before why her sister had married him. You could lean on a solid, reliable man like that. He would be an anchor.

Veronica bustled in. "We surely wouldn't have minded the OT, would we, honey?" She poured two more glasses of iced tea, set one down in front of Jeannette, and wedged herself into Ricky's chair holding the other. The Nerf football bounced off her ankle. "Ricky Calhoun," she said, "can't you do that someplace else?"

"I want to sit here with y'all."

Veronica lit a cigarette. "Listen to him. That boy's going to be a cracker all his life."

Jeannette winced. Sam put his arm around her. "How are you feeling, sweetheart?"

"I'm okay." She couldn't tell if he seemed like himself or not. Her heart sped up painfully, and she drummed the fingers of her left hand on her knee.

Ricky said, "Mommy, when is Auntie Rose coming over?"

Veronica looked over her shoulder at the clock and blew out a plume of smoke. "Soon. When the big hand's on the twelve, you see that?"

Ricky looked. So did Jeannette: twenty minutes. "I want her to come *now*," Ricky said.

"Lord, child, what are your parents? Boiled broccoli?"

Jeannette had watched her sister's family together since the time when Ricky was born. Were she and Sam about to walk into this kind of life? Would there be kids running around, toys strewn on the floor, meals squeezed around a tiny table? Jeannette tried to picture it. It didn't seem real.

Ricky bounced the Nerf off his mother's ankle again, unperturbed. "Auntie Rose is nice."

Veronica rolled her eyes. "Anyway." She turned to Sam and Jeannette. "Where do you folks want to have dinner?"

Sam said, "Tell you the truth, I don't know too much about what's around here. Us poor musicians can't afford dinner out."

Jeannette remembered what Plum Pudding had said about how she and the General had had Sam over to dinner. Musicians could eat out in blue-blood mansions. Drew said, "There's a nice little place over on Calvert. Flaherty's, you know it?" Sam shook his head. "Kind of a pub. They do steak and chicken and fish, all kinds of stuff."

"Sounds good," Sam said. "What do you think, Jeannette?"

Before Jeannette could answer, Veronica said, "It sure sounds funny to hear you call her that. Nobody here uses that name. She laid down the law a long time ago."

Sam said to Jeannette, "You never did tell me about your nickname."

His eyes were asking a different question. She could see it. He wouldn't speak up and spill the secret until she said so, but they didn't have much time before the sitter arrived, and she surely couldn't spend the whole night with her hand in her pocket.

"She never told you?" Veronica took another drag on her cigarette. For all she smoked, she did it so gradually that most of the cigarettes in the ashtray on the table were only half burned down. "I'd have thought you would, Nannie. It's a music thing and all, isn't it?"

Sam said, "Now I'm curious. So?"

Yes, it was a music thing, but it was tied to Reckord's Mill, and Aunt Gretchen, and Sam didn't know about the playground yet, or the kids, or Isabel. Everything had happened too fast for Jeannette to tell him. She still didn't know if she could.

She ought to try. If she was going to marry him, he would have to know her, wouldn't he? Even the things she wanted to hide. She swallowed. "It's because—"

Thump! The Nerf football ricocheted off the table leg, flew across the room, and smacked the refrigerator door. "Oops," Ricky said.

Veronica snatched the ball off the floor before it stopped rolling. "That does it. No more football for you, young man."

"But Mommy…"

"You can either sit here and play something else, or you can take the ball in the living room." Veronica lifted a finger to forestall argument. "No. I won't have Aunt Nannie's friend thinking we're raising you in the monkey house."

Sam coughed. Jeannette saw his mouth twitching.

"You decide," Veronica said, clutching the football in her lap.

Ricky slumped. "Okay. I'll go in the living room."

Veronica handed the ball back. Ricky left the room, dragging his feet. In another second, Jeannette heard the ball bounce off something hard, probably the side of the piano.

Veronica shook her head. "I don't know. What do you think, Sam, you figure on having a family someday?"

Jeannette's face got hot, but Sam didn't miss a beat. "I've thought about it, sure."

"Don't be in a rush, that's all I can say." As if the boys didn't light up Veronica's whole universe. "Once you've got 'em, you can't give 'em back."

Sam laughed. "I'm sure my mother felt the same way."

Jeannette had never heard him mention his mother before. She wanted to hear more, but at the same time, she felt like giving her sister a good sharp kick under the table for never minding her own business.

Veronica said, "I doubt you were a lot of trouble."

Sam shook his head. "More than you can imagine."

Jeannette thought she saw a shadow cross his face. What was this?

He squeezed her shoulders. "I have to tell you, though," he said to Veronica, "talking about having a family, it's kind of appropriate right now."

Jeannette's heart jumped into her throat. He turned to her and smiled. "Sweetheart, I think it's time, don't you?"

How could he? How *could* he? Jeannette ought to get mad. She had a right to decide when to talk to her own relatives, what to say... but he had that white-light glow again, lighting up the room, baffling her eyes.

Veronica leaned across the table, staring at Sam. "What's this, now?"

Sam spoke so calmly, anyone would have thought he had done this a hundred times before. "Veronica, Drew," he said. His free hand found Jeannette's under the table and lifted it out. She couldn't offer any more resistance than a boiled noodle. "Jeannette and I would like to tell you something. We hope you'll think it's good news."

He rested her hand on the table and lifted his own away. The ring gleamed.

For the longest second, silence filled the room. Even Ricky's Nerf ball had gone quiet. Nobody at the table moved. Jeannette didn't breathe.

Then, "Oh." Veronica's voice came out as a whisper. "Oh, my goodness."

Jeannette had expected a shriek. She hadn't expected her sister's hand to reach carefully, tentatively, across the table to take her own. "Goodness," Veronica said again. She touched the ring with her thumb. "Nannie, it's beautiful."

Her eyes met Jeannette's. Astonishingly, they brimmed with tears. The clock over the sink ticked twice as the sisters looked at each other.

Then Veronica let go of Jeannette's hand and sat back. "Well! You two!" She wiped her eyes with the back of her wrist. "Lord, you could knock me over with a toothpick." Brashness came back, syllable by syllable. "And you hid this from me? Jeannette Marie Reilly, you *hid* it?"

This was more like her. Jeannette realized she was shaking, maybe with relief. "Vee, I…"

"I don't believe it." Veronica rounded on Drew. "Andrew Calhoun, do you believe these two here?"

Drew's slow smile crept across his face. "Congratulations," he said. "Congratulations." He reached over to shake Sam's hand.

Veronica was laughing now. "And this has been going on *how* long? Not that long, it couldn't be, you just met! I had no idea my sister was such a sly thing!"

Sam laughed too. "I only asked her last week. After the concert."

"Why, you… you…" Veronica's eyes came back to Jeannette's face. Again, for the space of a blink, Jeannette saw something strange there. Then Veronica pushed her chair back. "Get over here," she ordered. "Both of you."

Jeannette stood up. Her sister's arms and the autumn-leaf smell of cigarettes wrapped tight around her. "Little sister," Veronica's voice said in her ear. "I love you. You know that, right?"

They hadn't said that out loud to each other for as long as Jeannette could remember. Why say what you already knew in your bone marrow? Before Jeannette could answer, Veronica let go of her, turned to Sam, and wrapped him in as much of a bear hug as a small woman could manage. "You take care of her, you hear? You take care of my Nannie."

"I will. I promise."

Veronica let go and looked up at him. "If she wasn't off her head for you, I wouldn't let you take her away. Not somebody she met two months ago. Consider yourself lucky."

Nobody had noticed Ricky come in. Now he jumped up and down. "Mommy! What's going on?"

Veronica said, "Your aunt is going to get married. What do you think of that?"

Ricky stared up at Jeannette. "Married?"

Veronica added, "And Mr. Sam here is going to be your uncle."

Ricky transferred the stare to Sam. "Are you going to live with us?"

"Well, no," Sam said. "Your aunt and I will have our own house."

Ricky's eyes went huge. "Aunt Nannie is going *away?*"

Good grief. Jeannette hadn't thought her nephews were that attached to her. Sam knelt down. "You can come and visit," he told the little boy. "We won't live far away."

"You won't?"

Sam shook his head. "We'll still be in Richmond."

"That's where we live," Ricky informed him.

Somehow Sam managed to keep a straight face. "I know," he said. A laugh bubbled up in Jeannette's throat.

Ricky thought this over, staring at this new uncle-to-be. Finally he said, "Will you play G.I. Joes with me?"

"You bet."

Veronica and Jeannette glanced at each other. Veronica grinned. Jeannette bit her lip to keep from laughing.

"Well," Ricky decided, "okay."

Somebody knocked on the door. Ricky shouted "Auntie Rose!" and flew out of the kitchen.

Veronica wiped her eyes again and rubbed her hands on her jeans. "All right. Time for us to get going."

After everyone else left the kitchen, Sam put his hands on Jeannette's waist. "How's your headache now?"

"Gone," she realized.

"Good."

Not the Maestro anymore, no more white light. That smile, and the brown eyes looking into hers, were precisely his own. If only he could stay like this all the time.

Drew stuck his head into the kitchen. "Just about ready. And by the way, your dinner's on us." Sam opened his mouth, but Drew shook his head. "No arguments. We're celebrating."

Veronica appeared beside him. Somehow, in the space of about thirty seconds, she had changed into sleek close-fitting slacks and a cowl-necked sweater. Normally her looks would have made Jeannette shrink into herself. Just for now, the world felt different.

"Come on, you two," Veronica said. "Let's eat."

♬

Afterward, when Rosalie from next door had gone home, and the kids were in bed, and Sam had kissed Jeannette good night in front of his future in-laws, Jeannette sat alone at the kitchen table with her hand spread out in front of her. The diamond sparkled.

Such a little thing. For such a big deal.

"Hey, little sister."

Jeannette looked up. Veronica stood in the doorway in her kimono. "Mind if I sit?"

Jeannette shook her head. Veronica came in and sat down. For a while, neither of them said a word. Jeannette saw a haze of tiny rainbows around the diamond, but when she blinked, they went away.

Finally she said, "I don't know what's the matter with me."

Veronica leaned forward. "It's okay. It's a big change."

Tell me you like him, Vee. Tell me I'm lucky. "I love him," Jeannette said.

Veronica's blue eyes were calm and steady. "I know you do."

Jeannette lifted her chin. "He loves me too."

"Yes."

If she had said *Of course he does.* Or, *he had sure better.* Wasn't that Veronica's job? To make sure her sister's life ran the way it should?

Jeannette said, "Were you scared when Drew asked you?"

"No, I can't say I was. But you and I are different."

Jeannette nodded. Then Veronica did say, "He's a nice boy, Nannie. I like him."

She didn't sound convinced. Words came up from the pit of Jeannette's stomach. "You aren't sure."

Veronica sighed and brushed her hair back over her shoulder. "Oh, honey, what do I know." Everything, didn't she? "He's not like us, I don't think. But that doesn't mean anything."

"Because he's from up north?"

"Up north? I don't care about that. You know what I mean. He's a different breed."

The stage. The white light. Plum Pudding and the Confederate General. Yes, Jeannette knew exactly what her sister meant and wished she didn't.

"He chose you, Nannie." Veronica's eyes were serious. "He chose you, and I'd say he knows his own mind. And you know yours. That's what counts."

Jeannette swallowed. "Okay."

Veronica reached over and put her hand over her sister's. To Jeannette's relief, the ring winked out.

CHAPTER ELEVEN

The beige brick building on Philadelphia's Lombard Street looked the same as it had the last time Sam saw it. Not one brick had changed, not one line of grout, as far as he could tell. He found a space on the street across from the front steps and hoisted his backpack out of the car.

After he couldn't go home anymore, this place had been the only home he had. Sam's feet remembered the depressions in the middle of the concrete steps from all the other shoes that had gone up and down them. He went up to the intercom by the entrance.

Apartment 2-J. How many times had he pushed this buzzer? In the old days, he would have heard, "Just a second, I'll be right down." Then, if he watched through the glass doors, he would have seen Gil appear on the wide flight of stairs, looking the way he always did, as if he had just rolled out of bed. As he hurried down the stairs, Sam had always kept his eyes on him, his best anchor and hope.

Now Sam reached for the buzzer. Late-afternoon sun still warmed the street, but a gust of wind bit through his denim jacket. The buzzer made a harsh squawk. After a pause he heard, "Sam?"

Gil's voice sounded tired, which it never had all the other times Sam had come here. More tired than it had sounded on the phone last week? Sam didn't know. "I'm here," he said.

"One sec. I'll buzz you in."

Another squawk, and the front door unlatched. Sam pushed it open.

Nothing had changed in here. The gun-metal-grey security desk in the corner of the lobby looked as unfriendly as ever. The guard behind it could have been any of the ones Sam always used to see, big interchangeable men in white uniforms. The varnished wood floor had the same long scratch in it, half-hidden by the navy rug, where somebody had probably once dragged a suitcase or packing crate over the boards. On the far side of the lobby, the old elevator with the brass grille waited for anybody brave enough to see if it still worked. Most people opted for the stairs, because even the six flights up to the top floor were manageable when you compared them with the possibility of getting stuck indefinitely somewhere in the middle. The grey stone fireplace had the same couple of blue plush chairs in front of it. The logs looked identical too. Sam had never seen them lit.

Once upon a time, he would barely have noticed any of these things. He and Gil would have been on their way upstairs together, drinking in each other's nearness as if they had not seen each other at chorus rehearsal two nights before. At college, they had to be colleagues and casual friends. Here, with Friday night in front of them and Saturday and as much of Sunday as they could steal until Sam had to get back to campus, they could be who they really were.

The wide flight of stairs, like the fireplace, harked back to the building's grander days. It had probably once been a luxury hotel for old Philadelphia money. Sam leaned on the railing and made his way slowly up.

His demons had never stopped gnawing at him in this place or anywhere else. Especially after that last fight with his father, Sam could not erase the winter-cold voice in his head or the memory of his mother's tears. Here, with Gil, the world made sense. Sam could not understand why the best thing in his life, the one thing he wanted most, had to be so wrong.

Sam got to the second floor. Here, a long strip of dark-green carpet covered the floorboards. The rows of doors on either side were painted beige to match the walls. Each door had a metal knocker and spy-hole in the centre. One of them, at the far end of the hall, stood open. From where he stood, Sam could see it.

He had been so scared the first time he came here. He'd hoped as hard as he could that Gil could not hear his heart racing. Gil had talked easily, cheerfully, as if the understanding he and Sam had reached only a few days before had been the most natural thing in the world. "It isn't much," he had said, talking about his place. "The piano's about all I could afford, furniture-wise. You'll see."

Sam had tried to laugh. "Gil, I live in a dorm. The walls are made out of cinder blocks."

In his strangest, most luminous, and most frightening dreams, Sam had never imagined being here. That first night, he had known, as stark and clear as the big icicles that had hung down from the roof, what this meant. What he was going to lose. Still, he had followed Gil down this hallway the way you would follow the light at the end of the tunnel.

Now Sam's backpack, the same one he had brought here that long-ago night, felt much heavier than it should have. With only a spare shirt, clean underwear, and a toothbrush and razor inside, it dragged on his shoulders. He went down the hall, counting the doors on either side: 2C, 2D, 2E...

The end of the hall came too soon. Here was the open door. Gil stood in the doorway, leaning on the frame.

His cheekbones and jaw stood out in too-sharp definition. His dishevelled hair looked less like he hadn't bothered to comb it and more like he didn't have the energy to try. His eyes, though, were the colour of a cloudless sky, and his smile still looked like the sun.

"Hey, you," he said.

Sam couldn't answer. He took one more step forward and reached out. He hadn't been able to do this when Gil was in the hospital bed, or for so very long before that.

Gil reached out too. His arms went around Sam, backpack and all.

It didn't matter that Sam could feel the hollow, too-thin chest under Gil's shirt and the hard line of his collarbone. The arms around Sam were as strong as he remembered.

People didn't know how AIDS worked. They babbled stupidity about avoiding contact and not touching bare skin. As Sam understood it, you couldn't catch the disease by hugging or any skin-to-skin contact that didn't involve actual blood. Right now, he didn't care. A death sentence would have been a small price to pay for this moment.

What a stupid way to think. He had more than just himself to worry about now. Jeannette was back home, waiting for him, with the ring on her finger that he had given her. He had wanted her to have that symbol before he came here; he should have known it wouldn't make any difference.

Gil let go and stepped back. "Come on in."

This place had been home when Sam had no other. Now his feet remembered the surprisingly deep pile of the beige carpet. On the wall by the door, the three Kandinsky postcards from the Philly Art Museum saluted Sam like the old friends they were. Through the narrow doorway to the right he could see a slice of the kitchen, the metal fridge and the calendar on the wall beside it. That calendar was another art museum product; Gil had always loved visiting the museum on his afternoons off. Sam was glad to see he had gotten hold of a new calendar, or maybe someone had gotten it for him. It showed a Matisse painting instead of Monet, and the date 1986 instead of 1982, but it hung in exactly the same place Sam remembered from the last time he was here. The fridge itself had the same row of round chrome magnets across the top.

By the time Sam followed Gil down the short hallway, he felt as though someone had taken a small but heavy hammer to his skin and made pinpoint bruises for every familiar object. There was Gil's stereo with its tall speakers. The record collection spilled out of the same stacked milk crates: green milk crate on the bottom, red in the middle, blue on the top. There, under the living room window, was the long black grand piano. And there was the old brown couch with the same worn cushions.

After the last morning in his parents' house, Sam had taken the train to Philadelphia and fled straight here. He had nowhere else to go. He and Gil had sat in the centre of that couch. As the afternoon sun slanted through the window and made squares on the piano and the floor, Sam had shut his eyes and put his head down on Gil's shoulder and let those strong arms hold the pieces of him together.

Now Sam made himself walk over and put his backpack down on the floor beside the couch, careful not to brush the armrest. In the doorway,

Gil said, "I wasn't sure what to do about dinner. I still can't cook worth spit." He laughed. "Some things don't change."

Some things didn't change? Nothing in this place had changed except Gil himself, leaning there against the wall as if he didn't trust his legs to hold him up. His white shirt hung too loose on him, and the end of his brown belt dangled down, showing how far he'd had to pull it in to hold up his jeans. His feet were bare. Sam could see every line of muscle under the skin.

If Sam let it, the cloud of pain hovering around him would rush in and swamp him so he collapsed in a lump on the floor. Gil didn't need that. Sam asked, "What kind of stuff do you have?" but didn't wait for an answer before he brushed past into the kitchen.

Nothing had changed in here either. Sam could have gone through these cabinets blindfolded. Between them and the fridge, he found a bottle of ginger ale, an open jar of Lucky Leaf applesauce, and a couple of boxes of saltines. Nothing else.

Gil followed him and sat down at the rickety kitchen table. That piece of paper wedged under one leg to hold it steady was probably the same folded-up notebook paper Gil had shoved under there the first time Sam cooked in here. "Gil Hart," Sam said, pointing at the pathetic array on the counter. "You call this *food*?"

Gil gave him a mock-sheepish look. "I don't get hungry very much."

"I can see why. I wouldn't either if I didn't have anything but dry crackers." Sam didn't have to ask where he could find a pen and paper. They had always lived by the phone. He tore a sheet off the spiral-bound pad and started scribbling as fast as he could. *Keep moving.* "You're going to have a decent dinner tonight," he said. "I'm going over to the co-op for groceries and then I'm going to cook for you. No arguments."

"But—"

Sam raised his head. "What did I just say?"

Their eyes met. The years in between might have disappeared. Sam had seen exactly that expression on Gil's face so many times, when he said the word *love*.

Sam folded up the list, creasing it hard, and slipped it in his shirt pocket. "Do you need anything besides food?"

"No, thanks. I'm fine."

If only. "Okay. I'll be right back. Don't go anywhere, you hear?"

Gil smiled. "Don't worry. I won't."

Sam pounded down the steps. Pathetic. He had lasted less than five minutes in that apartment. Narrow Delancey Street seemed to funnel the wind into a blade of ice that drove straight between his ribs.

At the co-op, he chose onions at the produce bin as if finding a perfectly round one would fix anything. He examined every individual stalk of celery and spidery green carrot top. He compared the weights of the five available whole chickens, sorted through a dozen bagged loaves of bread before picking one no different from any of the others, and sized up the brands of frozen orange and grape juice. By the time he got to the checkout line, the scream of pain in his head had damped down to a whimper.

The wind blew him back along Delancey Street. The grocery bags dragged on his arms. In the apartment, Gil still sat at the kitchen table. He eyed the bags. "Sam Kraychek, did you leave anything at the store?"

"Very funny. I hope I got everything."

Gil got up and came over to the counter for a look. He moved slowly, as if all his muscles were stiff; graceful Gil who had looked like a dancer on the podium. He opened a plastic bag at random and peered into it. "I can't imagine you didn't get everything. What's this? A chicken?"

Sam unpacked the onions and celery. "For soup. I hope you still have that stock pot of yours."

"I do, God knows why. Nobody but you ever used it."

Sam didn't have to ask where to put things or find things. He organized the groceries, dug the stock pot out of the cabinet above the stove, found the cutting board and a knife. You still had to toggle the kitchen sink's faucet a certain way to make it stop running. How bizarre that nobody had fixed it in all this time.

Gil said, "What do you need me to do?"

On their weekends together, he and Sam had worked side by side in here. Gil could get around a kitchen if you kept an eye on him. Tonight, if he, say, propped himself up against the counter to chop vegetables, if Sam had to take in the clean musk of his aftershave and the freshness of his clothes right beside him the way they used to be, Sam knew he would not make it through the evening. "You stay put," he said. "This is easy."

"I can at least put some music on."

Sam cleaned the chicken, put it in the stock pot, and covered it with water. When he lit the gas under the burner, the quick hiss of air blended with the first notes from the stereo in the living room.

It wasn't quite true that the piano had been the only piece of furniture Gil could afford, but it and the stereo were definitely the only two pieces he cared about. If he had put less money into them, he could have gotten nicer chairs and tables, but what did that matter? Chairs and tables were only "stuff." Music was essential.

Now quiet chords filtered into the kitchen. Sam stood still, holding the lid of the stock pot in the air. This piece? Now?

The first night Sam had come here, Gil had put a musical score on the piano and said, "I thought we could try this."

Sam had looked at it. "You're kidding, right?" You needed two pianos for Maurice Ravel's *Bolero*. There wasn't even room on one music stand for both scores. If the four hands tried to share a single keyboard, they'd end up in a tangled mess.

Gil grinned. "Kidding? Sort of. But I think we can make it work."

"How?"

"I'll show you."

They had sat together on the bench. Sam had known he should not be here. Back home, at the church where Sam had been baptized and where he had played the piano at Sunday Mass after Sunday Mass, gentle, white-haired Father Antony had explained in confirmation class that people who had "certain kinds of feelings" were not what God wanted them to be and would go straight to hell. And then there was Dad, the doctor, who had only ever mentioned queers once that Sam could remember, and that had been to make a comment about how such people had a disease of the brain. Sam had understood, that first night here with Gil, everything he stood to lose by letting his feelings lead him.

Now, on this night so many years later, Gil came back to the kitchen table. "Remember this piece?"

Sam put the lid on the stock pot and willed the water to rumble and boil as loud as it possibly could. "Sure," he said. "That was fun."

"You didn't believe me, as I recall, but the single piano version did work."

Sam turned away to chop the onion. "It did. You were right."

Yes, Gil had been right. Of the two of them, Gil had always been right.

The last night Sam had spent here was such a long time after the first one, but not nearly long enough. "I don't want you to hurt, love," Gil had said. They had been in the bedroom, lying together in the dark. Gil smoothed Sam's bangs away from his forehead, stroked his cheek with the touch that had always opened Sam's heart. "I don't want you to hurt, but I wish you didn't have to do this."

Sam chopped viciously. The knife clunked against the plate, and the onion vapour stung his eyes. How had he thought ending what he and Gil had would fix anything? He had never been able to go home anyway, after what he and his father had both said. He had lost his ties to home for good. And now Gil had this death sentence on him.

The music swelled. The *Bolero* was a single long crescendo.

That first night, he and Gil had sat together on the piano bench. With the first notes that came out of the instrument, ringing from the rich strings, Sam's fear had fallen away. How could he help it? His hands and Gil's brushed each other on the keyboard, and the long white keys rose and fell with perfect precision. He breathed Gil's clean scent, so near.

Now Sam wished he didn't have to hear the *Bolero*. Nothing would be powerful enough to stop up his ears.

Gil's voice cut through the rising melody. "I think that pot's boiling."

Steam poured out from under the stock pot's rattling lid. Boiling-over water hissed on the burner. Sam snatched a paper towel to wipe the onion juice off his hands and gave the knob on the stove a sharp twist. Gil laughed. "I think that might be the first time I've seen you make a mistake."

"Don't say that."

Sam hadn't meant for it to sound the way it did. For a moment Gil looked at him. Sam forced himself not to look away. Then Gil reached out across the table. "Hey," he said. "Come here."

Sam couldn't disobey. He scraped the onions into the stock pot with the chicken and the rest of the vegetables, simmering now. At the table he sat down and covered Gil's hand with his own.

The lean gentle fingers wrapped around his, and the music of *Bolero* wrapped around them both. Gil said, "Love, please stop blaming yourself."

"You shouldn't call me that."

Sam should have meant because of Jeannette. In fact, he should have taken his hand away again, because only one person had the right to hold it now, and she was a couple of hundred miles away. Nothing could have made him do it.

Gil shook his head. "No, I guess I shouldn't. It's just that I do still mean it."

The aroma of chicken soup filled the kitchen. There was no more comforting, homey smell in the world. Sam shivered. More than anything, here and now, he wished this place could be his home again.

He couldn't look at Gil. To the edge of the table, he said, "I don't deserve it."

It was true. He didn't deserve Gil's love any more than he deserved Jeannette's. He had told her the same thing, but she hadn't listened. Nobody listened or seemed to realize how hopeless he was.

Nobody except his father.

"The hell you don't."

Sam hadn't realized Gil had heard him over the music. He made himself look up. There was no laughter now in the blue eyes that watched him. Gil said, "Listen to me. I need you to hear something."

At that moment, the music reached its climax. The majesty of it filled the room. Sam and Gil sat and listened until the scorching final chords rang out. Sam felt them all the way up and down his spine.

That first night, he and Gil had laughed about cracked notes, fumbled page turns, and the splashes of sound that meant a desperate grab for a chord and a miss. The *Bolero* had filled Sam up like wine. When they got to the end, Gil had let go of the keys and turned to Sam. In spite of the fear that climbed up Sam's throat, he had sat still as Gil leaned forward and softly kissed his mouth.

Now the sound from the record player ended. Sam sat still, holding Gil's hand. For a few seconds, static drifted into the kitchen as the needle moved through the grooves on the record. Then the next piece began.

As soon as Sam heard the opening notes, he knew he should have expected them. Of course you would put Ravel's two greatest four-hands pieces together on a recording.

Gil picked up where he had left off. "Now, I'll be frank. I don't know how much time I have left. Nobody can tell me for sure."

Sam knew he had to listen, but he did not want to hear this. Especially not with the quiet, gentle melody going on in the background: the first movement of *Ma Mère L'Oye*.

Gil said, "I don't say that to be morbid. It's a simple fact. But I need to know that whatever happens to me, and whenever it happens, you understand it isn't your fault."

Sam couldn't keep Jeannette out of his head. Not with this piece going on. Did he owe it to Gil to tell him the truth; did he have to unleash that on him? Jeannette, who might say that this thing sucking Gil's life away was his own fault. *Most of those people, they do things they shouldn't.* Sam was supposed to link his life with hers. What had he done?

Gil said, "You did what you had to do for your own sanity, love. I know that business with your parents tore you up. I saw what it did to you."

He had. He had held Sam on the couch, lain beside him later in the bedroom and kept his arm around him, giving him a link to the world when Sam had been too wrapped in misery to move or speak and had only wanted to send himself into the dark and not come back. But Sam had been weak to let his father's rejection hit him so hard, hadn't he? He had been weak to decide he couldn't live with himself, if he was something his father hated so much.

Other people made different choices. Other people like Sam decided to be who they were, live openly with the partners they loved, and to hell with what anyone else thought. Sam knew that perfectly well. Gil himself had done it, living his life and washing his hands of the older brother who couldn't stand the "shame" Gil had dumped on their family. Sam had never had so much courage. He had never been able to forgive himself for destroying the home life he had loved, and more importantly, hurting Ma so badly. Maybe he should have been stronger. If he had been, Gil would not have reached the end of his road.

Gil said now, "Am I sorry we couldn't stay together? Yes. Did I miss you? More than I can say. But the fact that I chose to move on, and that I chose the person I did, was that your fault? Absolutely not."

The person I did. Those words reached Sam through the haze in his head. He didn't know that person's name. It struck him he would cut years off his life for five minutes alone with the bastard who had done this to Gil. Then he realized that whoever it had been, that person was probably already paying in a worse way than anything Sam could inflict.

Finally, some of Gil's other words caught up with him. *Did I miss you? More than I can say.* He thought Sam would forgive himself for that?

"Do you understand?" Gil said.

The third movement of *Ma Mère L'Oye* had begun. Sam tried not to follow its melody. "Yes," he said.

"Do you agree it isn't your fault?"

For a moment the music faded, burned out by anger. No, Sam would never agree. He would never forgive himself. He said, knowing how thin it sounded, "I'll try."

Gil raised an eyebrow. "I need more than that."

This movement was too short. It would be over in a couple of minutes. And then...

"When I think of your good heart, you do not seem so frightening to me."

"Oh, yes! I have a good heart, but I am a monster."

Sam could not sit here like this. The music dragged on him one way and Gil's hand pulled the other until he thought he must rip in two. He rushed words out. "I do have responsibility here, Gil. You have to admit that."

"You have a lot less responsibility than you're putting on yourself. What you were going through, I wouldn't wish it on anyone. You need to understand you had no control over what happened afterward."

The cheerful jingling harmonies from the stereo made Sam want to put his fist through the wall. He had to shut off the damn recording. "I do," he said. "I understand, but..." He couldn't let the anger out. Not here. He gently disengaged his hand. "I'm going to," he tried, and then escaped for the living room as fast as he could.

He snatched the needle off the record just in time. Another second and "Beauty and the Beast" would have started. Sam hit the power switch and stood in the silence, listening to his heart thud in his ears.

Gil's voice reached him. "What was that about?"

He stood in the doorway, leaning on the wall. Sam looked up into his face. Words did no good. In that instant, Sam thought that if he could have done it, he would have rewound the past or blasted it out of existence. All of it: Richmond, his orchestra, Jeannette, everything. He would have said to hell with the consequences, if he could have undone his worst mistake and if his future could have had Gil in it.

Now there was no future for them. No matter what Gil said, Sam knew that was his fault. He had held it in his hands and thrown it away.

He dragged his eyes away from Gil's face. "I'd better check on the soup."

"Sam."

Gil reached out, but Sam ducked aside. The gentle hand brushed his shoulder and fell away.

♫

Back in Richmond, in front of his apartment building, Sam had to pry his fingers one at a time off the Pinto's steering wheel. A steady rain had followed him all the way from the Maryland-Pennsylvania border. He and Gil had hugged each other one more time before Sam left, after the breakfast that Sam had gotten up early to cook to make sure Gil ate two decent meals in a row. The warmth of that last hug had faded too fast as the miles stretched out behind the Pinto.

Sam had to do something else now. He had planned it out on the drive back. He had to do it, because if he didn't, he would get in the car again and go straight back to Philly.

He hauled his pack out of the back seat. Rain splashed his face and dripped down the back of his neck. The three short flights up to his apartment felt steeper than he had ever noticed. He watched his beat-up sneakers climb them, mechanically, one step at a time.

It was only four in the afternoon. That meant *he* would still be at work. Sam would hear the one voice he wanted most. He did want it, didn't he?

He unlocked his door. The air in the apartment felt cold and dead.

If he stopped to think, he would never go through with it. He dropped his pack on the floor by the piano and went into the kitchen. Every step felt like wading through knee-deep mud.

His fingers didn't want to turn the dial on the phone. *Do it.* One number at a time. The dial spun with a noise like a zipper. Three digits. Six. Ten.

He could not sit down at the table. His knees wouldn't bend enough to step away from the counter. His heart beat so hard, he thought he might be sick.

On the other end, the phone rang. Once. Twice.

Click. "Hello?"

The ice in Sam's body dissolved all at once. He slumped against the counter.

"Hello?" the voice said again.

If he waited too long, she would think nobody was there. After all this time, watch her hang up.

He cleared his throat. His voice came out sounding tiny and scared. "Ma?"

Silence. It stretched out longer than Sam thought he could stand. Then he heard, "Liudas." It sounded like a sigh. And again: "Liudas. Oh, *mielas.*"

To the rest of the world, he had always been Sam. But he had belonged to her especially, had been *her* son, always, despite having his father's looks, and she had decided he had to have one name in her own language. She had translated his middle name to Liudas and called him by it since the day he was born. She called him *mielas* too, used the Lithuanian endearment so often that it could have been another name. Until this second, Sam had not realized how scared he had been that he would never hear her say either of those words again.

Now he heard something else: her tears. She must not cry for him anymore.

He wanted to reach through the phone line and put his arms around her. He wanted to erase every second of hurt he had caused her. "Ma. *Aš atsiprašau.*"

I'm so sorry. He had tried for a long while to cut the language out of his memory in case he could never use it again. The syllables with their light sibilance came back, and his tongue remembered them without trying. Saying them brought her that much closer.

Her voice. Her face. They, and the white house with the green roof, and the crab-apple tree in the yard, and everything that meant *home*, were coming back now, rushing in like a wave, bringing a lump up in his throat and sending warmth trickling back into his numb fingers. He heard a sniff. "*Viskas gerai, mielas,*" she said.

It's all right. It wasn't. It never would be, because he couldn't give her those five years back, but by God, he would do right by her now and forever.

"*Viskas gerai,*" she said again. Her briskness came back. "*Taip gera išgirsti tavo balsą.*"

Taip gera... It's so good, and something about... voice? *It's so good to hear your voice.* Sam remembered. Of course he did.

"So tell me," Ma said, switching to English. "Tell me everything. How you are, what you're up to, what..." Her voice caught. She tried to laugh, but Sam heard another sob, quickly stifled.

Nobody else laughed like her. He would hear it for real. Almost, almost he could tease her again, so he tried it. "Are you sure this is a good time? You're always busy."

"*Mielas.*"

In that one word, he saw the look on her face. Her eyes narrowed, the brows above them coming together in a V, her lips pursed the way they had been when she used to call him… yes, those words had stayed his head too. *Sunku berniukas*, pesky kid.

She said, *"Aš laukė ketverius metus. Pradėti kalbėti dabar." Start talking right now. I've been waiting all this time.*

Sam could have stood there and talked until it got dark out and the chorus gave up waiting for him and went home. He could have told Ma about Richmond and the river walk and his neighbourhood, and described the faces in the RSA until she saw each one, and told her about the Keatings and the board of directors, and the receiving line after the first concert. She would have drunk it all in and demanded more.

He had called, though, to say exactly one thing. His heart sped up. If he wanted to do right, if he wanted to go home again, this was the only way. "Actually," he said, "I do have one big piece of news."

"Well? Tell me."

He conjured her face in his mind as clearly as he could. "I'm going to get married."

Silence again. The phone line stretched between them, such a long way. Then she said, "Oh, *mielas.*"

Three syllables, but her voice did so much. That last day in her house when she had tried to stop him from leaving, when she had stood in the doorway to his bedroom while he threw his clothes and books in his suitcase. Standing there as if her small body could block the door and keep him inside. *"Don't do this, Liudas. You don't have to do this."*

Right now, he heard those words again in his head. That was silly. He was being the son she should have had.

"I'm sorry," he said. "That's a huge thing to spring on you all of a sudden."

She laughed. It was almost her laugh, but not quite. "I should say so! Now you *do* need to tell me all about it. Right this minute."

"Her name's Jeannette," he said. "Jeannette Reilly. She's my accompanist with the chorus." He had never written about her in his letters. After all, he had written so little.

"You met her this fall."

He knew what she was thinking, and he could laugh. "Yes, ma'am. It's sudden, I know, but you'll like her, I promise. She's really lovely. Has this great red hair. She's from South Carolina," he added, realizing he was rambling.

Ma said, "I can't wait to meet her."

"You two will get along fine. I know she'll love you."

"I'm not worried about that," Ma began. Then she stopped. Sam heard sounds in the background. A door shutting?

"Liudas," Ma said gently, "Dad's home."

No. It was the middle of the afternoon. Since when did the doctor get home before dinnertime? *No. No.*

Ma said, "He'll want to talk to you. I know he will."

Maybe Sam was imagining it, maybe he only heard his own loud pulse, but he thought he could make out footsteps in the background, coming closer. "Ma," he said quickly. "I don't think that's a good idea. Not right now."

"Please, *mielas*. It would make him so happy."

It wouldn't. How could she think so? She wanted to think Dad loved Sam. Sam could understand it, how she wanted the two people she loved most to love each other, but if Dad ever had loved his son, he couldn't anymore. Not since that last fight.

Ma said, "Let me put him on. Just for a minute."

Was his father standing right there in the kitchen? Did he know who Ma was talking to?

Sam heard, "Walter? Come in here, please."

More footsteps. Sam definitely heard them now. Then, "Yes?"

That same voice. Sam had heard it in his head so many times, hour after hour, day after day. *"Get out of this house."*

"He wants to talk to you, Walter. He has such good news."

Wants to? Sam felt like he was standing in a freezer. Dad might refuse to come to the phone. In fact, he probably would. That would be better.

Wouldn't it?

Ma came back. "One second, *mielas*." Was this his imagination too, or did her voice have the slightest tremor in it? "He's washing his hands. He'll be right over."

Sam heard the sink running. He couldn't open his mouth to answer Ma. The sink shut off. An instant of silence, and then more footsteps. Then, into the phone: "Sam?"

Jesus. That voice sounded exactly the way it always had, without one drop of emotion. His father could have been calling a patient. *"Mr. Varallo? This is Dr. Kraychek confirming your appointment on Wednesday."*

Hysterical laughter swarmed up Sam's throat. His eyes smarted. "Dad." If he only said one syllable at a time, maybe his voice wouldn't shake. "Hi."

"How are you?"

As if the last five years had disappeared like soap suds draining away down the sink. "I'm fine, sir." A whole sentence. Incredible. "Thank you. How are you?"

"Very well, thanks."

Sam's heart raced like a metronome in overdrive. What the hell should he say now? *What are you doing home?* Mistake: more crazy laughter tried to boil out of him, and he had to grit his teeth till they ached. Dad said, "Your mother tells me you have some news."

Get a goddamn grip! Sam clutched the phone so hard his fingers ached. "Uh, yes, I do. I wanted to tell you. Both of you. I got engaged."

At first he barely noticed the silence on the other end. Then, gradually, it settled on him. Dad was not answering. What was he thinking?

"You've always hated me! Let me give you something to hate!"

Dad remembered every second of that. No question. The horror of it closed over Sam's head. How had he dared to think he could change anything?

Then Dad cleared his throat. "That certainly is news. When did this happen?"

He could have been asking Sam when he'd gotten the oil changed in his car. "Last week," Sam managed. "Saturday."

"And the young lady's name?"

"Jeannette. Jeannette Reilly."

"Well," Dad said again. "I congratulate you both."

In the background, Sam heard Ma say something indistinct. Then Dad said, "Your mother wants the phone back. Take care."

That was it? That was *all*? "Yes, sir. You too."

He heard Ma say, "Walter, for heaven's sake, that isn't…" Dad answered something Sam couldn't catch. Ma laughed. Sam clutched the sound the way a drowning man would clutch a rope. "All right," Ma said, "but you could have done it yourself. Go on, then."

Footsteps moved away. Ma's voice came back. "*Mielas?*"

Sam leaned against the silverware drawer. "I'm here."

"Your father. Honestly, I don't know why he can't ask a simple question himself. Listen, mielas, you know I have to see you. It's been too long."

Too, too long. "Yes, ma'am."

"So I want you to tell me you'll come up for Thanksgiving. You and Jeannette both. That's what I wanted Dad to ask you about."

Thanksgiving. That was, what, three weeks from now? Sam tried to think. He could ask Jeannette about it tonight at rehearsal. Rehearsal. The ring. Should he make an announcement? He would have to, wouldn't he? People would see the ring. But Thanksgiving. Three weeks from now, Sam could go home.

His thoughts crashed into a wall. He would have to see Dad again.

"*Mielas?*"

She wanted this. She wanted this so much.

"Yes," he told her. "Okay."

She laughed again. "Well, you might want to ask Jeannette first. Just to be polite."

"Oh. Right." Sam tried to laugh too. "Okay. I'll see her tonight at rehearsal."

"You ask her and let me know for sure. Tomorrow?"

She wanted to know when she would hear from him again. She would not have to worry about that anymore. "Yes, ma'am," he said. "Tomorrow."

The hands on his watch had moved forward. He would have to be at rehearsal too soon. When he and Ma hung up, he dropped the receiver in the cradle with numb fingers and stumbled over to his bed. The mattress floated up to meet him.

♫

On the way to rehearsal, Sam parked in the Monroe Street lot and walked down to the river. He stood on the gravel path with his hands shoved deep into his pockets. Rain pocked the surface of the water.

The wind tugged at his hair, and beads of water slipped down his neck. He ignored them. Everything that had happened in the last couple of days banged around in his head. He'd better clear it out with a fast walk.

In this miserable weather, he had the path to himself. For some reason he didn't feel like walking.

Around the bend in the path, Belle Island waited. A long time ago, columns of men had marched down to this same river at bayonet-point. There had been wooden footbridges then between the bank and the island, knocked together sturdily enough to hold up under the concussions of boots. The men had crossed over and arrived on the island, where they would have to try to survive for months or years. A lot of them hadn't made it.

Sam couldn't get the picture of those men out of his head. They had been caught between bayonets on the one hand and that black hole on the other. Belle Island had probably looked nice enough from the outside, green maybe, tree-shaded. It didn't matter. A prison was always a prison.

The wind made Sam's teeth chatter, and the rain plastered his bangs to his forehead. He had been stupid to come down here in the wet. He turned away and left the river.

CHAPTER TWELVE

After the night when they told Veronica and Drew about the engagement, Jeannette didn't see Sam again until Monday's rehearsal. On Sunday he had to go up to Philadelphia to meet with someone there, a former colleague or something. He hadn't said much about it.

On Monday it rained. Jeannette borrowed Veronica's yellow umbrella and clamped her music under her raincoat for the walk to the Lewis Center. Her slacks were damp above the knees, and her practical shoes had shipped water by the time she got there. Sam's Pinto sat in its usual place by the dumpster. The little maple tree drooped dejectedly despite its brave colours. Jeannette hoped the tree would make it; she gave it a thumbs-up, as if a tree could see.

At least somebody had turned the heat on in the building. A week ago, Jeannette wouldn't have thought she would be so thankful for a blast of warmth. Down in the basement, Pink Sweater Lady descended on her. "Jeannie! How are you today?"

Jeannette shoved her left hand into her jacket pocket. "I'm fine, thanks, Mattie. How are you?"

She and Sam hadn't been obvious about their relationship in front of the chorus. Some people, including a bunch of the altos, had figured it out anyway. Pink Sweater Lady had cornered Jeannette in the ladies' room one evening to whisper, "So you and Sam are an *item!*" as if it were a piece of celebrity gossip. Jeannette didn't want to think about how they would react to the ring.

Pink Sweater Lady said now, "Oh, I'm doing fine, same-old same-old." Then, as if she'd read Jeannette's mind, she added, "Anything"—*nudge, nudge, wink, wink*—"new?"

What, did she have X-ray vision to see into Jeannette's pocket? Jeannette stepped back. "Oh, not much."

Just then, the rehearsal room opened. Sam stood in the doorway. "Evening, everyone. Come on in."

Everybody more or less lined up to say hello. The stand-throwing incident at the second rehearsal might have sent pacemakers into overdrive, but the first concert had cemented Sam's reputation as "the best conductor this group's had in a long time, and I mean a *long* time, and believe you me, I know what I'm talking about," as Spider/Gladys had announced one evening at the upstairs soda machine. People could overlook craziness when it came with a great big dose of white light.

Jeannette went in last. Sam smiled at her. "Hey, sweetheart," he said, too quietly for listening ears to catch. "How are you?"

He looked tired, on edge. Well, he had just spent the day driving in the rain. "I'm okay," she said. "How was your trip?"

"Fine." In two steps he was at the podium, opening his music. "Okay, folks. We're starting with the 'Hallelujah Chorus' tonight."

Jeannette had to rush to put her music up on the piano and fumble to the right section of Handel's *Messiah*. She bundled up her raincoat and dropped it next to the bench. It wasn't until she put her hands on the keys that she thought of the ring again, glittering under the light. She thought she heard somebody gasp, but that was stupid. Nobody could see her hand way up here.

Sam said, "We'll take it slowly. We have a lot to cover tonight, so don't over-sing." He turned to Jeannette, raising the baton. Their eyes met. The white stick hung suspended.

Abruptly, he brought it down. "I must be losing my mind. Before we start, folks, I'd like to share something with you all."

Jeannette swallowed. He was going to do this right now?

He said, "I know I haven't been with you all for very long, but you've given me such a wonderful welcome to Richmond. I think I should share this news with my musical family."

He turned to Jeannette. White light glittered around him.

"This is Jeannette's news as well as mine, and I hope she will forgive me for spilling the beans." He made the chorus wait, winding up the tension the way he strung out the last instant of silence before the final, crashing chord of a piece. Jeannette didn't dare look at the singers. "She has made me a very fortunate man," he said. "She has agreed to be the future Mrs. Kraychek."

Jeannette shut her eyes. She saw a yellow Formica tabletop and Veronica's hand covering hers.

Pink Sweater Lady yelped, "I *knew* it!" Somebody started to clap, and more people joined in. Applause filled the room and sloshed back and forth between the walls.

Pink Sweater Lady called out over the din, "Now, Sam, you can't think you're just going to start *rehearsal* now!" A chair scraped on the floor and her voice came closer. "Some of us have got to congratulate you two dear people!"

Good grief. Surely this could wait till break. Jeannette opened her eyes to see how Sam would stop it, but Pink Sweater Lady was already coming up to the podium, along with Spider/Gladys and a whole flock more.

The gaggle of altos stopped by the podium first and then clustered around the piano bench. Pink Sweater Lady got to Jeannette ahead of the others. "Congratulations, Jeannie, I *knew* this would happen! I was sure I saw something on your hand there!" Arms reached for Jeannette, hands stretched out to see the ring. She had never been so popular in her life. The clash of perfumes and hairsprays confused her nose. She peered between two women in front of her for a glimpse of Sam. Surely he would put a stop to this. They had work to do.

Someone else had come up to the podium. Jeannette saw Nathan's dark hair. Then the look on his face hit her, as quick as a blow to the throat. He looked as if he had watched some irreplaceable thing smash on the ground at his feet.

A soprano in a butter-coloured skirt and lemon blouse manoeuvred in front of Jeannette and demanded a look at the diamond. Jeannette held it out for inspection and lost sight of Nathan. Finally she heard Sam's voice, laughing. "Okay, folks. To be continued at break. Let's get to work."

Jeannette remembered she ought to be mad at him. When the crowd around her thinned out, she risked shooting him a look, not quite a glare, but maybe she could scrape herself together between now and break and ask him what on earth he'd been thinking. All those hands pawing at her made her want a shower this minute.

He met her eyes. The expression on his face took her straight back to her first-grade classroom when cherub-faced Davey Waters had to stand up in front of everyone for a whole period, because Miss Marilynne Thompson caught him putting a pocketful of caterpillars in Annie Callahan's desk. Jeannette had to clamp her lips tight together not to laugh.

Sam grinned and smoothed out the pages of his score. "Okay," he told the chorus. "Let's get down to business."

♪

After rehearsal, Veronica had waited up again. When Jeannette and Sam came in together, she only stayed up long enough to say goodnight. She didn't seem remotely embarrassed to be caught in her kimono. When Sam apologized for the late intrusion, she told him, "Don't fret for a minute. You're family now, you make yourself at home."

After she had gone to bed, Jeannette and Sam looked at the yellow kitchen table and then out at the dark living room. In tacit agreement, they went to sit on the couch.

Sam took her hand. "We won't keep your family up?"

"I doubt it." Jeannette pushed off her shoes and nudged them under the coffee table. Out in the car, with the heat blasting and finally drying her wet pants and socks, they had sat in silence for a few minutes until he asked if he could come in. He said he had something he needed to tell her. She said now, "You should hear the way Drew snores. Anybody who can sleep through that can sleep through anything."

At rehearsal break, he had asked her to come to his parents' house with him for Thanksgiving. He had looked so uneasy that she wondered if they were mad about his engagement, but he said they were thrilled, couldn't wait to meet her. She hoped that was true.

Now he began, "I think you should know something about my parents and me. You see, I haven't been back to Westbury in a long time. Not since I finished college."

Jeannette hadn't expected that, if she had expected anything. "Why not?"

"We had a fight. My father and I."

"What happened?"

Sam hesitated. "Well, Dad and I, we never really got along. For years we didn't, even when I was a kid." He spoke carefully, choosing words the way you would step between puddles on the sidewalk. "We were too different, I guess, but we're both stubborn. That's what my mother used to say. She called us her stubborn Kraychek men."

Jeannette remembered something Veronica had said only two nights ago. *I doubt you were a lot of trouble.* They had been talking about mothers, hadn't they? How kids gave their mothers trouble. And Sam had said, *More than you can imagine.*

Jeannette said, "Why did you and your dad fight?"

Sam shook his head. "It was so long ago. It doesn't really matter. I'd left Westbury, gone to college, gotten into music full-time." His eyes went to the piano against the far wall. "When I came back, I didn't fit in anymore. My father wasn't happy."

"Why not?"

Sam looked at her, reluctantly, she thought. "I was too different. You'll understand when we get there. Westbury is a particular kind of place."

A curl of anger woke up in Jeannette's stomach. Reckord's Mill had been a particular kind of place too. A particular kind of hole in the wall, where people watched out their front windows and whispered in the grocery store aisles and carried their bile with them to church to hear sermons about brotherly love. She said, "That's not fair."

"It wasn't my father's fault. Not really."

"But he didn't like you?" Drew's snoring notwithstanding, Jeannette had to remember to keep her voice down. Kids on a playground had taunted a little girl because of her hair, her mother, her music, but they hadn't been *family*, people she should have been able to trust. "He should have let you be who you wanted," she said. "He should have seen how amazing you are." She had never said that out loud.

Sam pressed her hand in the dark. "Thank you. But listen, I don't want you to think he's a bad person." He paused again. "We're just different. For instance, he's a doctor. He had a hard time understanding the music thing."

"That's still no reason for him not to like you."

Sam smiled, but a shadow of sadness hung on him. "You know, fathers and sons, it can be tough. I'm also the only one. That makes it harder for him."

That was true. Sam had no siblings. Jeannette had known that, but she hadn't quite realized how it might feel never to have that other presence keeping an eye on you, sticking a nose or a whole head in where it didn't belong, but ready to side with you against all comers. Sam had been so alone.

Another thought hit her. She didn't know why, except that Sam had said he hadn't been home in a while. "Did your father kick you out?"

He hesitated again. "Sort of."

"He *did*?" Hell, no. Home was home. Nobody had the right to tell you that you couldn't be there. In Jeannette's case, she hadn't wanted to be, but that was beside the point.

Sam said quickly, "It wasn't his fault. Not totally. We both knew we couldn't be under the same roof."

"What does that mean?" Jeannette's anger fanned hotter. This father, this future father-in-law, had better look out. He was a doctor? How good was he? Let him say one bad thing to Sam in her hearing and he would hope he was good, all right.

Sam said, "We both said some stuff, that last time we fought. It was my fault as much as his. More." His voice got husky. "I had to leave after that. But my mother, she... she tried to stop me."

That pain was as fresh as wet paint. Sam added, "The worst part was knowing how awful she felt. What I'd done to her."

Jeannette squeezed his hand. "You didn't do anything."

"I made my choices."

What did that mean? He made the choice to be a musician? That didn't give his father the right to kick him out of the house. Before Jeannette could answer, Sam went on, "I wanted to tell you about this in case things are a little strange when we go up there. Because I haven't seen them in a while. We won't fight, I promise."

"Are you sure I should go with you? Is it too soon?"

"No. Please come."

He looked like a scared boy again. Was he afraid she would change her mind and not go, maybe decide she didn't want to marry him? In this moment, when she saw how he needed her, she knew she would do that when the sky fell in. "Of course I'll come," she said.

He seemed to relax. "They're good people, they really are. I think you'll like my mother. She's pretty wonderful. And Dad... well, I know how he probably sounds to you, but he's not a bad person. He's done a lot. He grew up in a really poor neighbourhood, his father and pretty much everybody else who lived there were coal miners, but Dad got out. Went to med school, started his own practice. He was brave."

Maybe it was Jeannette's imagination, but Sam sounded like he was trying to convince himself about his father. She didn't care what this doctor had done or how poor of a neighbourhood he had grown up in. Jeannette herself had managed to go to music school, and look at Reckord's Mill. Sam's mother, though, he hadn't seen her in a long time, and he missed her. Jeannette was more than ready to like this unknown woman.

She asked, "What are their names?"

"My father's Walter, and my mother's Anna." This time, his smile looked real. "If I know her, she'll want you to call her Ma, like I do."

Mama. A hand reached inside Jeannette's chest and squeezed her heart. He saw it. "What's wrong?"

He still didn't know anything about Reckord's Mill, aside from the name. He knew that Aunt Gretchen had raised her and Veronica both but had never pushed to find out why. Soon, she would have to tell him. She would have to hand him that piece of herself.

Not tonight; not yet. She said, "I guess I'm just nervous about meeting them."

He touched her hair with the gentleness she loved. "You have nothing to worry about. They'll be thrilled."

She hoped. They might have ideas about what kind of woman their son should marry. This father sounded more than capable of that.

"I should let you get to bed," Sam said. "Thank you for hearing me out."

"Any time."

When they said goodnight, she held onto him longer than usual, standing there in the dark while the rays of the street lamp outside and the rays from the light in the kitchen blended on the carpet at their feet. She hated the thought of him going out into the wet night, back to his empty, chilly apartment.

Alone in her bedroom, Jeannette stared up at the ceiling. This father-in-law wouldn't look a thing like Sam. He would be old and grey, poky, with a face like a... yes... a shrivelled tomato. Doctor Walter Kraychek. Jeannette conjured up a wrinkly, disapproving frown and stuck out her tongue at it.

That helped. Laughing at herself, she burrowed into the warm dark under the covers.

CHAPTER THIRTEEN

The bridge over the Lackawanna River didn't disappear the way it had in Sam's dream. As Sam drove out onto the span, he clutched the steering wheel, as if that would do any good if the old concrete decided to buckle. It didn't. The flat grey river slipped past underneath, and the Pinto reached the other side.

Westbury.

No sun today, only grey cloud cover and a coating of snow. The clouds looked flat-bottomed, as if squashed against glass. The air in the mountains was so clear and cold at this time of year that you would think you could tap on it and it would shatter. Sam hadn't felt it yet, but he knew. Oh yes. He knew.

Jeannette sat quiet in the passenger's seat. Through Virginia and into Maryland, she had chatted with him about chorus and piano, Veronica and Drew and the boys ("Vee can't wait till Ricky starts school next year, but I feel sorry for his poor teacher, don't you?"), and Thanksgiving ("It'll be such a treat to have a real one, Vee makes stuffing out of a box and cranberry sauce out of a can"). When Sam told her that Ma wouldn't allow boxes or cans anywhere near the dinner table and promised that by the time they went back to Richmond Jeannette would be a full-fledged cook, she had laughed and squeezed his arm. "If your mama can make that happen, she must be able to walk on water."

She had gotten quieter as the car chugged north. After they crossed the Pennsylvania border, she huddled deeper into her corduroy jacket. Sam turned up the heat against the air that leaked through the car's lousy weatherproofing. For a while he thought she might have drifted off to sleep; after all, they had left Veronica and Drew's before daylight. When he glanced over, though, he saw her eyes open and watchful. Her face, jacket, and turtleneck sweater were all shades of creamy white. The brightest colour he saw was her hair spilling out from under her thin white cap. When he asked if she was okay, she said sure, but he saw how her hands held on to each other in her lap.

Of course she was anxious about meeting his parents. Any new fiancée would be. Sam knew he should say something cheerful, especially now as the car edged down Front Street behind a line of slow-moving traffic. Somehow he couldn't find enough breath to comment on the line out the doors at the A&P, or mention how long Westbury had needed a second grocery store. He certainly couldn't point back in the direction the car had come from and tell Jeannette, "If we'd turned left instead of right on Front Street, we would've passed Dad's medical practice on the corner." No doubt, after all this time, the front door at Westbury Medical was still the same shade of forest green, and the brass plaque on it—*Dr. Walter Kraychek, M.D., Family Physician*—was still so polished that you could check the alignment of your tie in it.

Sam had gone up the narrow flight of stairs behind that door countless times to his father's sterile, perfectly organized domain. As a kid, he had absorbed early on the fact that while everybody trusted his father, they didn't much like him. At least, they didn't talk and laugh with him the way they did with Ma. The other kids had always assumed Dr. Kraychek must be nicer to his own son than he was to other people; he'd be more patient, maybe, if Sam got scared when he had to have a shot or stitches. Sam hadn't often bothered to straighten those kids out. The plain fact had been that Dr. Kraychek hadn't had time for weakness or fear from anybody, especially not his own child. You could trust Dad to give you medicine that would make you feel better if you were sick, or stitch you up if you needed it, or set a broken bone. You didn't look to him to tell you everything would be okay, or say that you were being brave to swallow the horrible-tasting medicine or put up with the needle he slipped under your skin.

Thinking about that now, Sam gripped the wheel tighter and hoped Jeannette wouldn't notice. He drove down one last block on Front Street and made the left on River. Then, and only then, it hit him.

Home.

Memories poured in. Sounds: the old Greyhound bus chuffing up to the intersection of Front and Market to take passengers to the city. The hollow tolling of St. Francis's bell before Sunday Mass. The growls of competing lawnmowers on summer afternoons. The tune, or, yes, the twang, in the voices of neighbours calling hello to each other. And scents: the sharp crystal air in winter and the brown velvet incense in St. Francis. The camphor and cedar in bedroom closets, to guard good coats and sweaters against time. The potato and cabbage, sausage and spice aromas in everybody's mother's kitchen.

Home. In the five years Sam had been away, and the years before that at college, he had missed this place. In the worst moments of missing, he still hadn't understood how stretched-thin he had become.

The houses on River Street went past. One-storey brick with brown shutters, two-storey white with navy shutters, two-storey brick with kelly-green shutters. Each one was neat and square with a small square of lawn, a short flat driveway, and a mailbox by the curb. One summer, Rob Sheposky's father had put pumpkin-orange shutters on his brick house, and the street had talked about it for weeks.

Two blocks down. Three to go.

If Sam had been alone, he would have rolled down the window and let the freezing air in, to gulp it down and feel it fill him up. He still had enough of a grip to remember the girl beside him. Jeannette had told him she had never seen real snow. She was probably looking out right now at the white yards and white roofs and the piles of grey slush by the sides of the road, wondering what kind of purgatory she had gotten herself into. The thought made him want to laugh and made him want to reach over and squeeze her hand—the poor thing hadn't even brought gloves; he should have told her to make sure she did—and feel the hard real diamond on her finger.

Now, though, they had gone down another block, and Sam could only look at the road ahead. How many times had he walked along this same stretch? He had memorized the patterns of cracks in the sidewalk. Every fall, the maple trees on both sides of the road flamed scarlet. How many times had Sam raked those leaves out of the front yard and crunched the piles of them along the curb? He knew their crisp texture, their sharp, dusty smell.

One last stop sign, the intersection with Walnut Street. Sam's heart beat faster.

On the left, 515, 517, and there it was: 519. There was the stocky crab-apple tree, its branches clumped with snow. Behind it, he could see the two banks of bare azaleas that would bloom red in the spring, and the shingles of the white house, and the green front door to match the dark green roof. And there, in the middle of the front path, she stood waiting. A white scarf covered her hair. Her blue coat was the brightest thing against the white yard and grey sky.

Sam couldn't stop dead on the street. He forced the wheel around and pulled into the drive. Dad's old Fairlane sat at the end beside the house. How many times, over how many years, had Sam ridden in the back of that car? And that was before he had learned to drive it.

He finally managed to open his mouth. "That's Ma," he told Jeannette, nodding toward the front path. "Trust her to try to give herself pneumonia, waiting for us." His foot shook over the brake as he parked beside the Fairlane. It could have been a prop in an old black-and-white movie. "That's Dad's old car," he added. "I'm amazed it's still running."

"They made them tough."

Her voice quivered. Sam turned to her and saw how wide her eyes had gone and how pale her cheeks looked. Her hair was impossibly bright, like an oversaturated photo.

He put his hand on her knee. "Don't worry. Everything's going to be fine."

She looked at him the way the patient looks at the doctor who says it won't hurt. "You're nervous."

"Yes," he admitted. "But we'll be okay. Come on, let's not keep Ma waiting."

He got out of the car and opened Jeannette's door for her and helped her out and shut the door again. All the while he felt Ma standing there, watching. She held back long enough that he worried she might be mad at him after all. God knew she had every reason in the world.

He took two steps up the path (how many times had he cleared the snow off it, starting with the first winter he'd been tall enough to hold the shovel?) and then her heels clicked like scattershot on the concrete. Before he could worry about those flimsy dress shoes slipping on the wet, her arms and the cinnamon scent he had known all his life wrapped around him.

"Liudas. Oh, Liudas."

She was so small. The top of her head only came up to his shoulder. "Ma," he whispered. He was afraid to hug her too hard and hurt those delicate bones. Her scent wove together with the air, the white yard, and the dark lines of the crab-apple tree in the snow. Together they called to his heart and told him how long he had been gone.

"*Mielas*," she said. "I missed you so much."

Inside him, something let go. "I missed you too."

Sam's throat hurt. He could have stood there much longer, making up for all the times when he hadn't been here for her. She let go first and stepped back. "And this is your sweet girl," she said.

For a moment the cold bit through Sam's wool coat. "Yes," he said. He couldn't mind Jeannette being here now, sharing this. Not when she was the only reason he had been able to come back. He reached for her hand. "This is Jeannette."

For an instant Ma looked into his face. Sam didn't know why, but he saw Gil again, standing alone in his doorway with his clothes hanging slack on him.

Then Ma turned to Jeannette. "I'm so glad to meet you." Jeannette mumbled something that included the word "ma'am," and Ma laughed and said, "Oh, honey, none of that. You can call me Anna if you want, but Ma's even better."

It was so exactly like her that Sam couldn't help laughing too. He said to Jeannette, "What did I tell you?"

When she looked up at him, he thought he saw tears in her eyes. *What's wrong?* Before he could ask, Ma shooed them toward the door. "Let's get inside. You two must be freezing."

Sam said, "You're the one who's been waiting out here. Are you sure such an old lady should do that?" He could only say it because Ma would never get old, and he had to say something, because he knew who would be waiting on the other side of this door.

Ma held the door open. "*Sunku berniukas,*" she said. *Pesky kid.* "I'll give you an old lady. Is that how you talk to your mother?"

The warmth and the scent of the house hit Sam at the same time. The air smelled like cinnamon too, as if the scents of all the pies and Lithuanian pastries and spice cakes Ma had made over the years had seeped into the walls. Too long since Sam had breathed this. Much too long.

As a teenager, he would have given Ma some smart-alec answer when she asked him how he talked to his mother. He had always loved to see how far he could push it before she burst out laughing. Now, as the solid air gave way in front of him and then seemed to pull him in like a pair of embracing arms, he couldn't call up that smart mouth. Instead he said, "I'll only talk that way if she doesn't mind. Does she?"

"*Mielas. Žinote geriau.*" *You know better than that.*

Then the storm door shut behind them, and they were all inside in the narrow foyer, and in an instant like a photograph, Sam remembered how huge this same foyer had looked when he was a kid. A very small kid, for instance, no older than three, when he'd heard the front door open and come running.

Had he really done that? Jesus. Because the person on the other side of the door that day, the person coming in from outside, would have been...

Sam heard footsteps on the staircase now, coming down to the landing. He didn't need to look to see the beat-up pair of brown carpet slippers.

There was nothing to be scared of anymore. Everything that had happened was over and done. The footsteps came down to the landing and stopped.

He heard the door open and came running, calling back to the kitchen, "Mama! Daddy's home!"

Sam made himself look up at his father.

Ma's hair did look a little more silver now than it used to, but Dad's face had not changed. Sam looked at the older image of himself.

He knew it as well as he knew his own reflection. After all, they were the same eyes, the same hair, the straight nose and high cheekbones Sam saw every time he looked in the mirror. At forty, Walter Kraychek had looked closer to fifty and would probably stay that way for the rest of his life. Old age would not touch that stern, quiet face any more than it touched hard oak, or stone. Would Sam age the same way?

No smile on his father's face. Sam had not expected one. He also had not expected the ache he felt.

"Daddy's home!" Sam ran to the door, and sure enough, there was the bulging black doctor's bag coming in first, and then the pair of polished shoes with the laces neatly tied, and the pants with their sharp creases. And far away, above the collar of the white shirt, the face...

The tail of the memory flapped uselessly in Sam's head, like an incomplete movie reel. Had Dad smiled then? Maybe bent down to hug him? Sam would remember that, wouldn't he?

Dad said, "Sam."

It was exactly like the voice on the phone. *"This is Dr. Kraychek calling, regarding your blood test results."* Sam didn't feel like laughing now. "Dad," he answered.

The stillness said it all. Maybe this visit didn't matter much to Dad, or maybe he would have preferred that Sam had stayed away. Silence stretched out in the foyer, and Sam realized he didn't feel nervous anymore. Nothing but cold.

Then Dad held out his hand. "Good to see you."

"Good to see you too, sir."

They shook hands. Sam thought he heard Ma sigh. Well, this visit mattered to her. That counted for more than anything else.

She had always tried, Ma. She had reached out her hands to Sam and his father both, especially during the last couple of years before Sam had left, trying to hold the two of them together. Sam knew that was why she had told him the little of Dad's history she knew. Sam had never learned anything about his father from Dad himself. Not about medical school; not about the poor neighbourhood in Scranton, the place the locals had called Miner's Row, where Dad had grown up; not about the grandfather, Liuz Kraychek, with whom Sam shared a name. Apparently it hadn't been Dad's idea to give Sam his father's name. Ma had come up with that, as if a name might act as glue to hold the family together.

Sam had never understood why Ma had put up with Dad for so long, but she had done it. Now he could manage to do the same.

He reached out for Jeannette's hand. "Dad, I'd like you to meet my fiancée." At least they could see who had better manners, the doctor or the Maestro. "Jeannette Reilly, Walter Kraychek."

Dad gave her a visual once-over, the look Sam thought of as assessing symptoms. "Hello, Jeannette. I'm pleased to meet you."

Jeannette said, "Likewise, sir." Her voice, with its beautiful accent, sounded so much more alive than Dad's. Given that Dad had grown up in Scranton and his parents had both been Polish immigrants, he should have had the same twang as everyone else up here. He had stripped it out of his voice long before Sam was born.

Ma said, "Now, you two must be tired and hungry. Liudas, the guest room's ready. Go on and get your bags and get settled."

Sam was more than ready to escape, but to his surprise, Dad intervened. "I'll get the bags. Is your car unlocked?"

"Yes, sir." Nobody in Westbury worried about locking doors. "Thank you."

The blast of cold air from outside felt warmer than the foyer when Dad was in it. Ma said, "I'll get supper started."

When she took off her coat, Sam saw that she was wearing her favourite dress. Ma loved to wear blue because it set off her eyes so well. This dress was the colour of the sky, with a lace collar and a sash and a row of round pearl buttons up the back. She always joked that it made her look too young, but she had kept it for years and only wore it on the most special occasions. Sam understood what it meant that she had worn it today.

She hung up her coat in the foyer closet and reached for Sam's. He handed it over. "Do you need help cooking?" he asked.

"Not yet," she said. "Save up your energy for tomorrow. That's when I'll put you to work."

"Good," Sam answered. When her back was turned, he added quietly, "I've missed that too."

He wasn't sure if she heard. The front door opened again in a blast of cold. Dad brought the bags in, Sam's canvas-sided one and the screamingly chartreuse one Jeannette had borrowed from Veronica, who evidently saw nothing unreasonable about that colour for luggage. Sam took them both and headed upstairs.

He couldn't help but remember the last time he had been on this staircase. Thank God he had at least replaced his old suitcase. The one he had now wasn't much different, but he hadn't thrown it open on his bed that last morning, tossed his clothes into it, rammed his schoolbooks on top, and forced the zipper to close around the whole mess. (Ma stood in the doorway as if she could block it. "Don't do this, Liudas.") This suitcase hadn't thumped on each step on the long flight down.

Jeannette followed him down the upstairs hall. The same thin burgundy carpet he remembered covered the floorboards and the same cinnamon scent filled the air. Across the hall from the guest room, the door of Sam's old bedroom stood open a crack. He couldn't see in. That was fine. He didn't want to look at that room right now.

The guest room had white lace curtains in the windows, like a picture in an old storybook, and a white quilt with a pattern of roses on the bed. The bed had a four-poster wooden frame polished to a high gloss. The knob at the top of each post was carved in the shape of a pineapple.

Sam hoisted the suitcases up onto the quilt. When he could trust himself to sound normal, he turned to Jeannette. "What do you think so far?"

She was staring at something over the bed. Sam followed her eyes and saw the crucifix.

The brown plastic cross had always been there, with the white loincloth-clad plastic body of Jesus dangling on it. Ma and Dad had one in their bedroom, and there was another over Sam's old bed across the hall. All traditional Catholics had them.

Jeannette wasn't Catholic. She looked at the plastic cross the way she might have looked at an actual dead body hanging over the bed.

Sam remembered that when he had first left for college, packed up the clothes in his closet, and boxed up his favourite Civil War books from high school, he had thought about taking the crucifix too. The dorm room wall would look bare without it. You couldn't do something like that, though. Supposing your roommate would forgive you for religious freakhood, you still couldn't drive a nail into cinderblocks.

Later, during that time in college when everything had changed, Sam had wondered if his dreams might have been different if the crucifix had been there to protect him. If he had followed the rules, tried to stay a good Catholic in this wide-open new world, would the church have kept its son safe?

No point wondering any of that now. The crucifix was just a thing, a fake plastic thing no less. Jeannette shouldn't worry about it. Sam said, "Honey?"

She looked around. "What's that?"

"I asked you what you think of all this so far."

"Oh. Yes." She seemed to pull herself together. "Your mama's really nice."

Sam opened his suitcase and rummaged in it for the toiletries he would put in the bathroom. "I thought you'd like her."

The latches on Jeannette's suitcase clicked when she undid them. She said, "What were those words she used? Your mama?"

"Oh, that's right. I should have told you." Sam found the plastic bag he had put the bathroom supplies in and emptied it onto the quilt. "Ma is Lithuanian. That's where both of her parents were from. She still speaks

Lithuanian, and she taught me too." As he translated Ma's words for Jeannette, Liudas and *mielas* and *sunku berniukas*, another memory crept into his head. When had he last shared a bed with someone?

Jeannette laughed at *pesky kid*. She lifted a nightgown out of her suitcase. "So you're bilingual?"

That last night with Gil, as if Sam could forget it. He could not afford to think of it now. "Pretty much," he said. He examined the toiletries on the quilt as if he didn't already know what they were. Toothbrush, toothpaste. "I thought I forgot some Lithuanian, you know, when I didn't use it for a while." Razor. Miniature bottle of mouthwash. "It all comes back, though."

It all did come back. Gil's face in the dark, his sad eyes, his hand reaching to touch Sam's cheek. *"I don't want you to hurt, love, but I wish you didn't have to do this."*

Sam scooped up the handful of supplies and made for the door. "I'll put this stuff in the bathroom, and then we can do the ten-cent house tour if you want. One sec."

In the bathroom, he didn't turn on the light. His hands shook. The toothbrush fell into the sink and the mouthwash rolled off the edge of the counter and hit the floor with a cracking noise. Sam didn't bother to see if it was actually broken before he threw it in the trash.

CHAPTER FOURTEEN

Jeannette couldn't close her eyes, much less sleep. Okay. So it was dark. So the clock on the dresser said 10:32, and it would be at least seven hours till the sun came up. She still had no reason to get upset.

The guest-room bed smelled like lavender. The sheets had the stiff feeling that good-quality cotton took on when it had been washed a lot. Aunt Gretchen would have approved of the thriftiness implied there. Aunt Gretchen would not have approved of Jeannette getting between these sheets with a man under any circumstances other than marriage.

The old mattress sank down in the middle. The quilt came up to Jeannette's chin. In the dark, the room turned a uniform grey, featureless except for the green numbers on the clock and the ghostly curtains at the window. She could have been lying at the bottom of a bowl.

Sam had gone to sleep the minute he turned out the light. He had been tired all through dinner; no wonder, after the long drive today, on top of how it must feel to him to come home after all this time. The older folks were early-to-bed people too. Anna had urged Jeannette to stay up if she liked, make herself at home, help herself to anything in the kitchen. Jeannette had followed Sam upstairs, literally on his heels, and rushed to wash her face, brush her teeth, and get under the covers before he said goodnight. She didn't want to be alone in this house.

In daylight, it had looked like a nice enough place, a little worn but well-kept. Sam had shown her around all the rooms, except the one across the hall with the mostly-shut door. He had pointed out the master bedroom at the end of the upstairs hall and told her he had been born there.

His parents hadn't had time to get to the hospital, so his father had to do the delivery right here. "Ma said that was just as well. At the hospital, they'd have told Dad to stay out of the delivery room. Ma said nobody got enough hazard pay to do that."

Sam had drawn his first breath in this house. No wonder, by the time they had been here for an hour or two, it fit him like one of his button-down shirts. At supper, he and his mother had dished out plates of meatloaf and potatoes and talked back and forth in a mix of English and Lithuanian. Jeannette didn't follow all the words, but the tone and the looks the two of them shared told her everything she needed to know. That loving back-and-forth teasing squeezed her heart. *Mama.*

Jeannette herself had sat uneasily at the white Formica table, in the fourth chair that you could tell hadn't been used as much as the others because the white plastic cushion was thicker. Dr. Kraychek sat across from her. She and he carefully didn't look at each other, much less try to talk. Sam didn't seem to notice how tense she was. Maybe he should have felt strange too, after all this time, but on the other hand, why would he? The white table, the chair that had always been his as a kid, the sage-green floor tile, and the very walls seemed to welcome him back.

Now Jeannette put both hands on her stomach and felt for the ring under the covers. Sam slept on his side, facing away from her, but she could hear his quiet, regular breathing. She had no reason to feel so uneasy. They were engaged, after all, and besides, he hadn't suggested anything inappropriate or laid a finger anywhere he shouldn't. The crucifix could stare all it wanted.

The problem was, it did stare. She felt it. The walls and windows stared too. The creaky floorboards in the hall accused her, and the windows on the porch showed her a snowscape as alien and unwelcoming as the surface of the moon. Sam's old upright piano glared at her in the living room, and so did the television with its old-fashioned rounded face. Dr. Kraychek's brown leather armchair dared her to touch it with so much as a fingertip. Maybe Sam and his parents didn't realize it, but the *house* knew she didn't belong here.

She should feel like she did belong. These people were going to be her family. She would probably visit this house a lot. Somehow, still, none of it felt real. None of it felt safe.

She and Sam would go home on Sunday. Four days from now. Surely Jeannette could make it that long.

If only she could call Veronica right now. That was stupid. If the phone rang this late at night, her sister would think Jeannette had died. Even so, Jeannette would give anything to hear Veronica's voice, never mind if it was tight with panic.

She pushed the covers back and sat up. The mattress jiggled under her, and she held her breath until her feet touched the floor. She should have thought to bring slippers. This room didn't have a carpet.

Sam didn't stir as she tiptoed around the bed, stretching her hands out in the dark to feel for the furniture until she got to the door. At least the hall was carpeted. Someone had left a nightlight on in the bathroom. It illuminated a round patch of hallway. Jeannette didn't know where the main light switch was and wouldn't risk turning it on if she found it.

The only phone she had seen was in the kitchen. If she was serious about calling her sister, she would have to make it all the way down the stairs in the dark. So be it.

The staircase looked like a black tunnel. Jeannette made out a thin patch of light at the bottom, coming through the glass panes at the top of the door. Something to aim for.

She took one step down. The stair squealed.

The walls and ceiling pressed in. *You shouldn't be here.* The shadows seemed to have weight and heft to push back against her. Stumbling, she turned around and climbed back up to the landing.

What on earth was the matter with her? She was acting like a scared five-year-old. In the dark, the guest room door looked too far away. The other door, the one she had almost forgotten about, stood open a hair. Why hadn't Sam shown her that room? What was in there?

Jeannette shook herself. This was worse than the time she and Veronica had stayed up late on Halloween, because Aunt Gretchen wouldn't let them go trick-or-treating, and read ghost stories until they had to huddle together in Veronica's bed clutching a flashlight and listening to the floorboards creak. This house wasn't Bluebeard's castle.

What would be in a room Sam hadn't shown her? The most obvious answer was something that belonged to his father.

Dr. Kraychek hadn't told Jeannette to call him Walter. He hadn't told her to call him anything. Jeannette knew she wouldn't manage "Dad" or even "Father" if he, or she for that matter, lived to be a hundred. She had braced herself for a crotchety old curmudgeon who would make snide comments at the dinner table about Sam's job, or the studio apartment he lived in, or the fact that the RSA had to fight for its survival. She had promised herself that if he made one nasty remark, if he so much as looked at Sam in a funny way, she would stiffen her spine and lay down her fork and show him why you didn't cross a redhead.

He hadn't said a thing. He had kept his eyes on his plate, except when he looked politely and attentively at whoever was speaking. He seemed like a proper gentleman. So why on earth did he scare her so much?

She wouldn't worry about that now. The point was that this room, the mystery room, must belong to him, which explained why Sam wouldn't intrude on it. Maybe Dr. Kraychek had an office he could work in at home. That sounded like something a doctor might do. If she was lucky, it might have a phone.

She had to hear her sister's voice. Nothing else could have made her take those few steps to the mystery room and push the door open.

In the dark, she couldn't make out a thing. A shape by the near wall might be a desk, and something low and long under the far window might be a table. She tugged the door shut behind her and fumbled for a light switch. Yellow light flooded the room.

This wasn't an office. It was a bedroom.

The narrow bed under the window had a quilt on it, stitched out of navy-blue and white squares. An old teddy bear sat propped on the pillow. There was a round navy braided rug on the floor and a nightstand with a lamp on it and a single shelf down below. The lamp had a wooden base carved in the shape of a blocky, two-dimensional horse. The books on the shelf were tall and thin, with tell-tale yellow spines. Jeannette remembered the handful of Little Golden Books she and Veronica had read as children.

This was a child's room, but the child had grown up here. The shape closest to the door was, in fact, an old wooden desk, with a worn top and a straight-backed chair parked underneath. Another bookshelf hung on the wall above it. Jeannette made out a title: *History of the United States: Colonialism to the Modern Age*. The desk still had a cup in one corner, an actual white teacup with a green rim, with a handful of pencils and pens stuck in it. A ruler lay on the scratched wood.

There was a dresser too, made of the same plain wood as the desk, against the opposite wall. It had a small square mirror on it and a photo in a thin black frame. Jeannette went over and picked up the photo.

He looked so *young*. He wore a tuxedo, which should have made him seem older, but somehow it did the opposite. Fifteen years old at most. What had the occasion been? Behind him, she recognized the piano from the living room. He stood facing the camera, one hand resting on the brown keyboard cover. His smile looked exactly like himself.

Jeannette set the picture carefully back down. The glass and the frame had no dust on them. Neither did the dresser. She had a feeling she could go over to the long-unused bookshelf over the desk and run her finger down the spines of the textbooks without finding a single speck. That made sense. She would expect as much from the kind of housekeeper Anna seemed to be. But nobody had moved the furniture around in here, or taken the old children's things to an attic or basement, or brought in boxes or clothes from the rest of the house to pile up in the unused space. At Veronica and Drew's, an extra room like this wouldn't have stayed empty for five minutes. Even Aunt Gretchen, whose single-storey house had been twice as big as the apartment in the Belvedere, would have put this room to use quicker than you could blink.

Anna had not. Since the day Sam left, it had stayed shut, and spotless.

Why hadn't he shown it to Jeannette?

The lamp on the nightstand had a pull chain. When Jeannette tugged gently on the horse's tail, the light clicked on. She shut off the ceiling lamp and sat down on the narrow bed.

The lamp gave a soft yellow light. Maybe, a long time ago, a little boy couldn't sleep, and he turned on the lamp and sat up in bed and took one of his favourite books off the nightstand. He hugged his bear and looked at the pictures until sleep pulled up over him as softly as the blue-and-white quilt.

Jeannette turned off the ceiling lamp and eased back onto the bed. This one smelled like lavender too, but more faintly than the one in the guest room. The pillow had gotten thin from years of use. She set the teddy bear carefully aside, on the corner of the mattress against the wall. Then she pulled one side of the quilt over her, wrapping herself up in a cocoon, reached up to the nightstand and turned out the light.

♬

When she woke up, sun streamed in through the window. For a minute she didn't remember where she was. Then she saw a corner of blue-and-white fabric draped over the shoulder of her nightgown. Goodness. She hadn't meant to spend the night here.

The quilt looked hand-stitched. She unrolled herself carefully out of it and sat up. This room didn't seem to have a clock. Maybe the house was still asleep. She could slip back into the guest room, and nobody would have to know she had been here.

She was smoothing the quilt over the bed, tucking the corners back exactly as they had been, when a scent drifted into the room and made her mouth water. Bacon. *Oh, dear.*

Jeannette crept out into the hall. The guest bedroom was shut too, but the bed was empty, except for the white T-shirt and boxers neatly folded on the right-hand pillow. The sheet and quilt were pulled up smooth.

Jeannette sagged. Sam had woken up, seen she wasn't here, and probably gone looking for her. Had he thought to look in his old room? What if he hadn't?

What if he had?

Jeannette found her yesterday's jeans in her suitcase, pulled out a sweater and her bra, and turned her back on the crucifix to yank them on. Sam would worry if he couldn't find her, but he might not have gone through the house yet. She could slip downstairs and find him and say, who knew, she had gone outside for a minute. (In her nightgown, in the snow?) Or something.

She didn't run into Dr. Kraychek on the way downstairs. That helped. Apparently you didn't wear your shoes inside in this house, so Jeannette went down the front hall in her sock feet. She heard voices in the kitchen, Sam's and Anna's, and the bacon sizzling. The rich dark smell of coffee mingled with the smoky pork fat. Coffee always smelled better than it tasted. Her stomach growled.

In the kitchen, Anna said something indistinct. Jeannette caught the words "Philadelphia" and "friend," and then, clearer, "I don't know, *mielas*. I shouldn't say so, but…"

She sounded anxious. Sad? Jeannette stopped in the hall.

"Ma." Sam's voice had an edge to it. "I'm not sick, if that's what you're worried about. I told you that already."

Sick? What did he mean? And what about Philadelphia?

"No," Anna said. "It isn't that." Jeannette took another step closer. She could see into the kitchen now, a slice of the window over the sink and a corner of the white refrigerator. Anna said, "I'm worried about you, *mielas*. You know your own mind, but…" Her voice trailed off.

"I'll be fine," Sam said. His voice was gentle now. "You know this is the best thing to do."

Jeannette stepped closer again. Now she saw the corner of the table. Two hands rested on the white Formica, Sam's, and on top of his, a smaller hand with a gold ring sunken into the skin. "Liudas," Anna said, and then a string of syllables that sounded like a sad but lovely tune. After a moment, she added something else. A question?

Silence. Then Sam answered, quietly, three syllables Jeannette couldn't make out.

The smaller hand patted his and lifted away. "Good." Now Anna sounded brisk. A chair scraped back. Too late, Jeannette saw the older woman looking straight at her.

"Jeannette," Anna said cheerfully. "Good morning, honey. Come on in."

Jeannette forced herself to go into the room. Should she apologize for listening, or pretend she hadn't heard anything? But what did Sam mean, "sick?"

"I'm fixing some breakfast," Anna said. "We'll have bacon and eggs in a minute. Would you like some orange juice, or coffee?"

"Um. Orange juice, please."

Sam stood up. "I'll get it." He gave her a quizzical look as he got the carton of juice out of the fridge. "Was I snoring last night or something?"

"No, not at all." Did he know where she had spent the night? Was he mad? "I was having a hard time sleeping, so I got up."

"And found a different bed." So he did know. When he handed her the glass of juice, she couldn't read anything in his expression.

Anna, stirring scrambled eggs at the stove, looked around. "Weren't you comfortable last night, honey?"

"No, ma'am. I mean yes, I was." Jeannette backed up against the table, holding on to the cold glass. It was thick and heavy. "I was kind of restless is all. I didn't want to keep Sam up."

He drew out the chair at the head of the table for her and sat down in his own usual place. "So she ended up in my old room," he said.

Anna looked around again. "Did you? Oh, goodness, we don't use that one. I haven't been in there in a long time. Was everything all right?"

Through her nerves, Jeannette felt sure the older woman was… well, she couldn't lie, she wasn't that kind of person, but telling a fib. Dust didn't clean itself up. "Yes, ma'am." She was sitting in Dr. Kraychek's actual chair, and it hadn't bitten her. She hitched her back straighter and looked Sam in the eye. "The bed was very comfortable."

"It's as old as the hills." He looked away and took a sip from his coffee mug. "Almost as old as me, anyway."

Why didn't you want me to see your room? "It's a nice room," she told him, turning the glass between her fingers. It had bubbles in it, trapped forever under the smooth surface. "I like your lamp. And that picture."

"Picture?"

"On the dresser."

Memory lit up his face, sudden and surprising. "Oh, that's right. That was the day I had my first real concert. I played a Mozart concerto with the Lehigh Symphony. That was a good day, wasn't it, Ma?"

"Which day?" Anna brought plates to the table. Normally Jeannette ate cereal for breakfast, if that, but the scoop of scrambled eggs and the strips of bacon smelled irresistible.

"The concerto," Sam said. "Back in high school."

Anna laughed. "Yes, it was a good day, especially after." To Jeannette she said, "He wasn't a bit nervous, but maybe you can imagine, honey, it was a lot worse for me. I shouldn't have worried. He did us very proud."

That look went between them again. Jeannette remembered the strange words she'd overheard. The sad, lovely tune, *Ashtahvay* something. What did it mean?

Anna said, "Would anybody like toast?"

"Ma, sit down." Sam's face looked younger and more relaxed when he talked to her. He added, "I was impressed with my room, by the way. It looks just like it always did."

Anna sat and picked up her fork. "No need to change it. I knew you'd want it again, one of these days."

Jeannette remembered Sam's voice in the dark living room, telling her about the day he had left here for the last time. *My mother tried to stop me.* Jeannette saw this small, gentle woman closing the door on the memories of her son, keeping them safe in that timeless room, for... one of these days.

What had actually happened, the day Sam left? Would Jeannette ever find the nerve to ask?

"Better eat up," Sam said. "Ma's going to crack the whip today."

When Anna laughed, the sound hung in the air like gold. "Liudas, the poor girl won't want to be part of this family if you tell her things like that."

"It's the truth, isn't it?" Sam picked up his fork and took a scoop of eggs. "Ma has to make sure I can still cook," he told Jeannette. "I might have slacked off."

Jeannette plucked up her courage again. "He can cook," she told Anna. "He's great."

"I'm glad to hear it," Anna said. "Now eat, both of you, before it's all cold."

Jeannette pulled her plate closer and crunched a piece of bacon. *Part of this family.* Was that real now?

♫

Dinner took all day to fix. Now, looking at the loaded dining room table, Jeannette couldn't believe they had done so much. Sam said his mother's holiday meals always looked like this. Golden turkey, a big cream-coloured bowl of stuffing, cranberry sauce made from fresh berries, a dish of buttered peas and almonds, a pumpkin pie waiting in the kitchen. But that was only half of it. Sam had explained that his grandfather, Pete Gicos, had once run a Lithuanian diner in Scranton, and Anna would never consider a meal complete without some of her father's old recipes. So there were also peppery white sausages fried up crisp, and pillows of dough stuffed with potatoes and cabbage, and a baking dish full of something Anna called *kugali,* for which Jeannette had rubbed potatoes against a mysterious object called a ricer until her hands ached, and a cake flavoured with cinnamon and cardamom. At some point during the afternoon, when Jeannette had wanted to put her head down on the Formica table and fall asleep, Anna had asked her if her family had any heirloom recipes. "Not unless you count macaroni and cheese. The orange kind out of the box," she'd mumbled to Anna and Sam's laughter.

It had been worth it. Jeannette didn't know how they would eat half of this, or for that matter how the table held it all up. No question of using the kitchen for this meal. Jeannette had helped Sam lay out the dining room table instead, spreading the dark brown tablecloth, setting out the good white china and real silverware. She had taken a few minutes away from the cooking to call Veronica, finally, and say happy Thanksgiving.

"Gracious, Nannie, they'll make a chef out of you yet. You see if you can't bring some of that food home, you hear?" Jeannette didn't think that would be a problem. You could feed half of this neighbourhood with the spread they had made.

Dr. Kraychek sat at the head of the table and recited the brief grace. "Bless us, O Lord, and these Thy gifts..." Anna made the sign of the cross over herself. So did Sam. Jeannette timidly watched Dr. Kraychek carve the turkey with the expertise of long practice. When he handed you your plate, he could probably tell you exactly which muscle of the turkey's anatomy you were eating, not that she much wanted to know.

As he handed the plates around and started each of the side dishes in succession, Jeannette felt sure he was studying her. Those distant eyes, more remote behind the reading glasses he had put on to carve, examined her hands, her face, probably her hair too. She had followed Sam's example and changed for dinner into the one dress outfit she had brought. Surely he couldn't find fault with her modest skirt and blouse, though her hair, still too short for the bun, splashed her white sweater with too-bright colour.

After he passed the last dish, he turned to her. "So," he said politely, taking off his reading glasses and laying them beside his fork, "are you enjoying your visit?"

She wished he would put the glasses back on. He felt safer from a distance. "Yes, sir." She unfolded her napkin on her lap. Cloth napkins wouldn't last a minute at Veronica's. "Thank you."

Why did he look at her so closely? Could *he* possibly know about her late-night trespassing in Sam's old room? For goodness' sake, he couldn't read minds, or see through shut doors. She hoped.

He asked, "Do you like to cook?"

"Honestly, I've never done it much. I think I do like it, though, yes, sir."

"In this house, you'll certainly learn how."

Shouldn't you smile after you said something like that? And his voice sounded so flat, like he had tried to cut something out of it and done the job too well. Abruptly, Jeannette remembered how hard she had tried to sound like a Richmonder.

"Yes, sir." *Yay-us.*

He nodded and to her relief turned to his plate. Jeannette took the opportunity to cut a corner off one of the dough pillows. When the rich taste of potato and cheese filled her mouth, she caught her breath.

Across the table, Sam grinned. "You like it?"

Jeannette swallowed. "It's fantastic."

Anna said, "That's proper Lithuanian cooking. Pierogi just like my papa used to make." She nodded across the table at Dr. Kraychek. "Walter's mother, Mama Halina, she used to make them too."

Jeannette looked at Sam, confused. "I thought you said the family was Polish?"

Sam cut into a slice of turkey. "We are. Dad's family is. A lot of the recipes are the same, just sometimes they go by different names."

"Lots of potatoes," Anna said. "And cabbage. Poor folks' cooking."

Dr. Kraychek kept his eyes on his plate during the whole exchange. *Poor folks.* For some reason, Jeannette had a feeling he didn't like that. "I think it's great," she said firmly.

"That's good." Sam grinned again. "You'll be eating lots of it."

Now Dr. Kraychek raised his head. "Yes, we should talk about that. When do you intend the wedding to be?"

So formal, and so sudden. Jeannette wasn't surprised that Sam's face went still. His father's way of talking would make anyone uncomfortable.

Jeannette realized she knew why Dr. Kraychek scared her. He looked at you as if he was trying to see through you and found it too easy. Sam answered him, "Honestly, sir, we haven't decided that yet." It seemed to take him an effort to look at Jeannette. "What do you think, honey?"

"Um." She needed to drop that nervous stammer. "I don't mind. What would you rather?"

"I was thinking in the spring. Maybe May?"

Anna's voice brought warmth back into the room. "Goodness, you two. You don't let the grass grow, do you? Meet each other in September and get married six months later."

Sam's face relaxed. "May would be eight months, Ma."

Anna narrowed her eyes at him and sliced one of the white sausages into neat bite-sized segments on her plate. "Yes, I can count." She turned to Jeannette. "Now, don't let this boy of mine rush you. Are you sure that's enough time?"

Jeannette met her eyes and remembered Veronica's across the table. *He's a different breed.* Would Anna understand, if Jeannette told her she was scared, this had all happened so fast, she didn't know how to feel?

"Yes," she said. "It'll be plenty of time."

Sam said, "I was thinking too, if you don't mind, honey, I'd like us to have the wedding up here."

Jeannette hadn't thought about that at all. Before she could say anything, Dr. Kraychek asked, "Here? Do you mean here at the house?"

"No, sir. At St. Francis."

Jeannette thought she heard a sound from Anna, nothing as definite as a gasp, but a faint intake of breath. Dr. Kraychek said, "Are you sure you want to do that?"

"Yes, sir. If Jeannette doesn't mind."

All the eyes turned to her. Jeannette quickly swallowed the forkful of peas she had put in her mouth. "What's St. Francis?"

"It's the church where we always went to Mass," Sam said. "A couple of blocks away from here. I used to be an altar server, and they have a grade school all of us kids went to."

He wanted to get married in the church where he had always gone. Jeannette didn't want to go back to First Baptist, or anywhere near Reckord's Mill, for that matter. She didn't mind this, but why did Dr. Kraychek look so frozen?

"You do know they have rules," the doctor told Sam. "Regarding Mass attendance, and the marriage of a Catholic to a non-Catholic. And confession."

He seemed to put a stress on that last word. Jeannette didn't understand the silence that followed. Anna cut through it. "Jeannette, honey, you're not Catholic, are you?"

"No. Is that a problem?"

"It shouldn't be," Anna said. "Liudas, you know Father Antony isn't there anymore, of course. That's the priest who baptized him," she added to Jeannette. "There's young Father Fennessy now. I don't think he's too strict."

Dr. Kraychek said to Sam, "But you will need to discuss the situation with him. All of it, I feel."

What was that about? Sam had stopped eating and sat very still. "Yes, sir. I think we can reach an agreement."

Jeannette blurted, "What do you mean? What situation?"

Sam's fingers tightened around his fork, but he said calmly, "I haven't been to Mass in a long time. Sometimes the priests don't like that."

If this young priest, Father Fenny-whatever, gave Sam any trouble, he had better hope he didn't do it in front of Jeannette. As if anybody had the right to say you couldn't get married in the church where you had always gone.

Anna must have seen Jeannette's expression. "I wouldn't worry," she said. "Maybe while you both are here, you can go on over there and have a talk with him. I think he'll understand what you want to do, and why."

That last part was directed at Sam. Again, Jeannette felt like a second conversation was going on. She didn't have all the pieces to understand it.

Anna said, cheerful again, "For now let's not worry about it. Let's enjoy this good meal."

Dr. Kraychek nodded. "I agree."

Jeannette met Sam's eyes across the table. His face still looked taut. *Are you okay?* she wanted to ask. *What's going on?*

Maybe he heard the words without her saying them. He shook his head the slightest bit and his lips formed the words *Don't worry.*

Good grief. If that was what he wanted, she would do her best. Jeannette dug her fork into her square of *kugali*, trying to push her questions away.

♫

That night, Sam switched off the light as soon as Jeannette slipped into bed beside him, but this time he didn't turn away to go to sleep. He propped himself up on his elbow and put his free arm across her chest.

Her whole body tingled at the contact. She told herself not to be ridiculous. They weren't doing anything wrong.

He said, "I hope you didn't mind us putting you to work today." Faint moonlight came in through the lace curtains at the window and touched his face.

Jeannette shook her head. "I wish I could've been more use. You know I'm still pretty lousy in the kitchen."

"You did great. Besides, Dad was right. If you spend any time around Ma, you'll learn." He touched her hair. "I wanted to tell you, too, I'm sorry about all that church business at dinner. Are you sure it's okay if we get married up here?"

"Of course. We should." She hesitated, but she couldn't let go of this chance. "What did your dad mean about telling the priest everything?"

Sam sighed. "Well, they make you go through all this stuff. I don't know Father Fennessy. I almost wish it was still Father Antony, he was old-school but he knew me all my life. I'll have to go to confession at least and prove I'm still a good Catholic." His mouth twisted. "Not that I am. I haven't been to Mass in forever."

Since the day he had left this house? Jeannette asked, "Do I need to turn Catholic?"

She was serious, but he laughed softly. "No, I don't think so. Unless you want to."

She let herself say one of the many things she'd been thinking since they got here. "I didn't know you were so…" It sounded stupid, but she finished, "religious."

"I'm not, really. I used to be, but for a long time I've been what they'd call lapsed. If not a total lost cause." He smiled, but she saw a shadow behind it. "It would mean a lot to get married here. I hope they'll decide I'm still allowed."

"They'd better. I don't know why you wouldn't be."

He shook his head. Sadness there, always.

She was going to marry him. She had to understand this truth: they were going to share a life. She took a deep breath and reached up to smooth his bangs away from his forehead. "Sam, sweetheart, I don't want secrets between us, okay?"

He looked startled. "Why, sure. What makes you say that?"

"Well…" He wouldn't get upset, would he? She had the right to say something. "I didn't know about the church stuff, and…" She didn't have the nerve to tell him she had overheard his conversation with Anna that morning, or ask him what he'd meant by *Philadelphia* and *sick*. "I want to share things with you. Good things and, you know, not so good things."

As she said it, she realized what she had gotten herself into. She hadn't planned to do this now, any more than she had before, but she hadn't made any particular plan at all. If she didn't want secrets, she couldn't keep her own. "And there's things you don't know about me," she said. "Things I should tell you, too."

His mouth quirked. "Nothing awful, I know that."

"No. I mean, I hope not."

Now he looked quizzical. His hand moved over her hair. "Well, you never told me about your nickname."

He was teasing, but it was as good an opening as any. "I know," she said. This shouldn't take so much effort to say. You didn't know someone, and you handed him your heart, but she did know Sam now. That was the whole point. She said, "I asked my aunt to call me Nannie, a long time ago, and Veronica too, because of Nannerl. Mozart's sister. You know?" ("Nan Earl?" Aunt Gretchen had said. "Who on earth's that?")

Sam laughed. "No kidding? That's great. Is that the secret?"

Jeannette shook her head. "I wanted them to call me that because piano, music, you know, it was awfully important. Sometimes it was all I had. Because I didn't have my mother."

When had she said those words aloud to anyone? Her heart thudded in her throat.

Sam said, "I had the feeling something happened there. I didn't want to pry. I figured you'd talk about it when you wanted to."

"I do want to. It's hard to tell people, you know, because it was hard, growing up. My mother..." She looked up into his face. "She left. After I was born. I never met her."

"How come she did that?"

"She didn't marry my father. Or Veronica's." Jeannette shivered, never mind her long nightgown and the covers and the warmth of his arm around her. "The town didn't want her to stay. And Veronica, you know, she's tough, people didn't mess with her, but I looked like her. I mean like Isabel, my mother. People didn't like me either." She stared past him at the window, where the lace curtains framed a piece of dark sky. "And the kids," she said, "they were mean. They called us stuff. Bastards." *You know what your mother was, don't you?* Oh, those shrill voices, yelling the ugly words they had learned from their parents. All these years later, Jeannette knew that no child would have understood how deeply those parroted words would sink into her. To the other kids, they had been ritual playground taunts, the kind of things you threw out because it was fun to pick on somebody smaller and weaker than you, and then you moved on and forgot about it. The other kids, though, had families they took for granted and parents who loved them. They had never known how their carelessly flung insults had made Jeannette see herself.

Worthless, ugly, someone's discarded trash: Jeannette had carried that image of herself with her for a long time. Veronica had been too tough to let anyone else's insults take away her own worth, but Jeannette had been different. She still was. In spite of everything she had done for herself since then, she never forgot how it felt to be that lost girl.

She told Sam now, "Veronica and I, we didn't have anybody." After she said it, she shut her eyes. She couldn't help it. Now, maybe, he would see her the way she had always seen herself. No one apart from Veronica knew this much about her. No one else had gotten this close.

For a long moment Sam didn't say anything. Jeannette didn't breathe. Silence thickened and deepened.

Then, softly, he said, "You've got me."

Jeannette opened her eyes. Sam looked into her face. "Jeannette," he said. With his eyes holding hers, he repeated the words she had heard Anna say in the kitchen that morning, a beautiful tune, not sad anymore. She heard the syllables clearly: "*Ash tahvay mee-lyu.*"

"What does that mean?" she asked.

He touched her face. "I love you."

"I love you too. Oh, Sam, I love you so much."

She curled up beside him and rested her head on his shoulder. He held her. His spicy scent covered her like another quilt.

He was all she wanted. The crucifix could stare if it wanted. Aunt Gretchen could thrash around in her grave. Jeannette closed her eyes and drank in his nearness.

Her shivering died away. Tonight, she would sleep.

CHAPTER FIFTEEN

From the outside, the Holy Roman Catholic Church of St. Francis looked like a cathedral. A small one, maybe, but Sam had always thought that the tall spire and stone façade made it look like you should open the big wooden front doors and find carved pews, a flagstone floor and stained-glass windows on every side, and probably a marble pulpit and baptismal font, and an actual choir *loft* that did what the word "loft" said, and an organ. Definitely an organ. With a couple of keyboards and a spread of foot pedals. And a feast of stops—it would have to have those—to make the pipes sound like bells, and flutes, and trumpets.

St. Francis didn't have any of that. Sam stood at the altar on his wedding morning and looked at the sanctuary he had known all his life. The scratched baby-grand piano in the nearest corner was the same one he had played at all those Masses years ago. The ragged half-circle of chairs for the choir sat empty today. The windows along the sanctuary's side walls were made of panes of clear glass, about a hand's width across, and the ceiling had a handful electric bulbs in it. The plain dark pews and burgundy carpet seemed to swallow up what little light there was, so that the people in the pews had to peer at their Orders of Service. *Celebration of the Marriage of Jeannette Reilly and Samuel Kraychek.* The whole place felt like a burrow, spicy with dark-smelling incense.

Sam had been baptized in that wooden font up by the pulpit. Week after week, he had walked down to this altar rail to take communion. Back then, Father Antony would have been standing here holding the plate of wafers, Father Antony with his flyaway hair and milky eyes. If the old priest had been here today, instead of skinny Father Fennessy with his too-big surplice and nervous hands gripping the edges of the pulpit, would Sam have felt better? Would he have felt like any of this was supposed to happen?

He couldn't know. Father Antony had claimed his place in the flat green cemetery outside shortly after Sam had stopped coming home, so this morning Sam would recite his marriage vows in front of a priest who apparently had yet to get an actual marriage service under his gold braid belt. But the priest wasn't the only one who would hear him. The people in the pews would hear, of course, Ma and Dad and Jeannette's family and a slew of Westbury people Sam could barely remember, and along with them the crucifix that hung above the altar.

Some churches had gilded crosses with ornate carving. Some had fabric robes around the Son of Man and a crown of real thorns on his forehead. The crucifix at St. Francis had probably been carved decades ago. The cross was plain wood, as were the body and loincloth and crown and nails. The body's lurid white-painted skin seemed to glow in the dim sanctuary. You could see the drops of blood on its head and on the hands and feet as it hung there. If it had had bones, you knew they would all have been broken.

This is My body, given up for you.

Months ago now, Sam had knelt in front of this same crucifix and recited Hail Marys and Our Fathers for the salvation of his soul. He had done it after the session in the confessional booth in which he told Father Fennessy what he had done wrong.

Forgive me, Father, for I have sinned. No one else, not his parents, not the woman he was about to marry, could know what it had cost him to say the words aloud, or how often he had to rehearse them beforehand so he could get through them without breaking down. *I have had wrong and sinful relations with another man.*

Wrong and sinful. Gil. Oh, Gil.

Sam hadn't been able to say anything else, for instance tell the priest how long these "relations" had gone on, how often Sam had violated all the teachings of the Church. He had stumbled through the rest of the confession script: *O my God, I am heartily sorry for having offended You and I detest all my sins.* Sam had recited those words countless times since his first confession at age eight. His mouth didn't want to form them now. Detest? *I firmly resolve with the help of Your grace, to confess my sins, to do penance and to amend my life.* He had finished, sat in the confessional booth with the words ringing in his head, and waited numbly for the verdict. At least the booth's carved wooden screen had meant he didn't need to see Father Fennessy's face and read the judgment in it. Finally the young priest answered, in a thin, nervous voice that suggested he was in over his head, with the right words: *Thereupon I absolve you from your sins in the name of the Father, and of the Son, and of the Holy Ghost.*

After that absolution, Sam had knelt in front of the crucifix he looked at now and promised to amend his life. Now, today, he would do it for good.

The rear doors of the sanctuary opened. Sam saw his bride.

Sunlight caught her veil from behind and turned it into a glowing cloud. At a signal from Father Fennessy, the shaky-at-best pianist launched into an uneasy rendering of "Jesu, Joy of Man's Desiring." Jeannette, leaning on Sam's father's arm, started to walk down the aisle. Dad had agreed to escort her because she didn't have her own father to stand up with her.

The congregation rose in a solid block. Sam focused on Jeannette, trying to remember how often the two of them had worked together with the RSA's chorus, how they had played duets, how they had gone for walks beside the river. The brother-sister feeling between them had lasted so far, had made sense even, and neither of them had tried for anything different. Sam tried to remember that feeling, even though he knew it would all have to change.

The woman walking toward him now didn't look like the one he knew. In her white dress and long train, this woman was as fragile and beautiful as porcelain. Sam could never have touched her skin or kissed her cheek.

Soon he would take her hand. Father Fennessy would recite the words everyone knew: *to have and to hold from this day forward.* Sam would slip a ring onto that delicate finger and feel a cold metal band against his own skin. *As long as you both shall live.*

From above the altar, the sorrowful face of the Son of Man watched them all. *This is My body, given up for you.*

♪

The ballroom at the Greene House wasn't big, no bigger than the Lewis Center's green room. Green room, Greene House. Sam thought vaguely that the room should be cluttered with instrument cases and people's coats and jackets instead of the profusion of tables and white china.

He and Jeannette went in arm-in-arm. At every step, heads turned to follow their progress. Jeannette's hair glowed under her veil. Sam put on his best smile, which sat in front of his face like a shield.

The Maestro's wedding. Sam's title had sounded like a joke eight months ago, given that no one could say how long he would be allowed to keep it. Now it hung on him like a suit of armour. He had made good so far, he supposed. He and Jeannette had jobs to go back to in the fall. The RSA's future still hung in the balance; ticket sales this year hadn't improved enough to guarantee anything, but Sam had apparently filled enough seats at each concert that the board, or Bayard and Geraldine Keating at least, wanted him to do his best for another season. Meanwhile, he was doing exactly what he should in getting married. The RSA and its supporters could be proud of their young Maestro and his beautiful wife.

Sam was glad none of those people were here today. He and Jeannette had agreed that this day belonged to the two of them, and they both wanted to keep it separate from the rest of the world.

Sam guided Jeannette between the tables, shaking hands with guests and repeating the same words he used after concerts. "Thanks so much, thanks for coming, so glad you could make it." Behind his back, he rubbed his thumb across the band of metal on his left ring finger.

"Samuel." Jeannette's hands were shaking. Sam tried to keep his own absolutely steady so she wouldn't see how he felt. "Take this ring as a sign of my love and faith. In the name of the Father, and the Son, and of the Holy Spirit."

Thank God she had managed to get the damn thing over his knuckle. It had almost gotten stuck. Sam rubbed it again, covertly, as he smiled at little round Dorothy Demboski, one of his parents' friends, and listened to her bubble about how wonderful it was to see Sam again, she couldn't believe he was all grown up, did he remember how he and her nephew Henry had been "such troublemakers" back in third grade, and "your mother told us all about that job you got with the music, why, we all knew you'd go far, Sam, you were always so talented!"

"Thank you, Mrs. Demboski. That's so kind. It's wonderful to see you too."

Keeping Jeannette's arm through his own, Sam threaded their way between a couple of other tables to the family's station. Now, finally, they could sit down. Jeannette collapsed into her chair, and Sam sat beside her and took her hand.

It would be better if they were alone. At least she didn't seem to mind the way he held on to her. If they were alone, she could take off the gleaming white dress that felt like a ten-foot barrier between the two of them, and then he could look into her face and see the girl he had sat beside on the piano bench. Then everything would make sense. Of course it would.

The food was excellent, or at least everyone said so. Sam ate what was on his plate but didn't taste a thing. Jeannette chatted with Ma and Veronica, and Sam felt distantly surprised to hear himself and Drew joining in. When everyone's plates had emptied, a waiter located a microphone and announced to the room, "We'll now hear toasts from the best man and the matron of honour."

Drew stood up first. Jeannette had told Sam how shy her brother-in-law was, how hard it would be for him to talk to so many people at once. Sam noticed how tight he gripped the microphone, but Drew said steadily, "I haven't known Sam for very long. Not as long as a lot of you here, so I appreciate it even more that he asked me to be his best man. But one thing I do know about him for sure: when I look at him and Nannie together—I'm sorry, I should say when I look at him and *Jeannette*—I know he's the right man to make her happy."

Short and to the point. He sat down to applause, and Veronica took the microphone. When she stood up, all sultry curves in her navy silk dress, Sam wouldn't have been surprised to hear whistles. "First," Veronica said, "I have to thank y'all for being so nice to us." She flaunted her water glass in her free hand. The clear liquid swirled in the light. "You can tell we're not from around here, Drew and me," she said, "and you couldn't be friendlier. Now, I've got to tell you about this sister of mine."

Glancing sideways, Sam saw Jeannette blush. She was staring at her sister. That look said, *behave.*

Veronica said, "Drew can call her Jeannette if he wants, and y'all can do the same, but to me, she'll always be Nannie. She's my little sister. For the longest time, when we were growing up, we pretty much just had each other. We had an aunt too, but you know that's different."

Listening, Sam remembered what Jeannette had told him about Reckord's Mill, where she had grown up. Veronica's voice seemed to bring that place into the room with them, the great-aunt who had raised the two girls, the one-storey brick house with the tomato patch out back and the spinet piano Jeannette had practiced on for so many hours. Veronica went on, "Your sister's the one you tell your secrets to. She's the one you trade your dresses with and you do each other's hair. She's the one you look out for. And if anybody gives her trouble, why, you stand up for her with the last breath in your body."

Veronica looked down at her sister and Sam. Sam thought she focused on him.

"Now my sister's all grown up," she said. "She's found herself a man, and I'm here to tell her, I want her to be happy. I want nothing but the best for her, because I love her as much as I love my husband and my children. Maybe, if Drew here will forgive me, a little bit more."

That got some laughter. Veronica went on, "This man here, he makes her happy. He lights her up. When she first knew him, why, just to say his name she'd turn as pink as those azalea flowers outside."

More laughter. Sam couldn't help joining in, though he saw how Jeannette's mouth set in a line.

"So I know she's in love all right," Veronica said. "And I'm here to tell her husband, my new brother, that I'm glad she found him. I'm glad she wants to spend her life with him. But he'd better watch his step, and he'd better take care of her, because you know he'll have me to answer to."

The crowd thought that was hilarious. They couldn't see how her smile had disappeared. Her eyes rested on Sam's face.

The night Sam had told her and Drew that Jeannette had agreed to marry him, he had seen those eyes fill up with tears. He still remembered what she had said. "If she wasn't off her head for you, I wouldn't let you take her away. Consider yourself lucky."

Sam forced himself now to meet her look without flinching. *No monster anymore. I promised.* He nodded at Veronica. *I hear you.*

Her face relaxed. "That's about all I have to say, except that I love you both, and I wish you all the happiness in the world."

Everyone clapped as she sat down. Sam made himself join in. His palms felt numb, and he stopped as quickly as he could and put his arm around Jeannette again.

The waiter-cum-announcer took the microphone again. "In a few moments, the bride and groom will have their first dance."

Jeannette looked panicky. The two of them had practiced diligently for this, dancing to the record player in Veronica and Drew's apartment, but getting up in front of all these people was a different problem. Sam pushed his chair back and held his hand out to her as confidently as he could. "Ready?"

Her eyes said no, but her chin lifted. "Okay."

Somebody had drafted a teenage kid to operate the record player. Sam led Jeannette to the middle of the dance floor. She had taken her shoes off under the table, he saw, and hadn't put them back on. He would have to be extra careful.

He drew her into dance position. *Your hand on her waist and her hand on your shoulder.* Ma had taught Sam that years ago, when he was in high school and had decided that no amount of popularity would make disco moves look better than stupid. Ma had remembered enough about dancing from her "young days," as she put it, to give him a few lessons.

The record player started up. Sam and Jeannette had picked one of the songs Sam had learned to dance to, all those years ago: "When I Grow Too Old to Dream," played by the Glen Gary Orchestra.

Jeannette looked up at him, her eyes huge. "We haven't practiced in a while," she whispered.

He ignored all the other faces in the room. "Relax," he said. "You'll be great."

The music took Sam's feet and he started to move. Two steps to the left, two steps to the right. Over the last few months, Sam had taught Jeannette the foxtrot and waltz too. For this dance, with everybody watching, they had decided they should stick with the easiest one.

This record was actually one of Dad's. For as long as Sam could remember, Dad had kept a collection of big band records. You could turn that piece of the puzzle around however you wanted, it would never fit with the doctor's bag, the neatly polished shoes and wire-rimmed reading glasses and carefully pressed shirt. What did Glenn Miller have to do with those things? Or Benny Goodman? Or, for that matter, the Glen Gary Orchestra?

The music went on. The singer promised his love that even when he forgot how to dream, he would never forget her.

Listening to it, Sam couldn't help thinking about something Ma had told him once, about Dad. As much as he didn't feel like thinking about his father now, of all times, he remembered Ma telling him that she and Dad had met at the diner her father used to run. Dad had gone there for pastries and coffee while he studied for his exams, and Ma had noticed the "dark, handsome" boy who sat by himself in a corner, always poring over a thick book. Sam remembered Ma saying she had never let either of the other two waitresses have his table. She had brought Dad free refills of coffee without being asked and made sure she took him the freshest doughnuts, dusted with plenty of cinnamon. For all her best efforts, he had never said more than "good afternoon" and "thank you" to her until he got his diploma.

That med school diploma. Sam knew that despite the brand-new piece of paper that transformed the boy from Miner's Row into something better, Dad hadn't been able to save his own father. Liuz Kraychek had been dying of black lung disease, the product of all those years spent digging coal, by the time Dad got through with school. Ma had told Sam that part of the story too, how Dad hadn't been able to do anything for his father besides go to the hospital and sit beside a bed.

No. No hospitals, no beds with cheesecloth blankets, no windows with the rain dripping down. Sam focused on Jeannette and saw her staring down at their feet. He needed to see her eyes. "Honey," he said. "Look up."

She did, for one second. "I'll make us both fall down."

"No, you won't. Look at me."

She lifted her head again and this time kept it up. She had such striking eyes, that pure grey you almost never saw, without a hint of blue. Someday he wanted her to believe she was pretty.

Wife. What a word. *Husband* too, for that matter.

Over the speakers, the singer asked his love to kiss him once more before they said goodbye. Sam told himself that after this day was over, things would calm down. He and Jeannette would move into their new house and get set up. Everything would settle into a pattern. In the fall, when the new season started, they would be back with the chorus as a husband-and-wife team. They made a good team.

No monster.

Sam let the room slide out of focus, the white tablecloths, the glittering crystal and silverware, the multicoloured floral arrangements and the faces. All that mattered was right here in his arms.

The dance melody sailed up the scale. The last climax was coming. Sam let go of Jeannette's waist and pushed her gently away from him. They had never tried this before, but she spun away, clinging to his hand. Her white skirt swirled around her, and the veil glowed in the sunlight. He caught her back in. Her eyes were wide with shock, but she was so lovely.

He dipped her back over his arm as the final chord of the tune rang out. Her veil brushed the floor, and her red curls cascaded behind her.

When he brought her back up, to applause from the guests, the look on her face said *why, you!* He wanted to laugh. "See?" he said. "You were perfect."

She let him hold her long enough to smooth her veil down and catch her floral scent again. For a second, he felt light enough to float away.

CHAPTER SIXTEEN

After her first dance as Sam's wife, Jeannette sat at the family table while Sam danced the next song with his mother. While they were out on the floor, Veronica turned to Drew. "Drew, honey," she said, "can I get you out there?"

That would be a real surprise, Jeannette thought. "Uh, sure," Drew said. "Let's wait a little, though."

Veronica rolled her eyes at Jeannette. "I might have to borrow that boy of yours."

Jeannette laughed. "Go for it."

She couldn't believe how long this day had been. She wanted to be alone somewhere in a dark quiet place, so she could feel the strange new ring on her finger and understand what had happened to her.

The new Mrs. Kraychek. One of these nameless guests, at least to her, had called her that. Jeannette couldn't digest it yet. At the church, everything had seemed surreal.

When Sam took Jeannette's hand, his fingers felt like ice. That was the first shock. The second was the look on his face.

Father Fennessy's thin, reedy voice went on. "Samuel Kraychek, do you take Jeannette Reilly for your lawful wife, to have and to hold, from this day forward..."

Jeannette lost the thread. Sam was not looking at her or the priest. She followed his eyes to the crucifix, the face of the tortured man.

Maybe, Jeannette thought now, it had bothered him to have that thing hanging there watching them. It had certainly bothered her when she first saw it. Sam had stared at it until the priest's question mark woke him up: "Until death do you part?"

Now, watching her husband (what a word!), Jeannette remembered how he had drawn a breath and said, "I do." How those quiet words had rung with conviction.

Someone touched her shoulder. Jeannette turned around. She hadn't seen her father-in-law leave his seat, but now he stood behind her and held out his hand. "May I have the honour?"

"Um?"

Dr. Kraychek spoke like one of the medical journals Sam had told Jeannette he was always reading. "I believe a father-daughter dance is traditional," he said now. "I would like to offer my services."

Jeannette swallowed. Veronica said, "Well, go on, honey."

Well. After everything else that had happened today, why on earth not? Jeannette slipped her shoes back on and stood up carefully. "Thank you."

Could Dr. Kraychek dance? He acted like he slept in formaldehyde. With her lack of coordination, which she had no matter what Sam said, the two of them would be a perfect match.

Dr. Kraychek guided her to a place near the middle of the floor. She would have been happier on the fringes, though her white dress would get attention no matter where she was.

Another song started. Jeannette had time to recognize Bobby Darin's "Beyond the Sea" before Dr. Kraychek caught the beat and began to move.

Surprise almost stopped her feet. Sam had been as graceful out here as he was on the podium, but Dr. Kraychek was better still. Only the fear that he would trip over or step on her forced Jeannette to keep moving as he piloted them, with easy assurance, between the other couples. You could step out on a lake and walk on the surface of the water if you could dance like this.

Jeannette couldn't help staring at him as they made one circuit of the floor and then another. He looked as calm and distant as ever, but the way he moved, the way the music took over his body, told a different story. Who was he?

She blurted, "I didn't know you could dance. Sir."

Not the most gracious conversation opener, but he nodded politely. "Yes. It's been quite a number of years since I last did, but I do enjoy it."

He should relax his voice. His face. Suddenly she wondered what she could possibly say to make him smile.

"Sam's a good dancer," she said. Then, bravely, "But not as good as you."

Yes! The muscles around his mouth twitched. "I won't tell him you said so," Dr. Kraychek said. "His mother taught him the steps, as you probably know. I was surprised by his interest in learning, though not by his skill."

He *did* talk like a journal. Good grief. Jeannette's own twang came out stronger than usual, as if calling to the one she was sure he'd once had. "You knew he'd be good?"

Another twitch around the mouth. "Of course. He has rhythm."

How crazy to actually talk to this man. Jeannette didn't worry about her feet anymore. He moved too skilfully for her to make a misstep.

Sam had said his father hadn't understood about music. He had said the two of them were "too different," but Jeannette didn't see that difference so strongly now. Dr. Kraychek did know about music. Every motion of his body told her that.

Bobby Darin sang about a land on the other side of the stars. Jeannette listened to the sweet old lyrics and found herself wondering more than ever what had really happened between the two of them, the two "stubborn Kraychek men." She wanted to ask this man right now. She could have anything she wanted, couldn't she? She had the magic white dress.

Instead, she heard herself say, "Thank you again for the wedding, sir. It's beautiful."

He and Anna had paid for most of it. Veronica and Drew were in no position to help except for Jeannette's dress, Jeannette herself had no money, and Sam had just made the down payment on the house they would move into over the summer. Jeannette had never heard of a groom's parents footing the bill for a wedding before.

Dr. Kraychek nodded. "You are very welcome. We are delighted to have you in the family."

She thought she saw something then, behind his formality. In the eyes that looked so much like Sam's, she saw a familiar shadow.

Why? What had happened? What did he know?

Bobby Darin was promising now that he would never go sailing again. The song was ending. Confused, Jeannette wished for another second to ask her father-in-law some of the swirling questions in her head.

Someone took her arm. Sam's voice said, "Sir, may I cut in?"

"Walter Kraychek, I'm impressed!" That was Anna. "Let me sit down for a minute, and then I want my old dance partner back."

Dr. Kraychek stepped back from Jeannette. "I believe 'old' is quite correct," he said.

Anna took her husband's arm. "That's not what I meant, and you know it. Come on, let's leave these two to themselves."

She had the kindest eyes. Acting on impulse, Jeannette reached out to hug her. The veil drifted over them both.

"Thank you for everything," Jeannette said. The word she had always wanted to say came out in a whisper. "Mama."

Anna's arms tightened around her. "You're more than welcome, honey. You two enjoy yourselves."

Sam looked confused; no, Jeannette thought, he looked genuinely stunned. "I had no idea Dad could do that," he said. "Dance like that."

Jeannette laughed. "Really?"

The two of them started to move to the next song. "Not a clue," Sam said. He shook his head as if trying to clear it. "Neither of them ever told me." He glanced around toward the family table where his parents were sitting again. "I wonder why not?"

Jeannette studied him. "You and your dad don't know each other very well."

"No. Maybe we don't."

He looked sad again. Secrets, shadows: Jeannette didn't understand them, but they shouldn't exist anymore. She drew her hand out of her new husband's, put both arms around him, and laid her head on his shoulder.

Sam put his arms around her too. Holding her, he said softly, "You know, I'm looking forward to later. When it's just us."

She couldn't help shivering. "Me too."

The music cut off. People on the dance floor stopped in mid-step and looked around. Jeannette lifted her head again, reluctantly, and saw Veronica over by the teenage DJ, apparently haranguing him about something.

"Sorry, folks." Her voice, amplified by the microphone, cut through the room. "We need to change things up for a minute." Jeannette could see her mischievous grin from here. "This is for my sister. For old times' sake."

Oh, no. Jeannette looked at Sam in bafflement. A too-long pause, and then a harmonica tune she knew nastily well came out of the speakers.

Veronica's favourite song. Of course. Bruce Springsteen sang about the screen door and Mary's dress, and Jeannette glared across the floor at her sister. Not this, not now!

Sam, still holding her, laughed. "Your sister's a Boss fan. I should have known."

Jeannette shook her head. "She's too much. People can't dance to this, it's ridiculous! How did she even smuggle that record in here? I never saw it!"

"It's okay." He guided her head back down and kept his hand on the veil. "We'll just listen."

Listen? Jeannette had heard this song too often. Maybe because she was tired, or because of the warm pressure of Sam's hand on her hair, her eyes closed anyway as "Thunder Road" filled the room. Veronica and Drew's apartment, the chair in the kitchen, the *snick, snick* of scissors—the music brought it back. Jeannette, suspended, listening, understood what her sister wanted to send with her on this day, as Jeannette set out to find her own Promised Land.

CHAPTER SEVENTEEN

When Sam came up to the Greene House's bridal suite, carrying his and Jeannette's overnight bags from the car, Jeannette was standing in front of the window. She hadn't turned the lights on yet, but her dress had a soft sheen in the moonlight, and he could see the tint of her hair against her pale neck. She didn't turn around when Sam came in or when he put the bags down on a spare pseudo-antique chair. In the moonlight, she looked as pale as a porcelain figurine or a ghost.

He went up behind her, put his hands on her waist, and pressed his lips to the side of her neck. She was a real flesh-and-blood woman, with warm skin he could touch. "Hey," he whispered.

"Hi."

Her accent made even that one syllable sound like a fragment of melody. He said, "May I unlace you, ma'am?"

"Okay."

Sam undid the bow of the sash and ran its satin length through the hooks that went up Jeannette's back. *The new Mrs. Kraychek.* That was real, wasn't it.

The sash only undid one layer of the dress. A row of buttons lay underneath. Sam worked his way down it, gently pushing each tiny button through its hole. "They make these dresses complicated, don't they," he said.

"Uh-huh."

The fastenings could have been a chastity guard in themselves. Nobody would touch the bride until after the ceremony was over, and then it would be her husband's job to set her free from all the confining fabric. Sam undid the last button and realized the back of the dress had come fully open. He could see Jeannette's narrow spine, the strap of her bra and a single mole under her right shoulder blade. Her skin barely looked darker than the silky fabric he drew away from it. He felt a fascinated impulse to run one fingertip along those narrow vertebrae. "What happens next?" he asked.

She told him she had to step out of it, and took the corners of it from him and drew the lace sleeves off over her arms. "Could you hold the skirt, please?" she whispered.

What part of this mass were you supposed to hold on to? Sam bent down and carefully gripped as little of the fabric as he could. She stepped over the skirt, toward the window, one foot at a time. That would have been the moment for him to turn away. He had never seen her naked body before. If he turned away, she could put on her nightgown and nothing between them would have to change yet. Instead, though, he saw her hug herself like a child, standing in the moonlight with her bare skin exposed to his eyes.

He lifted the dress away, draped it over the dressing table, and put his arms around her. "You're shy," he said, kissing her neck again.

She nodded. Of course she was.

He knew she had grown up in a place where people had thought she was more wrong than orange shutters on a red brick house. They had judged her for something that wasn't her fault, something she couldn't fix, and had let her know about it every minute of every day. She'd had no mother, which alone was hard for him to imagine. Worst of all, she had never had the chance to try to be what people wanted. As far as they were concerned, she had been wrong from the day she was born.

She had tried hard to be strong. She had carved out a life for herself, which he admired, but he still saw a scared girl who needed a protector. She trusted him enough to show him that.

He rested his cheek on her hair. "You don't need to be shy," he said. "You're lovely, you know that?"

She shook her head. "You are," he said. "And besides, you know what?" She shook her head again. "I'm shy too."

That got her to look at him. It was the truth, or true enough: he had never shared anything like this with a woman. "Hey," he said softly. "It's just me. Don't be scared."

They needed to do this now. If you thought about it too much, it would only get more difficult. He turned her around to face him and touched her hair. Her beautiful eyes looked up into his face.

She needed a protector. A husband. He had to know he could be that for her. He hadn't wanted anything between them to change, but it had to, now that they had taken this step and bound themselves to each other. He had to know, right now, that he could be the man she needed. "We'll take our time," he said. "We'll do whatever feels right."

She whispered, "We could wait. It doesn't have to be tonight."

She was nervous. Her words said so, but her eyes, the same way he had seen before, said something else. Desire was waking up in her. He was hers, and she wanted him. With his fingertips, he stroked the side of her neck. "We could wait," he agreed, "but I think it might be good to try, don't you? Our first night."

Try wasn't the word to use. It was because he was tired. This would be easy another time. Any normal man would want to explore her body.

He saw her nervousness fade under his touch. He stroked her neck, her smooth bare shoulder and the line of her collarbone. "Let's try," he whispered.

She stood still, her hands at her sides, and didn't look away while he undressed. Any man would know how lucky he was to take her in his arms again and feel her bare skin against his. "There," he whispered." This isn't so scary, is it?" Except now his pulse sped up, and in the back of his head a faint warning voice said, *you can't*.

Not true. Sam willed himself to see the smooth line of her neck and the perfect swells of her breasts under her bra. She was his. Any man would want...

She reached up. Her fingertips touched his chest.

It had been so long. Sam closed his eyes. So achingly long since anyone had touched him. Soon his body would wake up too.

Except her touch wasn't the one he wanted.

Gil reached for the top button of Sam's shirt and carefully undid it. Sam lay motionless on the bed. He looked up into Gil's face as Gil went down the row of buttons, undoing them one at a time. Then the shirt lay open, and Gil gently drew the fabric back. "You're so beautiful," Gil whispered. "Do you know that?" Sam shook his head, too scared to breathe. Gil's fingers caressed Sam's bare chest. "Relax, my love," he whispered. He leaned forward, and Sam felt the warm pressure of lips against his skin. "Relax."

No. No. Sam forced his eyes open. Jeannette was touching his neck now, running her fingers lightly from his jaw down to his shoulder. *She* was the one he wanted, she had to be, there was no other way.

He caught her face between his hands and pressed his mouth against hers. He wanted her. His body throbbed with it.

Jeannette gasped. "Sam…"

"Come here." He heard how rough his voice sounded, but he could not stop. He caught her hands and pulled her to the bed and pushed her backward onto the pillow. Need screamed through his body. *Do this. Do it now.*

He slid his hands roughly under her back, grabbing for the catch of her bra. The hook resisted. He jerked and twisted it free and then caught the thin scrap of fabric and pulled it down her arms. Her breasts lay bare. He wanted them. He had to.

Her arms came up. She crossed them over her chest. "No." The panicked whisper reached him through the pounding in his head. "Don't. Please!"

For one instant he could have grabbed her arms and yanked them aside. For one instant he could have struck her face to shut her up.

A word sliced through the hot cloud in his head. *Rape.*

Shock poured over him. Oh, God. No. Please.

Monster.

He realized he was still holding the bra and let it go. "Oh, honey. I'm so sorry."

He should never have touched her. Never said a word to her. Hell, never hired her, all those months ago. He felt sick. She should throw on her clothes, stuff her things into her bag, and get out of here as fast as she could. Get away from him.

Total silence filled the room. Any second, she would leave him here alone. He would deserve it. He closed his eyes.

"Sam?"

Her hand touched his shoulder. He forced his eyes open but didn't dare look at her. Christ almighty, didn't she see what he was?

Words fell out of him, each as heavy as concrete. "I'm sorry. I'm ashamed of myself." It wouldn't do enough. He didn't deserve her forgiveness.

The mattress shifted as she moved closer. "Why?"

Why? She should be running away. Instead, she inched closer still. *Many men are far more monstrous than you...*

"What I just did," he said, as if he should have had to explain. "It was wrong. I scared you."

Another pause, with only the sound of her breathing in the dark. Then she said, "It's okay."

Okay? It couldn't be, didn't she realize? But she took his hand in hers, actually took it, and said, "I shouldn't have freaked out."

On the other side of the room, her white dress spilled over the edges of the dressing table and cascaded to the floor. Her left hand rested on his. The diamond glittered on her finger, and underneath it the new gold wedding band gleamed.

Till death do you part.

Sam made himself face her. He deserved disgust, anger. He didn't know why he didn't see them.

"I rushed things," he said. "It was stupid." More than stupid. What was it going to take, with him? What was he going to do with himself? "You know," he said, trying to smile, "I think maybe we should wait after all. We've had a long day."

"Are you sure?"

She looked so relieved. He didn't deserve her. "Yes." To prove to himself that he could do it without hurting her, he touched her face. "I'm sorry."

They changed for bed and slipped under the sheets and the ridiculous spongy comforter. She curled up against him. He turned out the light.

When he had finally given Gil the news, he started by saying he had bought a house. Gil had said, with that smile behind the words, "You must be doing well for yourself." Sam had explained it was a fixer-upper. He had to keep his voice steady, because he could give Gil the new address and phone number, but if he called, and if Jeannette answered...

Sam couldn't hide it forever. He didn't understand why he wanted to, or why it hurt so much to say, "There's something I need to tell you. I should have done it sooner."

When he did say the word *married*, Gil didn't reply for so long that Sam wondered if they had lost the connection. Finally Gil answered, gently, "Congratulations. I wish you both all the best."

The right words, but the tone said something else. Before the conversation ended, Gil put words to that too. "Be careful, love." He called Sam that, even then. "I don't want to see you hurt."

Lying under the canopy, with his eyes closed so Jeannette would think he was asleep, Sam knew that *his* getting hurt wasn't the problem. Who cared what happened to him? Especially after the way he had acted tonight.

Jeannette's arm lay across his chest, a slight, warm weight. Sam breathed carefully, not to disturb her. Sleep wouldn't find him tonight.

CHAPTER EIGHTEEN

Strands of Jeannette's hair clung to her cheeks and the back of her neck. She tugged the dropcloth smooth under her knees again and crouched over the roller pan, trying not to breathe the paint fumes too much. The smell made her sick, and the big creaky floor fan didn't clear the air, only stirred it around.

The new house needed so much work. Today Jeannette and Sam were repainting the downstairs hall. Sam had already finished the trapezoid of wall under the stair railing and moved on into the foyer. Jeannette didn't know why she couldn't keep up with him. Running a roller brush over the wall shouldn't be this difficult. She had pale yellow paint spattered on her arms and bare legs, like the reverse of freckles. Even when she scraped at them with her nails in the shower, they didn't always come off.

Today Sam had set up his old tape deck on the front staircase, which they had finished varnishing two days ago. A familiar song came out of the speaker. "When I Grow Too Old to Dream."

Jeannette loaded the roller up with paint. The sight of the sticky, glutinous stuff made her nauseous too. Her arm ached as she raised the roller to the wall, dripping a line of paint like a thick strand of spit.

Sam looked over at her. "We should stop pretty soon. It's twelve fifteen."

Another waft of paint smell caught Jeannette in the face. Her stomach turned over. "Do we have to go?"

Sam put down his roller and smiled at her. His expression bugged her, or would have if she'd had more energy; he looked like a parent chiding a little kid. "Honey," he said. "You know Geraldine and Bayard have been looking forward to this."

The Keatings had called three weeks ago to invite Jeannette and Sam to lunch. Jeannette had spent the time since then not thinking about it, except when she told herself something would happen to prevent them from going. "It'll be fine," Sam promised her now. "You'll have a good time, you'll see." He went back to painting, erasing the dingy white wall surface with a wide swath of soft yellow. Jeannette felt his contentment from where she knelt. It had the same glow as the colour.

Jeannette tried to think about her first dance with Sam at the wedding. With the song playing right now on the tape deck, she ought to be able to fill her head with good memories. Instead, she found herself thinking that the song wasn't really a wedding song at all. Too old to dream? What a sad idea.

She brought the roller up again. If only she didn't feel so *heavy*. She was probably just tired with all this painting and stuff. When Sam had brought her to see the house back in April, he had painted such a picture in her mind of how lovely it would be when they had it all set up. The living room had a deep bay window and double doors made up of tiny panes of glass, like something out of an old Victorian mansion. Sam had told her about the piano they could put down at the far end of that room, a black baby grand to replace both of their old spinets. She could imagine its rich sound filling the house when they sat down to play duets. The kitchen had an actual brick floor and tiled walls. All the rooms had high ceilings with cornice molding, dirty and dusty, of course, but when Sam talked her through how it would look when they had fixed it up, she saw it as clearly as he did.

He had been excited about the work. The day after they got home from their long-weekend honeymoon, he had gone straight to the hardware store for supplies and launched in. Jeannette tried to keep up with him, but she was starting to think she should have considered the whole business more carefully. They didn't need such a big house. They only had the barest kitchen necessities, and the couch from his place and the cheap queen-size bed they'd bought for the empty master bedroom, and her old bureau. No grand piano yet, though they had both sold their spinets to scrape a little money together. Jeannette hadn't thought she would mind parting with Aunt Gretchen's old instrument; goodness knew it had as many bad memories linked to it as good ones, but now she ached to think of it battered by unknown hands.

Sam had said to give the house time. She would see how perfect they would make it. But she couldn't stamp out the feeling that when it was all fixed, it would just be huge and empty.

"When I Grow Too Old to Dream" was still playing. Jeannette heard the line about the lovers sharing one more kiss and then saying goodbye. No, she and Sam really shouldn't have used this song for their first dance. How had she never noticed that line before?

Sam set down his roller. "Okay. Let's clean up."

Jeannette pushed the paint tray aside. She had made practically no progress, but he had covered a good section of wall in the foyer. Sad. Her knees ached as she stood up. She could tell him she felt sick. Maybe he would call the Keatings, and they could stay home.

He came over to her and put his hands on her waist the way he liked to do. "Are you nervous about lunch?" he asked.

Sweaty and paint-flecked or not, he was still beautiful. A new feeling stirred inside her, strong enough to push the nausea aside. Jeannette took a button of his shirt gently between her thumb and forefinger. "I kind of wish we had the afternoon to ourselves," she said.

"Now, honey, we've had lots of time to ourselves."

He had the same expression as before, like a parent talking to a child. Why did he do that? "I know," she said. She looked into his face, lightly turning the button back and forth as far as the thread would go. "But I mean I'd like to... you know."

He laughed. "Oh, is that it?" He ran a fingertip down the side of her neck and kissed her cheek. "Maybe later. How would that be?"

They had made love three times on the honeymoon. The first time had been hard. Jeannette had been scared, especially after what happened on their wedding night, but she tried to hide how she felt from him. That first night had left him so upset with himself.

He had made up for it on the honeymoon. He couldn't have been more careful, or gentle, and though it had still hurt more than Jeannette expected, afterward she found herself actually hungering for it again. The idea of it had always scared her. But with Sam—with her *husband*, the man who had chosen her—something had changed. For the first time, Jeannette saw lovemaking as something else: new and strange, certainly, but beautiful. It was the most intimate gift two people could share. She wanted to share it more with Sam, to be as close to him as two people could be.

But he hadn't seemed to want to do it again after they came home. They had been busy, trying to get as much finished on the house as they could before the RSA's season started in September. Sam had to get ready for the season too. This year, as he put it, he was still on trial. If they could keep things going as well as they had last year, by next May the RSA might officially be in the clear, and he could count on the job as long as he wanted it. He had to go into the new season loaded for bear. After the long days of work, he and Jeannette both just wanted to shower and sleep.

So now he said "Maybe later," and kissed her, and turned off the tape deck and scooped up his paint supplies to wash out. Jeannette didn't protest. When she bent down to pick up her tray, nausea settled on her again. It was going to be a long afternoon.

♫

The Keatings had a stone gatehouse. It stood empty now, unless they could afford to pay some poor nobody to stay there and keep fresh light bulbs in the lamps above the wrought-iron sweep. Judging by the size of the building, Jeannette thought, that person would probably have to sleep standing up.

As the Pinto climbed the long drive up to the main house, Jeannette pictured antebellum plantation owners driving their matched thoroughbreds under the spreading oak and beech trees. The wheels of the shiny, brass-outfitted carriages would have crunched on the loose gravel. The carriages would have swept past the gatehouse and thrown up dust or splattered mud on the faceless soul who came out to greet them.

The house appeared at the peak of the hill. Some plantation owners probably had gracious white mansions, or stately brick with fluted pillars, but this grey stone building looked more like a fortress. Sam parked on the gravel circle under, predictably, a magnolia tree. Jeannette wished it had been in bloom. The scent would have reminded her of Charleston.

Sam came around and opened the door for her. He always did that, which Jeannette used to find charming. Right now, she thought he had figured out that if he left her to herself, she would sit here all afternoon in the heat rather than walk up to the wide stone porch and knock on the door.

Another wave of nausea hit her when she stood up. It must have been the drive up the hill. Plus the day felt so heavy and humid, with a glaring white sky. Sam took her arm. "Are you okay?"

Jeannette brushed her hair out of her face. "Uh-huh," she lied. Maybe she would let her hair grow long again and put it back up in the bun so it couldn't glue itself to her skin.

"You look great," Sam said.

"Really? There's no paint on me?"

"I don't see any. You're lovely."

Jeannette's mint-coloured linen sundress had been another gift from Veronica. "You'll need nicer clothes now, honey, now that you're the Maestro's wife and all," as if Jeannette needed the reminder. And what did Veronica know about that anyway? The sleek, close-fitting dress felt like a costume. At least Jeannette could wear Aunt Gretchen's white shawl over it. "I'll try not to spill anything," she said, holding the shawl tight.

Sam squeezed her arm. "You'll be fine."

They went up the porch steps hand in hand. Sam walked as if this place was as much home as their own house on Calvert Lane, or for that matter, the little white house in Westbury. He gave the gleaming brass knocker three confident raps.

A voice floated out from inside. "Coming! Just a moment, dear."

To Jeannette's surprise, when the door creaked open the way a fortress should, Plum Pudding herself stood framed in it, instead of a butler or maid. Jeannette knew perfectly well she ought to think of the woman as Mrs. Keating, or Geraldine; the nickname business was silly, especially when Jeannette didn't want Sam treating her like a child. Here in this house, Jeannette clung to the name as a defiant shred of herself.

Today Plum wore a lilac blouse and skirt, but the same peacock twinkled at Jeannette from the blouse's collar. "Hello, Sam, so lovely to see you! Come in, dear. Jeannette, how pretty you look!"

Sam said, "Thank you for having us, Geraldine. This is a delight."

"You're more than welcome." Plum closed the door behind them and took each of them into a hug. Jeannette tried not to pull away from the powdery old-lady kiss on her cheek. "Let me take your coat," Plum said. "And Jeannette, dear, let's hang up your shawl, shall we? It's so very warm today, you won't need it a bit."

Jeannette handed it over resignedly. The cavernous foyer had a round table in the middle with a huge sparkling vase on it, probably crystal, full of tall flowers with thick stems and pink, lavender, and royal purple blooms. Each stem had probably cost five dollars at least. The ceiling was so far away that Jeannette practically got a crick in her neck trying to see it. An arched window let in too much of the white glare from outside, but at least it was cool in here.

"I thought we could have lunch in the sunroom," Plum said. "Not so formal, you know." Her mahogany cane tapped on the floor as she ushered them into a long, dark-panelled hallway. "I want to hear about everything," she went on. "Your wedding, the new house, all of these wonderful things you've been up to. Bayard and I have been thinking of you both so much."

Sam said, "That's very kind, Geraldine. We've certainly had a busy few weeks!"

The way the woman talked, Jeannette thought, you would honestly think they were all best friends. Maybe Plum and the General should have gotten an invitation to the wedding. Jeannette had probably committed some horrible social gaffe by not insisting on it.

Plum led them into a white room with a rich Oriental carpet and floor-to-ceiling windows. "Bayard, dear, they're here!"

Confederate General turned away from a side table. "Welcome, Mr. and Mrs. Kraychek." He wore the same grey three-piece suit Jeannette had seen before. Had he actually decided to look like one of those old Civil War prints, like the ones in Sam's books? He had the white hair and the beard; he probably had a stable on these grounds somewhere too, there was plenty of room for it, with a grey horse in it named Traveller. Except that the old prints didn't smile, which he did now as he came over to them, carrying a small tray that held four long-stemmed glasses. He said, "I would like to propose a toast."

"Yes indeed," Plum said, accepting a glass. Sam handed one to Jeannette and took one for himself.

"To the newlyweds," the General said. "Many years of happiness."

Plum said, "Hear, hear." She touched her glass to Sam's first, then the General's, and finally Jeannette's. The crystal chimed.

Sam said, "Thank you." White light hung around him. "You're very kind."

Jeannette sipped at her drink. Orange juice mixed with what had to be champagne. The bubbles stung her tongue. Maybe they would loosen it too.

Plum said, "Let's have a seat. Lunch will be ready in a moment or two."

The table had white linen on it and a white china vase with gilt edging. This was "not so formal?" The flowers in the vase had short stalks and tightly-packed magenta-and-purple blooms. Jeannette had a feeling Plum had chosen them. Sam drew out a chair for her, and when Jeannette sat, the rich floral scent hit her in the face. She set her glass down.

"Now," Plum said, "let's hear all about it. The most important part first. How was the wedding?"

Sam launched into the story. Jeannette listened to his description of Westbury as if she had never been there in her life. *Small town. Nowheresville.* He had said the same words to her once too, but now, in spite of his affectionate tone, they sounded snide and wrong. A chandelier hung over the table, glittering with white light. Jeannette looked down at her plate, heavy white china with a gilt edge to match the vase. The silverware had an elaborate pattern of scrollwork. Every piece had probably been hand-engraved by Paul Revere or somebody.

Sam was saying, "Before Jeannette and I went up there for Thanksgiving, I hadn't seen my parents' house in a few years. My old bedroom looked just like it did when I was fifteen. Worn-out bedspread and everything. I couldn't believe my mother hadn't changed it."

Jeannette remembered the hand-stitched quilt and its scent of lavender. Across from her, Confederate General sipped his drink and said, "We elderly folk are set in our ways. You young people need to bear with us."

Sam laughed. "Elderly? Bayard, you're hardly that."

White hair and a white beard did mean elderly, at least where Jeannette came from. A door opened on the other side of the room, and a young woman in a white apron brought a heavily loaded tray to the table. She had freckles and, Jeannette couldn't help noticing, bright red hair. "Here we are, Miss Geraldine," she said. "I'll set the things out for you."

"Thank you, Lisa. Oh, that does look nice."

The serving plates were all silver with filigreed edges. Jeannette should try to remember everything to tell Veronica about later.

"We'll serve ourselves," Plum said. "No need to stand on ceremony. Thank you, Lisa, you may go now."

On second thought, Jeannette didn't want to know what Veronica would say about a bona-fide maid. She already thought Sam was a different breed. These people were a whole different species.

The General started the first serving dish, laden with cold chicken, on its way around the table. Jeannette remembered Dr. Kraychek's hands carving a turkey.

"Now, Jeannette, dear," Plum said, "I haven't heard you say a thing yet. What do you think of your new house?"

Jeannette tried to manoeuvre a slice of chicken onto her plate with the heavy serving fork, though the bare thought of eating made her mouth want to glue itself shut. The piece flopped onto the edge of the plate. Only a stab with the fork saved it from tumbling onto the tablecloth.

She quickly passed the plate to Sam. "The house is very nice," she said.

Plum passed her a bowl of cut watermelon and blackberries and strawberries. Jeannette pictured the bright red, stain-inducing juice spraying everywhere, but she scooped up one piece of melon and one berry and transferred them to her plate. Plum said, "Do tell me about your house, dear. Sam told us there's much to be done with it?"

Jeannette swallowed against another twist of nausea. She wished she knew what was the matter with her today; this lunch would have been uncomfortable enough if she hadn't felt sick. "Yes, there is," she said. "Lots to do. We've been painting."

The General said, "Do you know, I've never painted a house? Not a single room. That seems like a skill everyone should have."

Sam said, "It's a skill I could do without. It's a lot more work than I thought."

But he liked it. Jeannette knew he did. Why would he pretend he didn't? Jeannette took a bite of chicken, which sat in her mouth getting soggy until she forced herself to swallow. Her head throbbed. At least they had glasses of plain ice water on the table too. Her stomach told her it would be a mistake to down hers at one swallow, so she picked it up and sipped carefully. Now and then she managed to interject a comment about the house, but mostly she listened while the others talked the work it needed.

After a pause in the conversation, the General said, "All this discussion makes me think this would be an appropriate time for something we had in mind. Do you agree, Geraldine?"

Plum beamed. "Certainly. Couldn't be better."

Jeannette wondered what they were planning now, but she wasn't left to wonder long. The General reached into the breast pocket of his suit coat. "Sam, Jeannette," he said. "Geraldine and I would like to make you a small gift in honour of your wedding. We thought it might help with your house projects."

Sam spoke up at once. "Oh, Bayard, you don't need to do that."

"Of course we don't." The General drew out a little ivory envelope. "But we want to. We also want to honour the difference you have already made to the Richmond Symphonic Artists, in one short year." He handed the envelope to Sam. "As you know, the RSA means a great deal to us. Consider this a token of our personal appreciation."

Sam opened the envelope and drew out a heavy ivory card. When he opened it, a small rectangle of white paper fluttered down. He caught it before it landed on the tablecloth.

"Oh." When he looked at it, the white light around him disappeared. For one second Jeannette saw his astonishment.

He looked up at their hosts. "Thank you so much. This is..."

"No more than you deserve," the General said. "Less, in fact, but I have to trust the rest of the board to assist me there. I'm confident they will, before the end of the season."

Sam cleared his throat. "We still don't know if..."

The General cut him off. "I do know. I said you would show everyone what the RSA is good for. You have. I have no doubt you'll continue to do it."

That was a compliment, Jeannette guessed, but the General looked so determined when he said it that she heard an unspoken "or else" at the end. And what did he mean less than Sam deserved? Sam's salary, maybe. The General wanted him to have a raise? Wasn't that asking a lot, when the orchestra didn't have much money?

Sam passed the card to her, slipping the piece of paper back inside. "Take a look, honey."

The card had two cutout white wedding bells on the front, decorated with gold swirls. Jeannette opened it and read, *To our Maestro and his lovely wife, on the occasion of their wedding, all best wishes for happiness and good fortune.* Plum had probably written it. The handwriting looked a little shaky with age but still elegant. Then Jeannette unfolded the white paper.

The number, written in a stronger, cleaner hand, jumped out and smacked her in the face. She couldn't earn that much with the chorus in a month.

Words spun in her head, *thank you, so generous,* but before she could say what she knew she should, a horrible feeling gripped her stomach, like iron hands squeezing and stretching it out of shape. For some reason she remembered the camphor scent of her little closet in Aunt Gretchen's house.

"I'm sorry." She dropped the card, cheque, and envelope on the table next to her plate and pushed her chair back. "Where's the bathroom?"

Plum said, "Are you all right, dear? You look quite pale."

"No, I'm... please, where's...?"

"Down the hall." The General's voice felt like a welcome blast of cold air. "Straight out these doors and down on your left."

Jeannette didn't know if she thanked him. She clamped one hand over her stomach and the other over her mouth and rushed out of the room, the terrible high heels skidding and clacking on the hardwood. She'd had no shoes good enough except the ones she had worn to her wedding, and with every step she expected to slip and twist her ankle and vomit right here, all over the dress and the immaculate floor. The dark hallway walls sped past her, and there was a door on the left and she dove through it and saw—thank God—a white porcelain toilet and one of those old-fashioned sinks perched on a pole. She collapsed on her knees on the hard, cold tile and dragged her hair out of her face, and leaned over the toilet and gave in to the spasms that wanted to rip her guts out.

Practically nothing came up. There was practically nothing in there, after all. Jeannette couldn't stand to look at the few strands of bile and couple of bites she had eaten swirling there in the bowl, so she reached for the chain and yanked it as hard as she could. The water carried her shame away.

She sat back on her heels. Her mouth tasted awful. The horrible noises she'd made had probably carried all the way down to the sunroom.

She had embarrassed Sam. That thought made her almost as cold as the chill from the tiles, seeping through her stockings and skirt. Why was she getting sick like this, anyway? *Heavy. Nauseous. Tired.*

She forced herself to her feet and turned the sink on. The cold water tasted as sweet as sugar. She rinsed her mouth again and again, then splashed more water on her cheeks. Her makeup would wash off. She didn't care.

Someone tapped on the door. "Jeannette? Are you all right?"

Plum. Jeannette straightened up from the sink. The door stood half-open. Her own face, in the gilt-edged mirror, looked like something out of a horror movie, pale and wild with dark circles around the eyes. She saw Plum's reflection behind her.

"I'm okay," Jeannette said. She felt too tired to care what anybody thought. Besides, a new idea had formed in some dark place in her head and loomed over her now, like a shadow.

Plum opened the door the rest of the way and stepped into the bathroom. "I'm so sorry, dear. I'm afraid you're ill."

"I'm all right." But Jeannette wasn't, was she? The shadow slowly took shape. *Heavy. Nauseous. Tired.* There was something else, too, that she hadn't thought about, hadn't wanted to think about. Hadn't Veronica gone through this? Hadn't Jeannette watched it happen, twice?

Plum asked, "Have you been feeling quite well lately?"

Jeannette could see both their faces in the mirror now. Plum was smaller than Jeannette was herself. No taller, for instance, than Anna Kraychek.

"I've been a little tired," Jeannette said.

Plum took her arm and turned Jeannette toward her with startling gentleness. "Forgive me for prying, my dear. I think this may be important. Have you been, shall we say, quite regular in everything?"

If only Jeannette were back in that little house. Anna would have listened. Jeannette thought she could have put her head on her mother-in-law's shoulder and told her—another wave of nausea made her thankful her stomach was empty—told her about the shadow that she knew had a name.

Right now, in this room, Jeannette had no one else. "No." It was barely a whisper. "I didn't have... I missed my..."

She couldn't finish. It should have come more than a week ago. It was still too soon to know, wasn't it?

Plum nodded as if she had expected no different. "I think you should see a doctor," she said. "Again, dear, please forgive me for prying. I understood you might not have a mother's advice."

I don't need yours! Jeannette couldn't say it, or the words that screamed louder in her head: *I'm not ready for this. I'm scared. I'm scared!*

"We needn't say anything about it just now," Plum said. "Sam was concerned about you. I'll go back now, shall I, and tell them you'll be along in a moment? I'll say you're feeling better."

Jeannette's neck felt stiff as she nodded. "Yes. Thank you."

Plum patted her arm. "Take your time, dear. There's no hurry at all."

After the cane had tap-tapped away, Jeannette stared into the mirror. Her own frantic eyes looked back at her.

Another woman might have looked just like this, once. A woman whose body had started to change and swell, rebel against her, and she had been so alone.

Mama.

CHAPTER NINETEEN

Lunch with the Keatings was miserable. Sam hadn't expected much different. He also hadn't expected Bayard Keating's exorbitant cheque, which felt to Sam like a bribe. A pat on the head for a job well done, with an implied *keep being good or else* tacked on.

Maybe that wasn't fair. Maybe the gift did come out of the Keatings' honest gratitude for a better-than-expected season. Sam couldn't work his way around to that idea, given that back when the Keatings' grand house had been built, a lapsed-Catholic coal miner's grandson (to say nothing about the rest of what Sam was) would have been about as welcome to walk through the front door as an infusion of bubonic plague. Sam would have been sent to the servants' entrance, if he had been allowed within a mile of the house at all.

On top of that, there was the apparent sickness that descended out of nowhere and hit Jeannette in the middle of the meal. Now, driving home with her beside him, as silent as she had been all afternoon, Sam tried to quiet the angry throbbing in his head long enough to sort out what to do.

Bayard's cheque burned in the breast pocket of his coat. That was not the worst thing. Far from it. The worst thing was the folded piece of lined paper that sat at home in the pocket of Sam's jeans, waiting for him.

He had gotten it two days ago. The handwriting on the envelope had jumped out at him from the pile of mail on the kitchen table. Jeannette had brought it in from the box; thank God the handwriting meant nothing to her and that there was no return address on the envelope.

Dearest Sam,

It's odd of me to write, I know, instead of picking up the phone, but I thought it might be best to keep this as private as possible. I wasn't sure when a call would be convenient for you.

Sam didn't need the paper in front of him to see the words again. He remembered every one.

I'm afraid I have some bad news. It's hard for me to write it, not so much for my sake—you know I've made my terms with this whole sorry mess—but because I would rather not force it on you. To keep it short, things aren't going well. My doctors tell me my "deterioration" is "atypically rapid," and they suspect I have another six months to a year at the outside. I have to say I believe them. These last few months, I've certainly been a better customer than usual at the hospital.

Sam drove numbly, clenching his hands around the steering wheel. Six months. A year at the outside.

I have to confess I'm writing to ask what I haven't before, that you will come up here again soon. I want to see you. This isn't to be morbid. It's only that seeing you would make me very happy.

It didn't help at all that Sam could hear Gil's voice saying the words. That insanely calm stuff about atypically rapid deterioration. And that seeing Sam would make Gil happy.

I hope you're well and that your wedding went perfectly. Those two words, your wedding, have a strange taste, but you know I wish you and your wife all the best.

When you have a chance, please be in touch. With my love,

Gil

Two days ago. The letter had come two solid days ago, and Sam still didn't have an answer for Gil, or the least idea what to say to the woman who sat in this car with him now.

Technically, he could tell her the truth. She knew Gil's name and that he was sick; after the wedding, Sam had finally told her that much about his "colleague" in Philadelphia. Keeping everything from her felt like sleeping on a pillow made out of rocks. She might not understand why Sam had to go tearing up there all of a sudden, when, except for that one offhand reference, he hadn't seen or mentioned Gil for months on end. Maybe she would realize you had to go when your friend was dying.

Friend. That was what Gil was. Plain and simple.

Driving mechanically, Sam remembered how Gil's handwriting had looked as neat and steady as ever. *Dearest Sam.*

Shit. *Shit.*

And now Jeannette was sick too, or something. Sam glanced at her profile. She stared straight ahead, close-mouthed. Stray curls clung to the back of her neck. Sam should ask her if she was okay, if she still felt nauseous. He couldn't do it.

Eventually he would have to open his mouth and talk to her. His wife. She had told him once that she didn't want secrets between them, and he had promised he wouldn't keep any (except the one she could never know). He had already lied once by omission by not telling her about the letter right away. And what could he say, what could he possibly say, to make her understand why he absolutely had to get to Philly, right now? He couldn't even tell her the name of Gil's illness, because that would bring her too close to the truth. She must never know why Gil mattered so much.

Sam shouldn't go up there and leave her behind. For one crazy second he thought about taking her with him. She would be company on the drive, they could stay in a hotel someplace, maybe go to the Philly art museum or something.

Christ, he really was losing it. As if, for instance, she could set foot in Gil's building. As if Sam could walk with her past the old fireplace and up those stairs, and they could go to the end of the hall and knock on Gil's door, and then Gil would open it, and he and Jeannette would be eye to eye.

They wouldn't, though. Gil was about three feet taller than her. Sam wanted to laugh, as sharp and sudden as needing to throw up, and then he wanted to cry, the kind of crying that would tear holes in your chest. He clenched his teeth until they ached.

He couldn't take Jeannette there. He shouldn't go alone. Gil was dying, and Sam couldn't do a damn thing.

By the time they got back to the house, his jaws felt as if they would never open again. In silence, he went upstairs with Jeannette, unzipped her dress, and turned away to change clothes. The pocket of his jeans crackled when he pulled them on. In that second, he could have jerked the letter out and wadded it up and thrown it in the garbage, or he could have gone to Jeannette and shoved it into her hand. Either of those things would have been wrong.

He tossed the envelope with Bayard's cheque in it onto his dresser. That was another thing. If Bayard knew what Sam actually was—*had been*, not *was* anymore—if Bayard knew that, he probably would have ripped up the cheque and stuffed it down his own throat before he had handed it across that fancy table. Sam yanked on his belt and left the room without a word.

Downstairs, he pushed aside the tape deck he had set up that morning and dumped paint into his tray. Hell, he might have to do this work alone. Served him right. He should have told Jeannette to lie down; he should have taken her a cup of tea or something. He was supposed to take care of her. At least he knew how to paint a wall.

After a few passes with the roller, he heard footsteps on the stairs. Jeannette brought her tray over to the paint can near him and bent to fill it. He asked, "Are you up for this?" He couldn't manage to look at her.

"I'm all right." She took her tray back to the part of the wall she'd been working on in the morning. He heard her roller creak as she coated it with paint.

The hell she was all right. The paper in Sam's pocket crackled again when he bent to reload the roller. He didn't want to stand there patiently smoothing paint on the wall. He wanted to open the door and tear outside and run until he ran out of breath and keeled over.

For one weekend, Jeannette could stand him being gone. Besides, he obviously wasn't the only closed-mouthed person in this marriage. If she had been sick this morning, she could have told him so, and they could have put off the Keatings and their payout for another day. What was the matter with her, anyway? Did she have a virus or what? She could at least tell him that.

He gripped the roller so tight that when he set it down, his fingers creaked. The handle had left red lines on his palm. He turned around to look at Jeannette. "Honey, I think we should talk."

When she put her roller down and faced him, hiding her hands behind her back, she looked like the kid who had been called up to the teacher's desk for passing notes in class. He said, "Do you remember about my friend Gil? In Philly?"

It was so hard to say Gil's name. Jeannette looked confused, no wonder, hearing this out of the blue. "Yes," she said. "Of course. How is he?"

Sam braced himself. His voice came out cold and flat, but steady. "Not well. I've been meaning to tell you, I got a letter from him the other day." Partially true. "We've been so busy I didn't bring it up." As good an excuse as any.

"You got a letter?"

He might as well get the worst over as fast as he could. "Yes. I'd like to go up and visit him again."

She registered that. "Oh. Can I come with you?"

Good thing he had already thought that through, or he might have said yes. It would have been safer in more ways than one. He said, "I don't think we should do that. The illness is progressing"—Christ, he sounded like his father—"and I'm sure Gil's not himself." When had he last been himself? Probably before this damn thing got him. "That's why I want to see him now, while we can."

And if Sam got up to Philly and Gil was in the hospital, and the doctors told Sam he couldn't go in, he would break down doors if he had to. "I thought I would go before the end of the summer," he went on. "Maybe not next weekend, since we still have a lot to do here, but the weekend after."

All she had to do was say okay, whether she liked it or not. Surely she could give him the single word he wanted.

She stared down at the paint-splattered canvas dropcloth. The blood climbed into her face.

Sam's fingers itched to clench into fists. "Honey. What are you upset about?"

She jerked her head up. "Why do you have to go?"

She had never raised her voice at him before. "Why can't I come?" she demanded. "I don't understand!"

He said the only thing he could think of. "Jeannette. Calm down."

"I don't want you to go! I don't want you to leave me here!"

For Christ's sake, she was hysterical. Sam went to her and caught hold of her upper arms. "Get hold of yourself." This was his own fault. He had known better than to say anything, but goddamn it, what else could he do?

She shouted into his face, "You're just mad at me!" Her eyes were tear-filled and wild. "I'm not good enough for you, and you're mad at me and you want to leave!"

What the hell? *You want to leave.* How could she think that? How could she dare?

Want to leave.

Dearest Sam...

Anger crashed over him. Anger picked up his hand and moved it so fast that his fingers blurred in the air. His palm connected with Jeannette's cheek hard enough to make his own skin burn. *Yes.*

She stared up at him. In her eyes, he saw what he had done.

Monster.

"I'm sorry." He let go of her. "Jesus Christ. I'm so sorry."

For a suspended second they stared at each other. Then Jeannette hid her face in her hands and sobbed.

Sam could not stand this. He put his arms around her. "Oh, Jeannette, don't. Please. I didn't mean to hurt you, sweetheart." He pressed a kiss on the top of her head. "I'm so sorry."

She ought to slap him back. That would only be fair. Instead she pressed her face against his shoulder, wrapped her arms around him, and held on tight. Hanging on to such a worthless piece of shit.

He touched her chin with a fingertip. "Let me see your face. I didn't make a bruise, did I?"

She raised her head. There was no mark on her cheek, but if anything could have made him feel worse, it was the helpless pain in her eyes. "Oh, honey," he said. He stroked her face as if he could erase what he had done. "I don't know what got into me." Not true. None of this was her fault.

As if she'd heard that, she said, "It's my fault. I was awful at lunch. I embarrassed you."

"No, you didn't," he said. Was she blaming herself for being sick? "Christ, even if you had, that doesn't give me the right to slap you. What was I thinking?" He tried to drag a joke out of the pit of his stomach. "Maybe I thought, I don't know, a woman's hysterical, you have to bring her around somehow."

He told her she had married a moron, which was a wild understatement. She didn't smile. Instead, so quietly he had to lean closer to hear her, she said, "I don't want you to go, Sam. I'm scared."

She ought to be scared of *him*. "Why?" he said. "You don't want to be here by yourself?"

"No." She hesitated. "I mean, no, I don't, but..." Her voice trailed off.

Sam could only think of two possibilities: either she actually was scared of him and didn't know how to say it, or could she possibly be chewing over what he had said about Gil? Could she already suspect there was more to the story than he'd told her?

He deserved anything she wanted to dish out. He would stand here and take it. "What is it, sweetheart? Tell me."

"It's... I'm..."

If only she wouldn't cry. He brushed a tear away. "Please tell me. It's okay."

"It's not. Oh, Sam, I... I think I'm pregnant."

What?

Sam realized he had stopped smoothing her hair. The air in the room seemed to have gone solid.

She couldn't have actually said that word. He ought to try to get to the bottom of it. "You're what?"

"I don't know for sure." Her voice rushed ahead, light and faint. "Maybe I'm not." He caught a few words here and there. *Feeling bad. Sick at lunch. Late with my...*

After a while he realized she wasn't talking anymore. He also realized he wasn't holding her, but didn't know when he had let go.

One word loomed in his head. He said it. "Pregnant."

"I'm not sure. It could just be a cold. Or something."

At least now he could hear her. "But you think you are."

Another babble of words. In the middle of it, he heard *Mrs. Keating*. "You told her?" he said.

"When she came in the bathroom. To find me. She said I should see a doctor."

She had told Geraldine. The two of them had stood there in the bathroom, presumably, and talked about it while Sam sat cluelessly at the table. Then Geraldine had come back and told him, what was it? "A bit of stomach upset. Nothing to worry about."

But she had given him a look, hadn't she. That twinkly-eyed look of hers.

"Pregnant?"

He didn't realize he had said it aloud until his own tone caught up with him. A little kid waking up from a nightmare: *it wasn't real, was it?*

Jeannette had gone so pale she looked ready to faint. Automatically he put his arms around her again. "Okay," he said, maybe to himself. "Okay. We'll figure this out."

Pregnant. A baby. Sam would be a father.

In some tiny, sane corner of his mind, he understood this was a good thing. He had a wife, he would have a child: that meant he was the man he ought to be, didn't it? But that small, sane voice could barely make itself heard through the cloud of panic. This couldn't happen now. Not yet.

Jeannette was talking again. He heard her say something about calling her sister, something about seeing a doctor. "Right," he said. "And then, once we know for sure, we can, you know, get ready." Fatherhood. What the hell did he know about that?

"Your trip," Jeannette said. "You should do it. I'm sorry I got upset."

Maybe it wasn't true. No matter what Geraldine said or Jeannette thought or anything, maybe it still wasn't true. But if it was, he and Jeannette were already in this together. Bound for life. Nothing could make that more permanent.

Could it?

He said, "We'll see. Let's find out about this first." As if they were talking about buying a new dishwasher.

"Okay."

She held on to him. In the silence and the smell of wet paint, Sam kept his arms around her, holding both of them up.

♬

Jeannette called Veronica and went with her to a doctor. The first test came back positive. Jeannette insisted on another opinion, as if this were a cancer diagnosis. The second test came back positive too.

She and Sam were going to be parents.

For the rest of the summer Sam flung himself into the work on the house. He did call Gil and tell him what was going on. "I'll drop everything if you need me to," he said.

Realistically, he couldn't. Gil answered, "I don't want you to do that. Do what you need to and come up when you can."

Sam could only sleep if he wore himself out every day. He and Jeannette painted and varnished and wallpapered. They picked a room for the, dear God, nursery. Sam made Jeannette take breaks from the work and lie down for a few minutes, or have a glass of ice water or lemonade. He didn't rest. From the time they got up until they collapsed into bed at night, he kept moving.

Ma was thrilled, or said she was. Veronica was too. Dad didn't say much. Sam didn't worry about what anybody said or didn't. He and Jeannette painted the nursery walls mint-green and looked at cribs and swings in a Sears catalogue. Through it all, he tried not to think about what was happening inside her body.

At the end of August, his season started. The RSA people would find out what was going on soon enough. Jeannette would only be able to play for the chorus through December because the baby was due by mid-February. Sam launched into the fall concert repertoire and worked harder and faster than ever. Life blurred with speed.

That couldn't last. Gil might only have six months.

In October, Sam couldn't wait anymore. Gil was still all right, so he said, but Sam didn't know what to believe. So one weekend, the last one before the first RSA concert of the season, Jeannette stayed at her sister's and Sam packed an overnight bag and drove to Philly. With each passing exit on the highway, the world slowed down. By the time Sam pulled into the parking lot behind Pennsylvania Hospital, time could have stopped completely.

No rain this time. The sky had the rich turquoise tint you only got on the clearest fall days. Sam went up the steps and into the lobby, where the smell of autumn leaves disappeared and the hospital miasma took over. The nurse at the desk might have been the same one he had seen the last time he came here, the day before he moved to Richmond. Gil was in room 20 this time. Sam went down to the end of the hall and found the door closed.

He had said he would beat down doors if anyone told him he couldn't come in here. It felt much harder to take the knob in his hand and turn it.

Gil was asleep. Sam took in the cheesecloth blanket and sterile sheets, the too-thin shape underneath them.

Had it really been more than a year since Sam had last come back to Philly, a year since that trip to Gil's apartment? The face on the pillow was still too thin, too pale, but Gil looked no worse than the last time Sam had seen him. At least not as far as Sam could tell. Right now, that was something to grasp on to.

Sam went quietly to the bed. The covers hid Gil's hands. Sam gently touched his shoulder and felt the sharp thin bone through the blue hospital gown.

"Gil?"

He had to say it twice. When the blue eyes opened, Sam let out his breath. Gil said, "Hey, you."

His voice sounded hoarser than Sam remembered. When he smiled, it didn't look quite the way it used to, as if he had to work for it. He was tired, Sam told himself. He had just woken up. "Hey," Sam said. "How are you feeling?"

"Okay. Better now."

Sam should have come up sooner. He should have forced it to work. Gil drew a hand free of the covers and waved at the plastic chair at the foot of the bed. "Sit down," he said. "Let's have a talk."

Sam moved the chair around, the same way he had before. It felt cold when he sat. Gil put his hand on the blanket, palm up. Sam covered it with his own.

"So," Gil said. "First I have to say congratulations. You've had quite a summer."

He wasn't the same. Sam felt it. The voice and the smile were both fading, though Gil held on to them with every breath. His eyes, almost as bright as the sky outside, were the only constant left.

Sam tried to smile too. "Quite a summer? You can say that again."

"How are you doing?"

He shouldn't have been the one asking that question. Sam said, "You know, I'm not sure."

Gil laughed. "Tell me."

His laugh didn't sound right either. Sam had already told him everything that mattered: how he, Sam, had been wrong time and time again, and it should have been him in this hospital bed. With the steady blue eyes watching him now, Sam tried anyway. "Well," he said, "for one thing, what's this shit about me being a father?"

It was supposed to be a joke, but Gil didn't laugh. "Why is it shit?"

"Oh, hell, Gil. You know me."

"That's not an answer."

You want me to say it out loud? Sam was not going to cry. He had done enough of that. He stared down at the top border of Gil's blanket and answered, "Because I fuck up everything I touch."

The cheesecloth fabric shifted. Gil's other hand slid free of the covers. Sam could not look up as those chilly fingers touched his cheek or when they moved over his hair, smoothing it once, twice.

Oh, hell. Sam was going to cry after all. That just about set the seal on everything.

Gil lowered his hand back to the blanket. "Do you know something?"

Sam made himself raise his head. Gil smiled as if the last few seconds hadn't happened and said in that hoarse gentle voice, "I used to wonder if I'd be a good father."

"You did?" Sam had never known that.

Gil nodded. "It was a long time ago, before I met you. It didn't last. I realized I wasn't cut out for it, but I'd see people with their kids, and I'd wonder."

Gil should have had that future, or any one he wanted. Words fell out of Sam's mouth. "I'll be hopeless."

Gil shook his head. His thumb travelled lightly over the backs of Sam's fingers. "You won't, love."

How the hell could he know that? How could anyone? Sam's voice seemed to have crawled away to hide, but he dragged it back out again. "Why not?"

"Because you care."

Sam struggled for breath. "I do. I mean, sure. But." He couldn't talk this way to Jeannette or Ma, and God knew he shouldn't bother Gil with it either when he lay here like this. "Jesus, Gil, a *baby*. Babies, you have to do everything for them, right? I mean, that's a few million chances to fuck up every single day."

Gil laughed. It sounded so tired. "Well, first you'll have to clean up your language."

Sam's throat ached. "Okay. Fair point."

"Do you know yet if it's a boy or a girl?"

What a strangely normal conversation. "No. The doctors said they'll be able to tell us around Thanksgiving."

"Do you have any names picked out?"

They ought to have lists by now. Sam admitted, "We haven't really thought about it."

"You know, I always liked Caroline. Even though Neil Diamond stole it."

Sam tried to smile. "How come you like it?"

"I don't know. The Kennedys, maybe. A Caroline would be a pretty girl. Graceful, you know, and elegant. It's a little old-fashioned too. I like that."

Caroline. Well, sure, it was a pretty name. Sam tucked it away in the back of his mind. Sitting here with Gil, he could let himself not think about the baby. Only for now. Only for a few minutes.

Gil asked about the wedding. Sam shouldn't have been able to talk about it, not here in this place, but he found himself telling about the church and the priest, how Jeannette's dress had looked, the food and the dancing, as easily as if he were reading a story. Halfway through his description of the dancing—"Jeannette's sister Veronica made everybody listen to 'Thunder Road'"—he realized why. He was, in fact, telling a story, about something that had happened to somebody else. The person sitting here beside this bed, holding Gil's hand, would never have gotten married. The person sitting beside this bed had only ever loved once.

When Sam finished talking, the two of them sat quiet for a while. Sam held Gil's hand and understood that this was where he ought to be.

Then Gil said, "By the way, how did your wife feel about you coming up here?"

His wife. Yes, Sam had a wife, obviously, but couldn't they hold off on using that word for another minute or two? He said, "She was okay with it."

"Really?"

"Well, not at first. She came around."

Gil's fingers tightened around Sam's. "How much does she know?"

Why did he care? Sam didn't want to talk about it. "I told her you and I were colleagues. And friends."

"That's difficult."

Well, yes, Sam had lied to Jeannette. Fine. What else could he have done?

Gil said, "Have you thought maybe you should tell her more?"

No. Absolutely not. Sam heard himself say, "She wanted to come up here with me. I said we probably shouldn't."

"I can understand that."

Could they leave this alone for now? But real life closed back in, no matter how tightly Sam clung to Gil's hand and tried to push everything else away. Sam did have a wife. She was expecting a baby. He had... Jesus Christ, he had gotten married, and he and Gil had been...

"Gil," he said, "listen." He had to say something before it was too late, if only he could find the words. "I didn't marry her because... I mean, I..."

"Love, I understand."

Sam caught his breath. "No. No. You don't. Because I married her, but..." There it was, the simplest thing in the world. "I love you. Always. You know that, don't you? I love you." *I never stopped loving you. I never should have left. I'm so sorry, Gil.*

Gil pressed his fingers. "I know that. I love you too."

Sam didn't care if he never said another word or moved a muscle again. He would sit here beside this bed as long as he had breath in his body.

They talked about where Sam was staying tonight, how his new season was starting out, and the concert next weekend, as if Sam cared about that. Gil asked how the chorus was doing this year. "Better," Sam said. "Maybe I did scare them into shape." When visiting hours ended, he didn't want to get up. "Are you sure I have to?" he asked. "I could get an extra blanket and camp out. This floor looks clean enough."

Gil laughed, a quiet shadow-sound. "They'd chase you out. Go on and get a decent night's sleep."

"All right. But I'll see you in the morning, okay? First thing."

"I'll be here."

Sam pressed his cheek against Gil's hair, felt his too-thin shoulders again and caught the scent of hospital detergent. "Goodnight," he said. He kissed Gil's cheek. "See you tomorrow."

"Goodnight, love."

By now the sun had gone behind the hospital, throwing the building's stark shadow across the parking lot. The air felt much colder than it had before. Sam hurried to his car, wiping his eyes. He would be back tomorrow.

♫

At seven in the morning, Sam's bedside phone in the Motel 6 rang, dragging him out of sleep. He pushed the blanket away and fumbled for the receiver. "Hello?"

"Mr. Kraychek? This is Jonas Caruso from Pennsylvania Hospital."

Sam sat bolt upright on the hard mattress. "Yes? What is it?"

"I'm sorry to call so early. Mr. Hart hoped I would reach you before visiting hours."

Sam threw the covers back and stretched the phone cord as far as he could, grabbing for his clothes on the floor. "What happened? What's wrong?"

"Mr. Hart is still stable. His condition has not changed since last night. He asked me to call because he felt it would be best if you did not visit this morning."

Sam stopped, holding one leg of his jeans. "What? Why not?"

"He felt it would be best if you went straight home."

"I don't understand. I told him I'd see him today."

"Yes." Caruso's voice sounded polite but distant. "He mentioned your wife."

"Jeannette's fine." Sam hadn't heard otherwise. "Look, I don't know what this is about. I don't even know how you got this number. Put Gil on the phone, I want to..."

"Mr. Hart said he thought it would be best if the two of you did not talk. He told me where you were staying so I could find the number."

Sam barely heard the second half of that. Gil didn't want to talk to him? What the hell? "I don't believe you," he said. "Something happened. Something's wrong with him. Why won't you tell me what's going on?"

"Mr. Kraychek, I assure you Mr. Hart asked me to say exactly what I have said." How could the man sound so damn calm all the time? "He felt it would be best if you went home to your wife. He also asked me to tell you not to forget Caroline."

Caroline? Who the hell was that? Then Sam remembered, but he didn't care. Nothing in the world mattered except Gil, who was so close but so far away. Sam's hand clenched around the phone. "Why can't he tell me that himself?"

This time the voice had real sympathy in it. "He felt it would be difficult for you both."

Sam stood by the bed in the dark. His jeans dragged uselessly on the floor. Gil wanted him to go home to his wife and the baby. Caroline. Gil felt it would be best if he and Sam didn't see each other.

"Mr. Kraychek?"

Sam wanted to throw his clothes on and drive to the hospital and barge into Gil's room right now. But that wouldn't work, would it, because Gil was right. Gil was always right.

"Mr. Kraychek, are you still there?"

I love you. They had both said it. "Yes," Sam said. "I'm here."

"I'm sorry. I realize this is unexpected."

Sam sat back down on the bed. The mattress felt like concrete. "No. I understand. Tell Gil… tell him I understand too. Please."

After they hung up, Sam kept his hand on the phone for a long time, in case. It didn't ring again.

Never mind. He could do something else. A letter, or another call, once he was back in Richmond. He could call from his own house like a normal person, and he and Gil could have a normal conversation. Maybe, after a while, Sam could come back up here. He and Gil had cleared the air, so to speak.

It wasn't true. Sam knew it, but he buried the knowledge in the deepest place he could find. For now, he would go home.

CHAPTER TWENTY

"What'd you say he was doing again, honey?"

Jeannette sat at the old kitchen table in her sister's apartment. She had pushed her chair all the way in so the yellow Formica would hide the barely-there, but still foreign, curve of her stomach. "He's visiting a friend," she told Veronica.

Her sister stood at the counter, chopping onions for spaghetti. "I thought he had a concert coming up."

"He does," Jeannette said. "We do. The first RSA concert is next weekend." Jeannette sipped at the glass of Sprite her sister had set in front of her. She had been nauseated most of the afternoon, but now for some reason the smell of the raw onions made her mouth water. She hated the back-and-forth swings between sick and ravenous. "He wanted to go to Philadelphia sooner," she said, "but we had too much to do on the house. His friend is sick. That's why he had to go now."

Veronica glanced over her shoulder. "Sick? What's the matter?"

Jeannette had finally asked Sam the same question. He had said he would rather not talk about it. Jeannette didn't want to admit that to her sister or say how uneasy it had made her feel that Sam wouldn't tell her such a simple thing. "Some kind of cancer," she said. The lie tasted sour in her mouth. "He told me, but I forget."

Before Veronica could answer, Ricky ran into the kitchen with C.J. toddling behind. "Mommy! Stick 'em up!"

The jet from the orange squirt gun nailed Veronica on the calf, soaking her jeans. Veronica whirled around on her son. "Ricky Calhoun! You take that out of here this minute!"

C.J., giggling, ran over to Jeannette's chair. "Auntie Nan!" He pawed her lap the way a little dog would, looking for a treat. His hands were wet and sticky.

Ricky whined, "Mommy, I'm *hungry!* When do we eat?"

"The sooner you leave me alone, the sooner I get this done."

What *did* C.J. have on his hands? Jeannette caught one of them as it slapped her thigh again. "C.J., what did you do to yourself? Is this paint?" It was. He had left green fingerprints on the leg of her white pants. "Where'd you get this?"

"Can we have a snack?" Ricky demanded.

"No," Veronica said. *Chop. Chop.* "Dinner's soon. You'll spoil your appetite."

C.J. beamed up at Jeannette. He didn't seem to notice she had asked him something. Age two and a half and the boy couldn't string a handful of words together. Jeannette thought Veronica should be concerned. Looking closer, she saw a streak of purple on the little boy's face and smears of orange on his shirt. "Child," she told him, "you're a mess."

"Aunt Nannie! Look out!"

Squirt! The water hit Jeannette on the shoulder. "Ricky!" she snapped. "Didn't your mother tell you to take that someplace else?"

Veronica turned around from the cutting board. "Ricky, you leave your aunt alone. Give her a paper towel and tell her you're sorry. And wipe up this water on the floor."

"Mommy, I'm bored. I want to go outside."

"Well, you can't right now. Nobody can go with you. Clean up that water like I told you."

Jeannette could have gotten the paper towel faster herself. Water soaked into the thin sleeve of her flowered blouse. Ricky swiped at the puddle he'd made on the floor and brought Jeannette another towel. "I'm sorry, Aunt Nannie."

"Okay. Thank you." Jeannette blotted at her sleeve. The towel wouldn't do anything for her pants. C.J. had probably ruined them. She'd liked these pants, but that was what she got for wearing white in October.

Ricky said, "Aunt Nannie, can't *you* take us outside?"

"No, honey. Not now."

"Why not?"

"Because I'm not in the mood."

Ricky stared up at her. "Why are you always cranky?"

Jesus! Before Jeannette could snap something, Veronica said, "Ricky, Aunt Nannie doesn't feel so good."

"Because she's going to have a baby?"

"Yes. Now you leave her alone, like I told you."

"When's Daddy coming home?"

"Soon. And I have to have this food ready for him when he gets here. So you and your brother go find something to do for twenty minutes, all right?"

Ricky looked at the clock. "When the big hand is on the twelve?"

"Yes. That's all I ask. Now scoot."

Ricky corralled his brother, who had been crawling on all fours around and around the chair legs. "C'mon, C.J." The two of them went out.

"You know they'll soak the living room with that gun," Jeannette said.

Veronica shook her head, scraping the onion into a saucepan. "Honey, at this point I don't care." She opened a can of tomatoes and dumped them on top of the onion. "I wish Drew wouldn't have taken that weekend shift. He's at the office enough as it is."

"He wants the extra OT?"

"That's right. He's got this house idea on the brain." Veronica stirred a packet of Spatini into the saucepan. The smell filled the kitchen and made Jeannette's stomach growl. Veronica added, "I guess I can blame you for that, Nannie."

Thump, from the living room. "Ricky," Veronica yelled, "what was that?"

"Nothing, Mommy. We're playing Nerf."

"Lord." Veronica shook her head again. "Pray they don't crack their heads open."

At the very least Jeannette ought to get up and offer to make the pasta. "A house would be good," she said. "The boys could use the extra room."

Veronica turned around from the saucepan, brushing stray hair away from her face. "Extra room to destroy things. I tell you, Nannie, ever since Drew saw that house of yours, he's been going half crazy."

Jeannette realized her sister looked awfully tired. Drew was gone a lot more these days, working every hour he could. Even with Ricky in kindergarten this year, Veronica had plenty on her hands. Jeannette shouldn't have barged in to stay with them this weekend.

"He thinks we're going to get a place like yours," Veronica went on. "He goes on about how great it would be to have all that space. I keep telling him we'll never afford it." She stirred the sauce, looking over her shoulder at Jeannette. "I still don't know how your Sam did."

Jeannette felt her blush starting. "I told you, the house needed a ton of work. It still does. It wasn't all that expensive."

"It looks expensive."

"We're both working, though. And that's another thing," Jeannette added quickly. "I'll have to quit in the spring. Sam's kind of worried about it." She would have had a hard time explaining why she didn't want Veronica to know about the check the Keatings had given them, or about how, as Sam had told her, Confederate General had promised the board's "involvement and support" when it came time for her to stop work. A raise for Sam couldn't wait until next season.

Veronica looked at her, stirring steadily. "Somehow I have a feeling he'll manage."

She had always said Sam was a different breed. Now Jeannette had married into that breed. Jeannette winced. "Vee, you know his parents. You saw their house. His family's not rich."

"I didn't say they were. He has good friends."

"He's good at what he does."

Veronica filled another saucepan with water at the sink and dropped in a pat of butter. "And he's lucky. That's a good thing for him and you, honey. I'm saying nothing against it."

You are. Jeannette couldn't say it, the same way she couldn't get up from the table and take the box of noodles out of her sister's hand.

Veronica broke the pasta into the water. "It'll be tough at first, with the baby. You know that." Jeannette wished she didn't. "Sam's a good provider, I don't doubt that for a minute," Veronica said. "He'll take care of you." She had once said he had better. She didn't say things like that anymore.

To distract herself, Jeannette tried to think about the nursery. She and Sam had put all the other projects on hold and finished it last weekend. They had painted the walls green and put up green curtains with white polka dots, and they had bought a new white crib and a changing table and a rocking chair. They hadn't had time for much else in the way of details or decorations, but they would make up for it later. The baby wouldn't care one way or the other, right?

Jeannette told herself that by the time the baby was born, she would be ready. Meanwhile, Anna had enough enthusiasm for them both. She had promised Jeannette a shopping trip to Scranton over Thanksgiving, by which point they would know if the clothes should be blue or pink.

And they would have to start thinking about names. Jeannette could only think of one, which didn't fit no matter how she turned it. *Mother.*

Thump. "Ricky Calhoun," Veronica shouted, stirring the boiling noodles, "if you wreck that living room I'm going to hang you up by your toenails."

Ricky ran back in, giggling. "Really? How do you do that?"

"You don't want to find out. Now could you please try to be quiet for thirty seconds? Aunt Nannie doesn't know what she's in for, having a baby of her own." Jeannette wished that were true.

The front door opened. Ricky shrieked "Daddy!" and flew out of the kitchen.

Veronica muttered, "It's about time. Anybody would think he didn't have a home to come back to."

Drew came into the kitchen with both of his sons hanging off him, one clinging to each leg. "Hey, all," he said. He put his briefcase down on the kitchen table, knocking the ashtray aside. "How are things?"

Veronica snapped, "Don't put that there. I'm about to set out dinner, don't you see?"

Drew moved the briefcase to the floor. "Ricky, go wash your hands for supper. Help your brother," he added, prying C.J. loose and setting him on his feet. He went to Veronica and kissed her neck. "What's the matter, hon?"

Veronica brushed him off. "Too busy. And those boys have been climbing the walls all afternoon. Nannie can tell you."

Drew turned to Jeannette. "Couldn't you take them to the park or something? It was a great day out."

Veronica splatted pasta onto plates. "Drew, she's pregnant. She doesn't want to spend the day running around after those two monkeys."

"You used to take Ricky out to play when you were pregnant with C.J."

Jeannette knew Drew wasn't picking on her, just making a logical point. Even so, her blush climbed up her neck and into her cheeks.

"First babies are harder," Veronica said. "A man wouldn't understand that." She nudged him aside, but more gently, and reached for the sauce on the stove. "Now clear off and get changed or whatever you need to do. This'll be all set in a minute."

After he left, Jeannette said quietly, "I'm sorry, Vee. I should help more."

Veronica shook her head. "Never mind him." With her back to Jeannette, she ladled sauce onto a plate. "You have enough of your own business to deal with."

Jeannette made herself stand up. She didn't have to wear maternity clothes yet, but to herself she looked like a foreign object. She went over to the stove and touched her sister's shoulder. "I can help if you need me. Really. Anytime. Sam and I aren't far away."

Veronica turned to look at her. She did look tired, her hair more straggly than sleek. With a shock, Jeannette saw the first traces of crow's feet at the corners of her sister's eyes.

"Oh, Nannie, I know you're not. It's just…"

"Just what?"

Veronica shook her head. "Never mind." She went back to ladling sauce. "Look, tell you what you can do right now. Find me that parmesan cheese in the fridge, and there's some lettuce and tomatoes in the drawer you can wash off. We'll have a salad."

Jeannette set the can of cheese on the counter and dug in the crisper for the lettuce. After she and Veronica wedged the plates and the salad bowl on the table, they were still miraculously alone. Jeannette wanted to say, *I love you, Vee, I promise,* and tell her, *I'm still here. I didn't go away.* When Veronica set the cheese can on the table, their eyes met. Words hovered on Jeannette's lips.

Ricky burst in. "Can we eat? Can we eat?"

Drew followed, hauling C.J. over his shoulder like a sack of potatoes. "Mmm. Smells great, girls."

Veronica said, "All right, then. Everybody sit."

Jeannette wedged herself back into her chair. Veronica had her hands full corralling the boys and trying to keep enthusiastically slurped sauce off the floor. Jeannette poked at her own plate, trying to swallow the nausea that crept up her throat.

♬

On the night of the first RSA concert, Jeannette stood in the Lewis Center lobby waiting for her sister to arrive. Veronica hadn't wanted to come tonight, but Jeannette had worked on her during their visit, promising a comp ticket, and Drew had agreed to stay home with the boys. Finally, on the Wednesday before the show, Sam had called to invite her himself. At that point Veronica had given in.

Jeannette wanted her sister here tonight because soon she, Jeannette, wouldn't be able to come to any concerts anymore. Not to rehearsals either. She tried not to think about how it would feel, spending all those hours in the big empty house with little whoever-it-was.

"Evening, Mrs. Kraychek."

Even the ushers knew Jeannette, which was embarrassing because she couldn't tell them apart. They were all blocky college-age boys in red vests and black pants, so alike you would think you could order a box of them, like crayons.

"Hello... um..." She sneaked a glance at this one's black-on-gold name badge. "Eric."

The boy had wheeled a loaded hand cart over to the small table by the door, and now he unloaded three boxes of programs and another collection box for ticket stubs. "How are you tonight, ma'am?" he asked.

"I'm very well, thanks. How are you?"

"Fine, thank you." Eric set a wad of programs on the table and pushed the still-full boxes underneath, where the dangling edges of the red tablecloth would hide them. "Got to make sure we have enough books for tonight," he said. "Gonna be a full house."

Jeannette hadn't paid much attention to ticket sales lately. "Is it?"

"Sure." The boy grinned. "Mr. Kraychek's pretty popular, you know that."

A full house. Sam would be pleased. Jeannette wondered when the RSA had last gotten any such thing. How had Sam managed to do so much?

"Can I get you your program, ma'am?"

"Thank you."

Jeannette took the program and moved away from the table, rolling the sleek book between her hands. People would start arriving soon. She ducked into a nearby corner.

Sam had gotten back from Philadelphia on Sunday and arrived at Veronica and Drew's promptly at six to pick her up. He had stayed for dinner, eating leftover spaghetti with every sign of enjoyment and listening to Ricky's breathless barrage about school. "Uncle Sam, know what? My friend Jack, he brought his fire truck for show and tell, it has a light that goes around and around. And know what? We're gonna have a Halloween party and we get to dress up and I'm gonna be a pirate. Mommy got me a eyepatch and a real sword, 'cept it's plastic." Sam (who had told Jeannette once that his only regret about his name was what happened to it when you added "Uncle") nodded and exclaimed in all the right places, and Jeannette, keeping an eye on Veronica, saw her sister relax under the warmth of his charm. "Brother mine" got a hug and a "You come by any time, that boy of mine adores you" when it was time to leave.

Jeannette hadn't felt so easy. Veronica didn't know what to look for, but Jeannette saw the wall of white light up around Sam like a shield. In the car, after he had turned on the heat against the settling October chill, she asked, "How did your trip go?"

He shook his head. "Let's leave that alone, okay?"

So Gil wasn't doing well. Jeannette had known that. And Sam didn't want to talk about it. It was his business, not hers, but she couldn't quit thinking about the fact that they were supposed to have a life together.

Now, in the Lewis Center, the lobby doors opened. People came in, a trickle at first that swelled to a stream. Jeannette saw elegant dresses, sparkling jewellery, elaborate feathery hats and polished dress shoes. She would never wear such a glittery look herself, but she couldn't help a glow of satisfaction about her own new dress. She had sprung for it out of her last paycheque: midnight blue, with an empire waist to hide her changing shape, and long sleeves that stressed her narrow wrists and small hands. Sam had admired her that evening before they left the house. She had told him she wanted the Maestro to have a pretty wife. Soon, her body would change too much, but she would try not to think about that.

Instead she admired the crowd coming in. Really, she couldn't guess when the Lewis Center had last gotten so full. Then, in a brief lull, Veronica appeared.

No sequined top and slit skirt; no slinky, curve-hugging silk dress. Veronica wore a plain brown skirt that fell to the tops of her perfectly ordinary flat shoes and a white blouse that buttoned up past her collarbone and revealed nothing of the bust or arms underneath. Where and when had she gotten those clothes? She had pulled her hair back into a twist and carried her corduroy jacket over her arm, as proper as a Victorian schoolmarm.

Eric the Usher greeted her. "Evening, ma'am. Ticket, please?"

Jeannette woke out of the shock. She had Veronica's ticket in her purse. She plunged out of the corner, digging under her compact and purse pack of tissues.

"Right here." She handed the ticket over. "Eric, by the way, I'd like you to meet my sister, Veronica Calhoun."

Eric tore off the top half of the ticket and handed Veronica the stub. "You're Mrs. Kraychek's sister? Pleased to meet you, ma'am. Have you been to a concert before?"

"Yes," Veronica said. One syllable. It took Jeannette a second to realize what was wrong with that. Veronica added, "It's been a while."

"Glad to have you back. You enjoy it, now."

Sam had put them in the prime seats, as always. Rich people seats. Veronica draped her jacket neatly over the back of her seat and opened her program book. "What are we listening to tonight?"

"Vee, why are you talking funny?"

Veronica looked at her over the top of the booklet. "Everybody here knows you, don't they? That boy by the door certainly did."

"What does that have to do with…" Then Jeannette understood. She felt like she had swallowed an egg-sized lump of ice.

Veronica nodded and went back to her program. "So. Let's see what we have here."

Jeannette slid down in her seat and opened her curled-up program book, not that she needed to look to see what the orchestra would play. No chorus tonight. The chorus was rehearsing for nothing but *Messiah*, all of it, for the December concert, exactly the way Sam had dreamed last year.

He had done it. He had filled this house. And now Veronica dressed funny and spoke funny, and Jeannette wished she could slide clear under the seat so that no one would see her and come up and start talking. *Everybody knows you.* She wished she could have told her sister that wasn't true.

The concert started with one of Mozart's most popular symphonies. You heard it all the time, on the radio, in movies, in TV commercials. Jeannette watched heads nodding in the rows in front of her as the violins launched into the theme. Mozart wrote catchy tunes, except you could hear this one two ways. On the surface it sounded light and fun. If you listened closely, you could hear the tension underneath, strange harmonies and shadows. Sam would never let a piece be exactly what people expected. As he guided the orchestra through it, the music sounded edgy and raw, the veneer of gentility so thin that the real and tormented soul lay exposed underneath.

Sam could do that. He could open a door, take you by the hand, and guide you through into a world you had never imagined. *Here,* the music said. *This is how life tastes. Try it and see.* The notes came to life, and Jeannette hung on each one. When the piece ended, Sam turned to the audience and embraced them all with his smile. Jeannette clapped until her palms stung.

The house lights came up after two curtain calls. Veronica picked up her purse. "Just going to the girls' room, honey."

Jeannette stood up too. "I'll come with you."

"That's all right. I know where it is."

"No, I need to use it too." For some reason, Jeannette didn't want to let her sister out of her sight.

They got as far as the back of the hall. In a momentary crush near the door, someone touched Jeannette's arm. "Evening, Mrs. Kraychek."

She looked up. It was Nathan Woods.

Jeannette had barely noticed his presence in the chorus since the past spring. She'd had far too much else to think about. Now, looking up at him, it struck her again how tall he was. She had gotten used to seeing him in some bright colour or other; he had a whole array of polo shirts in every colour of the rainbow, but tonight he wore a grey suit, white shirt, and navy tie. In the drab colours, he looked strangely extinguished. In contrast with Eric the Usher, who had greeted Jeannette with the same words, Nathan didn't look relaxed or friendly. There was something distant about him, something cold.

Jeannette drew herself up. She had never liked him and didn't now, but as the choral accompanist and Sam's wife, she had to be polite. "Evening, Mr. Woods." It felt funny to call him that; she had never really called him anything before. By the door, people were moving again, and Veronica started to follow. Jeannette stopped her. "Vee," she said, "this is one of the singers in the RSA chorus."

She introduced the two of them. Veronica gave Nathan a quick "Nice to meet you," and then said, "Excuse me, I need to find the ladies'," and disappeared through the hall doors.

Jeannette thought that was unnecessarily rude. Nathan didn't seem to register it. He asked her, "So how are you?"

Innocuous words, but Jeannette didn't like his tone. She could have sworn it had an edge behind it. He knew she didn't like him, maybe, and he thought she might make trouble for him with Sam? She wished she didn't feel uneasy standing here alone with him.

"I'm very well, thank you." At least she could match his chilly politeness. "How are you?"

"Fine, thanks."

Another pause. After a too-long second, he said, "I haven't had the chance to congratulate you on the coming arrival."

Sam had told the chorus about it, this time with Jeannette's approval beforehand. It made sense to let them know she wouldn't be back in the spring. Of course it had subjected her to ridiculous amounts of feminine giddiness from Pink Sweater Lady and her fellow altos and rounds of Twenty Questions about every baby-related topic they could think of, no matter how embarrassing. "Thank you," she answered.

"You're due in February?"

Jeannette lifted her chin. It felt barely decent to discuss such a thing with a man, especially this one. "Yes."

"The chorus will miss you."

That caught her off guard. Did he mean it? She certainly didn't expect *him* to miss her much. "I hope to come back later," she said, "when the baby's old enough."

Baby. The word sent a chill down her spine. *Mother.*

He said, "We'll hope you will."

Another searching look. Then he said, "All the best to you, of course," and turned on his heel and vanished as quickly as Veronica had.

What had that been about? Jeannette stood where she was, reflexively putting a hand on her stomach, as if that would help if the nausea started up again. That look on his face. He had seemed so *unfriendly*. All right, she didn't like him, but she had never been rude to him. She had hardly ever exchanged two words with him before. Why should he should look at her that way?

She found herself thinking about the night Sam had told the chorus about the engagement. The look on Nathan's face when he had come up to the podium, as if he had lost something that meant the world to him. That was ridiculous. He had no business looking like that either.

"Excuse me, aren't you Sam's wife?"

Jeannette turned to see a woman in a green-and-yellow feathery hat bearing down on her. Another donor, or a board member, somebody Jeannette didn't know. She couldn't talk to anybody now. "I'm sorry," she said, backing away. "Excuse me."

In the lobby she hesitated. She didn't want to go to the ladies' room, where she might find her sister in her schoolmarm outfit, and she couldn't stand around here either and risk running into Nathan again. Instead she hurried down the side hallway past the restrooms, to a backstage access. One of the ushers patrolled nearby but made no move to stop her as she pushed through the door.

This was the green room. It wasn't green at all, more white and brown, but that was what you called these places: combination rehearsal rooms, coat checks for the orchestra, and reception halls when you needed one. It was empty now, except for scattered jackets and open instrument cases. Jeannette leaned against the closed door and listened to her own hard, unsteady breathing.

She didn't know why she felt so shaken. Maybe she could go and find Sam. Nobody would interfere. Even he might not mind, in the middle of a concert or not, if she told him she wasn't feeling well.

And she really wasn't. Nausea gripped her. If only it would leave her alone. If only the baby would settle down and grow or whatever it needed to do.

If only it wasn't there at all.

What was wrong with her? She must not think such things.

If only it would disappear.

No. No. Nobody thought like this.

The nausea spiked. Jeannette scanned the room frantically and pounced on a plastic trash can just in time. She doubled up over it.

If only she could make it go away.

This was her punishment. She straightened up, choking down the sour taste in her throat. You thought awful things, and you deserved to get sick. At least it never lasted very long, because she didn't eat much anymore.

The green room had a water cooler in the corner. Jeannette poured herself a paper cup and drank it slowly. She had Tic-Tacs in her purse, back in the hall. She would go and get one and sit down to wait for Veronica, if her sister hadn't gotten back ahead of her.

Everything would be okay. Jeannette smoothed her skirt, opened the door, and let herself back out into the lobby, willing the world to stop spinning.

♫

The mint helped. More than that, Jeannette had the music. Modest Mussorgsky's *Pictures from an Exhibition* would raise the dead right out of the ground.

Sam had said the piece was over-played. All the great standards were. You would never think it to watch him lead the orchestra.

Jeannette sat up straight in her chair as the solo trumpet began the opening fanfare. You would have to be dead indeed if you didn't sit up when those sharp silver notes lanced the air. The deep brass and low strings joined in, and the earthy-sounding chords filled the room like the smell of pine.

When Jeannette was in high school, her teacher had let her try to learn the piano version of this piece. She'd had to figure out for herself that she didn't have the physical power it demanded. At first she had been disappointed when she practiced until she ached all over and still couldn't make the piano sing the way she wanted. Now she didn't know how one piano by itself could compete with the rainbow of sounds in this hall.

The second movement, "The Old Castle," had been the only section she played well. She closed her eyes now and let the ghostly litany wrap around her. In her mind she saw ruins, collapsed turrets and crumbled walls, the only remnants left of past and lost things.

Near the end of the movement, she opened her eyes to watch Sam. His face in profile had the intensity she only saw when he and the music were wrapped together. He might lock the door on his own thoughts sometimes, shut everyone—even her—out of his soul, but here, in this hall, that soul lay out in the open for everyone to see.

Past and lost things. Jeannette thought of Sam's mysterious colleague in Philadelphia. She didn't know anything besides Gil's name, didn't know what terrible struggle he was going through, but she knew he meant something to Sam. A lot.

Jeannette watched her husband now and understood. He was scared. His friend was very sick, Philadelphia was too far away from Richmond, and Sam couldn't be there all the time in case something happened. Maybe he didn't want to worry Jeannette with details. Maybe he would have liked to talk to her about it, but with the new house and the baby and everything they had to deal with, he thought he shouldn't.

Jeannette watched him onstage, under the light. He was so beautiful. *I love you*, she thought to him. *I know you must hurt. I want to help.* Tonight, before they left this hall, she would find a time to tell him she understood. She would tell him that he could share his sadness with her, however dark it was. She wanted to share everything.

"The Old Castle" faded away. The Pictures continued. Jeannette watched as the motions of Sam's hands and arms created every note: moments of intimacy and tenderness and moments so powerful the walls should have shivered and crumbled to dust. He created them all as if they had never happened before.

The last movement, "The Great Gate of Kiev," roared with brass, chimes, and tympani, and ended with final crashing blows on a huge copper gong. The sound blended without a break into the roar of the audience as they scrambled to their feet.

I'm so proud of you. Jeannette stood up with everyone else and clapped and clapped, while Sam faced them and bowed. After three curtain calls the audience didn't seem to get tired, and the players onstage drummed their heels on the floor, calling the Maestro back out to join them. Sam reappeared one last time, and Jeannette felt sure he looked straight at her. She blew him a kiss, blushing in the dark to think that she, of all people, had the right to love him.

The hall buzzed with talk as the house lights came up. Jeannette caught words like "incredible" and "out of this world." Veronica had joined in with the standing ovation. Now she bent down, collected her purse and drew on her jacket. "That was very nice."

Nice? Veronica truly was hopeless when it came to music. Jeannette laughed and took her sister's arm. "Well, come on and let's tell Sam you thought so."

Veronica gently disengaged herself. "No, honey. I'd better get home."

"What? Why? We were going to drive you."

"I know. But it's not far, and it's nice out, and Drew'll be waiting up."

Come to think of it, Jeannette hadn't seen Veronica smile once all evening. "Vee, come on," she said. "Sam wants to see you, and you don't want to walk home by yourself." Never mind that Jeannette had done it for weeks, back when she had first started her job. "Let's go say hi," she said. "I'll make sure he doesn't stay too late."

Veronica didn't answer but let Jeannette take her arm again. Jeannette didn't bother with the outside backstage access. The usher by the stage steps, another face she didn't recognize, waved her past. "Evening, Mrs. Kraychek! Great concert."

Of course Sam's dressing room was overflowing with people. That time Jeannette had come here alone in the dark felt like a thousand years ago. Now the receiving line went halfway down the hall. Jeannette could have pushed her way through, but these were all orchestra players in their regulation black, and she wouldn't budge in front of them. Veronica didn't protest at the wait. She stood silent, holding her purse.

Someone tapped Jeannette's shoulder. "'Scuse me? Mrs. Kraychek?"

It was the woman in the green-and-yellow hat that Jeannette had seen at intermission. The long feathers waved in their own personal breeze, like fronds of seaweed. She had florid orange hair too, Jeannette saw, and a round, pink face, and she beamed like a friendly toad.

"Yes," Jeannette said. "That's me."

The woman put out her hand. "I'm Barbara Whitaker. Babs." She had sunshine-yellow nail polish on. "I'm, gosh, it sounds silly to say, I'm a patron, I guess. This is my husband Skip. We've got RSA season tickets this year."

"Oh. That's lovely." Jeannette shook hands with Babs and with a small sandy-haired man in a sand-coloured suit, whom you would never notice while you took in his rainbow of a wife. "Did you enjoy the concert?" she asked.

"Oh, sure," Babs said. "Why, we don't know much about music, but we've heard a ton about Sam. We're new in Richmond, moved here in August."

Now Jeannette heard the thick twang in the woman's voice. Deep South. Texas? Mississippi?

Babs went on, "Skip joined the Rod and Skeet Club, and there's this dear man there, you know him, Bayard Keating."

"Yes. Of course."

"Well, he told Skip we just *had* to come hear this group. He said, 'That Sam Kraychek is a marvel!' And his wife Geraldine, she's the nicest lady, isn't she? She says to me, 'He has the loveliest wife, too. She's a redhead, dear, just like you.'"

Jeannette tried not to let her face show anything. Just like her?

Babs went on cheerfully, "Now, I wouldn't say our hair looks the same at all. Yours is much prettier. Lord, I bleached mine and did every dumb thing to it for years, you can tell, can't you?" At least she didn't give Jeannette time to answer. "But I saw this pretty redheaded lady, and I knew who you were, knew it right away!"

Jeannette said, "It's very nice to meet you. Please, let me introduce my sister." Veronica had been staring off into space, and Jeannette had to tug on her arm to get her attention. "Veronica, this is Babs and... Skip, was it?"

"That's right," Babs said. She reached out at once for Veronica's hand. Skip apparently was the silent partner in the marriage; he and Drew would have gotten along like a house on fire. "Veronica?" she said. "What a nice name."

Veronica drew herself up. "Thank you. Where are you from, Babs?"

Why had she asked that? Her voice sounded as flat as a spatula.

"Arkansas," Babs said cheerfully. "We always say Searcy, but really it's this little town called Bald Knob. Bald Knob, can you beat that?"

"What brought you to Richmond?" Veronica asked.

"Well, Skip here, if he don't mind me saying, he did real well in the automotive business, and when it came time for him to retire, we thought we'd see what life's like in the big city. We like it fine so far. People here are real nice."

The line had been moving slowly forward. Now Jeannette could see the door to the dressing room. Sam would be shaking hands with everybody, the way he did.

Another voice came through the murmur around them. "Excuse me. Do pardon us. Thank you so much, dear; I do beg your pardon."

Plum Pudding had a frond in her bonnet too, in an understated shade of lavender. It came past a row of orchestra people and waved up alongside the Whitakers.

"Hello, friends, hello." Plum's face creased into papery wrinkles when she beamed. "How lovely to find you all together."

She must have clothes in every shade of purple known to man. And she must sleep in that peacock brooch. Jeannette said, "Good evening, Mrs. Keating. So nice to see you."

"Now, Jeannette, dear, I can't have that anymore. Do call me Geraldine."

The General towered over the group. "That's right. You mustn't stand on ceremony with us, you know!"

Plum asked Jeannette. "How are you feeling tonight, dear? Are you quite well?"

"Yes. Thank you."

Babs leaned forward, making the green-and-yellow plumes twitch. "Why, what's the matter?"

Jeannette blushed again, torn between annoyance at having her personal business discussed and relief that she still didn't show enough for people to know right away. Plum answered for her. "Babs, dear, our Jeannette is"— she leaned forward too, to murmur—"in a delicate condition."

Jeannette saw comprehension dawn over Babs's pink face. "Oh! Well, for goodness' sake! Congratulations!" She wrung Jeannette's hand again. "When are you due? Is it a boy or a girl?"

The whole line could probably hear her. For a second Jeannette wished she could knock that silly feathery hat right off. "February," she said. "And we don't know yet."

Babs rounded on Veronica. "So you'll be an aunt!" she trumpeted. "I'll tell you, Skip and I, we don't have kids, but I just love his sister's babies. We spoil 'em all the time, and then we get to send 'em home!"

Veronica's face was a perfect blank. "Yes," she said. "My husband and I are looking forward to it."

Plum said, "So you see, Babs, it's very important that we show our support for our Maestro at this special time. We don't want him or Jeannette to have to worry about a thing."

Jeannette sucked in her breath. That meant money. Rich people always thought they could speak in code, and everybody else would be too stupid to catch on. Was that why the General had manoeuvred Sandy Skip into getting concert tickets, when he and Babs probably didn't know which end of a violin was up? Milk it wherever you found it?

"Yes, indeed," the General said. "As we mentioned before, Jeannette, the board will demonstrate its support in a particularly concrete manner."

He winked at her. Beside her, Jeannette felt her sister stiffen.

The General went on, "I'll bring this up with Sam, too, of course, but I can take the liberty of hinting to you that we won't find it necessary to wait until next season. After all, the holidays are around the corner."

Babs cut in, "I tell you what, you folks need any help, just put me and Skip down for whatever. This concert tonight was real nice. And," she added to Jeannette, "your husband, he's a looker, all right!"

Maybe the floor would open up. Maybe Jeannette could disappear.

Veronica said, "I'm sorry, folks. I need to be going."

"Vee, no." Jeannette clutched her arm again. "Please. Look, there's only a couple more people ahead of us."

"It's true, dear," Plum said. "Do stay. By the way, you look lovely this evening. That skirt suits you."

Veronica gently detached herself. "Thank you, but I do need to go. My husband's by himself with the kids."

The General was quickly solicitous. "Do you need a ride home? Our car is right out front."

Jeannette said, "No, Sam and I were going to drive her. Please, Vee."

"I'm fine." Veronica smiled then, but Jeannette could have been looking at her through glass. "It's a short walk. Goodnight, Nannie. Goodnight, folks."

She walked away. Jeannette watched her figure get smaller and smaller along the gauntlet of people behind them.

Babs said, "Well, it's true, kids are plenty of work!" She winked at Jeannette. "Better you than me, honey, but I do wish you all the best."

The line moved forward again. Jeannette blinked hard. Now the dressing room door stood open in front of them, and there was Sam, the white light gleaming on his collar and gold studs. "Evening, everyone!"

Plum said, "Good evening, dear. Marvellous performance," and the General boomed, "Magnificent. Simply magnificent. Sam, you know our new friends, don't you? Russell and Barbara Whitaker."

Russell? Jeannette felt herself brushed aside as Babs reached forward for yet another handshake. "No," she said eagerly, "we didn't meet you yet, but we've heard plenty about you. So this is a real orchestra you've got here!"

Sam laughed. "I hope it is. I'm so glad you could make it tonight." He looked at Jeannette. "Honey, where's Veronica?"

Jeannette's voice felt thinner than tissue paper. "She had to leave. She was worried about the boys."

"But—" Sam began.

"I know. She couldn't stay."

"She couldn't," the General affirmed. "I offered her a ride myself, but she said she didn't mind the walk."

Sam didn't look pleased. "Well, it isn't very far."

The open door jumped. One second Jeannette was looking at her husband, and the next second the walls blurred and skewed sideways. They righted themselves again and left her struggling to breathe.

Plum caught her arm. "Dear! Are you all right?"

Sam's warm, strong hand closed around Jeannette's. "Come sit down," he said. "You've been on your feet too long."

She let him lead her to the room's one hard-backed wooden chair. The Keatings and Whitakers fussed behind. Jeannette heard Babs say, "Does she need some water? Skip, go find her some water."

"I'm all right," Jeannette whispered. Her head felt stuffed with cotton. The spindles on the chair dug into her back. If only everybody else would go away, and she could be here alone in the dark again, like that night before everything happened. If only, in fact, she could turn the clock back to that time.

Sam's face floated above her. "Just rest," he said. "Take it easy for a minute."

He and the others moved back to the door. Plum said something Jeannette couldn't catch. Jeannette stared up at the cool white ceiling, which thankfully held still.

More people, more voices. The chair sat in the corner of the room, opposite the long mirror, so Jeannette didn't have to see anybody. With Sam in the doorway, apparently nobody could see her either. She closed her eyes. The line must be moving along. Sam said the same words again and again: "Thank you. Thanks so much. So glad you came." Each time, they sounded fresh and real.

Finally the door shut. Sam sighed. Jeannette opened her eyes and sat up straight. She had to remember the concert, how Sam needed to talk to her.

"That's that," he said. He looked worn out. "Thank God."

Jeannette started to get up, but he shook his head. "I'm going to change clothes. You keep resting."

He went into the closet of a bathroom. Jeannette didn't need to stay in this chair. She knelt on the floor to stack his scores neatly in his briefcase. When she slipped the baton into its case and set it alongside the pile, the bathroom door opened again. "Jeannette, what are you doing? I told you to stay put."

She looked up at him. In the jeans and sneakers and button-down shirt, he looked more tired than before, as though the concert clothes had been a suit of armour propping him up. His cheeks were flushed, and dark circles stood out under his eyes. Jeannette carefully got to her feet. The room stayed still. "I'm fine," she said. "Don't worry."

"Fine? You almost fainted back there."

"I'm sorry. I didn't mean to."

He shut his eyes tight and rubbed his forehead. "I know you didn't. I wasn't blaming you."

She went to him and touched his arm. Through the clean shirt, it felt feverishly warm. The hair at his temples was wet with sweat. "Are you mad at me?"

He let his breath out sharply and opened his eyes. They looked like dark pools. "Of course not. I'm worried, that's all. I don't like you being sick."

"I'm not. Pregnant's different."

She knew why he didn't like it. He was dealing with enough sickness. "I'm fine," she said again. Carefully, she smoothed the damp bangs away from his forehead. "I know you're stressed," she said. She conjured up the beautiful melody of "The Old Castle" and wrapped it around herself. "You can, you know, tell me about it."

He stepped back, away from her hand. "About what?"

"Your friend. Gil."

His face went still. "We don't need to discuss that."

She moved closer to him. "Sweetheart, you're upset." Only the picture of him there onstage, showing his soul to them all, let her keep going. "I want to help. I want to share it."

"You can't." Two syllables, dead and final.

"Why not?" Now anger warmed her. "I don't understand why you won't talk to me. For God's sake, I'm your wife!"

He looked just like his father. Immobile face and cold eyes. "You think I don't know that? I know exactly what my responsibilities are."

What did he think she was saying? "Sam." Half afraid to do it, she touched his cheek again, surprised to feel natural flesh warmth instead of finger-burning cold. "I love you, you know that. You take care of me fine. It's only, sometimes I feel like you don't talk to me."

"This is not something I need to talk about."

She made herself say it. "That's not true."

A taut line of muscle ran from his jaw down the side of his neck. "Jeannette. You have enough to deal with. We both do. The last thing I need is for you to worry about something that doesn't concern you and make yourself worse."

Make herself *worse*? What did that mean? More sick? More of a hassle for him?

"Of course I'm stressed," he said. "We're going to have a child. I need to be sure we're ready. The house, our finances, everything. I want you to be healthy."

"I am. I'm fine."

He ignored that. "And that means not upsetting yourself unnecessarily. The situation with Gil is my responsibility. I never should have mentioned it at all."

Frustration spilled out of her before she could stop it. "Sam, please, you can trust me, you can talk to me! I don't know why you don't think so!"

"I asked you before to leave this alone."

It would have been better if he had slapped her again. His voice was so cold; his eyes belonged to a stranger. Anything would have been better than this.

Maybe he saw how she felt. More gently, he said, "Now, it's late. We need to get home so you can get to bed."

She let him help her on with her jacket. The maple tree by the dumpster had gotten bigger since last fall, but this evening Jeannette had thought some of the bottom branches looked sickly and drooping. The old Pinto sat in its usual spot. Sam had talked about getting a better car. He didn't want to drive a half-trustworthy battered can once they had more responsibilities.

He put his briefcase in the back and made sure her belt was fastened securely. He worried about those things. She wanted to tell him he didn't have to, everything would be fine, but she couldn't. Not when he seemed so far away from her.

The belt had to stretch farther than usual now. Jeannette looked down at it as Sam pulled out of the space. By the time this was over, it would have to reach a lot farther yet.

If only it wasn't true.

Her husband didn't want to talk to her. Part of the reason for that was what she carried inside her body.

If only she could make it go away.

She let the words stay. The dark street flowed past on either side as they drove home in silence.

CHAPTER TWENTY-ONE

The baby was a girl. By the time Sam and Jeannette had the nursery furniture in place and a couple of drawersful of tiny pink and white clothing, Jeannette had taken Sam's hand and put it on her stomach to feel the next milestone. Sam tried not to let her see how that faint tap against his palm sent ice water trickling down his spine. Dear God. There really was a little person in there.

As the calendar flipped forward into December, Sam had a harder and harder time sleeping. The RSA would give a full *Messiah* performance this year, exactly as he had promised last fall. The board had approved a raise in Sam's salary, effective in January. Where the funds were coming from, God only knew. Sam imagined Bayard Keating levelling one of those pistols he must have at the men around the boardroom table and ordering them to turn out their pockets. Jeannette would end her tenure with the chorus soon. In February, the world would change. Meanwhile, in Philadelphia... but Sam would not think about that.

When insomnia hit, which it did more nights than not, Sam slipped out of bed and went to the nursery. When it—she—was born, he would be scared to breathe in this room. In the dark, he made out the crib's pale mattress through the railing and imagined a tiny shape in there. Suppose, when she was sound asleep, he did dare to reach in. Suppose he laid his hand on her back and felt the rise and fall of her breathing.

The day of the last *Messiah* dress rehearsal, two days before the concert, Sam woke up after a few hours of dozing. Jeannette lay asleep beside him in her usual pose, curled up on her side. She always put her hair up at night. Her red ponytail slipped down the back of her neck, making her skin look pale and fragile.

Sam eased closer to her, trying not to jostle the mattress. She had such a hard time getting to sleep. When he slid his arm under the sheet and rested his hand on her stomach, she didn't stir. The sheets were smooth and clean. Jeannette's skin was warm, faintly scented with the violet soap she used. The baby was quiet; sleeping too? Sam breathed the nearness of his wife and daughter.

After a while, Jeannette sighed. Her hand moved under the covers and settled on Sam's. "Hey," she whispered.

Sam kissed the back of her neck. "Did I wake you?"

She eased over onto her back and reached up to touch his face. "No. I think I just woke up."

Sun warmed the blankets and turned the white ceiling pale yellow. Sam propped himself up on one elbow to look at his wife's face. She had faint shadows under her eyes, but her cheeks had a rosy tint, warmer than her creamy-pale nightgown. Her smile reassured him. He asked, "Did you sleep okay?"

"Uh-huh. Did you?"

He didn't want her to worry about his insomnia. "Pretty well." He touched her stomach again. The taut curve of it, through the thin fabric of her nightgown, still seemed foreign to him. "How are you and the little one today?"

"Okay. She's being quiet, I think."

They always called the baby "she" and "the little one." They still hadn't talked about names. Some people did say you should wait until you saw the baby so you could pick a name that fit. Jeannette said, "I'll get the spare bedroom ready today."

Ma and Dad were coming down tomorrow for the concert. Sam would have to hope for some real sleep tonight or, more likely, pour a couple of gallons of coffee down himself in the morning. "Take it easy," he told Jeannette. "Don't strain yourself."

This morning she actually looked happy. "Don't worry," she said. "I can put sheets on a bed. I want to make sure everything looks good when they get here."

"It'll be fine. They'll love the house."

"Ma will."

Sam laughed. Ma had asked a couple of hundred questions at Thanksgiving and demanded to know why they hadn't brought pictures (the only ones they had were of the house in its "before" state, which Sam didn't want Dad to see), while Dad had only managed a comment or two about property values and mortgage APRs. Sam said now, "I think Dad'll be impressed too."

It was good to see Jeannette cheerful. The two of them had certainly had problems, and Sam knew whose fault that had been. If he thought about it, though, they had covered most of the major life changes now. Marriage, a new house, a baby on the way. When the baby was born, he and Jeannette would find their new footing. Life would get into some kind of pattern. Sam would be a better husband and would do his best to learn about fatherhood. It would have been nice if he could have asked somebody how it worked, for instance the one person who ought to know, but he and Dad had never had that kind of conversation.

When he left for the office, Jeannette walked him to the door to kiss him goodbye. Her white slippers engulfed her small feet, and her terrycloth bathrobe hung open, showing her stomach and the pale hollow of her throat. "Go back in the kitchen where it's warm," he told her. "And drink your tea." He made a cup of peppermint for her every morning.

"I will. See you late, I guess?"

"Around ten. But don't stay up if you don't want to. And if you need anything, you call, okay?"

She smoothed his bangs in the way that channelled Ma. "I will. I promise."

Sam knew he shouldn't worry yet about the biggest phone call of all, but every day it inched closer. He had a feeling Jeannette wouldn't go into labour when he was right there to take care of her. The call would definitely find him at the office. When he got there this morning, he shut his door, picked his way between the stacks of music on the floor, and opened the *Messiah* score on his desk. Lydia would answer if the phone rang in the main office. Sam tried to pretend he wasn't straining to hear it through the walls.

If he didn't know every note of *Messiah* by now, and every downbeat, cue, and cutoff, he was a lost cause. With the dress rehearsal tonight, though, and only coffee to keep his brain running, he couldn't leave anything to chance. A lot of money rode on this concert, which mattered. Ma and Dad had never been to an RSA concert before, which mattered more. And the music mattered most of all.

The RSA had come a long way in the past year. They could never have done this tour de force last December, even if the board had approved the expenses. Maybe Sam shouldn't have gotten hung up about the Keatings' wedding gift. It didn't seem possible, but maybe he had deserved it.

The music danced in his head, the way it should sound tonight, the way it should sound two days from now when he and his musicians sent their best shot at it out into the world. Sam was so caught up in it that he didn't hear footsteps coming down the hall. The knock on the door catapulted his heart into his throat.

"Come in." It came out as a squeak.

Lydia opened the door. "Phone call for you. Relax, it isn't Jeannette. It's from Philadelphia. Someone at Pennsylvania Hospital?"

She didn't know what that meant. Sam had not told her about Gil. He pushed his chair back.

This couldn't be anything serious. Maybe Gil knew about the concert (How? Had Sam mentioned it back in October?) and he was calling to say good luck. Or having Jonas Caruso say it for him, if he still thought he and Sam shouldn't talk.

Sam followed Lydia down the hall to the main office, one foot in front of the other. Maybe Gil had decided it was okay for them to talk after all. Maybe Sam would pick up the receiver and hear something like, "Good morning, Maestro, how are you?" Gil might even feel better, and his voice would sound like himself again.

Sam reached for the phone on Lydia's desk. His fingers didn't want to close around it, but he picked up the receiver. "Hello?"

"Mr. Kraychek? This is Jonas Caruso calling."

The unshakably calm veneer had a hairline crack in it, and Sam knew. He stared at the corner of Lydia's desk, at a dark knot in the wood. "Yes," he said.

"I'm very sorry to tell you that Mr. Hart passed away this morning."

One minute Sam was standing in a room with a solid floor and solid walls. The next, he hung in space, holding the cold, clunky phone receiver in his hand.

"Mr. Kraychek?"

Sam didn't want to open his mouth. He didn't want to move, ever again.

"Mr. Kraychek, I'm very sorry."

"Thank you," somebody said. Sam felt his lips move, so the voice might have been his.

Caruso said, "I'm afraid I have no information regarding funeral arrangements. I understand Mr. Hart's brother will take care of that. If you like, I will learn what I can and pass it along."

Gil's face on the pillow, that first visit. *You would think I didn't have a brother.* Gil's body lying in a casket. "No," Sam heard the strange person say. "That isn't necessary."

"You would rather not be informed about funeral arrangements?"

"No. I would rather not."

Silence. After a while, Caruso said, "Mr. Kraychek, is there anything I can do?"

Sam felt his lips move again. "No. Thank you."

"I'm very sorry. Please accept my sympathy."

Sam didn't know if he answered. The receiver was in his hand, and then it wasn't. The knot in the desk hovered in front of him.

The hospital. Sam saw it all again: the corridor with rooms like tissue boxes, the rain on the window, the supply closet, and the heavy smell of laundry detergent.

I love you.

Gil's hands on the blanket. His too-thin fingers, his hollow cheeks. His eyes, still the same shade of blue.

I love you.

"Sam."

Somebody touched his shoulder. Sam couldn't move.

"Sam?"

Lydia. Yes. This was her office. Her desk. "I'm sorry," Sam said.

"For what? Sam, what's wrong?"

A hand touched Sam's face. It didn't belong there. Sam turned his head.

Lydia's eyes, behind her glasses, looked like big blurry marbles. A strand of steel-coloured hair curled under one ear. Sam could see each one of the lines at the corners of her mouth. Her lips moved and her voice reached him. "What is it? Tell me."

As if he could. As if anyone would know what it meant that this one person was gone forever.

"A friend," he said. The syllables sounded blank and empty. He had to work for each one. "A friend of mine, in Philly. He died this morning."

Lydia's wide eyes went wider. "Oh." A hand closed around his arm. "I'm so sorry."

I'm sorry. It had never been enough when Sam said it. He wished he could crawl into a hole in the dark.

Lydia said, "You need to sit down. Stay here a while. I'll give you some space."

He stood still as she moved around him, scooping papers up off her desk. They rustled. "The door will be locked," she said. "Don't worry about the phone." He heard the door shut behind her, and then it was just him and the desk and the phone and the harsh white winter light through the window.

He did not want to move again. It hurt—oh, how it hurt—to pick up one foot and take one step, then another.

Lydia's chair had brown plastic cushions and a swivel seat. Sam dropped into it and put his head in his hands.

Suppose a knife gashed your palm. You didn't feel it at first. You only saw the blood well up on your skin.

The office smelled of ink and paper. Through his fingers, Sam saw the neatness of Lydia's desk. One stack of papers here, another there. A pen holder with ballpoints in it. A box of paper clips. The desk itself looked old and worn, with dark lines in the grain.

At first you didn't feel the knife that cut you. Then your skin woke up out of numbness, and the pain turned into a line of fire.

Sam closed his eyes. In the dark, time unspooled.

Suppose Gil had not gotten sick. Suppose Sam had left, sure enough, and Gil had gotten involved with somebody else, but that person had been healthy.

Suppose later on, Gil and that person had broken up, and Gil had called Sam to say hey, I was thinking about you, how are things? And then suppose the rest of it had gone exactly the way it did, with Sam moving to Richmond, Gil staying in Philly... but Gil had not been sick.

Sam floated in the dark. He and Gil would have talked every now and then, the way they did in real life. "Maestro, how are you?" They might have visited once in a while. And when Sam had a major concert—say, the first time he conducted all of *Messiah*—Gil would have taken the train from Philly to Richmond, and Sam would have met him at the station.

Pain seared through Sam's body, not only a line of fire but a branching tree that dug into every cell and scorched along every nerve. Gil had told him to go home. *He felt it would be best. Your wife. Caroline.*

Sam could not move. He sat, eyes closed to shut out the harsh white light, and let the pain take him.

CHAPTER TWENTY-TWO

Jeannette had finished wrestling the brand-new fitted sheet onto the brand-new guest bed when the phone rang. She had to puff her way down the hall to the master bedroom to answer it. At seven months, normal clothes and normal walking had become a fond memory.

She picked up the phone. "Kraychek residence."

"Jeannette, honey. It's Ma."

Jeannette still usually called her "Anna" in her head, as if to remind herself that the older woman was only a borrowed mother. Aloud, she said, "Hi, Ma, how are you?"

"I need to talk to you. Do you have a minute?"

She didn't sound right. Jeannette sat down on the bed, hoping the news wasn't that Anna and Dr. Kraychek couldn't come down for the weekend and the *Messiah* concert after all. "Sure," she said. "What's going on?"

"Liudas asked me to call you. He's had some difficult news."

Jeannette knew perfectly well who Liudas was. She still had to process it before it made sense. "Sam asked you to call me? But why? He's at his office, he could have called himself."

"I know. He thought it would be better if I told you."

Jeannette automatically looked around for the nearest trash can, which stood by the ironing board in front of her closet. "What's wrong?"

Anna cleared her throat. "He had a phone call today, from Philadelphia. His friend Gil passed away this morning."

Jeannette felt a kick at her insides and clamped a hand on her swollen stomach. "Gil—Gil died?"

"Yes." Anna's voice sounded light and too far away. Over the phone, you shouldn't be able to hear all the miles between Richmond and Westbury. Anna said, "Liudas is taking it pretty hard."

Jeannette could have guessed that. She remembered the aftermath of the last concert, that horrible *I never should have brought it up*. She knew exactly how Sam's face would look when he came home tonight.

And he hadn't wanted to call her himself. Dear God. He had gotten the news, there in his office she guessed, and he had been able to pick up the phone and call his mother and ask *her* to tell Jeannette. As if, what, he couldn't stand to talk to his own wife at a time like this? As if Jeannette wasn't good enough?

A shriek started somewhere deep inside her. By the time it reached her throat, it had shrivelled into a whisper. "Why didn't he call me himself?" *Why? Why? Why?*

Anna's voice reached out for her. "He didn't want you to be upset. Especially now. He wasn't sure he could be calm about it, so he thought it would be better coming from me."

"But... but..." Jeannette couldn't find the words to say how much worse it was that he had done it this way. *He's shutting me out. Nailing the door up!*

Anna said, "I told him no matter how upset he was, you might still rather if he called. He said he thought it was best if the two of you didn't talk about it. At least not right away."

No! No! "Why does he do that?" Jeannette realized how helpless she sounded. Tears came out of nowhere. "Why won't he talk to me? What did I do wrong?"

"Honey," Anna began.

Jeannette couldn't listen. "He's going to walk in here looking like somebody ran over him with a truck, I just know it, and he won't let me help! He won't talk to me! Why? Somebody please tell me why!"

"Jeannette. Calm down, now. You need to try to calm down."

Jeannette closed her eyes. She was snuffling and whimpering like a child, and she couldn't do anything about it. Anna said, "Get a tissue. Do you have any right there? I'll hold on so you can go get some."

"I have some." Jeannette stretched over to her side of the bed and fumbled for the box on the nightstand. Her stomach hated being pulled like this. Too bad.

She blew her nose. When she quieted down, Anna said, "Listen, honey, I know this is hard. Liudas can be very private about some things."

Jeannette knew that. Did she ever. "I'm his *wife*," she mumbled into a fresh tissue.

"Yes, and he wants to do right by you. You know that, don't you?"

Jeannette guessed she did. "But I don't understand." She sniffled again. Ugh, she'd dripped onto her turtleneck. God knew she never wanted to wear this orange maternity monstrosity again: *it's the Great Pumpkin, Charlie Brown!* She said, "Wouldn't it be right to talk to me?" You didn't say that to a mother-in-law. Essential rule of marriage: never tell her when her son is wrong.

When Anna answered, she didn't sound irritated. If anything, mystifyingly, she sounded nervous. "Honey," she said, "you know, sometimes people go through things. Things happen to them. And then they decide they want to change something, so they have to let the past be the past."

What was this? "I don't understand," Jeannette said again. She wrapped the wet tissues in a clean one and wadded the ball in her palm. "Do you mean something happened to Sam?"

She had never been clear why he had gotten estranged from his parents. And then there had been all that business with the church. Too many secrets. She was too tired to deal with them.

Anna said, "He went through a difficult time a while ago, when he was in college."

"He told me that. A little, anyway."

Anna hesitated. "There were things he wanted to change, afterward."

"Like what?"

"I can't really speak for him, honey. I'm sorry."

Of course she couldn't. Jeannette should have known better. "I shouldn't ask."

"No, you want to know. That's natural. But, you see, Gil was part of that time. And I think Liudas is trying to think how to manage it."

Manage what? How did you manage the fact that your friend had died? "What does he want me to do?"

Anna spoke carefully, choosing the words one at a time. "I think he'd like to be left alone about it."

Of course he would. "He doesn't want me to say anything."

"I think he'd rather you didn't. Just for now."

Except it wouldn't be "just for now." "He wants me to act like I don't know about it?" Jeannette heard her voice spiralling up again, accusing. "Pretend everything's normal?"

"I would give him some room," Anna said. "Let him decide whether to bring it up."

Jeannette shook her head. The tears were coming again. She should act more grown-up than this.

As if Anna saw into her head, she said, "I know this is hard. Please try to remember, honey, he's doing the best he can."

"I don't understand *what* he's doing."

Long pause. Through her own gulping and sniffing, Jeannette thought she heard the other woman sigh.

Anna said carefully, "Jeannette, I don't know how much Liudas told you about that time in college. What happened. He did tell you he left home for a while."

"Yes." Jeannette wanted to say, *He told me his father threw him out.* Except she wasn't going to cast it up to this woman that Dr. Kraychek had done something bad, too, on top of complaining about Sam. She did add, "He told me you didn't want him to go."

"Yes. I tried to talk him out of it. I couldn't." Another pause. "When I watched him leave, I didn't know when, or if I would see him again. I don't know if you can imagine that."

She still hurt. Jeannette could hear it. "Ma," she said quietly, "please tell me what happened."

"Oh, honey, it's not mine to tell." Before Jeannette could protest, Anna went on, "Liudas and his father had a disagreement. They'd had others before. A lot of the time, they didn't see eye to eye. That last time, they both said things. Hurtful things."

Almost verbatim what Sam had said. "What did they fight about?" Jeannette tried to remember what Sam had said about that. Music, wasn't it? What Sam wanted to do for a living?

Anna didn't say so. She said, "That isn't mine to tell either."

This didn't feel right. What harm would it do to say, "He didn't like Sam's choice of career?" Surely such an old fight didn't matter anymore. "But…" Jeannette cast around, trying to put threads together. "But Gil was involved somehow?"

"Liudas and Gil were friends at that time. Gil was part of a world that I think Liudas decided he had to stay away from."

What did that mean? Jeannette had the strangest feeling that Anna was trying to tell her something without actually saying it. Anna went on, more steadily now, "My point, honey, is that none of us did things right, back then. Liudas felt he'd made mistakes. I know that. His father and I, we haven't talked about it much, but I think we both made our share too. Over and over, I thought about what I should have done, what I should have said, so Liudas wouldn't have had to leave." Those words had no hidden agenda. They were about a mother's pain, pure and simple. "I never want another time when he's so far away from us. So what I want to say to you is, please, try to be patient. I know Liudas wants to do right by you. He wants to do the right thing. If he makes mistakes… well, we all do."

Jeannette was more confused than ever. Was she saying if Jeannette wasn't careful, Sam might leave? Jeannette had never considered the possibility. God help her if he ever did. And what was all this about mistakes? Sam knew it was a mistake not to talk to her, Jeannette, but he couldn't help it?

Jeannette mumbled, "You're still coming down tomorrow, right?"

"Yes. We are."

One word came out of Jeannette's gut. "Good."

When Anna laughed, it felt like spring sunlight. "Everything's going to be all right, honey. Try not to worry."

That was fine to say. Once in a while, though, Jeannette would trade "going to be" for "is." "Okay," she said. "I'll try."

"Now, let's talk about something happy. How's our little girl doing today?"

That was happy? Jeannette tried to muster some enthusiasm. "She's fine. She was kicking a few minutes ago. She's quiet now." She still had a hard time not saying *it*.

"Oh, honey, I know you'll think I'm a broken record, but you can't imagine what it's going to be like for you. It's the most wonderful thing."

If you want this baby, you can have it. Her. The words went through Jeannette's head before she knew it. Then she heard them, and how wrong they were, but in the same second she realized how desperately she wished she could do exactly that: hand this little human, this strange occupant of her body that made her nauseous and stretched her all out of shape, over to somebody who loved and wanted and would care for her.

Mama.

Out loud, she said, "I'm nervous."

Anna laughed. "Of course you are. Everyone is. I know I was."

"You were?" Jeannette would have guessed Anna had practically been born knowing how to change diapers.

"Oh, sure. Why, honey, I'll tell you something. A week or two after Liudas was born, this one day I thought I'd done something awfully wrong. I don't even remember what it was anymore, do you believe that? Anyway, Walter was at the office and we were still new in the neighbourhood, and I was out of my head with worry. So I called up our neighbour, Mrs. Rabinowitz. She was one of these tough old ladies that looked like she was carved out of wood. I cried and told her whatever it was I'd done, and said I knew I'd made the most awful mistake, and do you know what she told me?"

"What?"

"She said"—Anna made her voice nasal, with an edge on it like a carving knife—"*Of course you did. And you'll make a lot more. And he will survive them all.*"

In spite of herself, Jeannette laughed. "Did you feel better?"

"Can you believe it, I did. That was one no-nonsense old lady."

For a minute they were both quiet. Jeannette thought, *Mama. Grandma.* The baby would have a grandmother. That was some comfort. Then Anna said, "I should let you go, honey. I'm sure you're busy."

Jeannette didn't want her to hang up. "Not really. I was just fixing the guest bed for when you get here."

"I can't wait to see your house. From what you told us at Thanksgiving, it sounds lovely."

"It is. It's kind of big."

"It'll fill up fast. One baby can make more difference than you'd ever think."

Jeannette pictured C.J. and Ricky tearing around the apartment. Maybe a girl would be quieter. It was her only hope.

Anna said, "Now, I should go sort out our packing for the weekend. Will you be all right, honey?"

Jeannette's heart sank right down into the soles of her swollen feet. "I guess."

"You will. We'll see you tomorrow."

"See you tomorrow."

After they hung up, Jeannette sat on the bed, looking miserably down at her drip-stained turtleneck. She looked ridiculous. Between now and the end, it would only get worse. She wished she could get this thing out of her body and be done with it.

Now she was supposed to sit here and wait for Sam to get home, looking like someone had yanked all his teeth out without Novocain, and she wasn't supposed to say anything to him about the only thing he would have on his mind. She could go to bed and pretend to sleep, but she would have to deal with him eventually. Tomorrow. You couldn't sleep forever.

She wished she could. Just lie down and sleep until after the baby was born.

If only they had a piano. Jeannette missed her spinet, and they hadn't gotten the grand yet. She had a harder time playing now; she had to push the bench farther back than she liked to fit her stomach in, and she had to reach around the bulk of herself for the keys. Still, when she sat up in front of the chorus, she forgot about her swollen stomach and her aching back and feet, and Sam up there on the podium looked like the man she had fallen in love with a year ago. In those moments, everything did seem all right.

But soon she wouldn't have moments like that again. No more chorus for a long time. She would be stuck here in this huge house, drifting around like a ghost, with only a shrieking baby to keep her company.

No. Jeannette hauled herself to her feet. The silence in the house pressed in on her like fog. She wasn't going to sit here and let it swallow her.

Sam didn't want to talk about Gil? But Jeannette did. She wanted her husband to talk to her.

I love you, Sam, don't you see that? Why didn't he trust her? What didn't he want her to know? What was the… what had Anna said? The "world he had to stay away from?" Why did Gil matter so much, and why wouldn't Sam tell her?

Jeannette was going to do something. She couldn't call Veronica for help, because even Veronica didn't talk to her like she used to. That was wrong too. Veronica felt like she and Jeannette belonged to two different worlds now, as if Jeannette had, for the first time in their lives, gone somewhere where her sister couldn't follow. Jeannette would have to fix that, but right now there was no time. She had to take care of this other problem first, and she had to do it by herself.

The cab had a twenty-something black driver with enormous hair. Not long ago, Jeannette would have had to work up her nerve before she could get into a car alone with a strange black man. Now she didn't care. When the cab pulled up in front of the Lewis Center, she opened her mouth to tell the driver to go around back but changed her mind. She could go in the front. She was the Maestro's wife, after all.

She picked her way up the flight of wide, shallow steps, holding onto the brass railing. A welcome gush of warm air met her in the red and gold lobby.

The security guard looked up from his desk. "Afternoon, Mrs. Kraychek."

Good thing Jeannette had at least changed out of the pumpkin shirt. This lobby shouldn't make her want to shrink into a ball anymore. "Hello, Mr. Johnson."

"Are you here to see Mr. Kraychek? Would you like me to call his office for you?"

Jeannette hitched her purse higher on her shoulder and wrapped her wool coat around as much of her as she could. "No, thank you. I'll go ahead over."

"Yes, ma'am. You have a good day, now."

"Thank you. Same to you."

To get to the offices, you had to go through to the backstage access and past the dressing rooms to the rear staircase. You could take the stairs down to the basement or up to the narrow brown hallway that looked like the ones you got in old school buildings, with beat-up linoleum and a smell of dusty wood and narrow windows that didn't let in enough daylight to cancel out the permanent shadows. Sam's office was up there.

Jeannette reached the staircase and hovered in front of the door that led outside. Through its small square window, she saw the maple tree by the dumpster. It had long since lost all its leaves. The bottom branches looked sickly for sure. That wasn't a good place for a tree, trying to force its way up through concrete.

Sam's Pinto sat in its usual place. Jeannette drew a breath and reminded herself why she had come here.

I love you, Sam. I want you to talk to me.

No secrets.

If she didn't do this now, she never would. Clamping her purse tighter under her arm, she marched up the stairs.

Sam's office was at the end of the hall. He had said once he thought it must be a converted broom closet. It had enough room for one small desk and two chairs, and it had a sliver of window that looked out onto Jefferson Street. Sam, being Sam, had filled up the desk, and the windowsill, and whatever part of the floor he didn't actually need to walk on, with music.

The RSA's main office was a slightly bigger room opposite the stairway landing. When Jeannette came into the hall, Lydia Holland, Sam's orchestra manager, was on her way in there. She saw Jeannette and stopped with her hand on the doorknob.

"Jeannette! What brings you here?"

Lydia was a no-nonsense woman, much taller than Jeannette. Jeannette swallowed and drew herself up as straight as she could. "I want to see Sam. Is he in his office?"

Lydia's only softness came from her old-Virginia lilt. "Yes," she said. "But right now he's…"

"Busy. I know. I just need to talk to him for a minute."

Lydia let go of the doorknob. "Do you want me to get him?"

"No, thank you." Jeannette could manage to find her own husband. "I'll go down myself."

She walked away. For some reason she felt sure Lydia was watching her. Well, Jeannette wasn't supposed to be here, and no doubt Sam was in a terrible mood.

Her footsteps sounded too loud in the hallway. She had better get her thoughts together. *Sam, I talked to your mother. She told me about Gil. Sweetheart, I don't like you keeping everything to yourself.* He would go silent. She could see his white face, the set line of his mouth. *I want you to talk to me. I told you I didn't want secrets.*

So what if he got angry. She was angry too. *I should never have brought it up,* he had said, as if she were a stupid child who couldn't handle anything.

By God, they would have an actual child on the scene soon. Sam would have to hope Jeannette wasn't as helpless as he seemed to think. He didn't want her getting upset about things that didn't concern her? This did concern her. He was her husband, and he had...

...let the past be the past...

What did those words mean? Who *was* Gil, anyway? As Jeannette stood here on her two feet, she was going to get some answers.

Her own breath and pulse were so loud in her ears that she had put her hand on the doorknob of Sam's office before she heard the voices. Or, to be more accurate, one voice. A deep, rich, chocolate voice, murmuring something Jeannette couldn't make out.

Another sound came through the dusty old wood. Someone crying.

Jeannette turned the knob. The door opened.

The harsh light through the window back-lit the scene. Sam sat with his back to the door. He was hunched forward in his chair, his head in his hands. He was sobbing.

Jeannette froze. She had never heard him cry before. She had never heard any sound, ever, with so much pain in it.

If he had been alone, she would have run to him. She would have wrapped her arms around him and begged him to share his hurt with her. She would have taken it all on herself if she could.

She couldn't go to him. He wasn't alone.

Nathan Woods sat in the chair next to Sam, so close to him that no sliver of light showed between their two bodies. His arm, in its bright green shirtsleeve, was wrapped around Sam's shoulders. Jeannette heard him say quietly, "It's not your fault. Don't ever think it's your fault."

Sam seemed to run out of tears. He wiped his face with the back of his hand. "I should have gone back," he said, so low that Jeannette barely caught it. "Why didn't I?"

"Angel, you were dealing with so much. He wouldn't want you to torture yourself like this. I know he wouldn't."

Angel. Jeannette couldn't keep quiet. Words barrelled up into her throat and out through her mouth, which opened by itself to let them go.

"What's going on?"

For the space of a heartbeat, nothing happened. The words rang in the air. Then Nathan looked around. His arm didn't leave Sam's shoulders. When his eyes met Jeannette's, she saw, clear as day, *You're not welcome here.*

Sam turned to face her. She had never seen him look so tired. "Jeannette." He didn't sound alarmed or angry, only exhausted. "Why are you here?"

Jeannette's prepared words sprouted wings and flew away. "I," she stammered. "I came because..." Nathan still hadn't let go of him. The black man's eyes stayed on her, watchful, unfriendly. "Sam," she said, "please, tell me what's wrong."

Sam looked at Nathan. At *Nathan.* Who asked, as if Jeannette wasn't standing right there, "Does she know?"

Sam drew his chair back from Nathan's and disengaged himself. "I assume so." To Jeannette he said, "You know Gil died this morning."

He sounded like he didn't care about *her* at all. Terror put out feelers in Jeannette's stomach. "Yes," she said. "Your mother called."

"Then you know what's wrong."

"Yes."

"And you came here because?"

"Because I... because..." The fear climbed up the insides of Jeannette's stomach, lining that swollen cavern, clinging to her flesh. "Sam, why didn't you call me? Why did she have to? *Why won't you talk to me?*"

Her voice came out as close to a scream as it ever got. Down the hall, the main office door opened.

Nathan said, his voice as dark and flat as deep water, "Jeannette, this isn't a good time."

"Who are *you* to tell me that?" She was yelling now. "How dare you tell me not to talk to him? He's *my* husband! *Mine!*"

Somebody came down the hall. Somebody gripped Jeannette's elbow. "What's the matter here?"

Lydia. Jeannette yanked her arm away. "I want to know what's going on!" she shouted. "I want somebody to give me answers right now!"

A heat haze blurred the air around her, but the tentacles in her stomach stretched and spread and she felt so cold, so very cold, because a new idea blew in on an icy breeze.

...let the past be the past...

...a world he decided he had to stay away from...

...and the television in Veronica and Drew's apartment, the newscaster talking about the mystery disease, AIDS, and the way Sam's face had looked...

No. No. Nonono.

Sam had stood up. Jeannette made out that much through the blur of terror, but Nathan was faster. His tall dark shape loomed up, swelling, sucking the air out of the room, and then he was in front of her and his hand caught her arm and he pulled her after him, down the hall and through the doors to the stairway landing. Before she could protest at how hard his fingers gripped her or how he had dragged her along so her feet hardly touched the ground, he took her shoulders and pushed her, gently but firmly, down onto a step.

"Put your head down." His voice didn't sound like chocolate now. It sounded rough, like tree bark that would leave your fingers scraped and bloody. "Between your knees."

She couldn't do it. Her stomach got in the way, but for some reason she tried anyway, craning forward till her chin bumped against her own distended belly. From somewhere far above, she heard him say, "Sam doesn't need you sick right now. He doesn't need you passing out. Get a grip on yourself."

Who the hell was he to talk to her like this? And where was Sam, anyway? Shouldn't he be here with her? Shouldn't he *care*?

The dizziness faded. Jeannette raised her head, brushing stray hair out of her face. Nathan stood over her with his arms folded.

Surely she was dreaming. None of this was really happening. In a minute she would wake up on the spare room bed at home, where she had, yes, drifted off after she got the sheets on, because she didn't sleep well these days.

Nathan said, "Listen. I don't know how much Sam wants to tell you. It's not my place to say a damn thing. But if you come tearing down here like this, and you get sick, or something bad happens, he can't handle that."

He was staring down at her like a judge. Jeannette didn't know why she should be scared of him, but she was. Oh, she was.

"And," he went on, "I don't want you getting any wrongheaded ideas about what you just walked in on, so I'll tell you right now, your husband is faithful to you. You understand?"

No. She didn't. Her anger had drained away like bathwater when you pulled the plug. Now the cold from the step under her seeped up into her body and met the branching cold in her stomach. She should tell this man off. Instead she heard herself whisper, "You're mad at me." When she was the one who should be angry.

"Yes. You're making it worse for him. And I don't sit back and watch that happen to someone I love."

Someone he *loved*. Jeannette couldn't process the word. Pieces of a puzzle, scattered in wide-apart corners of her brain, began to squirm toward each other. They reached out, found matching protrusions and empty spaces, slotted into place... but they must not.

Nathan's voice softened. "You don't mean to hurt him. I believe that. You don't know what the deal is, do you."

"No," she whispered. "I don't." She didn't want to know. All she wanted was to be back in the house on Calvert Street, smoothing a fitted sheet on a bed. Or maybe she wanted to be further back still, at Veronica and Drew's. Maybe she wanted never to have left that place, with the yellow Formica table and the chairs squashed in around it and the faces and voices she understood.

"It's not my place to tell you," Nathan said. Almost Anna's exact words. It was nobody's place to tell Jeannette anything, and that was fine with her. Nathan said, "For what it's worth, I think Sam should come clean with you. I'll tell him that. He's made his choices, and he's doing his best to stick to them." Jeannette wished she had the strength to stick her fingers in her ears and sing "The Star-Spangled Banner" the way you did to shut out the taunts of children, if you were brave enough. She never had been. Nathan went on, "I respect that, even though I don't agree with what he's doing, and I don't think it's fair to him, or you. But for now, I can tell you he called me when he found out about Gil because he thought I would understand. I came here because I do understand. That's all."

"Okay," Jeannette whispered.

Nathan looked down at her. His face seemed to fill her whole vision. He didn't look like a judge anymore, not the human kind who would wear a black robe and sit on a bench. He looked much worse than that. Why did people think God was white?

"You love him," he said.

"Yes." Oh, God, yes. Even if, right now, she wished she had never seen his face.

Nathan shook his head. "There's going to be tough times. No matter how you cut it."

Jeannette didn't know what that meant either. She didn't want to.

Nathan said, "Try to hold on to one thing. Sam never meant to hurt you. When he thinks he's hurt somebody, he doesn't forgive himself."

"Okay." She would have said anything. Done anything. Whatever it took for everybody to leave her alone.

Footsteps came down the hall, and the door to the landing swung open. Sam came over to her and took her hands in his. He looked so tired that every nerve in her body ached for him. "I'm so sorry, honey," he said. "It's a tough day, that's all. Later on, we'll talk about everything, I promise."

She nodded. *We don't have to. Please. Don't tell me.*

"Let's get you home." He helped her to her feet and waved away Nathan's offer to get a cab. "I'll drive her. It's not far." He led her down the stairs to the back entrance. "We should get you a better coat," he said, opening the door to let her out ahead of him. "That one's not warm enough."

She let him take care of her the way he always did. The puzzle pieces squirmed and twitched in her head, wanting to join together like the links of a chain.

The maple stood by the dumpster. In the harsh winter light, it drooped like a tired old horse whose time was done.

By the time Sam came home from the dress rehearsal of *Messiah*, which he'd driven back for after he dropped her off at home, Jeannette had taken the hottest shower she could stand and crawled into bed. The shivering didn't stop all night. It hadn't stopped the next morning when she woke out of a hazy half-dream in which she was trying to climb an endless flight of stairs under harsh white light. She found Sam in the kitchen. He had made a pot of coffee, and he turned around and smiled at her as if nothing at all had happened yesterday.

"Hey. Did you sleep okay?" He pulled out her chair at their small round table. He had already dressed and shaved, and he looked fresh and clean; she found herself thinking of a branch of a pine tree with clear drops of rain on it. By contrast, she was bloated and puffy in her rumpled bathrobe, her face swollen, her feet stuffed carelessly into beat-up slippers.

"Uh-huh," she lied. "Did you?"

"Pretty well. I'll put your tea on."

She should ask him how the rehearsal had gone. She couldn't.

When the tea was ready, he brought her a mug. He sat down across from her, set his coffee down, and reached for her hand. "Honey, I know we need to talk."

This close, she saw the tiredness in his face and a small red line on his chin where he had cut himself shaving. Her stomach churned when his skin touched hers. She tried to pretend it was the smell of the coffee.

"I know you're worried," he said. "I haven't been fair, not talking to you."

The puzzle pieces had inched closer together in her mind, and now she had to strain every nerve not to let them join. "It's okay," she said.

"It's not. I know that. I haven't wanted you to worry, and you know, I've been going a little crazy with everything on our plates. I didn't think I should burden you. But you're right, I need to be honest with you."

His eyes—still such a beautiful colour, even with the shadows around them—looked straight into hers. He took a breath. He was going to tell her the truth, or a lie, it didn't matter which. She didn't want to hear it, and she tried to open her mouth to stop him, but the shivering got worse and her knees, wedged in under the table, started to shake, and then the table itself began to tremble.

"Jeannette!" In one quick motion he stood up and pulled his chair around next to hers. "What's the matter?"

"I'm cold. Just cold."

His hand felt cool on her forehead. "Oh, sweetheart, I think you've got a fever." He got up again. "Stay right there."

She sat. His footsteps went away down the hall and disappeared up the stairs. She gripped her hands tight together, but that didn't stop the chills that shook her.

He came back in with the thermometer and took her temperature. A hundred and one. She wasn't surprised. She had done this to herself, flying down to the Lewis Center through the freezing cold like a crazy woman. She let him lead her back upstairs to bed.

His parents arrived that afternoon. Jeannette submitted when Sam insisted Dr. Kraychek should take a look at her. She held another thermometer in her mouth, took deep breaths, and felt surprisingly indifferent about her father-in-law examining her misshapen body. Dr. Kraychek was methodical and detached. There was no danger to the baby, he said. Did anything hurt? She shook her head. She didn't feel sick, really, except for the nausea that wouldn't go away and the shivering that didn't let go, despite three layers of covers. Dr. Kraychek gave her Tylenol to bring down the fever.

On Saturday morning, Anna made chicken broth. She brought a steaming bowl up to Jeannette at lunchtime and sat by her to make sure she finished it. "Do you want me to stay here with you tonight?" she asked.

Jeannette shook her head. "I'm okay, Ma." She had finally stopped shivering. Maybe it was the Tylenol. "You should go to the concert."

"I hate to leave you here by yourself."

"I'll be fine." Jeannette spooned the last of the broth up. She didn't much want it, but Anna's word was law for now. "I feel better today."

"You do look better. Yesterday you were awfully pale." The older woman studied her. "I know this is a tough time."

Tough times. Nathan's voice floated through Jeannette's mind. Jeannette handed the bowl back. As she looked into her mother-in-law's kind, steady eyes, she wanted to demand to know why she, Anna, hadn't stopped all this from happening. She could have, Jeannette knew. Sam would have listened to her.

She could have stopped Sam from getting married.

Jeannette couldn't talk to any of them. Not Sam (God, why did he still have to be so beautiful?), and not to this woman, who had locked up the memories of her son in an immaculate bedroom. Anna had been through enough. So Jeannette only said, "It'll be all right. You go to the concert, and then later I can hear about it."

That evening, they left her in bed with tissues and tea, the bottle of Tylenol, some cough drops, and a stack of magazines. Jeannette accepted Sam's kiss and promised she wouldn't wait up for him if she needed to sleep. She wished him good luck and told him how sorry she was she couldn't be there. All the while, in her mind, she saw the flight of stairs from her dream, and the white light glittering down on her.

Then the door shut downstairs, and the house fell quiet. With nothing left to stop them, the puzzle pieces leaped into motion.

Sam's voice in his mother's kitchen: *I'm not sick, if that's what you're worried about.* Jeannette hadn't had any idea, back then, what he could mean. Now she did, and she understood what Gil had died of; the memory of Sam's face during that news broadcast at Veronica and Drew's told her enough. Anna: *A world he had to stay away from.* Jeannette knew what that meant too. She had known ever since Nathan had fit another piece in: *He's made his choices and he's trying to stick with them.* Sam had used the same word once. *Choices.* She had thought he meant music.

Jeannette sat up in the bed, propped up against the headboard with a pillow behind her back, wrapped in her nightgown with the blankets over her. The cup of tea sat untouched on the bedside table. Her own body didn't seem to belong to her. She felt as if she were watching somebody else, some other woman far away, with a distended stomach and swollen feet and straggling red hair.

Another woman who shouldn't have had a child.

The pieces slotted into place. Sam's sadness. His anger. The white light that he used as a mask, wrapping it around himself so that she couldn't reach him. The way he hadn't told her about Gil, and then what he had said to her later.

Jeannette understood. She had been so *stupid*.

Anna knew. Nathan knew. Dr. Kraychek surely must. More pieces slammed into place. *I was too different.* Oh, yes; proud, reserved Dr. Kraychek could have been beyond angry to hear such a thing about his only son. Angry enough to throw him out of the house. And his own words, the doctor's, over the Thanksgiving dinner table: *You will have to tell the priest about your situation. All of it, I feel.*

Jeannette had sat there and heard it all, the family business, the church business, she had seen Sam's face on their wedding day as he was about to say the words that would bind him to her for life. The whole thing had played itself out in front of her eyes, and she had been too *stupid* to know.

Sam was... was...

He wants to do right by you. Anna again. And Nathan: *Your husband is faithful to you.* And Anna: *Let the past be the past.*

Veronica, so long ago: *He chose you, Nannie.* But also, *He's a different breed.* Veronica, the one person who had always been there, who had walked away after that last concert and left Jeannette alone.

"Oh," Jeannette whispered. "Oh." The voices blended and swirled in her head, louder and louder, until she couldn't bear it anymore, and she couldn't keep her distance from that other red-haired woman on the bed. She was falling through the air, back into her own body. Its weight dragged on her. The intruder in her belly kicked and pushed and prodded.

"What can I do?" The choked words rang out unanswered in the empty bedroom.

Above all the other voices, one stood out loud and clear: Sam's. *I love you. You've got me.*

Did she? Did she? But he was not what she had thought. He was something she could not understand, something she never would understand, and he, that person, had held her, touched her, made promises to her...

The baby kicked again. Jeannette lifted her fist high in the air and swung down, hard.

If only she could make it not be true.

Her fist stopped dead in the air. She could not do that. Must not.

"Oh!"

The shivering started again. Jeannette dove under the covers, huddling there like a rabbit in a burrow, squeezing her eyes tight shut. *What can I do?*

In another time, in another place, another woman might have thought the same thing. A woman with red hair and scared eyes, who had nobody in the world to help her. Right now, Jeannette wished for that woman as she had never wished before in her life.

Mama!

CHAPTER TWENTY-THREE

S am knew things could have been worse, going into the *Messiah* performance. Jeannette could have gone into labour that evening. Ma and Dad could have gotten into a car accident on the way down from Pennsylvania. The roof of the house could have fallen in.

Sam kissed his wife goodbye, made sure she had everything she needed within reach of the bed, and left the house. When he got to the basement rehearsal room for the chorus warm-up, he put his briefcase down by the piano and opened his score on the stand while the singers filed in. *Leave me alone. All of you go away.*

There was one person he wouldn't have minded seeing, one voice he would actually have been glad to hear. It didn't come, and Sam knew why it shouldn't. That call to Nathan's office two days ago had been the biggest mistake of all. How had Sam let himself do such a thing?

The noise in the room swelled. The blend of voices, chairs shifting into position, and scores rustling should have acted on Sam like a gulped glass of wine, especially tonight. Instead it splashed around him like waves around a rock stuck in the mud. Maybe if he sat still, he could freeze like this and never have to move again. They could carry the stool out with him still on it, and somebody else could take his place and do something useful up here.

I'm sorry. He thought the words again, or maybe they had never stopped. Tonight he didn't have enough to give. *I'm sorry, Gil.*

He didn't notice the noise had died down until somebody called his name. "Sam?"

The voice belonged to Ralph Wilder, the bass from the chorus who had made the mistake in that memorable rehearsal a long time ago, of calling Mozart's C minor Mass "just a piece of music." Considering you could still see the scratch on the floorboards from the flung music stand, Sam knew he should consider himself lucky he still had a job.

"Yes?" he said. "Was there a question?" The chairs were full, and all the eyes were on him. Sam didn't glance at the back row of basses. Nathan had to be here by now. Sam couldn't afford to care.

Ralph asked, "How's Jeannette?"

"I'm afraid she couldn't be here tonight. She isn't feeling well."

She would have felt worse if he had said what he meant to, that morning. He had spent all night thinking about it. If he brought Gil out of the past and showed her what had happened so that it would never happen again. If he told her. If he promised.

He had been about to do it. He had taken her hand, there at the table, and said, "I need to be honest with you." He had taken a breath, to have one last moment with Gil's face in his mind, and to remember all that they had been. He had opened his mouth to say, *Jeannette, sweetheart, please don't be scared, but I have to tell you...*

Then her hand had trembled in his, and the whole table shivered. She was sick. He could not make her feel worse. The words he had meant to say dried up and blew away.

Now, when he told the chorus she was home sick, women shook their heads in sympathy. From the alto section, Mattie Sinclair trumpeted, "Is it the morning sickness?"

Jeannette would curl up and die if she heard that. "No," Sam said. "She has a virus. Nothing serious."

Mattie said, "Oh, what a shame! But listen, you tell her we still have to have a shower for her."

A big to-do would be the last thing Jeannette wanted, but Sam saw the sentimentality on every female face in the room. They all thought it was lovely, their very own Maestro and his wife having a baby. "That's very kind," he said, "but we have a concert to put on tonight. Everybody stand, please."

No concert warm-up should have dragged so much. The singers sounded decent, but Sam had to force his arm to move through the air. The baton seemed to weigh a hundred pounds.

Gil's voice prodded him: *They need more from you.* Sam could not give it. He thought of Handel's name on the score and tried to conjure up an old man in a white wig, leaning over Sam's shoulder. *All right, boy, what are you going to do?* That didn't make a difference either. It only meant one more person for Sam to fail.

Sam's muscles ached. His arm didn't want to move anymore. In his head, Gil said, *What's the matter? This isn't the Sam I know.* He couldn't afford to be the person Gil had known anymore.

The final "Amen" seemed to crawl past. After it ended, Sam knew he should say something inspiring. Thank the singers for their hard work and tell them that tonight the RSA would take Richmond by storm, that people would remember this concert for years. The air sucked at him, waiting for the right words.

"Okay," he said. "I'll see you onstage soon." He picked up his briefcase and left the room.

Out in the hall, Lydia was waiting. "Done already? You still have time."

"They're ready. They'll be fine."

"Are you okay?"

Sam couldn't say the right thing. "No."

"What's wrong? I mean, I know the other day was—"

"I need to sit down. I'm going upstairs."

She didn't stop him as he went past her to the stairwell. Behind him, choristers came out into the hall. Sam caught the words "tired" and "not himself" before the basement door swung shut, cutting off the sound.

In his office, he dropped the briefcase on the floor and fell into the chair in front of the desk. In half an hour, something like that, he was going to get onstage in front of that audience. Ma and Dad would be watching. Sam should want to do his best for them. Certainly for Dad, who might finally understand why his son had become a conductor—but who the hell was Sam kidding? Dad would never understand that. Sam could do his best at just about anything and it would never be enough for Dad.

One pair of arms could have helped him right now. One voice could have lifted him out of the grey pit he lay in. He would never have those arms or that voice again. They had left the world forever.

What's the point? Shit, God, I know you don't listen to me anymore, but can you give me something here? Can you give me one fucking reason why I should get out of this chair?

Behind him, the door opened. Lydia again, no doubt. Sam should have locked the damn thing. He didn't bother to turn around.

"Hey."

Sam started up. "Who's there?" As if he did not know that voice.

"It's me," Nathan answered. "I thought you might be here."

He came over to Sam's chair. For some reason Sam could not stand up or pull away. Nathan's arms slipped around from behind and held him.

This must not happen: Sam knew it as clearly as he knew anything. They both had to be onstage soon. Lydia might walk in any second.

Sam didn't care. His head rested against Nathan's chest. Somehow, for a heartbeat or two, the weight he dragged felt lighter.

Neither of them spoke. Outside, the hall was silent. Sam put his hand on Nathan's arm. A gleam of light through the window found his gold wedding band. It glared at him against the sleeve of Nathan's jacket, but just for now, Sam didn't let go.

♫

When Sam stepped onto the podium that night, the white light poured into him like water into a jar. The audience's anticipation lifted him up. He turned to the players and saw rays of energy, like a spiderweb, connecting them to each other and to him. The baton's grip fit into his palm. The stick seemed ready to dance on its own.

With the first downbeat, the *Messiah* journey began. Sam listened to the tight, clean rhythms and the perfect phrasing. The motion of the baton twined together so tightly with the sound that Sam thought he could have let go of the stick and trusted the music to hold and move it.

The watching eyes in the hall disappeared. Sam looked at his chorus and saw the same light that filled him reflected in their faces. When he met one pair of eyes in the back row, he didn't look away. The only reason he could stand up here and do this now was because Nathan had given him the strength to try.

The music slipped past, one signpost after another falling away behind, as Sam held onto each note of the constantly-shifting kaleidoscope around him. Into the "Hallelujah" chorus. The audience got to its feet and trumpet and tympani made the stage shiver. *King of Kings, and Lord of Lords!* The hall should have exploded with the hugeness of it. And too soon, much too soon, into the gorgeous soprano solo, *I know that my Redeemer liveth,* and the bass aria interwoven with a silver trumpet solo: *The trumpet shall sound, and the dead shall be raised!*

Finally, into the last chorus of all. *Worthy is the Lamb that was slain!* The hall rang with the chorus's joy. The music flowed out of the air and into Sam's arms and hands. This was easy. This was home. How had he thought otherwise? The Amen rolled like a river. Sam held out the grand pause before the final chords, stretching the silence to the breaking point. Then one last peal, the chorus sending their sound into the hall and beyond to the night sky itself, the tympani and organ roaring together, and it was over, it was finished. They had done it.

Sam stood on the podium with the music beating in his blood. The baton lay on the stand, his score open to the last page.

Applause crashed in. Sam raised his head, looked over the orchestra to the back row of the chorus and found the one pair of eyes he wanted. A moment of contact. Neither he nor Nathan needed anything else.

Then he turned around and faced the audience. They were on their feet, clapping and cheering. No empty seats tonight. Sam held out his hand to his musicians and passed the applause on to them.

Lydia waited in the wings. A trail of mascara had sneaked down her left cheek, behind her glasses. She caught Sam in a hug; this from the woman who limited physical contact to half-second handshakes. "You are something else," she told him. "I hope you know that."

Sam had to get to the reception. Before he went to the green room, he gave himself one minute alone to sit the table in his dressing room, close his eyes, and try to shut out all the noise from outside.

We did it, Gil.

Behind his closed eyes, he saw Gil healthy again, standing on the college podium with that radiant energy filling him. Somehow it wasn't so terrible to remember. It ought to have been, when that face was gone forever, but Sam held it in his mind. *We did it, Gil. You would have been proud.*

Soon, Sam had to go out and meet all the faces that waited for him here tonight. For one last minute, he stayed at the table. His hands gripped each other tight.

I love you, Gil. That will never change.

♫

Chaos in the green room. Lydia manoeuvred through the crowd to stake out a place for Sam near the door and brought him a plastic cup of ginger ale. Faces crowded in. Sam tried not to laugh as the white-tie and evening-dress crowd employed purses, elbows, and stiletto heels to jostle for a place close to him.

The RSA's donors were the most aggressive. Sam smiled and shook hands with people who he knew perfectly well were a lot more interested in being seen at the symphony—and talking to the Maestro—than in listening to actual music. You did whatever it took to keep the concerts coming. Besides which, these people had no doubt helped float Sam's salary raise. He understood now that pride only got you so far.

Among the board members, Sam had achieved more than a few conversions. Tonight he saw men he hadn't seen since the contract signing. They wrung his hand and presented their wives and children with an enthusiasm that made Sam feel like a revivalist preacher. One of the men, who had a round flushed face that suggested he had brought his own supply of wine, told Sam, "I'll admit, Mr. Kraychek, two years ago I would've said no show like this could happen. Good for you, son."

Son? How old would Sam have to be before he stopped getting comments like that? And, speaking of which, where were Ma and Dad?

As he wondered that, the circle around him shifted and a new face appeared. Sam saw everything that had just happened onstage encapsulated in Nathan's smile.

The singer said, "I have some folks here who say they know you."

Sam should have noticed them right away. Nathan's height made it hard to see anyone else. Ma's eyes swam, and a trace of a tear clung to her eyelashes. She stood there, trim and neat in her white blouse and beige skirt and long blue coat, with her hair twisted back in its usual bun. No diamonds on her throat, no gold bangles in her ears, but she looked better than any of the velvet- and chiffon- and makeup-clad women.

She didn't hug him. Instead she reached out with one hand. "Liudas."

He took her hand between both of his and felt the softness of her white wool glove. She said, *"Mielas, aš nežinau ką pasakyti."* I don't know what to say.

"Kad niekada neįvyksta," he teased her. *That never happens.* *"Ar jums patinka tai?"* Did you like it?

She shook her head. *"Ką manote?"* What do you think?

Sam switched to English to answer. His Lithuanian didn't feel as up to speed as it should have. "I'm not sure what to think. I haven't gotten a hug yet."

She looked at him. *"Aš liedžiama?"*

Sam had to think about that one. *Liedžiama,* from the verb *liesti,* to allow. Was she asking if she was allowed to hug him? What kind of craziness was that? "Ma," he said, *"noriu apkabinti dabar."* I want a hug right now.

She laughed. That was better. *"Sunku berniukas,"* she said, *pesky kid,* and reached out for him. Her head rested against his shoulder, and her cinnamon scent hung in the air. *"Mielas,"* she said, *"aš esu labai tavimi didžiuojasi."* I am so proud of you.

It couldn't last long enough. Dad stood there watching, and Nathan too. When Ma let go, she turned to the singer. "Thank you again for finding us, Mr. Woods. We didn't know what to do with ourselves in this crowd!" Her briskness had come back. Sam noticed how much her Westbury accent stood out here and how lovely it sounded.

Nathan said, "My pleasure. When I saw him"—a respectful nod at Dad—"I thought he couldn't look that much like Sam and not be related."

Sam swallowed. Two days ago, in Lydia's office, he had told Nathan everything about himself and Gil. He had told him about the college chorus, about deciding he couldn't work for Gil anymore, about the note he had written and pushed under Gil's office door. He had told him how Gil had come to find him in Bond that night, and instead of dishing out the repulsion and disgust Sam had thought he deserved, Gil told him that the note had been the most unexpected and beautiful gift.

Nathan had listened. And when he asked what had happened, why Sam and Gil had split up, Sam had told him about the last fight with Dad. *My father threw me out.* He had explained how he had gone back to Philadelphia, how Gil had helped him put himself together again, but how in the end, the strain had been too much. *I couldn't live with myself.*

All of that went through Sam's head now as he looked at his father and Nathan. What would Dr. Kraychek say if he knew Sam had discussed such private business with someone like the singer? If he could have seen, only a few hours ago, that same man with his arms around Sam in the office? Sam didn't have to guess.

Ma said, "We should head back to your place, *mielas*. It's getting late."

Sam pulled himself together. "That's fine. I think we'll be done here soon."

Dad cut in. "You should do what you need to."

The words sounded so curt that Sam took a reflexive step back. Then he realized he had done it. A current of anger ran up his spine. What the hell could Dad be mad about now?

His father said again, "You should do what you need to. We know you have work to finish here."

Trust Dad to tell Sam what his job was. "That's true," Sam said, "but I think we're—"

"Aside from which," Dad interrupted, "we can't leave yet. I haven't told you what I thought of your performance."

He sounded like he was going to take Sam to task about something. God knew he couldn't do what Sam had just done if you marched him up to the podium and aimed a cannon at him. The hell with it. Sam propped the right smile in place and said, "I'd like to hear what you thought."

"It was outstanding."

What?

Dad held his hand out. No smile touched his mouth or the eyes behind the glasses. He said, "I always understood you were talented, of course. I did not realize how much."

This had to be some sort of joke. Numbly, Sam put his hand out too. Hugging Dad would be unheard of, but the handshake set the seal on the words Sam couldn't believe he had heard.

Ma said, "Well, for heaven's sake. I would just about say he's talented."

The tension snapped. Sam couldn't help laughing. As he did, he remembered something else, forgotten in the long blur of the preceding months. He said it before he could change his mind. "I think you're talented yourself, sir. I never knew you could dance."

Sam had never seen his father blush. A blush meant a lapse in control, a surrender. Now, though, Dad looked as if he had swallowed a too-hot gulp of something.

Ma said, "He certainly can." Sam wanted to hear more, concert reception or not, crowded green room or not. She seemed to know that. As if they had been alone, she said, "Why, I remember the first time he showed me how. We'd only been seeing each other a few weeks. He brought an album over to my dad's house and put it on the stereo, and next thing I knew, we were spinning around the living room like Fred Astaire and Ginger Rogers. You could say he swept me off my feet."

Sam couldn't believe his ears. He tried to picture the skinny, dark-haired kid from Miner's Row guiding a blue-eyed girl around a makeshift dance floor, twirling her around and leaning her back over his arm so that her gold hair brushed the carpet. Except Dad hadn't been only the kid from Miner's Row anymore. He had the overlay of medical school, he was Dr. Kraychek then, and his father had died with the coal dust in his lungs.

Dad cleared his throat. "That might be a slight exaggeration."

Ma shook her head. "It's not. You can trust me on that."

Sam had to push his luck. Right now, in this place, he was the Maestro. He could have what he wanted. "But what happened? Why didn't I ever see you dance before?"

Dad seemed to have found a point in the middle distance to stare at. He didn't answer, but Ma said, "Oh, we did it for a while. After we got married, before you were born, in the evenings we used to put a record on and dance just like that, in the living room. Then when you came along, I would put you down on your blanket and you would watch us. You loved music already, back then."

Nathan caught Sam's eye and grinned. Sam tried to bring back a memory of a tune playing on the stereo, probably one of Dad's big band records, and maybe a blurred picture of Ma and Dad gliding across the living room floor. He couldn't do it.

Ma said, "No, you wouldn't remember. You were too little. By the time you turned three, we didn't do that anymore."

"Why not?"

Ma smiled. "Oh, I don't know. We were always busy, somehow. And tired. Dad was building the practice, you know, working late a lot."

Sam looked at his father. Dad was still staring off toward the card table where Lydia was pouring out plastic cups of ginger ale and wine. Ma said, "When you wanted to learn, though, *mielas*, when you got older, I did wish he would have taught you himself." She put her hand on Dad's arm. "I'd have liked for you to learn it from him."

For an instant Sam saw it. Instead of Ma, Dad showing him how to stand in dance position: *your hand on her waist, her hand on your shoulder.* Dad showing him how to feel the beat of the music and let it guide his feet, how to lead a partner through the steps. Ma had been a good teacher, yes, but Sam would have liked to learn from the best.

Ma's touch on his arm seemed to have tugged Dad out of whatever place he was in. He focused on Sam. "We shouldn't monopolize your conversation," he said. The blush, if it had been one, had gone. His face looked as remote as ever. "We had better get going."

Sam wanted to stop him. He wanted to ask, *Why didn't you teach me? Why couldn't we share that?* If they could have, would things have been different?

Too late now. Too many years and too much trouble in between this moment and that one. Sam said, "Okay. I'll see you back at the house."

After Ma and Dad had gone, Nathan stayed long enough to give Sam a hug. "You were incredible tonight," he said. "By the way, your dad's quite a character."

Sam wished the two of them could have sat somewhere and talked everything over or simply been quiet together. There was no time for that. The stragglers had to be ejected, and Sam had to collect his things from the dressing room, and the drive home stretched out in front of him.

He turned up the heat in the Pinto, but the cold still bit through his wool coat and gloves. He kept thinking about what Ma had said. *I would have liked you to learn it from him.*

Why couldn't Dad have taught him to dance? Sam drove onto the bridge across the James, glancing at the lights spangling on the water below. Dad had claimed not to understand how Sam could choose the crazy profession of music, but Sam had watched music take him. Why hadn't the two of them ever been able to talk about things? Why had they spent their lives on opposite sides of a wall?

Sam could only think of one reason. The fights, the silences, the fact that Sam had never been good enough: all of that told him how he had plunged into his father's life like a brick crashing through a window. Dad had never wanted a child.

Sam gripped the wheel and stared straight ahead at the flat concrete span. He could ask Ma about it when he got home. No doubt she was waiting up for him. He could say, *listen, did Dad*—what? Wish Sam hadn't been born?

No. Sam couldn't do that. Ma wouldn't want to answer that kind of question. Besides, if Sam asked it, he would get much too close to another truth: how he felt about what was going to happen a couple of months from now.

Maybe, tomorrow morning, the sun would warm the bedroom again. Maybe Jeannette would feel better, and Sam could lie beside her and tell her and their daughter both about the concert. He had a home, a family. Any normal man would know how lucky he was.

And Dad had actually used the word *outstanding*. Sam should not forget that.

He kept his eyes on the road and drove on. Behind him, disappearing in the rear-view mirror, the river glittered in the dark.

CHAPTER TWENTY-FOUR

Without the piano, Jeannette would not have made it through the final two months.

The grand arrived while she and Sam were in Westbury for Christmas, playing the role of a family, opening presents under the tree. Somehow Jeannette played along. White light glittered down on her all the time.

Apparently Sam had made arrangements with the movers and given Lydia Holland a house key so she could let them in. When Sam and Jeannette got home from Pennsylvania, he told her to close her eyes and led her into the living room. Jeannette looked at the long, sleek, black shape under the bay window and felt her mouth open in spite of herself. It was more beautiful than she had hoped.

Sam said it was a Christmas present, technically for both of them but more for her. "I know how much you've missed it," he said. When he looked at her that way, she would have given years off her life to forget that horrible afternoon in his office and the endless days that had followed.

They had never talked about any of it. The Richmond *Times-Dispatch*, which had ignored the RSA for years, sent a critic to the *Messiah* performance, who proclaimed the event "the height of the season's celebrations." Afterward, Anna and Dr. Kraychek were in the house, and then there was Christmas shopping, and a visit to Veronica and Drew and the kids, and then the trip to Westbury. Jeannette had let all the busyness sift over what now lay between her and Sam, as easily as river silt would cover a stone.

He seemed as willing to let it go as she was. Neither of them mentioned Gil, or Nathan either. Maybe Sam thought she hadn't put the pieces together. Maybe he assumed she still didn't know anything. She wished she didn't.

With the holidays over, the RSA's season resumed. Sam went back to the office and rehearsals, and now Jeannette had nowhere to go.

Funnily enough, she didn't feel scared about giving birth. It ought to terrify her, especially when she knew how much it would hurt. Somehow that didn't seem to matter. Sam asked if she wanted to see if Veronica could come and stay sometimes, so she wouldn't have to be alone so much, but Jeannette didn't want anyone in the house with her. Only the piano.

She had to pull the bench out farther than she liked to play, and her arms were practically straight. Some people said babies could hear music in the womb. This one surely would, then. Jeannette hoped the poor thing wouldn't grow up to be a pianist.

She didn't talk to the baby. A lot of mothers would have. Veronica had chatted all the time to Ricky and C.J. before they were born. Jeannette didn't, because as she sat alone on the bench with the listening emptiness of the house around her and the wonderful keys moving under her fingers, a seed planted deep inside her started to put out its first tentative shoots.

She had to be crazy. No sane person would walk away from her husband and child. Not if she had a choice.

Sometimes her thoughts terrified her. She would sit on the bench literally paralyzed with fear, her hands frozen on the keys. Sometimes she felt so unbearably sad that she had to stop playing, run to the hall bathroom for tissues, and have a good cry. Sometimes she wanted to call up Veronica and tell her everything, or call up Anna and tell *her* everything, or, why on earth not, call Sam at his office and tell him what she was thinking and beg him, plead with him, to give her a reason not to do it. Say anything he had to. Lie if necessary.

That was the problem, though. He would surely have to lie.

She couldn't stay with him. Not like this, pretending the truth didn't exist, pretending he wasn't the person he was. A normal mother, a decent woman, wouldn't have wanted to leave her baby behind too. Certainly not with a man who was *wrong*.

Jeannette thought, over and over, about another woman who had abandoned not one but two babies. Isabel had not had a choice. The town wouldn't have let her stay. Wherever she had gone, she probably couldn't have dragged two helpless children along with her. Jeannette, though, could take this child.

God help her, she didn't want to. The baby was Sam's. He had invaded her body the same way he had invaded her life.

During her first days alone in the house, Jeannette sat at the piano and let her fingers run over scales and arpeggios, and then over Haydn sonatas, elegant crystals of sound that had nothing to do with the chaos in her head. She didn't so much as glance at the *Hungarian Dances* or Ravel's *Ma Mère L'Oye*, and she tried not to imagine what she had once pictured all the time: herself and Sam sitting here at their very own piano, filling the house with their music. And she never, ever, stopped playing to touch her stomach in response to a tap or kick from the baby, and never said a single thing out loud while she was in the house alone.

That last part, at least, was stupid. If the baby could hear at all, there inside her, it—she—already knew Jeannette's voice.

She noticed, as hours and days passed, that her fingers felt stronger. Sight-reading came easier. Her hands moved more readily over the keys than they used to, and her mind responded faster than ever to the markings on the page and the sound she heard.

Years ago, she had sat at her Aunt Gretchen's old spinet and talked to it through the music she played. That piano had known her better than any person. Now this piano put out feelers, reaching for her, and though Jeannette knew she must never love it too much, she didn't know how to hold back. That wasn't how you made music.

You talked to the piano. You told it the things you couldn't say aloud to any person. When Jeannette actually faced Sam at the beginning and end of each day, she felt as calm as still water because she let all the hurt and bewilderment and anger out when she was alone. Only the piano knew the rest of the story.

Only the piano knew what she wanted to do now. The seed inside her put out roots and leaves and dug itself in deep. Day after day, as Jeannette's delivery date got closer, she told the piano what she would do after that date was over. How hard it would be to go through with the plan. How terrible, sometimes, it made her feel; but also, how desperately she wanted it.

On what turned out to be the last day, she took out her book of Chopin Ballades and opened it to the piece she had learned long ago, the piece she had heard Sam play the first day she met him.

Her fingers traced the light ascending melody in the first measure, and she remembered the sidewalk outside the Lewis Center, the hot September sunlight, the maple tree pushing up between squares of concrete. The battered grey Pinto and the boy who pulled his briefcase out of the back seat and hurried into the building.

She wished she had never seen him. Even so, as she played, she remembered again how beautiful that boy had been. How his music had poured out and welled up in the stairwell like a rising lake. How Jeannette had known that she could never sound like that, her hands had never been strong enough to make the piano sing that way.

They were strong enough now. Either that, or this piano itself chose to help her. She must not love it too much, because she would miss it too much. Its bass sounded as soft as velvet and as strong as oak. The treble rang like chimes.

When the second melody began, the cradle song, the notes rocked back and forth like arms cradling a child. Jeannette thought of the empty crib upstairs, the rocking chair, the dresser waiting with its load of sleepers and onesies, the flower stencils she and Sam had finally put up on the walls. She thought of Sam standing by that crib, or sitting in the chair with a small bundle in his arms.

As the melody turned dark, the left hand sinking into the lowest register in a growl of clashing notes, Jeannette remembered her wedding night. How Sam's lips had hurt her mouth, how he had pushed her back onto the bed and wrenched at her bra, how angry and lost he had looked.

He never wanted me.

The melody rose again out of the bass, no triumph here but an ecstasy of pain. The notes shouted, *I don't belong here! I want to go home!*

When the cramps started, Jeannette thought she had an upset stomach again. She would make it to the end of the piece and then run for the bathroom.

The pain came in waves. By the time she played the last chord, she knew what they were. She kept her hands on the keys and her foot on the pedal while the sound rang in the room.

The house looked lived-in now. Besides the piano, the living room had a comfortable plaid sofa and armchair, a sturdy coffee table for books and mugs, and in front of the smaller window, a plant stand with a spider plant on it that trailed green fronds to the floor. Someday a little girl might play on the carpet with a book or blocks or a doll. Her father would sit at this piano and run his fingers over the keyboard. The little girl would leave her toys and come over beside him and stand on tiptoe to see the keys.

Jeannette waited for the sound to fade. Then she dried her eyes and pulled herself to her feet.

She called the RSA office. Her voice sounded as calm as snow when she told first Lydia and then Sam that it was time. Sam answered breathlessly that he would be right there and hung up.

Jeannette went carefully up the stairs to the bedroom. She was standing by the bed, checking the contents of the overnight bag one more time, when the truth slapped her in the face. This was really happening. She was going to have a *baby*.

She crumpled onto the bed and clamped her hand over her mouth to hold the sobs back. God help her. All of them. Especially the poor defenseless child inside her, ready to come out.

Mama.

After a couple of minutes, the door opened downstairs. Sam must have broken every speed limit and run every red light between here and the Lewis Center. "Honey?" His voice came up the stairs, riding on panic.

Jeannette swallowed hard. "Up here," she quavered and hauled herself up off the bed.

He took the steps two at a time. She heard the impact of his shoes on the bare wood. By the time he came in the bedroom, she was reasonably calm, closing up the bag, turning around to face him. "It's okay," she said. "We have time."

He looked so young. She had seen that scared boy's face before, in a dark apartment. "Are you all right?" he asked. "Are you ready?" She saw exactly the same thought hit him: *This is really happening.* He ran his hand distractedly through his hair.

She went to him. Gently, half wishing she had never done this before, half aching to think she might never do it again, she smoothed his bangs away from his forehead. "It's okay," she said again. "We'll be fine."

Maybe some fragment of her real thoughts reached him, moving straight from her mind to his through her fingertips. "Jeannette," he said. "You know I love you, right?"

She could have blurted out everything. *I'm sorry. You should never have met me. None of this should have happened.* She could have told him what she wanted to do and how sad it made her. Another cramp came before she could speak. He saw the spasm in her face and snatched the bag off the bed and caught her hand.

"We should go," he said. "Can you walk? The stairs?"

She made herself laugh. "Yes, I can walk. How do you think I got up here, silly?"

One thing at a time. She leaned on his arm and let him lead her out of the room, one foot in front of the other.

♫

It hurt.

They gave Jeannette drugs, she didn't know what kind. One of them involved sticking a needle in her spine. That hurt too, but nothing, anywhere, could have been as terrible as the pain that wanted to rip her apart.

Sam wasn't there. Fathers weren't allowed in the delivery room. Instead there was a doctor, the same one she had seen plenty of times before, but everything felt dreamlike and wrong, and she didn't know why he should stand there staring at her when she was sweating and helpless, her swollen stomach straining against the hospital gown, her knees bent, her most private part open to the air and his eyes. At first she hated him and wanted him to go away. When the pain got worse, she stopped caring.

Then, somehow, after a time she couldn't measure, the slow tide of herself came back in. She was sitting up in the bed, exhausted, aching from the waist down. Someone, a clean, slim figure in a white uniform, held out a white-wrapped bundle.

Jeannette let the fabric touch her arms. The weight of the bundle settled on her. She looked down into it and saw…

…a tiny, pink, squashed face, tight-shut eyes, pursed lips, and such a minuscule hand.

Something dropped straight through Jeannette's body, burning like a bolt of lightning.

Daughter.

She stared at the tiny face. The little hand twitched against the white wrapping. In another second she would have brought up her free hand to touch it, stroke each of the impossibly small fingers, caress the little cheek.

The door opened. "Jeannette." Sam hurried to the bed. He was still wearing his overcoat, for some reason, and he looked so tired, with dark circles like bruises under his eyes and black stubble on his chin. "Are you okay, sweetheart?" He bent to kiss her. She closed her eyes when his lips touched her cheek.

She had to remember. She had never known who he was. With her eyes still closed, she lifted up the bundle. "You can hold her."

The weight left Jeannette's arms. The room smelled of floor cleaner and fresh sheets and soap and disinfectant, and a hint of what she would have known anywhere: Sam's clean, spicy scent.

For a moment everything was quiet. Then Sam whispered, "Oh."

Jeannette didn't need to open her eyes to see his wonder. His voice caressed the shape in the bundle. "Baby girl. Look at you."

His arms were strong enough to carry that child. Now Jeannette had to remember what she was going to do.

♪

She chose a Friday to go through with it. Fridays were best, because Sam didn't work late. Jeannette packed a bag with the things the baby would need for one afternoon, and a suitcase with the things Jeannette couldn't do without, and called a cab.

She only had a narrow window to do this. For the first week after they came back from the hospital, Sam had stayed home; a special dispensation from the RSA. Now he had gone back to work but with later mornings and earlier evenings when he could swing them. Within the next week or so, his parents would come down to meet their granddaughter. Jeannette had to have gone through with her plan by then.

The baby slept against Jeannette's shoulder while she stood on the porch and waited for the cab. Good thing the weather was so cold. That way Jeannette didn't notice the aches she still felt in her stomach and legs, or, for that matter, the ice inside her.

The birth certificate said Caroline Anna, which sounded ridiculously long for such a tiny creature. Sam had chosen the name. Jeannette had let him pick whatever he liked, because it wasn't as if she had a right to a say. Sam didn't like leaving for work in the morning, and when he got home, Jeannette knew she could hand the bundle over the minute he walked in the door. He had also taken over most of the nighttime feedings. That was just as well.

The weight on her shoulder had gotten heavy by the time the cab pulled down the driveway. Jeannette got in the back while the driver loaded the bags in the trunk. Her voice did not shake when she gave him Veronica's address, the same way it hadn't trembled two hours ago when she had told Sam goodbye.

He had thought she meant goodbye for the day, of course. The driver shifted the cab into reverse, and Jeannette looked over the bundle on her shoulder at her wedding ring. Maybe she should have left it, along with the diamond Sam had given her. She could leave them with Veronica. They would be the least of the things she was leaving behind.

It would be all right. Veronica might not understand—in fact, Jeannette knew she wouldn't—but sisters helped each other, no matter what. And the baby would have people to take care of her. And Sam...

If the plan worked, by the time he found out what Jeannette had done, she would be on a train headed back to the place she never should have left. Not Reckord's Mill. Even if Aunt Gretchen's house had still belonged to them, Jeannette wouldn't have wanted to see it again. No: Charleston. At least she could be in a place where her voice would fit in, and she would be a tiny drop in a sea of people and could start over. She knew about starting over and digging out a new life. The idea didn't scare her as much as it might have. After all, another woman had done the same thing once, a long time ago. Jeannette knew that if she hadn't laid eyes on her mother by now, she probably never would. Still, she hoped Isabel was out there somewhere, living a life she had built for herself.

Jeannette shouldn't worry about Sam. He couldn't have a claim on her anymore.

The cab rolled down the street and left the house behind. Jeannette did not look back.

CHAPTER TWENTY-FIVE

After Sam and Jeannette came home from the hospital, with their daughter a living, breathing reality, Sam tried not to notice how wrong the world felt.

He had more than enough to distract him. He couldn't help thinking that most fathers probably didn't hover around the crib the way he did, but he didn't want to take his eyes off that little life. When his daughter lay awake, looking out at the world, he felt sure she was watching everything and wished so much he could know what she thought about it. He couldn't remember why he had been scared to touch her. When he lifted her into his arms, and she nestled on his chest and hid her face against his neck, it felt like a missing piece of his soul had slotted back into place.

Jeannette did not feel the same way. Dr. Esterson at the hospital had thought she might have post-partum disorder. She hadn't been able to nurse the baby the first time she tried, and she either couldn't or wouldn't try again. At home, she made up formula and gave feedings and changed diapers, always quietly, shut in on herself, as if she were taking care of a plastic doll. Sam could never resist talking to the baby (who, if she could have understood him, would have known her father was a doting fool), but Jeannette didn't do the same. She didn't say much to him either.

They'd had to choose a name at the hospital. Sam had known what name he wanted since the first look at the baby's face, but Jeannette ought to have the first say. She was tired, she told him. She couldn't think straight. When he suggested the name he had carried in his head for months, she agreed right away.

She didn't seem to care about much of anything. Sam tried to tell himself this was a passing thing. Ma and Dad would be down soon to help; Ma had sent her granddaughter so many kisses over the phone that anyone would think she wouldn't have much left to do in person. Veronica, too, was thrilled to be an aunt, and had in fact offered to come over and help Jeannette whenever she wanted, but that brought up another thing Sam didn't understand. Jeannette had said no.

If Jeannette had wanted to keep the baby all to herself, it would have made sense. She didn't want that either.

Sam tried not to worry. Life was a blur anyway, between work and the nursery. Things would get better. Jeannette would recover, and they would settle into a routine at home. Sam told himself these things over and over, day after day, and when he held the baby, he let himself forget everything else. That was why, the day the world turned inside out, it caught him blind.

Friday, February 27, two weeks and a day after Carrie's birth. A beautiful day, a welcome break in the middle of Richmond's grey and gritty shift from winter to spring. Sam sat at his desk with his copy of Bernstein's *Chichester Psalms* open in front of him, trying to study for the midseason March concert. Sun poured in through the window behind him.

Footsteps in the hall, a knock on the door. Lydia said, "Phone call for you. Do you know a Veronica Calhoun?"

Sam shut the score. "Veronica? Sure. That's my sister-in-law. What's up?"

"I don't know. She said it was urgent."

Sam got to his feet. Maybe Jeannette felt sick. Maybe she had let Veronica come over after all, and the two of them thought he should come home. The walk to the phone in Lydia's office was too damn long. Someday, he hoped, it would stop feeling like a walk to the gallows.

He picked up the receiver. "Veronica?"

"Sam. Thank God."

She sounded terrified. Sam gripped the edge of the desk. "What's wrong?"

"Sam, listen, I don't know how to tell you this. I don't know what to do."

This couldn't be Veronica. Veronica always knew what to do. Fear scrambled up Sam's throat. He demanded, "What's going on? Is it Jeannette? Tell me what's wrong."

"Yes. It's Nannie. Listen, you need to come over here. Can you? Right now."

"Here? Where?"

"My place. Please."

Sam asked the only thing that mattered. "Is Carrie all right?"

"She's fine. I have her here. Please come."

Afterward, Sam could never remember the drive, except for the jagged edges of buildings against the strangely perfect sky. Veronica was waiting in the Belvedere lobby. Sam saw her red-and-black kimono through the glass doors, saw her holding a bundle against her shoulder. He got inside and took his sleeping daughter from her without a word. The baby's warmth in his arms let him breathe again.

Veronica looked half frozen, as if she had been standing out in the cold for hours. Her eyes were red, and her usually sleek hair looked tangled. "Come upstairs," she told him. She didn't sound hysterical now, only exhausted. "We have to talk."

They sat at the yellow kitchen table. C.J. played with blocks in the living room. Sam held the baby against his chest and felt her breathing as Veronica told him what had happened. "I don't understand it," she said. She brushed tears away. "She wouldn't tell me why."

Sam took in the information a shred at a time. How Jeannette had arrived here unannounced with the baby, a bag, and a suitcase. How she had told Veronica she needed help.

"I wanted to call you then," Veronica said. "I said, Nannie, what are you doing? I said, this is your husband, you need to talk to him. She wouldn't let me call you. I never saw her like that before. She said if I picked up the phone, she would turn around and leave and never talk to me again. I was so scared."

She reached into the pocket of her kimono. Somehow Sam already knew what she would set on the table between them. He wanted to shut his eyes against the sight of the thin gold band, empty and lost, and the diamond glittering like an angry eye.

Jeannette had told Veronica she was going back to Charleston. "She had money for a train ticket," Veronica said. "She wanted some extra for a month's rent. I asked her what she was going to do." She rubbed her eyes again. "She said she would figure it out, she would find something."

The words settled on Sam like snow. He could believe Veronica had never seen her sister like that before. Jeannette, go off alone, with no plan in the world?

Veronica said, "I begged her to tell me why. I said, things happen in marriage, there's misunderstandings. If you love each other, you hang on and find a way to fix it. I said, having a baby can make everything seem harder. She didn't listen."

So Veronica had done what Jeannette asked. She had given her money and promised to keep the baby with her until Sam got home. "I think she wanted me to wait to call you until the end of the day, but I couldn't do that. You had to know."

She wanted you to wait to call me until she got away. Sam opened his mouth. "She left here not long ago?"

Veronica nodded. "I called you as soon as I could. I mean, I couldn't think too well."

Another husband might have gone tearing off to the train station. Sam sat still.

Veronica said, "The worst was how she left the baby." She nodded at Carrie, still fast asleep against Sam's shoulder. "She barely looked at her. She didn't say goodbye."

Her voice trailed off. She ducked her head, but Sam saw a tear fall onto her lap.

She didn't understand, but Sam did. That day in his office. Nathan's arm around his shoulders. Jeannette's eyes full of tears: *How dare you tell me not to talk to him? He's my husband! Mine!* Sam had thought she didn't realize what she saw. How could he have been so stupid?

He had decided he couldn't tell her what he was. That had been useless, hadn't it. She had put the pieces together herself.

Monster.

She had left the baby. In spite of everything, she had left the baby with him. From someplace far away, Sam realized how close he had come to losing everything.

Veronica was saying something. Sam had been staring down at the yellow table, the purple grape juice stain on it, but he made himself look up again. "Sam," she said, "what is this about? Is my sister going to come back?"

Jeannette shouldn't come back to him. "I don't know." Sam's voice sounded dead. "I'm so sorry, Veronica."

"Do you understand this? Do you know what happened? She never told me things were bad with you two. I mean, I know you have a busy schedule and all, but..."

Veronica was strong, she had always taken care of Jeannette, she had never been afraid of a thing. She was afraid now, and helpless. That was Sam's fault too.

He could not tell her why her sister had left. Instead he said, "Did she say she would keep in touch with you?"

"I told her she had to."

That was something. One of them, at least, would know if Jeannette was okay.

Veronica said, "I just don't know how she could do this. Nannie isn't... she wouldn't..." Her hands twisted together on the table. "I should be mad at you, I guess, but my God, I can't even do that!" Her laugh sounded more like a sob. "I'm knocked clean sideways. I don't know what to do about anything!" Sam couldn't nod, couldn't tell her anything so trite as *I know.* "And you," she said. "You and that poor little baby. What are you going to do?"

Carrie had nestled her face against Sam's neck. One hand, barely visible at the end of her soft flannel sleeve, rested on the top button of his shirt. Sam laid his own hand on her back. His palm spanned her shoulders so easily. Against his fingertips, the bare skin at the base of her neck felt like velvet.

What was he going to do?

The beautiful day had shattered and his marriage lay in ruins. He had hurt so many people. Jeannette. Veronica. Ma and Dad and Gil. Nobody could hope for redemption when they had made that many mistakes.

Poor baby was right. He couldn't imagine a worse excuse for a father. Right now, he was all she had.

Veronica watched him, waiting for him to say something. Sam couldn't speak. He focused on the soft rise and fall of his daughter's breathing, the only reason he had to keep going.

CHAPTER TWENTY-SIX

Jeannette had expected a rush of relief when she found herself alone and free in Charleston, the city that had once been home. She hadn't expected an ache like a severed limb with the stump left unstitched and hanging.

She found a one-room apartment that could hold a narrow bed, a second-hand couch, a small table and a couple of chairs, and a few plants. Nobody was going to help her make meals anymore, so she bought a couple of cookbooks. At first she thought about looking for a music job, teaching piano lessons if nothing else, but then she tried to go to a choral concert at her old alma mater, Charleston Southern. She thought that would help her remember who she had been before Richmond, but she had to leave before the first half ended. After that, she decided to shut herself away from music for a while.

Instead she got a job in the quietest place she could find: a branch of the public library, a few blocks away from her apartment. There, she didn't hear so much as a radio. She learned to lean on the rhythm of shelving books, bending to the cart and stretching to the racks. She held on to the smells of paper and binding glue and the solidity of the books, like bricks, between her hands.

Meanwhile, a thread connected her to Richmond. She didn't want it, but Veronica was the only family she had left. When they talked on the phone, Veronica would say, "Nannie, how are you making it?" and Jeannette would say she was fine. Veronica asked if she needed any money, and Jeannette said no, the job paid plenty for her expenses. She could have thought about a car if she wanted, but that made her wonder if Sam had replaced the Pinto, so she stopped thinking about cars.

Veronica had changed. Once upon a time, she would have bodily strapped Jeannette to the sofa in the old apartment before she would have let her walk out the way she did. Now Veronica didn't so much as mention Sam's name on the phone. The first time she brought up the baby— "Nannie, your little girl needs you, don't you see that?"—Jeannette hung up on her. Veronica didn't mention the baby again.

She did, though, send Polaroids. Those envelopes arrived in Jeannette's mailbox every few weeks or so, usually with a sheet of notebook paper wrapped around them. The paper always had a sentence or two on it in Veronica's handwriting. Jeannette quickly learned how to slit the envelopes open and slide the contents out so that she only saw the notebook paper or the white backs of the photos. She transferred them sight unseen into the drawer of her bedside table.

She could have told Veronica the truth about Sam, who he was, how the marriage with him had never been real. She wasn't sure why she didn't do it. Maybe she would have felt too stupid. Besides, she didn't dare think about her marriage too much, or she wouldn't be able to drag that amputated stump around anymore.

She thought Sam's name only when she had to remind herself of why she had left. He did not try to get in touch with her; she had given her number and address to Veronica but told her not to pass them on. Maybe Veronica had obeyed, maybe she hadn't, but Sam seemed to understand why Jeannette wanted his silence.

He ought to understand. He knew perfectly well.

The days went on. Somehow Jeannette had been in Charleston for a week, then a month, then six months. She walked to and from work. She shelved books. She grew out her hair and put it up in a bun. Even though she didn't look at the photos Veronica sent, for some reason she let them keep coming. Veronica didn't ask if she had seen them or what she thought. The Polaroids accumulated in Jeannette's drawer and snippets of information accumulated in her mind, from the couple of sentences her sister sent along with each one. *She smiled yesterday,* one note said. Another: *She can hold her head up.* Two more: *She can roll over. Sit up.*

Jeannette imagined a calendar with pages flipping through the months. One year: *Nannie, she took her first steps yesterday, we're so proud.* A second year: *Nannie, she's learned so many words, you wouldn't believe it.* Jeannette didn't ask about her—Carrie—when she and Veronica talked, so Veronica might not have known this, but Jeannette held the date of her daughter's birth in her head. If anyone had asked her how old the baby was, she could have told them down to the day.

♫

Time moved on. September 28, 1990. Back in Richmond, Carrie was two years, seven months, and sixteen days old. That weekend, Veronica came down to Charleston for a visit.

Jeannette and her sister had visited a handful of times before. Jeannette wouldn't go back to Richmond, at holidays or any other time, so Veronica stole an occasional weekend away from the ever-growing boys and the new house she and Drew had bought north of the city. Her visits had a peaceful vanilla-pudding blandness. Jeannette breathed her sister's closeness and the familiar cigarette smokiness and tried to pretend that the two of them were girls together again. In her little apartment, they could have been back at Aunt Gretchen's, before the world took hold of either of them.

Up until this visit, Veronica had always played along. She would fill Jeannette in about Drew and the boys but didn't say a word about Sam or Carrie. Instead she and Jeannette talked about Jeannette's job and the people she worked with: chatterbox Miriam at the circulation desk, officious library manager David who waved his Master's of Library Science around like a flag, daydreaming Peter who sat behind the info desk drawing charcoal sketches in a notepad. Jeannette didn't mind any of them; in fact, she had come to see them all as a quirky but harmless substitute family. Veronica liked hearing about them, or said she did. She and Jeannette went for walks along the Battery, ate the meals Jeannette had learned to cook, and talked about nothing in particular until it was time for Veronica to catch the train back home.

Every visit had gone the same way. This time, though, Jeannette felt a difference as soon as she met her sister at the train station. Veronica stepped off the platform carrying her canvas overnight bag. She had on tight-fitting jeans and a plaid short-sleeve shirt that left nothing about her shape to the imagination. Jeannette liked to see her looking young again, liked to notice male heads turning as the two of them walked through the station lobby, but she didn't like Veronica's expression when they got into the taxi Jeannette hailed to take them back to the apartment. Her sister had something to tell her. Jeannette didn't want to hear it.

Veronica waited until they got to Jeannette's place. Then, as they sat together at the little kitchen table with glasses of sweet iced tea, with the sun spilling in on them through the single square window, Veronica said, "Nannie, I need to talk to you. I want you to promise you won't get mad."

Jeannette's stomach tightened. She kept her voice light. "I won't get mad unless I have to."

Veronica set her glass aside. "No, you need to hear me out. I want you to be happy, Nannie, God knows I do, but things have got to change. This has all gone on too long."

Jeannette wanted to get up and walk away. How dare Veronica challenge her about anything? She had no idea, no *idea*, what Jeannette had lived through, and Jeannette knew exactly how long "this" had gone on. Down to the day.

Veronica's eyes held her. For some reason Jeannette couldn't push her chair back. She folded her arms across her chest. "Vee, I know what the situation is. You don't have to tell me."

Veronica shook her head. "You don't know all of it. You don't want to talk to Sam, you don't want to hear about him, I understand that. But you should know where things stand with him."

Jeannette flinched at the sound of Sam's name. She couldn't stop herself and it made her angry. "I don't care where things stand."

Veronica put her hands down flat on the table. "Nannie. I still don't know why you're so mad at him. I don't understand what he did."

"He lied."

The words fell out of Jeannette's mouth. Behind them, the truth boiled up, as scalding and angry as it had been the day Jeannette left. Worse: it felt like she had forgotten how to swallow pain during the time she had spent away. As if, during those last couple of months in Richmond, she had grown calluses to protect her heart, but now those had dissolved.

"Lied?" Veronica said. "Lied how? About what?"

Jeannette could tell her. She could throw it down on the table between them. *He never wanted a woman. He's sick and messed up. He used me.*

The words burned a path from her gut up her throat. She could say it, and then Veronica would know exactly what Sam had done. Jeannette could picture her sister's anger, how she would turn it against that pathetic excuse for a husband and father. But before she could open her mouth and let it out, she saw Sam's face again in the dark studio apartment the night he asked her to marry him.

He had looked so lost. Jeannette saw him as if that night had happened yesterday. Almost four years ago, and she hadn't managed to forget.

The words washed away. Jeannette felt worn out. She said, "He never really wanted to get married, I don't think. He never had time for me."

Veronica leaned forward again. "You mean he didn't treat you right? He left you on your own too much?"

Jeannette thought he might as well have. She remembered those months when the two of them could have been living on opposite sides of a wall. "Yes."

Veronica reached out. Jeannette couldn't help taking her hand. Their fingers laced loosely together on the table. Veronica said, "Nannie, honey, I wish you would've told me. You were lonely, and then you had the baby. I know that's hard. I could have helped you out."

Could she? By then, things had gotten strange between them, and Jeannette hadn't stopped to put them right. Now Jeannette managed, "You had your hands full."

"Well, sure. They were never too full for you, though. You know that."

Jeannette swallowed. Yes, right now the two of them could have been girls again. Veronica could have been charging across the playground to rescue her sister from the tow-headed brats. Jeannette couldn't let Veronica see how, this time, the big sister couldn't have fixed what was wrong.

Jeannette said, "I felt like I didn't know him." That was true. "And then the baby. I couldn't love her, Vee." Of course she couldn't, when she didn't want to.

"Nannie, sometimes that happens. They call it 'failure to bond.' There's things you can do about it."

Jeannette hadn't tried. "I can't do anything about it now," she said. "She doesn't know who I am. She wouldn't want me around."

God, it hurt. Veronica saw it: she closed both her hands around Jeannette's. "That's what I wanted to talk to you about, honey. Can you listen to me a minute?"

Jeannette blinked back her tears. "Okay."

"Here's the thing," Veronica said. "Sam, now, he and I talked before I came down here. He wanted me to tell you that he isn't going to ask you for a divorce. He said, this is exactly how he put it, he wouldn't hit you with one more thing after all his other mistakes. I think I know what he meant now."

She didn't. Jeannette tried to absorb what Veronica had said. Sam and her sister had discussed all this without her.

Veronica said, "You see, honey, if he served you with papers and all, he could take full custody of Carrie and no questions asked. He wouldn't have to give you visitation or anything."

Fog filled Jeannette's mind. Divorce. They probably should have done that a long time ago. Sam already had full custody of Carrie. Jeannette might never see her daughter again. She had already known that, hadn't she?

Veronica went on, still holding Jeannette's hands between both of hers, "So the thing is, he doesn't want to do that to you. Legally, he could," she added gently, "because of the way things went down." She meant Jeannette leaving, of course. "But if the two of you talked about it, if you figured out a plan, you could still spend time with Carrie. See her when you wanted."

Jeannette swallowed. She had all those photos in her bedside table, but she didn't know what her daughter looked like. What kind of mother acted like that?

Veronica finished, "I know this is all hard for you, honey. But like I said, I think it's gone on long enough. You and Sam need to sort things out so you can both get on with your lives. And, Nannie, that little girl deserves to have her mama."

Mama. Carrie didn't know anything about having a mother. Jeannette's throat was so dry her voice came out in a whisper. "Does she know about me?"

Veronica nodded. "She knows she has a mommy. She knows what you look like. Sam showed her pictures."

Carrie was so young. Two years, seven months, sixteen days. Did it mean anything to her to look at somebody in a picture? Jeannette had never seen a picture of Isabel. She and Veronica had grown up with nothing at all.

Veronica must have been thinking the same thing. Watching Jeannette's face, she said, "You know your baby deserves better than we had."

Jeannette couldn't answer. Veronica went on, "I have to tell you one thing, though. Sam's a terrific father. With what you said, you'd think maybe he wouldn't be, but that baby is his whole world." She finished, "So I told him I'd tell you all that. I won't tell you what you have to do, honey. Nobody can decide that but you. I just want you to think about it, that's all."

Jeannette nodded. Her brain seemed to have filled up with cold molasses. She didn't know when she would be able to think about anything.

Veronica squeezed her hands and let go. "Now, I'll tell you what, I'm starving after that train ride. How about you fix me one of those suppers you're so good at."

Jeannette managed to smile. She wouldn't call herself a good cook: functional was more like it. "Okay."

As she moved around the galley kitchen, putting the meal together, she and Veronica went back to their usual vanilla-pudding conversation.

Jeannette chatted about the library, Peter's sketchbook, Miriam's gossip, while in her head the Polaroids rattled and slithered around in their drawer as if they could yell for her attention. A little girl who was walking and talking, who *knows so many words, you wouldn't believe it.* A little girl who had only seen her mother in photos.

She deserves better.

♫

The day Jeannette disappeared, the future stretched out in front of Sam in a series of insurmountable peaks. If anyone had told him then, "Two and a half years from now, the RSA will be thriving, your daughter will be walking and talking and getting prettier every day, and she will think her father is the greatest person in the world," he would have laughed, if he managed to answer at all. The world had turned into a nightmare. He survived because one tiny life held him accountable.

During those first months, three people helped him keep it together. One was Veronica. She had said she should be mad at him and didn't know how right she was, but her love for her niece trumped everything else. That day in her apartment, when Sam's legs would finally support him enough to walk and he trusted himself to drive home, she put her arms around him and Carrie both and held on tight. "You call me, you hear? If you need anything, you call. I don't care if it's the middle of the night."

If she had known why Jeannette had left, she probably would have chased him out of her apartment with any weapon she could find. Strangely, as Sam went slowly down the stairs with the precious burden in his arms, he no longer cared about his sins. He only had enough energy to put one foot in front of the other. At home, with Carrie settled in her crib, he called his parents. Ma answered. He told her briefly that Jeannette had left him and Carrie, and he didn't know when, or if, she would be back.

"Oh, Liudas. *Aš atsiprašau.*"

I'm so sorry. She had said exactly the same thing when he had told her about Gil's death. He remembered that. And she did not throw out a barrage of questions: *What do you mean? What happened? How could she?* In fact, she did not sound as shocked as she should have been. He didn't have the energy to wonder why.

She and Dad arrived at Sam's house before noon the next day. They must have left Westbury at dawn. Sam met them at the door with Carrie. Ma took her granddaughter in her arms and whispered, "*Saldus mažylis. Toks gražus.*" Sam remembered those words: *Sweet little one. So beautiful.*

Dad said very little. Sam had braced himself for an interrogation. He had thought he might stun them all, when Dad asked the inevitable "Why did your wife leave?" and say, "Because she figured out what I am."

The question didn't come. Dad did ask if Sam knew where Jeannette was and if she had been in touch with him. Sam told him about Charleston and Veronica. Dad only nodded. Then he asked to hold the baby.

In that moment, as he watched his father settle Carrie in the crook of his arm, Sam realized he could still feel things. Once upon a time, Dad had delivered a baby right there in the house on River Street, because he hadn't had enough time to get Ma to the hospital. Sam pictured the master bedroom, the late-afternoon sun slanting in through the lace curtains, the gold-haired woman on the bed and the young man standing beside her.

Now Ma said, "*Mielas,* I remember that look on your dad's face. He looked the same way the first time he saw you."

Was that true? Sam didn't know. If he thought back hard enough, could he remember those arms holding him? Could he remember the wonder in that face? He wished he could, but with everything that had happened since, he didn't dare believe it.

At least the house felt alive again with his parents in it. Ma was another of the three people who kept Sam going. When she worked with him in the kitchen or worked around him while he sat at the table with Carrie, she managed to tease him out of himself. "I don't know, *mielas.* You have so much to learn now. Do you think you're up for it?" From anyone else, the same question would have frozen him. Her face said she knew he could take care of anything. She should not have loved him the way she did, but he took it without question.

After a few days, Dad had to go back to work. Ma stayed on for two more weeks, helping with feedings and changings and laundry. The day she left, a Saturday, Sam drove her to the train station and came back to a house that felt bigger and emptier than ever. Carrie had gotten used to being held all the time and fussed when he tried to put her down in her crib. He found his *Chichester Psalms* score and sat on the couch with her in his lap and the music open on the cushion next to him. The notes didn't make any sense.

He must have been more tired than he knew, because when the doorbell rang, it jerked him out of a half-doze. Carrie was fast asleep against his shoulder. He took her with him into the foyer and looked through the glass panes by the door.

Nathan. When Sam saw him standing there, he couldn't get the lock undone fast enough.

"Hey." Nathan smiled. "I know it's awfully pushy to drop in on you like this. I'll go away if you say so."

"No. Please, come on in."

The chilly March draft swirled through the foyer. Nathan shut the door carefully behind him. "I was in the neighbourhood," he said, "and I thought, I haven't met that little girl yet. I'll just barge on over and see if they're home."

"We're glad you did." Carrie was awake now. Sam turned her against his shoulder so Nathan could see her face. Her big eyes looked up at him solemnly.

Nathan touched her cheek with a fingertip. "Oh, now, look at you." He bent closer. "My sister's little girl must have been this small once, but I don't remember. Look at those eyes." He glanced up at Sam. "Blue?"

Sam had to look away. "They're grey." Jeannette's eyes.

Nathan nodded. After a pause, he said, "Pretty girl, can you come here?"

Sam let him take her. She didn't fuss at the new person. Nathan cuddled her and said, "She says, 'Daddy, who's this, now?'"

Sam couldn't help smiling. The baby looked tinier than ever in Nathan's arms. Did the view seem different to her, all the way up there?

Nathan studied her. "You know, I think you look like your daddy. You have his face."

"My mom thinks so too," Sam said. "Poor thing."

Nathan shook his head. "I don't think so." To Carrie he added, "Now, I wonder if your daddy has any coffee around. You think I could make him some?"

Sam laughed. "Coffee? I wouldn't last long without it."

Nathan told Carrie, "Then let's do that. I'll put some coffee on, and you keep Daddy company. Deal?"

Sam sat at the table with his daughter while Nathan moved around the kitchen as confidently as if he had been in it dozens of times. The house felt warm again. For now, that was enough.

So Nathan became the third person who helped Sam get through. On weekends, the singer stopped by to visit. He checked in with Sam now and then at the office and brought him coffee and sometimes a sandwich at chorus rehearsals. Sam let himself lean on that friendship. And sometimes, on weekends when Nathan stayed into the evening, Sam would put Carrie down for the night, and he and Nathan would sit together in the living room. Often they didn't turn on the lights. They sat together on the couch, looking out the bay window at the dark quiet street, and Nathan put his arm around Sam's shoulders. The first time he did it, Sam thought he should pull away, but Nathan said, "I think Dad needs somebody to hold him too." Sam couldn't deny it.

Weeks became months. Months stretched out to a year. Somewhere during that time, it became natural for Sam to exchange a kiss with Nathan when they said goodnight. Later, for the first time, Nathan came up behind Sam in the kitchen, slipped his arms around him, and held him the way you held the person you loved. That felt right too. Sam felt his soul opening up again in a way he had thought it could not. He never forgot Gil. He never forgot Ma and Dad either. Somehow, in spite of the shadows, what he and Nathan had bloomed and grew strong.

To the rest of the world, including the RSA people and Sam's in-laws and parents, they were colleagues and good friends. Sam knew Nathan felt restless; he was too proud of it, he told Sam one evening, to want to keep it to himself. "I want the world to know you're mine." Sam felt the same, but as right and radiant as what they had was, Sam couldn't convince himself yet to let the world see it. It could still cause too much pain. He couldn't go through that again, not yet, as much as he wished he were stronger.

One year, then another. Sam watched with astonishment as his daughter grew. First smile, first laugh, first steps and first words. His little flower had beautiful eyes and dark hair and a face that, yes, was the same shape as his own but with finer, more delicate features. As small as she was, she wrapped him firmly around her finger.

In the fall of 1990, the RSA went into its fifth season with Sam as music director. At the dress rehearsal for the first concert of the season, Sam looked out at his orchestra and wondered how he and they had come this far.

This first concert would be orchestra only. The chorus was preparing for *Messiah* again in December, their third full performance of it under Sam's watch. For this fall program, Sam had originally planned all Beethoven, but over the summer he had changed his mind. The concert would open with Beethoven's "Edgmont" overture and end with the *Eroica* Symphony, but between the two, Sam had inserted the orchestral version of Ravel's *Ma Mère L'Oye*.

He shouldn't want to touch that piece again. Lately, though, Carrie had fallen in love with "Cinderella" and "Beauty and the Beast." Maybe reading her favourite bedtime stories had put the idea in his head. After he programmed it, one idea led to another.

He and Jeannette needed to settle things. Neither of them had filed for a divorce, but eventually they would have to. The situation had dragged out long enough. Sam asked Veronica, when she went down to see her sister at the end of September, to tell Jeannette that he, Sam, wouldn't ask for divorce first. That would have let him take Carrie away for good. Despite the fact that she had shown no interest in her daughter, and despite the fact that for his own sake he would have done it gladly, Sam couldn't make himself punish Jeannette that way. Not after the rest of what he had done.

Veronica did it and reported back that Jeannette was thinking things over. Sam pushed the uneasiness out of his mind while he focused on concert prep. Maybe Jeannette wouldn't decide to do anything. She hadn't done anything after all this time.

The dress rehearsal for the fall concert went well. After five years together, Sam and the players understood that they could count on each other. When rehearsal ended, Sam went down into the house and found Nathan in the second row, with Carrie beside him.

She had started coming to work with Sam when she was only a few months old. Sam had gotten to the point where he couldn't in all conscience ask for Veronica's help much anymore. Veronica insisted she loved to do it, but she had plenty to do with her own two, plus the move to a new house the summer after Carrie was born. Any halfway-smart person would have found a good nanny, but Sam couldn't stand the thought of leaving Carrie with a stranger. The plan he and Lydia came up with had worked out better than Sam dared to hope. The RSA people became a kind of extended family for Carrie, who absorbed music along with the air she breathed. Sometimes Sam thought that had a lot to do with the way she was.

Now she saw him coming across the stage and jumped out of her seat. "Daddy!" Watching her run still made him nervous, she might trip and fall so easily, but she got to the bottom of the stage steps at the same time he did.

He caught her up and hugged her. "Hey, baby girl. How come you're down here? I thought you were helping out Aunt Lydia upstairs."

She looked up at him. "Uncle Nathan bringed me."

Nobody had told her to call Nathan "Uncle." She had come up with that herself. Her voice had a lisp and a Richmond lilt in it, and her solemn, funny sentences so often made Sam want to laugh, but she hated that. He kept a straight face. "Did he?"

Nathan came up to them. "That's right," he said. "I wanted to watch for a while, so I asked Lydia if I could bring Carrie down. She was a good little audience."

Sam smoothed Carrie's hair away from her face. "I bet you were. Did you like the music?"

She nodded. "Daddy, I come see the concert."

She said it as if she had been mulling it over all day. Sam had to swallow another laugh, but he was surprised. She hadn't come to any shows before, and he hadn't known she thought about them at all. He said, "You mean the concert tomorrow? You want to see it?"

"Yes."

By now he should know not to underestimate what she thought about. He said, "Well, but you were going to visit Aunt Veronica tomorrow. Don't you want to see Aunt Veronica?"

She shook her head. "I come see the concert."

Sam heard Nathan cough. He said, "Honey, concerts take a long time, you know? You might get tired."

She shook her head. "Not tired. I see the concert."

She didn't raise her voice or whine the way other kids might have. Stubborn Kraychek *men*, was it? Ma should have seen this. Nathan had turned his back on them, and Sam saw his shoulders shaking. *Big help you are.*

As if Nathan heard the thought, he turned around. "Tell you what," he said. "If she wants to be in the audience, she can sit with me."

Sam shook himself. The point was that a not-quite-three-year-old couldn't make it through a whole evening. "It would be too much for her," he said. "I don't think she's ready."

Carrie patted his cheek to get his attention. "Daddy," she said firmly. "I ready."

Sam burst out laughing before he could help it. Never assume she didn't listen or couldn't understand. Carrie gave him her most reproachful look—*how could you?*—and he pulled himself together as quick as he could. "Okay," he told her. Maybe this was why he'd programmed the Ravel. "You can see the concert with Uncle Nathan."

That night, after she had gone to sleep, Sam called Veronica. "I'm afraid there's been a change in plan."

"What's up?"

After all this time, anything unexpected still made her nervous. Sam knew the feeling. "Nothing serious," he said. "It's just that your niece informed me today that she's going to watch the concert."

Veronica laughed. "Did she, now?"

"In no uncertain terms. You know she can make up her mind about things."

"She sure can." Veronica hesitated. "Do you want me to come?"

She preferred to avoid the Lewis Center, Sam knew. Too many memories. "That's okay," he said. "Nathan's going to be there. He'll take care of her."

He couldn't help holding his breath every time he mentioned Nathan. To his relief, Veronica accepted it without question; she had come to see the singer as a friend and had noticed nothing different yet. "Okay," she said. Another pause. Then, "Sam, I wanted to tell you, I talked to Nannie yesterday."

Sam's hand tightened around the phone. "Did you? What did she say?"

"Nothing much. Except, this time she asked about Carrie."

Sam's chair seemed to shudder under him. He and Veronica had always tacitly avoided discussing the fact that for two years and more, Jeannette had not seemed curious about her own daughter. He tried to keep his voice calm. "Really?"

"Uh-huh. She didn't say anything about, you know, what you and I talked about." The divorce business. "She just wanted to know how Carrie was doing. And she said, 'She's a pretty girl.'"

Sam knew Veronica had taken a recent picture of Carrie down to Charleston with her in September and had handed it to Jeannette personally. He had never been sure whether or not Jeannette had gotten all the other pictures Veronica had mailed. For all he knew, she had thrown out every envelope when it arrived.

So she was taking an interest now. That was good. They did have to resolve things. Sam didn't want to tell Veronica that he felt like a pair of icy hands had closed around his chest.

"That was about all," Veronica said. "We didn't talk long."

They never did. Once, things had been different between the two of them. Sam said, "Thank you for telling me."

Veronica cleared her throat. "Of course. Well, you tell me how the concert goes, okay? Tell me how our little music fan likes it."

Sam's laugh felt hollow. "We'll keep you posted for sure."

After he hung up, he went upstairs and quietly opened the door to Carrie's room. She was curled up under the pink-and-white blanket, hugging her brown plush bunny. The night light bathed her soft cheeks and closed eyes.

Sam went to the bed and sat down on the edge of the mattress. Carrie didn't stir. A strand of dark hair lay across her cheek, and he smoothed it away.

Suppose Jeannette were here right now. Suppose she could walk into this room and see this little girl.

No.

Sam knew exactly how wrong that was. Jeannette had the right to talk about Carrie, ask about her, see her if she wanted.

No.

Sam leaned forward and kissed his daughter's cheek. "I love you, baby girl."

He whispered it, not to wake her. Then he got up and went out, shutting the door behind him as if it could hold out the world.

♪

Jeannette called the Lewis Center two days before the RSA's October concert. She didn't recognize the name of the woman who answered the phone at the box office, but she put on her strongest South Carolina accent just in case. "I'd like to reserve a ticket for Saturday's concert, please."

"Let me see what we have."

During the pause, Jeannette looked at the photo of Carrie she had set up on her nightstand. A pair of grey eyes, identical to the ones Jeannette saw every day in the mirror, looked back at her.

The woman came back to the phone. "We have a couple of seats left in the lower orchestra. You have more choice if you'd like to sit closer to the back, but of course you don't get as good of a view."

"I'd prefer the back," Jeannette said. "Do you have anything in the very last row?"

"The last row?" The woman sounded as if she couldn't in all conscience sell a seat there. "Yes. I can give you V 115, that's in the middle section, or V 22, that's on the aisle near the left-hand door, or..."

Jeannette cut her off. "That would be perfect. V 22, please."

"Very good," the woman said. "You'll pick it up at Will Call?"

"Yes."

"Your name?"

Jeannette had thought this through. "Reilly. Marie Reilly." It sounded stupid, as if she were a character in a lame spy movie, but she wouldn't take any chances.

"Very good, Ms. Reilly. We'll see you on Saturday."

Jeannette hung up and reached for the photo of her daughter. Veronica had given it to her at the end of their last visit, handed it to her out of her purse right before she got on the train. This time she hadn't put it in an envelope. Jeannette had had no choice but to see it.

The little girl in the picture had Jeannette's eyes and Sam's face. Her smile was sweet and shy. Jeannette had sat in the taxi and stared at the photo all the way home.

When she got back to her apartment, she had sat down on the bed and opened her bedside drawer. After all this time, the Polaroids had gotten jumbled, but Veronica had written the date on the back of each one. Jeannette had sorted them out chronologically, looking only at the backs of them. Then, finally, she had turned them over.

The first ones looked like the infant she remembered. Flipping through them felt like watching a sped-up film of a growing plant, but the grey eyes were always the same.

That afternoon, holding this most recent picture in her hand, Jeannette had made a decision. Now, today, she had followed through on that decision by calling the Lewis Center. She knew she had to do this. It still felt like madness.

On Saturday morning, the day of the concert, Jeannette packed an overnight bag and put the picture in her purse. The taxi let her off at the train station. Nobody in Richmond knew she was coming. She wouldn't have to talk to anybody if she didn't want to.

The train left on schedule. Jeannette sat by the window, bracing herself against the rocking of the car and watching the scenery flow past. The rails carried her north for the second time in her life. The first time, her sister's apartment had been waiting for her, and a new job with a terrifyingly real conductor. Now Jeannette unzipped her purse and took out the photo. She didn't need to look at it anymore; she had memorized every detail of the little girl's face, but holding it felt like an anchor.

Tonight's concert would only be a start. Jeannette didn't expect to talk to Sam, and surely Carrie wouldn't be there. Toddlers (Carrie still counted as a toddler, right?) didn't sit through two hours of orchestra music. Jeannette would watch Sam on that stage while he did the thing that had made her fall in love with him. Nothing else would ever be as hard. After she survived it, then later she might, for instance, pick up the phone. Meanwhile, nobody had to know what she was doing. Veronica would have probably would have insisted that Jeannette come and stay with them, but no power on earth could have gotten Jeannette to go to that new house, sit at that same old yellow table, and listen to the boys bang and shriek around the way they always had. Jeannette's heart held together, barely. Let her sister put a Bruce Springsteen album on the stereo and the pieces would fall apart.

When the train arrived in Richmond, Jeannette tucked the photo safely back into her purse and found a cab to take her to the Ramada Inn two blocks down the street from the Lewis Center. She tried not to notice how close they were to the old Belvedere, but as the cab went down Jefferson Street, she couldn't avoid seeing the James River slipping past, lit with orange and gold in the sunset. She made herself eat a sandwich at the Bain's Deli next to the hotel. Then she went back to her room and took her concert clothes out of the overnight bag.

She had thought a lot about what to wear. In the end, she had decided on the same black wool skirt and grey blouse she had worn to that first chorus rehearsal so long ago. Veronica had never persuaded her to get rid of them. The skirt fell below her knees, and the blouse buttoned up to her chin, erasing as much of her as possible.

Her hair was her biggest fear. After only two and a half years, she couldn't hope that the RSA people she had known wouldn't be there anymore. If she waited for that, Carrie would grow out of all recognition. Obviously somebody might recognize Jeannette's face; she would have to take her chances with that, but her hair had always been the beacon that drew unwanted attention. She wound it up into the tightest, smallest bun she could.

Her long, shapeless tan coat extinguished her almost down to her plain black shoes. When she looked at herself in the mirror, she thought she had never seen a more nondescript face than the pale, unmade-up, mouselike one that looked back at her.

She left the hotel at the last possible minute. It felt strange to walk to the Lewis Center carrying a new purse and no music. Her fingers darted to the shirt collar again and again, checking that every last button was firmly fastened.

She didn't go behind the building. Sam's Pinto, if he still had it, might or might not be there, and the maple tree might or might not have hung on this long. Jeannette didn't want to know. She went straight up the front steps to the lobby doors.

The woman at Will Call didn't recognize her. "Reilly? Yes, ma'am, right here." Jeannette handed over her money and took the ticket with sweaty fingers.

The usher handing out programs didn't look familiar either, but that didn't mean much. Jeannette kept her head down and shuffled past, sticking out her hand in time to catch a booklet. Nobody said, "Hey! Aren't you...?" She ducked into the dim hall and dropped into her seat in the back corner.

The RSA people who remembered her would be down in the lower orchestra, in the rich people seats. Jeannette opened her program and tried to forget the night she had sat in that lower section with Veronica and Drew. *"So that's what he looks like! Not bad at all, Nannie. I can see the appeal."* She opened her booklet to the program for tonight, avoiding a glimpse at the inside front cover where Sam's picture would be.

She hadn't bothered to ask what was on tonight's concert before she bought the ticket. Now she found the page. Words on the program jumped out at her as if they had been written in red ink. *Ma Mère L'Oye*, Maurice Ravel (1875-1937).

How could he? How *could* he? Jeannette snapped the program shut and fumbled under her chair for her purse. Forget it. This had all been a mistake.

The house lights went down. She froze.

A creak as the stage door opened. Footsteps. Jeannette forced her head up. The concertmaster, Victor Goodstein, had come onstage. He stood next to the podium and bowed, then turned around to tune the orchestra.

Jeannette could not sit here. Nausea gripped her as the tuning sounds filled the hall. Her seat was on the end of the row: she wouldn't bother anyone if she slipped out this second, while she still could. The door looked so far away.

The tuning stopped. Silence. Then the stage door creaked open again, and now Jeannette could not have moved a muscle if someone had held a knife to her throat.

She closed her eyes. That much she could do. The applause began again, and those were his footsteps on the stage floor, and she knew without looking how he would face the audience, how he would smile.

As the applause faded, she opened her eyes. He was already turning away, but she saw his face. For one instant she could have sworn their eyes met.

She must have imagined it. He turned to the orchestra and picked up the baton. The music began.

During the "Edgmont" overture, Jeannette kept her eyes closed. She didn't need to look at Sam to see the motion of the baton or the way his face looked in profile. The melodies wrapped around her like iron bands. She had walked away from music. Now it pulled her in, as if to punish her for the long absence, and closed over her head so that she felt sure she would drown.

After the overture, she had a minute or two to drag herself up to the surface and breathe. Then the Ravel began.

This time, Jeannette could not close her eyes. They locked on Sam's face, his hands, the white baton. Memory took her straight back to the basement rehearsal room and that first night. The guiding motions of his hands as intimate as a touch on her body.

His apartment, in the dark. His face in the faint light through the window. *"Jeannette, will you marry me?"* What was he thinking now? This piece had belonged to the two of them. In this moment, with the white light on him, did he remember her?

In the final movement, chimes rang and the harp's glissandi sparkled in the air. Jeannette could not raise her hands to applaud when the last chord faded. Beside her, in front of her, people stood up to clap and cheer, but over their heads she could still see his face.

The house lights came up. He had disappeared backstage, the audience had begun to stand and stretch and leave the hall for a break, and finally Jeannette could move too. She reached under her seat again for her purse.

In the red-and-gold lobby, she headed straight for the glass doors. She had forgotten about running into anyone she knew. All that mattered was to get out of this building as fast as she could.

She almost collided with someone. At the last second, she realized who it was and ducked back against the wall.

That man. Nathan Woods. By some miracle, he had not seen her. Give her a second to catch her breath, and then she could sneak past and...

Then she saw why he hadn't noticed her. Someone else had his full attention.

The little girl was so *small*. Jeannette stared at her smooth dark hair, her profile, her sunshine-coloured dress with a sash tied in a neat bow at the back.

He, Nathan, held her hand. An older woman, someone Jeannette didn't know, was talking to them both. Jeannette heard, "You must be Sam's little girl. How old are you, sweetie?"

"Two and three-quarters."

The shy lisp was almost too low for Jeannette to hear. She clung to it. *Two years, eight months, three days.*

She couldn't move while they stood there. After a minute or two, they headed off toward the other side of the lobby. Jeannette didn't take her eyes off the yellow dress until more people moved across her vision and hid it from sight.

Her breath came back. Ice trickled up and down her spine. That man. With her daughter. For a crazy second she wanted to dive into the crowd and snatch the little girl away.

The lights in the lobby flickered. The crowd moved back toward the doors of the hall. Jeannette let herself drift back to her seat.

She barely listened to the *Eroica* Symphony. The white stick danced in the light but could not hold her attention. Where, in this sea of people, was the yellow dress? Jeannette scanned the crowd in the dark, trying to make out Nathan's head sticking up above the rest. She felt sure Carrie was still with him.

How dare he? Him and Sam both. How could they do such a thing?

By the end of the concert, she knew what she had to do. She would not leave this building until she had marched right up to Sam and told him she knew all about him. Knew what he was. Would not tolerate him exposing their daughter to that.

There was a meet-and-greet afterward. Jeannette put on her coat, clamped her purse under her arm, and gripped her rolled-up program tight. She followed the crowd down the hall to the green room.

As soon as she stepped inside, she saw Sam in the middle of the room. White light fell around him and set him apart from the rest of the throng.

How could he still be so beautiful? How was that fair?

She gripped her program tighter. She probably knew people in this room. They would see her, maybe storm up and accuse her of abandoning their Maestro. She didn't care. Nothing in the world mattered except to get to Sam and throw every stab of pain she had ever lived through back in his face.

She took one step toward him. On the other side of the room, the crowd parted.

"Excuse us, folks. Excuse us for a second."

Jeannette didn't know how she could hear the dark-chocolate voice from where she stood, but she did, loud and clear. She saw the yellow dress. Then, peering between the people closest to her, she saw Sam bend down and hold out his arms.

"Here's my girl."

His voice reached her too. Maybe the room had gone quiet. Jeannette saw her daughter let go of Nathan's hand and run to her father.

As Sam caught her up, someone stepped in front of Jeannette, blocking her view. She pushed her way into another gap between people without a thought about rudeness or the danger of being recognized. She couldn't stand to lose sight of Carrie again.

The yellow dress looked so small and bright against Sam's black tailcoat. Carrie hid her face against her father's shoulder and twined her arms around his neck.

"Hey, there," Sam said. He rested his hand on the little girl's hair, and Jeannette saw he had no wedding ring. How long ago had he stopped wearing it? "What's the matter, honey?" he asked.

Something about him had changed. It took Jeannette a minute to realize what it was, and then she knew. The white light had fallen away.

Somebody—Nathan—was saying, "There's a lot of people here." Jeannette couldn't take her eyes off her husband. She saw him kiss Carrie's dark hair. "It's okay, baby," he said. Nothing could erase that voice from Jeannette's memory. "I've got you."

What had Veronica said? *She's his whole world.* Anybody with eyes could see that.

The past sucked at Jeannette. If she looked back at her own childhood, such a long time ago in such a different place, would she find protective arms holding her? A gentle voice telling her she was safe? Aunt Gretchen had tried, yes; she had done her best, but the plain fact was she had never wanted the burden of two little girls in her own old age. No one had ever said it out loud, but Jeannette and Veronica had always known it.

No. Jeannette could scour her past for the kind of love she saw right now, the love Sam had for the child in his arms, and find only a parent-shaped emptiness.

No one noticed her as she slipped away. The glass doors of the lobby opened and let her out into the night.

♪

Nathan said, "I was impressed. She did a great job."

Sunlight streamed into the kitchen. Sam sat at the table with Carrie in his lap. She was still sleepy after the long day yesterday, and now she dozed with her head against his chest. The rich smell of percolating coffee filled the room.

Nathan said, "She was a little lady." The coffee finished, and he took the pot off the burner and filled two mugs on the counter. "And, you know, she was really listening. She had her eyes on you the whole time."

Sam couldn't help liking that. "I'm glad she made it through. That was a lot to take in."

Nathan went back for the half-and-half carton and the sugar bowl. "I think she liked it. You've got a little musician in training there."

Sam stirred half-and-half into his mug. He must still be tired too; he felt like he had a sack of concrete strapped across his shoulders. The concert had felt long. The Ravel had been part of that, no doubt, and he had worried about Carrie, though it turned out he didn't need to. But the strangest thing, which he still couldn't get out of his head, had been the woman he had seen in the audience.

He hadn't mentioned her to anyone. She had been all the way in the back, and Sam hadn't even gotten a clear look at her face, much less her hair.

He couldn't have said why she made him so uneasy. He had to be imagining things, between the Ravel and the talk with Veronica on Thursday.

Nathan sat down on the other side of the table. In Sam's lap, Carrie stirred. She looked up at him with sleep-confused eyes. "Hey, honey," he said. "You okay?"

She thought about that. She always woke up slowly, taking the world in bit by bit, as if she were putting puzzle pieces together in her head. "Yes," she decided.

"Would you like some apple juice?"

She nodded. Nathan started to get up, but Sam said, "I'll get it. You've been doing all the work." He lifted Carrie onto her booster seat.

She had been so patient last night. As Sam poured the juice into her yellow plastic cup, he remembered the crowd in the green room. So many people, familiar ones and unknowns both, but after one overwhelmed moment she had recovered quickly. She had held on to the edge of his lapel and stayed calm and quiet while he greeted all the faces. Somehow the job had felt easier with her there with him.

He set the cup down in front of her on the table. She was wide awake now and picked it up eagerly. Sam had sat down again with his coffee when the doorbell rang.

Nathan glanced at him. "Expecting anyone?"

"No."

"Probably somebody selling something."

Sam set the mug down. Salesmen didn't show up on Sundays.

Carrie put her cup down too. "Daddy, I get the door?"

The bell rang again. Nathan said, "I'd leave it. Those people can be so rude."

Sam pushed his chair back. Carrie looked at him expectantly. "No, honey," he told her, "you stay here."

Nathan said, "Really, I wouldn't bother."

Sam shook his head. "I'll be right back."

He went into the hall. It couldn't be anything. It wasn't. And yet cold wrapped around him, and when he looked through the glass panes by the door, he already knew who he would see.

Leave it. Walk away. He could not be so stupid. If nothing else, she would have seen the cars in the driveway. She knew he was here.

Sam forced his fingers to turn the deadbolt. The door swung open.

She looked tiny, like a bird. She stood there on the porch with her purse clamped under her arm and her shapeless tan coat unbuttoned, showing the high-collared silver blouse and the black skirt that hung past her knees. Behind her, down on the street, a cab pulled away from the curb.

She had combed her hair back from her forehead and twisted it into a tight bun. Her wide, scared eyes (he had seen that exact shade of grey every day for the past two and a half years) rested on his face.

"Jeannette." The syllables dropped out of his mouth.

She swallowed. Her shoulders went back and her spine straightened, but her voice still huddled up small. "Sam. I need to talk to you."

He could have said so many things. *After all this time, you show up here?* Or, *You could have picked up the phone.* Or, *Really? Well, I don't need to talk to you.*

He had to do better than that. He stood aside. "Come in."

She stepped into the foyer, scanning it as if she expected a trap to slam shut around her. Before he could begin to think what to say, offer an empty piece of politeness like taking her coat, or tell her he had a guest in the house, she said, "I want to talk about Carrie."

Sam went still. Incongruously warm sunlight played on the walls. "Yes?" he said.

Jeannette faced him squarely. Her voice had a backbone in it now. "Yes. I don't like the way things are for her. I don't think she should..."

"What's going on?"

Nathan. Sam could not turn his head, but he heard the deliberate footsteps coming down the hall. Carrie had to stay in the kitchen. She must not hear any of this. Sam had one instant to offer up that prayer, if it was one, before Jeannette's purse landed on the floor with a noise like a door slamming.

"How *dare* you?"

Her face had gone from white to scarlet. She rounded on Sam with her fists clenched. "How dare you have him in this house? How dare you let him be around her?"

Her fury paralyzed Sam. He could not open his mouth. Jeannette shouted, "I know what you are! You shouldn't be allowed to keep her! You're not fit to be a father!"

The words sank into Sam's brain. Through a red mist, he remembered his daughter's small fingers holding the edge of his lapel. Then rage crashed over him and swept everything else away.

"You left her!" His own voice roared in his ears. He had never felt so angry, not in the fights with Dad, not in the worst times with the woman who stood in front of him now. "You walked off and left her and never gave a damn! Where the hell do you get the nerve?" His hands burned. More than anything, he wanted to slap her face so hard she would wear the mark of his fingers forever. "Get out of here! Get out of this house!"

In the kitchen, something thumped on the floor. Little feet ran and stumbled in the hall. Carrie burst into the foyer. "Daddy!"

Through the red haze, Sam saw her terror. Her face was flushed, her eyes wide and full of tears.

The fury blew away. She ran to him, and he bent down and caught her. She clung to him, shaking, and buried her face against his shoulder.

Sam straightened up, holding her, keeping his hand on her hair like a shield. "It's okay, baby girl." Nothing mattered except that she must not be hurt. He faced his wife. "Jeannette, you need to leave." He couldn't believe how calm he sounded. "We aren't going to do this in front of her."

Jeannette's cheeks were on fire. She looked absurdly small in the oversized coat, her thin chest heaving under the silver blouse. She stared at Carrie. Then she covered her face with her hands and burst into tears.

Oh, hell. What could anyone do about this?

Nathan said, "I'm sorry."

Sam had almost forgotten he was there. "I know I should go," Nathan said, "but I don't want you to deal with this alone."

Sam found his voice again. "I can handle it."

Nathan shook his head. "Do you mind if I stay?"

A lump sprang up in Sam's throat. Jeannette hung there between them, crying. "No," Sam said. "It's fine. If you're sure you want to."

"I do."

In Sam's arms, Carrie had stopped shivering. She must not be in the middle of this. The last thing Sam wanted to do was let go of her, but he kissed her hair and said, "Honey, could you go back to the kitchen with Uncle Nathan?"

She shook her head, hard, and held onto him tighter. In some other world he might have smiled.

Jeannette needed to get herself together. Still holding Carrie, Sam bent to pick the purse up off the floor. "Jeannette," he said. "Let's sit down, okay?"

She nodded and let him lead her to the living room doors. Another time, she had closed her eyes so he could walk her in here and surprise her with the new piano.

They sat on the couch. Sam held Carrie in his lap. Nathan had followed them as far as the doorway. Now he met Sam's eyes, nodded, and quietly left the room.

"I'm sorry," Jeannette gulped. "I'm sorry."

You should be, goddamn it. Sam couldn't find the anger anymore while Carrie hung on to him like this. He ought to keep a box of tissues in this room. With one hand, he managed to unzip Jeannette's purse and dig through until he found a little pack of them, which he passed to her.

She mopped at her eyes. Mascara stained the white paper. "I'm sorry." When she looked up at him, he saw a frightened girl. Dear God, he had once known that face so well. "I didn't mean," she tried. "I shouldn't have said…"

You damn well shouldn't have. Sam swallowed the words for Carrie's sake. "You were upset," he said. His voice slipped almost automatically into the gentle tone he used to use with her.

"I didn't expect," she began. She waved the tissues in the direction of the hallway. "I thought... I hoped you'd be by yourself."

"I understand."

Strangely, he did. Of course Nathan would have been the last person in the world she wanted to see, especially here in the house she and Sam had fixed up and lived in together. Of course that had been a slap in the face. Sam could only imagine what kind of nerve it had taken for her to decide to come here at all.

"When did you come to town?" he asked. Another thought hit him. "Does Veronica know you're here?" She didn't, did she? Surely she would have warned him.

Jeannette shook her head. "No, I didn't tell her. I came up yesterday. For your concert."

That explained one thing, at least. "So you were there. I thought I saw you."

"You did?" She looked scared again. "I didn't want you to. I sat in the back, I didn't want anybody to recognize me. I'm sure they don't want to see me anymore." She was right about that, but Sam wouldn't say so now. Not when she was already hurting so much. She hurried on, "I shouldn't have come here like this. And I didn't, I really didn't mean to start a fight. It's just..." She waved the tissues again helplessly, this time at Carrie, who sat huddled and silent in Sam's lap, hiding her face against his chest. "She... you know..."

She what? *You walked away and left her. You don't have rights anymore.* Sam bit the anger back again. He was supposed to know better.

Jeannette went on, "Her pictures. I have them. And I thought... oh, Sam, it was such a mistake. I don't want her to... to not have..."

In another time, in another place, she had told him how music meant everything to her because she had no mother.

Memory came back, whether he wanted it or not. The guest room in his parents' house, Jeannette's head resting on his chest, the dark wrapping around them both as she whispered how hard it had been for her as a child. How much she had wished for the woman who had never been there.

She didn't want Carrie to live the same way. "I know," he said as cold settled on him. "I know what you mean."

His mind raced ahead. If Jeannette asked for custody, even shared custody. If she wanted Sam to give Carrie up for a single day out of a year, much less weeks or months, how could he stand it?

Or if she went to a judge and told him what her husband was…

"Daddy?"

Carrie had raised her head. Sam forced himself to breathe. "Yes, honey?"

She pointed to Jeannette. "Who is that?"

Sam glanced at his wife. She was watching him, her face pale and anxious.

She's nobody. Nothing to us. Dear God, he wished he could say it. If Jeannette wanted to, if she went to a judge and told him what Sam was, she could take Carrie away whether Sam consented or not. No judge would leave a child with a parent like him.

His little girl looked up at him, her beautiful eyes round with worry. Her mother's eyes. He said, "This lady is very important. She's your mommy."

Carrie knew what the word meant. She knew that other kids, for instance C.J. and Ricky, had mommies who lived with them, though she had never asked why hers did not. Sam watched her thinking. She always thought so carefully about things.

She said, "Mommy?"

Sam swallowed. "That's right. She's the lady we looked at in the pictures. Do you remember the pictures?"

Carrie nodded. Sam believed she did remember, though he hadn't been sure what the photos might mean to her. She turned her head to see Jeannette.

Jeannette smiled and wiped her eyes again. "Hi there, Carrie." Her voice trembled. "You're such a pretty little girl, you know that?"

Sam couldn't help wondering how it must feel to her, hearing her daughter's voice for the first time. He said to Carrie, such a strangely normal thing to do, "What do we say, honey?"

She whispered, "Thank you."

Jeannette told Carrie, "I haven't seen you for a long time, not since you were very small. You've gotten so big." She looked ready to cry again.

Dear God, this was all so fucked up. Nobody could put it right. Least of all Sam, who had caused it.

Carrie looked around at him. She looked scared. All of this had to be confusing; people were upset, and she didn't understand. A thought came into Sam's head, and he made himself say it before he could decide not to. "Carrie, could you do me a favour? Mommy's a little sad, but I think we could cheer her up. Could you give her a hug for me?"

Carrie looked at her mother, and then back at him. "Okay."

Sam let go of her, but she stayed on his lap to hold out her arms to Jeannette. Jeannette leaned forward.

Sam could have held them both. Jeannette put her arms around the little girl and closed her eyes. Sam saw the peace in her face. His chest ached as if it wanted to cave in.

After a moment, Jeannette opened her eyes again and looked at him. Sam heard the question she didn't ask and couldn't say no, not when he knew how much this meant.

When she lifted the little girl into her lap, Carrie reached anxiously for her father. It took all of Sam's self-restraint not to take her back. "It's okay," he told her. "Sit with Mommy for a little while, okay?"

She wasn't happy about it, but she obeyed. Jeannette touched her face, probably trying to coax a smile. "I saw you last night at Daddy's concert. Did you like it?"

No doubt she had seen Carrie with Nathan. That explained why she had appeared on the doorstep today. Carrie nodded, too shy to speak. Sam put in, "That was your first time in the audience, wasn't it, honey." For her, he kept his voice calm, as if they had all seen each other dozens of times before.

Jeannette smiled. It looked more real now. She said to Carrie, "Do you like listening to music?"

Carrie nodded. Almost inaudibly, she whispered, "Daddy has a piano."

In another world, Sam would have wanted to laugh, especially since the piano sat right there for everyone to see. But it had once been Jeannette's piano too.

Jeannette didn't seem to notice the sting of it. "She knows the word piano?"

That did make Sam smile. "I think she could tell you the names of all the instruments in the orchestra."

Jeannette laughed. Actually laughed. She said to Carrie, "Is that right? Do you know the word orchestra?"

Carrie looked at her mother as if to say *Of course, silly, who doesn't?* "Yes."

Jeannette said, "And your daddy plays the piano, doesn't he. I bet you watch him sometimes."

Sam wondered how she had known that. Carrie nodded again. Then she said, "I going to learn to play too."

She said it exactly the way she had said she was coming to the concert: as if it was something she had thought about carefully, weighing the pros and cons before she made a decision. Jeannette's eyes met Sam's. Before he knew it, they were both laughing.

Through the shock, Sam saw poor Carrie fix him with her reproachful look. He pulled himself together. "We know you want to learn to play, don't you," he said. "Once your hands get big enough."

Jeannette had always taken cues so quickly. "I'm sorry, sweetheart," she told Carrie. "I didn't mean to laugh at you."

Carrie looked up at her. Sam watched the two pairs of grey eyes studying each other.

Carrie said, "It's okay." A strand of Jeannette's hair had escaped her bun and strayed down her cheek. Carrie reached up with one small hand and touched the vibrant red. "Mommy's hair is pretty."

Jeannette blinked. "Thank you." She smoothed Carrie's bangs away from her forehead with the gesture Sam knew so well. "Your hair is pretty too."

Sam's whole body felt as if someone had been pummelling it with a mallet. At least now he saw what he needed to do. "Carrie," he said,

"Mommy and Daddy need to talk for a little while. Could you go and keep Uncle Nathan company?"

She looked up at him, then back at Jeannette. "Okay."

The three of them went down to the kitchen. Nathan sat at the table with his untouched coffee in front of him. When they came in, he pushed back his chair and stood up.

For a moment the silence tightened. Then Jeannette cleared her throat and took one step toward the table, then another. The sun through the window touched her hair. She held out her hand to Nathan.

Nathan looked as incredulous as Sam felt. Jeannette said, "I... I'm glad to see you again. I hope you're doing well."

"I'm very well, thank you."

Jeannette nodded. She let go of his hand and came back to stand beside Sam.

Sam found his voice. "Could you keep an eye on Carrie for a little while?" he asked Nathan. "I think we're going to take a walk."

"Sure thing."

Carrie ran to him. "Take your time," Nathan said. "We'll hold the fort here."

Sam led Jeannette back to the foyer and opened the front door for her. He knew where they needed to go.

♫

Honey-yellow sunlight danced on the river. Jeannette walked along the gravel path, matching her step to Sam's. A slice of sky and sunlight separated the two of them.

She felt dizzy. She hadn't honestly thought she would go through with the trip to the house. After a few hours of lousy sleep, she had woken up too early in the hotel room and had planned to go straight to the train station. In the end, though, she couldn't shake the memory of the yellow dress. Her daughter had been too near, too real. Jeannette couldn't walk away a second time.

The gravel path crunched under her and Sam's shoes. On such a beautiful day, they had the walk to themselves. That came as a relief. Jeannette had walked here alone plenty of times, when the city had been new and strange and Veronica's apartment too full of noise to give a crowded mind some space. She had walked here after the man beside her now had burst into her world like a comet tearing across the sky.

She still didn't know Sam. She had never known who he was, but maybe she could try.

She said, looking up at him, "Carrie's beautiful. You're doing such a good job with her."

It sounded strained and wrong, as if Jeannette had any right to pass judgment on what kind of job Sam was doing. He seemed to understand anyway. He said, "She's the best thing I've ever had."

Jeannette wanted to tell him she knew that. Before she could, he said, "Jeannette, listen. I don't expect you to believe this, but I'm sorry for everything. I never wanted to hurt you."

Jeannette remembered the stairwell at the Lewis Center and Nathan staring down at her. *When he thinks he's hurt someone, he doesn't forgive himself.* Somehow, she found she believed that too. She said, "I know."

The green curve of Belle Island took shape around a bend in the path. Pine trees made spiky silhouettes against the clear sky. When Sam and Jeannette came abreast of the island, Sam stopped walking.

Jeannette stopped beside him. The water plashed quietly. On the street beside the path, a couple of cars hummed past. Sam didn't turn to look at Jeannette. He stared straight out at the island and said, "So we should talk about Carrie."

Jeannette knew what he was thinking. She moved closer to him. The slice of air between them was as thin as a pencil now. She said, "Sam, I don't want to take her away."

Now he did turn to her. His eyes were dark and deep. He said, "I don't want to lie to you. Not now. You know what I am."

Jeannette kept her voice steady. "Yes. I know you're... well..."

"Gay." He pushed the word out, one sharp syllable. "And you should know, too, that Nathan and I are..." Now it was his turn to hesitate. Colour climbed into his cheeks. "He's my... the usual word is 'partner.'"

Jeannette felt herself shivering. She pulled her coat closer around her. "You mean you're involved. Like in a relationship." She didn't know how that could work between two men, didn't want to know. The thought made her stomach twist.

"That's right," Sam said. His voice sounded clearer now, steady, as if what he had said so far gave him courage. "We love each other. That's pretty much all there is to it. He's been there for me, helped me when I needed it. More than I deserved."

We love each other. Jeannette looked into his eyes and tried to understand. She heard herself say, "You loved Gil."

She wouldn't have thought she remembered that man's name. Certainly she had tried to forget it. Pain tightened Sam's mouth. He said, "I did. Very much."

He had loved someone and lost him. Before Jeannette realized what she was doing, she reached out and put her hand on his arm. His corduroy jacket felt soft and chilly under her fingers.

He didn't move at the touch. He said, looking her in the eye, "You should know that you would have grounds to take Carrie away if you wanted. Because of Nathan and me. Any court would back you up."

"No," Jeannette said. "I wouldn't do that."

"Are you sure?"

The colour had left his face again. His mouth was set. Jeannette looked into the brown eyes she had loved and realized in a rush that she did know this man; she always had. "Sam," she said. Her hand tightened around his arm. "I wouldn't do that. I don't want to hurt her, or you."

She and he had sat side by side on a piano bench. They had shared music, their fingers moving together over the keyboard, her hands answering the motions of the baton in rehearsal. He hadn't been able to tell her the truth, but their souls had touched each other. Nothing would change that.

She said, "You tried not to be that way. Gay." The word made her blush.

He looked surprised. "Yes."

"Because of your parents?"

He nodded. "You remember when I said I couldn't go home?" His voice sounded softer now, more tired. "That was why."

Jeannette had guessed that. "So you tried to be what they wanted."

"That's right."

Jeannette wondered if Anna and Dr. Kraychek knew the truth now, if Sam planned to tell them or thought he could, or if he had to keep carrying the secret and pretending on the outside. She realized how lonely that had to be. She ought to know how it felt when the world judged you and shut you out because of who you were.

She said, "About Carrie, though." She should have thought this through on her own first, tried to figure out what she did want. After all this time, things had still managed to happen too fast. "Where I live now," she said, "it's a studio apartment. I couldn't even have a bed for her." Saying it made her think how tough it would be to squeeze a child into that little space, how upset Carrie might be to find herself away from home and her father. That thought hurt. "It's just that I want her to have a mother," she said. "I'd like to see her sometimes, have her be able to talk to me when she wants. I don't know if you can imagine what it's like, growing up without that."

Sam shook his head. "No, I don't think I can. You're right. She needs you in her life."

"The custody stuff, I don't know. She wouldn't want to be away from you, but if I can just see her." Veronica had said *visitation*. It sounded like a place to start.

Sam nodded. The colour had come back into his face. "You can come up and stay with us any time you want. When she gets older, maybe we can work it out so she can go down sometimes and stay a while with you."

"Yes. I'd like that." Jeannette managed a laugh. "I'll have time to get a bigger place."

Sam smiled. It looked real. "Okay," he said. "Maybe we're going to be okay."

"We are."

He had been standing with his hands in his jacket pockets, but now he took one hand out and put it over hers where it rested on his sleeve. She felt its warmth all the way up to her shoulder.

"We should head back," he said. "Give the babysitter a break."

Babysitter. The idea of Nathan being around Carrie, helping take care of her, still made Jeannette's insides tighten. He cared about her, though. Jeannette had seen that already, in the little time she had been around them.

Carrie had people who loved her. When Jeannette had found Nathan at the house, seen him and Sam together after everything it had cost her to come and face her husband, it had whipped her into a frenzy of fear. But to call Sam an unfit father, God knew Jeannette had no right to that. Not after what she herself had done.

Jeannette knew too well how it felt when you didn't have much of anyone to love you at all. Carrie deserved much better. Jeannette would never deny her that.

She took Sam's hand. "You're right. We should get back."

The sliver of air between them had disappeared completely. They walked back along the path together, hand in hand, leaving the island behind.

EPILOGUE

Sam sat at his parents' kitchen table. Thanksgiving dinner had been eaten and the leftovers put away, and Sam had tucked Carrie into the bed that used to belong to him and made sure she fell asleep. Now he had asked Ma and Dad to sit down for a minute so he could talk to them.

The white Formica table gleamed. Sam wanted to raise his head and look his father in the eye. Dad was the one he had to tell, Dad specifically, and this time there would be no shouting, no storming upstairs to throw clothes into a suitcase. Sam knew he should look up and meet the eyes that looked like his own reflection in the mirror. He ought to be old enough by now, wise enough.

He couldn't do it. Instead he spoke to the table. He did keep both of his hands out in front of him where he could see them, where there could be no clenching them around his knees or clutching them together in his lap like an angry kid. In his own ears, his voice sounded quiet and steady. He told Ma and Dad that he had something to say to them, something he knew they would not like to hear. He said he knew how disappointed they would be, and he was sorry. "You know what I am," he said. "I think you know I tried to change it, but I couldn't."

Then he told them about Nathan. "One of my choir members, you met him." Still he could not look up. He felt sure Dad's stare was drilling a hole through the top of his head. "I don't want to hide this from you, or I'm lying to all of us. Nathan and I are in a relationship. He loves me, and I love him."

After that, the words ran out. Sam sat still. Anything could happen now. At least, if the world fell apart again, he had another home to go to, and a life waiting for him there.

Someone touched his hand. Someone's warm fingers rested on his own.

Sam's head came up. Ma's eyes were huge and bright, but when she spoke, her voice was steady. "I know you, *mielas*. And I don't believe there's a thing wrong with you."

Sam couldn't take that in. Not right away. Ma went on, "You tell me you have someone in your life that you love. That's all I need to know. You're who you are, and I wouldn't ask you to change." Then, keeping her hand over his, she looked at Dad. "If anyone does think he needs to, they can take it up with me first."

Sam couldn't believe his ears. Ma had never, in his hearing, questioned Dad or told him she thought he was wrong. Never in all the years of fights and strain between her husband and son. She had done it now, with no trace of anger, but loud and clear for the world to hear.

Now Sam managed to look at his father. Dad's face looked as calm and remote as it always did, but he had heard what Ma said. Beyond a doubt. Sam felt sure he saw a hairline crack in that veneer.

Dad said, "Anna, I wasn't going to suggest that." His voice had no more emotion in it than the day he had told Sam to get out of this house.

Ma said, "I should hope not. You did tell him that before."

They all knew what that meant. Dad turned to look at Sam. For the first time in his life, Sam saw his father look unsure, uneasy.

Dad said, "I have made mistakes."

Sam thought he should have had to collect his jaw off the table. Dad, admit a mistake? His father went on, "I was worried for you. What you were. It terrified me."

Terror? Dad? Sam couldn't fathom it. Dad said, "I felt you were embarking on a life that would involve a great deal of danger and hurt. There was nothing I could do to stop you."

Out of the chaos in Sam's head, a few words managed to come out. "Dad, I didn't choose this. It's how I am."

The doctor's eyes rested on Sam's face. "I realize that," he said. "I had to understand that I could not fix it. Cure it."

He had wanted to change it. Hell, Sam had wanted the same thing. But how had Dad thought throwing Sam out of the house would fix anything? Why hadn't he said something instead? Told Sam he was worried, given him someone to talk to instead of shutting him out?

Ma might have felt Sam's temper boiling to the surface. Her fingers tightened around his. Sam said, struggling to keep his voice even, "Why didn't you tell me how you felt?"

Dad looked at him steadily. "I've already explained that. There was nothing I could do."

Jesus. If Sam opened his mouth, he thought steam might pour out of it. He didn't trust himself to say anything.

Ma spoke up instead. "Liudas is right to ask you that, Walter. I've wondered too. Not just why you didn't talk to him about this—why you didn't talk to him about anything."

Like the dancing. Like the fact that Dad loved music too, that it moved him the way it moved Sam. That was something they could have shared, but Dad hadn't let it happen.

Dad's face looked more open now than Sam had ever seen it. Dad said to Ma, "I think you know why."

"I've tried to guess, but I haven't been sure. And he doesn't know." Ma squeezed Sam's fingers again. "He's never known why you had such a hard time, all these years." Sam understood what she meant: such a hard time being a father. He remembered what he had wondered the night of the *Messiah* concert, if Dad had actually wanted a child. Ma said, "I think you would be right to tell him."

Dad looked at them both. Sam didn't know what to think. If it was true that Sam had shown up in his father's life like a burglar breaking into a house, Sam wasn't sure he wanted to hear it.

Dad didn't say that. Instead, he began a story, the first and only story he had shared about himself.

It began on Miner's Row: Coalco Road. Dad said, "The old cast-iron signpost called it that, at the intersection with Lackawanna Street, but to us it was the Row. No one ever called it anything else."

Sam listened, caught up in amazement at the simple fact that Dad was telling him this, breaking solid decades of silence. Dad described the Row steadily, neutrally, as if he had been talking about a place he had heard of or maybe visited once in a while, rather than the place tied to all of his earliest memories. Sam wondered what would happen if he didn't see his parents' house for the next thirty years. Could he describe it with the same kind of detachment? It felt strange, and sad too.

The Row had consisted of a line of ramshackle houses made out of boards slapped together, with identical concrete pads in front where nicer houses would have had porches, and identical narrow windows, and inside, identical floor plans of tiny rooms and dark hallways. A person could have gone blindfold into any house on the street and found his way to any room. Dad explained how people didn't lock their doors. No one had anything worth stealing, and anyway, everything, down to the clothes on your back and the food in your stomach, belonged to the Pennsylvania Coal Company.

"The management used my father and the other men like him," Dad said, with no trace of anger. "They considered them dim-witted Polacks, only good for brute labour." He added that his mother had always been unhappy. "Even when I was young," he said, "I remember how every day she seemed to fade a little more."

In Dad's words, Sam saw the grandparents he had never known. Liuz, whose name Sam shared, had been stockier and burlier than Dad and Sam himself, with the kind of body that could bear up under the abuse of the coal mines. Halina had been thin and pinched, worn out with the effort of trying to keep body and soul together, and trying to keep the house clean when no amount of scrubbing would get rid of the coal grime.

She had faded under that life, yes, but she had not always done it quietly. Dad remembered streams of reproaches against his father. Liuz could never earn enough money to get his family off the Row, didn't know enough English or have enough skills to find different work, seemed willing to let his family sink into this hopeless life like sinking into quicksand, without so much as a wave for help. "My father was a gentle man," Dad said. "He would rather laugh than get angry. He did what he could, but it was never enough."

So Dad had planned his own escape. He had buried himself in his schoolbooks and aimed at college and medical school. Once he got there, he had lived at school and gone back to the Row as little as he could. "I did not want my classmates to know where I had grown up," he said. "Doctors did not come from the Row."

Then, in his last year of school, his father got sick. Sam knew how Dad had stayed at the university until the bitter end, refusing all distractions until he had the diploma he had worked so hard for. Then he had gone to the hospital, where his mother had finally managed to take Liuz. It had been too late. "When I saw him," Dad said, "I knew no treatment would help. Even now, black lung is often fatal. One can't easily reverse years of corrosive damage to the lungs."

He had stayed at the hospital while his father died. As far as he knew, Liuz never knew he was there, or knew what Dad had managed to accomplish. Dad said, looking Sam in the eye, "But I had become a doctor, for whatever good it did."

Sam tried to take all of this in. Though Dad's voice still held no emotion that Sam could hear, for the first time in his life, Sam could see what his father must have felt. How Dad had known, growing up, that his own father had in some mysterious but definite way failed his family. How much it had meant to Dad to get off the Row when his father hadn't been able to. How hard Dad had worked to get his medical degree, and how useless that piece of paper had seemed as he sat and watched Liuz die.

Looking at the face that was so much like his own, Sam thought about what a difference it might have made if Dad had shared any of this when

Sam was younger. Sam would have listened. He had been that kind of kid. He didn't know why, but the thought made him ache.

For now, he didn't interrupt. Dad went on with his story, moving forward a handful of years to the time right after he and Ma had gotten married, when they were living in Westbury and he had started his practice. Becoming a doctor had gotten him out of Scranton, at least. It had helped win him the beautiful girl with the gold hair whose father owned his own diner; the beautiful girl who loved to dance. When she got pregnant, Dad said, "We agreed from the beginning that she would go to the hospital when the time came. I had studied gynaecology in school but had no intention of practicing it."

Sam had changed that. When "the time came," as Dad put it, and Ma's call reached him at the office, Dad had gotten home to find his plan torn to pieces. Ma wouldn't leave the house. "She was sure you were coming too quickly. She told me she wouldn't set foot outside under any circumstances."

Sam looked around at Ma. Up until now, he had been listening to Dad so intently that he had almost forgotten she was there. "You said that?" he asked.

"I did," she said. "Your father didn't like it one bit." Mischief woke up in her eyes. "I showed him I wasn't the only stubborn one in his house. My child wasn't going to be born in a Fairlane."

Dad picked up the thread again. He had gotten Ma upstairs and resigned himself to delivering a baby. Sam had always pictured dispassionate Dr. Kraychek going through the steps of the process as methodically as you would mow a lawn.

"I won't expand on the details," Dad said. "Some of them are rather unpleasant." Sam thought he might still be right about the dispassionate part until Dad went on, "You need to understand one thing, however. Childbirth can be dangerous. If anything went wrong, or if I made a mistake, I had no one there to help me. I could have lost you both."

In that sentence, it was real. Sam saw what he had tried to imagine after Carrie was born: his father, as a much younger man, standing at a bedside in late afternoon sun. The woman on the bed, her body distended and her eyes wide with pain, was the woman he loved. Sam felt the truth of that love as sharply as a hand squeezing his heart.

The young doctor had known that his wife's safety, even her survival, and the survival of the child inside her, might depend on skill and knowledge he wasn't sure he had. Sam looked at his father now and saw how afraid he had been.

Sam had to clear his throat to get words out. "You did it, though. We were both okay."

Dad nodded. "Fortunately, we had no complications."

Ma said, "And you know, if we'd gone to the hospital, Dad wouldn't have seen you until later. This way, he saw you before I did. I never did think that was quite fair."

"I'm afraid it couldn't be helped," Dad said. "But yes, the risk had its benefits."

Then and there, as he brought back that moment, his veneer dissolved. Sam saw the expression he had been much too young to remember. He had felt the same wonder himself, the first time he saw his daughter.

Sam understood. He had not crashed into Dad's life like a brick through a window. Even now, after what Sam had said tonight, his father loved him and always had. Sam could not wrap his mind around it.

Dad said, "Your mother has a point. I might have been wiser to talk more with you while you were growing up. You may see, though, why I made the choices I did."

Sam realized he did. Dad had watched his own father fail and worried, day after endless day, that he would do the same. It had been safer to be chilly and distant, not to let anyone see his weak side. Sam swallowed. "I do see, Dad. I get it."

"If I had done things differently, you and I might have been closer. I have thought about that more often than you may realize." Dad's expression didn't change, but his voice had the smallest tremor in it as he went on. "Perhaps I should tell you too that the day you left here"—Sam knew exactly which day he meant—"I understood immediately what I had done. But by then it was too late."

Sam knew the last thing he should do now was cry and make a fool of himself. Neither he nor his father had ever mentioned that last fight to one other. Sam had thought they never would. Now he imagined Dad sitting frozen-faced in the kitchen on that last day, hearing the front door slam behind his son, knowing he had made a terrible mistake but deciding already, in that heartbeat, that he couldn't fix it. How could you fix what you'd done wrong if you were never supposed to be wrong in the first place?

You could have come after me, Dad, Sam thought. *You had to know where I was going.* But Sam hadn't wanted to be found. Maybe, if he had reached out in the days and weeks after that last fight, things could have been different. He had made his choices too.

Now it took every ounce of his self-control to say, in a tone that sounded almost as calm as Dad's, "All things considered, we're hanging in there."

His father's mouth twitched. "That's true. We are."

Later, alone in the guest room that he and Jeannette had shared years before, Sam lay back in bed and looked up at the grey ceiling. His daughter was fast asleep across the hall. From downstairs came the quiet night-noises Sam had known all his life: the creak of Dad's recliner in the living room, the hum of the kettle in the kitchen as Ma made her nightcap of tea. Sam was here in this place that had known him all his life. He wasn't the boy he had been or the man he had tried to be, but somehow he still belonged.

Maybe he was all right just as he was. Sam lay in the dark and let that hope fill him.

The End

AUTHOR'S NOTE

To the Reader:

There are so many books to choose from, and reading time is precious. Thank you for spending your time with *To Love A Stranger*. I hope you enjoyed it!

Please check out the Book Club Guide that follows, and especially please consider exploring the Twitter feed, #TLASMusicProject. I would love to hear about your experiences with music, pieces that have been important to you, music you've heard or performed yourself, or anything else you would like to share about how music has made a difference in your life. If you're new to live performances of classical music, please consider checking out a concert. The players will thank you, and this music—which, as Sam says, can change the world—needs you to help it thrive!

ABOUT KRIS FAATZ

Kris Faatz (rhymes with skates) is a pianist, writer, and teacher. Before finding its home with Blue Moon Publishers, her debut novel *To Love A Stranger* was a finalist for the 2016 Schaffner Press Music in Literature Award. Kris's short fiction has appeared in a number of journals, including *Kenyon Review*, *Potomac Review*, *Reed*, and *Glassworks*.

Kris holds Bachelor's degrees in music and engineering from Swarthmore College and a Master of Music from the Peabody Conservatory. She has also been a contributor at the Kenyon Review Writers Workshops and the Sewanee Writers' Conference.

When not at work, Kris can often be found cooking or baking one-handedly so she can also hold up a book to read. Favourite writers include Barbara Kingsolver, Terry Pratchett, Jane Austen, Richard Adams, F. Scott Fitzgerald, and John Steinbeck. Kris also loves hiking and exploring the outdoors. She lives in Maryland with her husband Paul and cats Alafair and Templeton, who, like cats everywhere, know who's really in charge.

Connect with Kris online:
Blog: https://krisfaatz.com/journal/
Facebook: https://www.facebook.com/kristinfaatz/
Twitter: @kfaatz925
Goodreads: https://www.goodreads.com/user/show/18974118-kris-faatz
Youtube: http://bit.ly/2beRP1z

BOOK CLUB GUIDE

1) Who is your favourite character in *To Love A Stranger*? Least favourite? Why?

2) Sam becomes a conductor, knowing it's a risky career choice, because he can't imagine doing anything else. Have you ever felt that way about a job or project? What was that like?

3) Sam and Jeannette are very different from each other, but both are passionate about music. Sam says, "music can change the world." Do you think music could have that kind of influence? Why or why not?

4) Why does Sam try to "live straight"? Do you think he has valid reasons for doing it?

5) Sam's relationship with his father is complicated. Why do you think Walter had/has such a tough time with fatherhood? Can you relate to his experience?

6) Have you ever felt judged because of something you are (as Sam is) or because of something that happened to you (as Jeannette is)? How did you respond?

7) Have you ever found yourself, as Jeannette does at the end of the book, in a place where you have to reconsider something you've always thought was true? What was that experience like?

8) After the end of the book, how do you think things will go for the characters? What do you think Carrie's childhood will be like?

9) If you could tell Jeannette one thing, what would it be?

10) If you could tell Sam one thing, what would it be?

Extra credit! Go to a live performance of classical music: an orchestra concert, an opera, a solo performance, a chamber recital, etc. Afterward, send out a tweet with the hashtag #TLASMusicProject and share what you heard and what you thought.

WRITE FOR US

We love discovering new voices and welcome submissions. Please read the following carefully before preparing your work for submission to us. Our publishing house does accept unsolicited manuscripts but we want to receive a proposal first, and if interested we will solicit the manuscript.

We are looking for solid writing—present an idea with originality and we will be very interested in reading your work.

As you can appreciate, we give each proposal careful consideration so it can take up to six weeks for us to respond, depending on the amount of proposals we have received. If it takes longer to hear back, your proposal could still be under consideration and may simply have been given to a second editor for their opinion. We can't publish all books sent to us but each book is given consideration based on its individual merits along with a set of criteria we use when considering proposals for publication.

THANK YOU FOR READING
TO LOVE A STRANGER

BlueMoon
PUBLISHERS